PRAISE FOR
JEAN-CHRISTOPHE VALTAT AND *AURORARAMA*

"He is funny, intelligent, lyrically precise, and frequently self-aware."
—JAMES WOOD, *THE NEW YORKER*

"A magnificent achievement, balancing serious intent with arch humour. It's also beautifully stylish, replete with inventive steampunk iconography and fantastical characters in a stunning polar setting."
—ERIC BROWN, *THE GUARDIAN*

"The novel glides on silver skates from the surreal to the absurd to the languorously decadent ... Irresistible."   —LAURA MILLER, *SALON*

"Combining Arctic adventure with Victorian fantasy, this page-turner is as sparkling and colorful as the northern lights."
—*SAN FRANCISCO CHRONICLE*

"*Aurorarama* [presents] one of the most thoroughly conceived alternative universes I've ever encountered."   —*WIRED*

"*Aurorarama* tells a tale of political intrigue (secret police! Eskimos! *Prisoner*-esque hovering airship!) with some truly lyrical prose."
—*io9*

"Jean-Christophe Valtat's *Aurorarama* follows steampunk's basic conventions, but its influences and setting are of a different species. Narrated as a trans-Arctic alterna-history, *Aurorarama* harks back to Jules Verne, Raymond Roussel, and Marcel Allain and Pierre Souvestre ... This surrealism is largely what distinguishes *Aurorarama* from standard-issue steampunk ... *Aurorarama* mesmerizes less for its intricate plot twists or descriptions of steam-powered gizmos than for its extraordinary dramatization of the birth and death of a civilization."   —ERIK MORSE, *BOOKFORUM*

"[*Aurorarama*] entrances and delights. You could spend years picking apart the sly references and the particular myths, poems, novels and songs that inspired Valtat, or you can simply enjoy it for the experience. Valtat is making his American debut in a big way ... With his remarkable enthusiasm and bravery, it's completely possible he'll conquer the world."   —JESSA CRISPIN, NPR

"*Aurorarama* is perhaps what Jules Verne would write if woken from the dead and offered a dose of mushrooms ... An enjoyable amalgam of thriller, fantasy, and polar adventure, topped off with a sprinkling of anarchist intrigue ... Valtat's world is ingeniously imagined and peopled with an alluring cast." —JACOB SILVERMAN,
THE NATIONAL (ABU DHABI)

"Marvelous, perfect, and perfectly marvelous! ... [*Aurorarama*] promises to attract discerning and sophisticated readers galore, those fans of the fantastical who are tired of second-hand visions and stale conceits ... Valtat's novel is *Little Nemo in Slumberland* as retold by a trio of Jeff Noon, Steve Aylett and William Burroughs. I can hardly wait for its sequels." —PAUL DI FILIPPO,
THE BARNES & NOBLE REVIEW

"As well-written as it is well-imagined ... *Aurorarama* explicitly blends conventional narrative pleasures with the logic of dreaming."
—*STRANGE HORIZONS*

"*Aurorarama* is an experience to be savored." —*MAKE* MAGAZINE

"The prose is gorgeous, undeniably so." —*SAN FRANCISCO
BOOK REVIEW*

"A terrific storyteller, Valtat mixes humor and poetry, romance and politics into a surprisingly thoughtful page-turner about social revolution." —MATTHEW JAKUBOWSKI, *PASTE MAGAZINE*

"[Valtat] has a magical sense of shape and a gift for lyrical prose that are rare in modern writing." —*LA CROIX*

"Valtat [is a writer of] beautiful energy." —*LE MONDE*

"The most noteworthy contribution to steampunk in almost two decades ... *Aurorarama* rejuvenates an entire subgenre, adding creativity and accuracy (historical and, more importantly, tonal) to a field that risks being defined solely by corsets and airships. Beyond its importance in legitimizing steampunk, *Aurorarama* is a sparkling read—breathing, human characters wandering amok in one of the most captivating cities in fiction." —*PORNOKITSCH*

LUMINOUS CHAOS

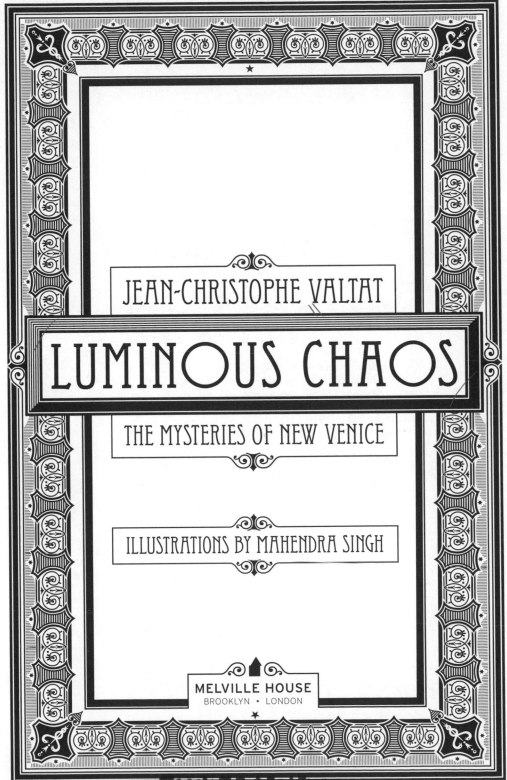

JEAN-CHRISTOPHE VALTAT

LUMINOUS CHAOS

THE MYSTERIES OF NEW VENICE

ILLUSTRATIONS BY MAHENDRA SINGH

MELVILLE HOUSE
BROOKLYN · LONDON

LUMINOUS CHAOS

Copyright © 2013 by Jean-Christophe Valtat
Illustrations © 2013 by Mahendra Singh

First Melville House printing: October 2013

Melville House Publishing   8 Blackstock Mews
    145 Plymouth Street   and   Islington
    Brooklyn, NY 11201   London N4 2BT

mhpbooks.com   facebook.com/mhpbooks   @melvillehouse

Library of Congress Cataloging-in-Publication Data

Valtat, Jean-Christophe, 1968–
  Luminous chaos : a novel / Jean-Christophe Valtat ; [illustrated
by] Mahendra Singh. — First edition.
      p. cm. — (The mysteries of new Venice ; Book two)
  ISBN 978-1-61219-141-6 (hardback)
  ISBN 978-1-61219-142-3 (e-book)
1. Anarchists—Fiction.   2. Time travel—Fiction.   3. Paris
(France)—Fiction.   4. Steampunk fiction.   I. Title.
  PQ2682.A438L86 2013
  843'.914—dc23
                                        2013027517

Printed in the United States of America
        1 3 5 7 9 10 8 6 4 2

CONTENTS

"Parisian literature of the byways has its own methods, and its purveyors are shrewd enough to know what will be tolerated and what enjoyed by their peculiar class of patrons; transcendental toxicology and an industry in idols worked by criminals intercommunicating by means of Volapük may be left to them."
                              —A. E. Waite, *Devil Worship in France*, 1896

"Of Paris, what am I to say? All of it was of course a delirium, a tomfoolery."   —Fyodor Dostoyevski, *The Gambler*, 1865

EPISODE I

EVERY DOGE HAS HIS DAY

I

The Divorce with the Sea

On that sunny St. Mark's day in 1907 A.B.—After Backwards—the white Buildings of New Venice bristled with flags and were heavy with banners, while all along the thronged embankments a cheering crowd waved through a colourful whirlwind of streamers and confetti. As far as the eye could see, a canalcade of ribboned gondolas paraded under draped bridges, crushing brittle pancakes of ice with their gleaming gilded prows.

It was a great day for New Venice, but for Brentford Orsini it was the worst of his life.

He sat under a canopy in the leading gondola, with a look on his face so sombre that Dürer's *Melancholia* might have patted him on the back and offered to buy him a drink. Even his mind's eye was frowning as he remembered that this was the very same route he had taken, barely more than a year earlier, on his way to kick the Council of Seven out of the City they had dishonoured. What for? What good had it done? Weren't they all almost back to where they'd started?

The crowd above him seemed a noisy, bothersome blur. He wouldn't have been surprised if they had stoned him and shouted abuse, or, more aptly, jeered at his naïveté. That would have made more sense than this masquerade, which mocked everything he had ever made or meant.

Today was the day when, after a year of rule that had passed as quickly as a dream, he was to hand over his position as Regent-Doge to his elected successor. There was nothing wrong with this in principle: after all, he himself had penned the part of the City and Commonwealth Charter that regulated the Regency until the legitimate Doges, Geraldine and Reginald Elphinstone, came of age to govern the City of New Venice and the Northwasteland Commonwealth. He had not even been personally defeated: the charter did not allow a regent to be a candidate for his own succession. This should have been his triumph, a testimony to his ability to protect the wintering ship of state and to his integrity in giving back, as promised, the rudder that he had snatched from the senile hands of the Council of Seven.

But no: every time Brentford looked to his left and saw Peterswarden wearing the robe and golden stole of the Regent-Doge, he felt like the King of Fools.

❆

Brentford's reign had started off well, though, with the admittedly gruesome but nonetheless rather positive news that the entire Council of Seven had been engulfed in a crack while crossing an ice-cutting field, shortly after the uprising that had banned them from New Venice. It had happened a few miles away from the city, and for some weeks it had been a favourite excursion among New Venetians to snowshoe or skate to the place of the accident, where heads of reindeer frozen in their struggle could still be seen protruding like puzzled chess knights on an infinite white square. Brentford had felt not so much sorrow as a certain sense of safety, which, he now discovered, had been illusory.

If Poletics had a taste, it would be bittersweet. The moments of pure enthusiasm that had followed Geraldine and Reginald's Restoration as the direct descendants of the city's founders, the Seven Sleepers, along with the advent of something like a republic, had progressively evaporated, leaving—what a surprise—a more motley, complicated reality.

To begin with, the Forty Friends, though far away from the city they funded, had not appreciated the always rather subservient Council of Seven being replaced without their assent. Their investments, already on the wane before the revolution, had dwindled steadily ever since. That had not saddened Brentford, as economic autonomy was his ultimate goal, but it had infuriated certain classes of citizens, mostly tradesmen and shopkeepers, who suddenly discovered a passion for democratic debate exactly proportional to the drop in their income.

Then the Senate of the Seven Sectors, the first ever to be freely elected—by women as well!—and on which Brentford had relied to carry on the reforms, had proved somewhat prone to bickering and rather receptive to lobbying, when not, Brentford suspected, to the odd outright bribe. On the whole, Brentford refrained from forming any highfalutin theory of human nature, but he had to admit that he was disappointed.

Still, he'd had high hopes that when the elections came, Pieter Van Reimerswaal, the former Chancellor of the Exchequer for Everyday Entertainment and Exceptional Events, a clever, pleasant, and serviceable man, would win the necessary majority. The unexpected candidacy of Peterswarden, a notorious supporter of the Council of Seven—and the brain behind that most Machiavellian of schemes, the Inuit People's Ice Palace—had been an ill omen and a political masterstroke, which Brentford was pretty sure had originated with the Forty Friends and the local lodges that supported them. As a Scandinavian, Peterswarden had naturally lobbied to get the votes that depended on the wavering senator from Niflheim, but even worse, he had used his anthropologist's knowledge of the Inuit world to somehow convince Igjuktuk, the Inuk senator from the new Inuvik Sector, to tip the scales in his favour. Brentford had fought hard for Inuit civil rights, and felt the result of the elections as a bloody backstabbing. He doubted that the Inuit had forty words for snow, but he felt he could use forty words for betrayal.

The cortege eventually arrived at the long Polar Pier and its covered walkway, which led to a white building lined with Doric columns and a tower topped by a meridian globe: the Markham Marina. There, moored a few feet above the ground, softly bobbing in the sharp April breeze, floated the *Dukedominion*, the luxurious ceremonial airship reserved for such official occasions. Made on the Pennington design, it was elegant and spectacular, with its aluminium envelope shining in the pale polar sun, the characteristic dorsal fin running the whole of its length. Its most striking feature, however, was the gilt heraldic figurehead of the New Venice sea lion curling its powerful fishtail around the keel and defying the ice-fields with its spread wings and sharpened claws.

The party, mostly officials and their guests, disembarked from the gondolas and headed towards the airship, while the crowd looked on from behind fences or from the private ice boats strewn across Marco Polo Bay. Colourful balloons in the shape of the sectors' animal totems could be seen floating all around, while much higher, silvery tethered aerostats harvested power from the storms and auroras—one of Brentford's projects, which filled him with a bitter pride.

He couldn't help comparing this procession to his own investiture the year before, or seeing the changes in the faces that frolicked and downdolphined in the frothy wake of power. His former mistakes passed all around him in fur coats, sashes, and top hats, mostly former secretaries and servants of the Council, some justly resentful and some whom he had thought better of purging and who, taking his leniency for weakness, had been waiting for the first occasion to bubble back to the surface. As to those who had pandered to him before realizing that was not the right approach, they were now eager to ignore his presence, staring through him as if he had become a ghost.

But Peterswarden, of course, had been his most egregious miscalculation. He had been deeply involved with the Council's darkest plots, but Brentford had deemed it sufficient punishment that the Northwestern Administration for Native Affairs and the Inuit People's Ice Palace had been, respectively, reduced to rubble and emptied of all meaning. He had proposed Peterswarden as a chair for the charming but small Academy for Arctic Anthropology and forgotten all about the man, whom he'd dismissed as a simple underling. But Peterswarden, after all, had started as a polar explorer. That required not only toughness and shrewdness but also a sound understanding of networking, fundraising, and public relations, all of which he had used very effectively to orchestrate his comeback. And now there he was, tall, lanky, wiry, and wrinkled, in ceremonial robes and *corno ducale*, soberly saluting before he stepped up into the ship, while Brentford was reduced to a mere spectator of his own, spectacular downfall.

By and by the guests filled the luxury cabin that ran all along most of the keel. There again, no effort to impress had been spared: on each side, the round ports that joined the dark blue carpeted floor to the panels and mouldings of the gilded ceiling alternated with Arctic-themed oil paintings and carved allegories, all executed in a curvy, intertwined Art Nouveau style. At the far end, raised by two half-circular steps, was the double throne of the Dauphin-Doges, topped by convoluted statues of Boreas and Neptune and framed by figures of Dawn and Night.

There sat Reginald and Geraldine, wrapped together in their black velvet cloak, their clever eyes restless in their little pale faces. To Brentford the presence of these adorable Siamese twins was more a worry than a relief. Their sheer improbability surely incarnated something of New Venice, but even in this they were more heraldic than useful, and doomed to remain so in an increasingly lonely way. Worse, were they ever to be taken seriously, God knew what would happen to them. He suspected that it would be his next mission in the city to protect them from harm.

He could count on Gabriel for support in this, he supposed, as much or as little as anyone ever could count on Gabriel d'Allier for anything. But Gabriel himself (who now nodded at him discreetly from the back of the crowd with a little half-clownish, half-sorry grimace) was also about to leave the service of his two pupils the Twins, and would remain as far as possible from the hassles of a *poletical* life that he scorned.

Beyond Gabriel, Brentford's past allies were glaringly absent. Captain-General Mason, dependably independent, had asked to be discharged with the change in administration, as if it prompted him to feel he had somehow failed New Venice, and his successor, a taciturn Anglo-Alsatian officer named Kurz, could barely conceal his impatience with democracy. Since their support had been decisive in last year's coup, he supposed the Sophragettes could be counted upon (if, indeed, they still existed!), and likewise the Scavengers, but if it came down to that, it would really signify that he was back in the open, and with a target painted on his back.

He sighed as, with everyone aboard, the *Dukedominion* was unmoored and, with a whirring of her enormous electric propeller, started slowly to ascend over the ice fields and water leads of the ocean. There was a general silence, and a certain apprehension, for the ship was not the safest that ever flew, and the modest circle of a few wobbly miles that she completed on such days as this one was probably the most ambitious trip she could ever attempt. But the tension relaxed a little when from both sides of the throne a choir intoned the New Venetian Hymn, Purcell's "Song of the Cold Genius,"

> See, see, we assemble
> Thy revels to hold,
> Tho' quiv'ring with cold,
> We chatter and tremble.

It was the cue for the ceremony to begin. Peterswarden walked to the side port halfway along the keel, which was decorated with a Tiffany stained glass depicting a rather convoluted allegory of Justice. There, the purple-clad Elected Elders of the House of Honours and Heraldry presented him with both a nosegay of greenhouse roses and the Vera, a golden ring on a blue velvet cushion. He took oaths over it, a long mechanical series of formulaic promises meant to reassure the assembly of his submission to the Dauphin-Doges and the Senate, although it was well known by all that he actually controlled most of the senators. Then, a little square window was opened in the porthole itself, letting in a cold draft that made everyone shiver, and in profound silence, Peterswarden threw the ring overboard, while uttering the ritual formula: "We espouse thee, O sea, as a token of our perpetual dominion over thee."

The crowd burst into applause and Brentford felt a pang of jealousy. Marrying the frozen sea from the lofted airship had been his towering moment, and poletical questions aside, it made him sick to watch Peterswarden stepping into his enchanted shoes. It was like seeing another man marrying one's childhood sweetheart.

Peterswarden, who for once could barely hide his own emotion, walked back to the pulpit. It was now time for the new Regent-Doge's address. Brentford barely listened, busy as he was fathoming the bubbling well of his own black bile. From time to time he emerged, picking up some snatches that, unsurprisingly, did little to brighten his mood. He felt that every word was projected towards him at full speed, like a phantasmagoric ghost of his worst fears about the city's fate. Finally, this torture came to an end, and his sigh of relief got lost among the turncoat cheers and the sycophantic handclaps.

Suddenly, when everyone thought the ceremony was over, a voice rang out from aft.

"Sir," Reginald cried, raising himself and Geraldine from their throne, "we have a present for you."

Had something been forgotten in the protocol? Peterswarden looked up from his pulpit, visibly annoyed. Obviously, Brentford thought, he didn't like the reminder that, as a Regent, he was just a stand-in for the Dauphin-Doges.

The Twins walked towards him among the puzzled, murmuring guests, a little silver icebox in their gloved hands.

"Actually, it is a present and a pledge," Geraldine explained, as they arrived at the pulpit. "A token both of our trust in you and of your commitment on our behalf."

"I'll gladly take both the present and the pledge, Your Most Serene Highnesses," Peterswarden answered with his cool polar explorer's nerve, bowing slightly towards the Twins, his bony hands protruding from his wide sleeves.

Reginald opened the box, and, both twins tiptoeing forward in unison, Geraldine took out a little block of ice that she put into Peterswarden's upturned palm.

"Here," Reginald said with a straight face, "we are proud to offer you a little ice from the pole. Will you promise to watch over it and give it back intact to your successor?"

A hush fell on the audience. Peterswarden could not but accept the unpleasant gift and the ridiculous, impossible mission that went with it. "I promise," he said in a voice he strove to keep as dignified as possible. The block was already beginning to thaw, both burning and drenching his hand.

"Then we are satisfied. We declare the ceremony completed," Geraldine said, as the Twins turned their backs and solemnly pranced back to their throne among the stunned onlookers. Brentford could feel himself wince with pleasure at the trick. It was not, however, very strategic. But then who was he to give strategy lessons?

As the *Dukedominion* made a labourious U-turn and the crowd dissolved in a scandalized buzz, he spotted Gabriel leaning against a port, his brow resting on his arm as he watched the landscape intently, as he had done during the whole murderous speech.

"Diadems—drop—and Doges—surrender—
Soundless as—dots—on a disk of snow"

he declaimed pompously as Brentford approached.

One had to be a trained d'Allierologist to know that there was, first, a sneer behind the quotation, and, second, no malevolence in that sneer. Gabriel, after all, was in the same leaking boat as Brentford.

"It certainly looks as if the fog is rising," Brentford answered, as the private joke demanded. "How was your day?"

"The six-month one? Not so bad, as a matter of fact. Thanks to you, I must say. But, unlike you, I never deluded myself that it was going to last forever."

"How wise of you. I don't think your pupils have profited much from your wisdom, however."

"How did you find our little addendum to the protocol?" interrupted Reginald, who had silently joined them, arm in arm with his Siamese sibling. He wore the mischievous grin, not exactly smug but irritatingly close, that Gabriel had come to know by heart.

"I'm sure the Regent-Doge found it quite *thrilling*," answered Brentford. "Don't tell me you had something to do with it," he added, turning to Gabriel.

"Bah. So little it is not worth mentioning. Don't you think the little bug—that is, their Most Serene Highnesses, can come up with their own ideas?" he answered, ruffling Reginald's head in a good-humoured breach of every conceivable etiquette. They could have been triplets, the three of them. But Brentford could feel the filigree of regret that ran through their routine, surely because he shared it, too.

"Already plotting behind my back, are we?" interrupted Peterswarden. The thick nest of courtiers that surrounded him guffawed in unison.

Brentford turned slowly towards him.

"Why should we plot? Aren't we still in a Republic?"

"I am the living proof that we are," Peterswarden answered with barely concealed irony. "I simply hope you bear me no grudge over my victory. Let us make peace."

He offered his hand. Brentford took it reluctantly, and felt how cold and wet it still was from the ice block. Their eyes locked for a short uncomfortable while. Democracy or not, Brentford had found, politics often came to these showdowns of savage hypnosis.

Peterswarden relaxed his grip and, lightly touching Brentford's arm, motioned him towards the porthole.

"You see, it is well known in my line of work that in ancient times, when a king was not deemed able to guarantee natural growth and protection for his people anymore, he was quite simply put to death. Shouldn't we all rejoice that we live in more enlightened times?"

Before Brentford could sharpen his answer to this unusually bald threat, Peterswarden had already turned his back and moved off.

"As for their Most Serene Highnesses," he hissed towards the Twins as he left in the midst of his escort, "They can be assured of my wholehearted commitment."

Meanwhile, while all backs were turned on the dwindling *Dukedominion*, a hooded, faceless woman with bare feet picked up a little golden ring from the ice field. But that has nothing to do with the rest of this story.

II

The Midnight Mission

Back in the city, Brentford had agreed to meet for a late snack with Gabriel and the Twins, though he did not expect much solace from this private farewell ceremony. For the time being—a chilly stretch of starry night—he was walking in the rundown Pleasure Island district, his head in the blur of his breath, his fists clenched deep in his greatcoat pockets, his hobnailed shoes squeaking hastily on the glazed greyish snow. Pleasure Island, despite its name, was nothing like a red light district. As a matter of fact, it was barely lit at all. And there was not much to see there, anyway, besides grim rows of warehouses and workshops and, between them, deserted moonlit wharves with skeletal T-Rex cranes vaguely clanging in their sleep. But the place was dear to Brentford's heart. It was here, at the end of this street, in the former factory of the Société Hyperboréenne d'Exploitation Industrielle de Tabac et d'Allumettes Nordiques, that Helen Kartagener had once saved the city with her incantations to stop time. And it was here that he was working on the project that would help him overcome the blue devils of early retirement and, he hoped, also help him to play a new part in the city's future. It was now on its way to becoming the Polar Phalanstery for Possible Poletics, a cultural centre for local creativity and a forum for ideas that could benefit the community. No doubt Brentford would see the usual crowd of crackpot dreamers with plans for telepathic mail networks, compulsory Esperanto, hothouse naturist colonies, or petrol-powered vehicles all come a-flocking. Whether any of them could invent something as absurd as this city in the Arctic remained to be seen, though.

Past the gate, he crossed the inner yard towards another archway, until he reached a double door that pretended to resist his push a little, like an old private joke. His gas lantern left wide Rorschach patches of darkness untouched, but it was enough to see that the whitewashing and the tiling had made some significant progress, which gave him good reason to hope that the place would open as planned.

But inspecting the phalanstery was not quite the reason for his visit. He let himself slide down the wall and remained seated there in spite of the sneaky cold, the gas-lamp at his side, his arms around his knees, allowing thoughts to drift through his head. It was here, he reflected, in this very hall, that Helen had not only reassembled the excavated bones of the Polar Kangaroo but had seemingly resurrected it. It was here that she had, well, made love to him, in a way that had left his mind as much befuddled as enlightened. It was here that he had seen her for the last time, dead (well, in her own way) from having stopped the flow of time over the city when Delwit Faber's Lobster Girls had cut the power lines with their claws. If she had any idea what he should do now he would certainly listen to it. And wasn't his own oblique shadow, moving on the adjacent wall, drawing her clear-cut profile?

"Helen?" he asked in his head.

"Are you a child?" his own voice answered, knowing exactly what Helen would say. "Coming to me when another boy kicked you in the shins?"

"Thanks for the kind words. They're exactly what I need right now."

"No, what you need now is a lesson. You wouldn't have come here otherwise. You wrote the rules of a game and you don't want to accept a defeat that's not even yours. You do not accept it, yet you embrace it. You not only feel humiliated, you've let your opponent see how you feel. You were taught to act with pride, and your pride is racking you."

"Well, I could have said that much myself," Brentford replied, wincing.

"Of course. But I'll say what you can't bring yourself to say: let the bastard be, Brentford, let him glow with the notion that he humbled you. That's what will lead him to his own demise."

"I'm not sure I understand."

"To admit that proves you're wise."

"But I don't feel like it."

"Then don't listen to the advice of that old, stupid Helen."

He was about to apologize when the door creaked disapprovingly and a shadow slid into the room, quickly followed by a man.

"Your, er . . . Excellency?" the man said tentatively, as he raised his own lantern.

He wore the the navy blue, gold-striped topcoat and small top hat of the Boreal Beadle Brigade, which had been founded a few months earlier as a counterweight to the Gentlemen of the Night. Another ghost of Brentford's reign coming to haunt him, then.

He got up with a sigh.

"Yes, beadle. How can I be agreeable to you?"

"I was looking for you, Your Excellency. You have been called by the Regent-Doge."

"On what grounds? I have no official duties that would justify such a late call."

The beadle looked embarrassed.

"I haven't been told, Your Excellency. But they insisted that it was urgent and important."

"Has something happened?"

"I can't say, Your Excellency." The man hesitated, looking ill-at-ease.

Brentford mulled it over. For a while, he considered refusing flatly, just to see what would happen, but he felt reluctant to further embarrass the beadle. Maybe Peterswarden had counted on that too—the famous Orsini manners.

And that is how Brentford found himself in the back of a propelled police sled, speeding through meringue monuments and crossing blancmange bridges over quiet tinfoil canals.

Much to his surprise, he wasn't taken to the Blazing Building, but further away, to Maurelville, where he quickly recognized the observation tower and the bridge that marked the entrance to the sturdy neoclassical buildings of the Kane Clinic.

He was ushered into a meeting room, and was surprised to find the whole Senate of the Sectors assembled there, huddled in the dim light around a long mahogany table, where Dr. Playfair, the new Gestionnary-General for the H.H.H., stood behind the Regent-Doge like a menial waiting for orders.

Here was, it seemed, a government that made its decisions at night and acted at night. Clearly something big was in the works, and some distant part of Brentford stirred, vaguely elated to be a part of it. He noticed a human shape in a shadowy corner of the room, wrapped in blankets on a three-wheeled litter, but before he could make any more out, Peterswarden spoke.

"Ah, Mr. Orsini. We are relieved that you could join us."

The Regent-Doge did his best to sound straightforward, but Brentford could sense the uneasiness of the senators surrounding him. Brentford also noticed that he wasn't offered a seat, which made him feel as if he were somehow on trial. What the pole was going on in here?

"We are sorry to have disturbed you at such an hour, but as you can see, you are not the only one whose presence has been requested. There is a general consensus among us that little can be done about the present matter without your cooperation."

"You flatter me, your Most Serene Highness," answered Brentford, almost feeling the canker sores bursting in his mouth as he gave Peterswarden *his* title.

"We took the risk of bringing this agonized man down here in the hope he would talk to you and explain the situation himself," Peterswarden went on, indicating the sick man on the stretcher, "but I am afraid he has passed out for the moment. This is what we have gathered, however. The man is a French explorer, called de Lanternois. The Health Angels found him beyond the city limits just in time to save his life, if not all his limbs. We first thought he'd been on his way to the pole, but he appears to be on a mission, and, more exactly, asking for our help. Not on his own behalf, mind you, but on behalf of France."

Brentford almost snorted at the idea.

"France is calling New Venice to its rescue?"

"Well, Paris, more exactly. It appears that the last few Parisian winters have been exceedingly harsh. Polar harsh. Life has been, from what we gather, completely disorganized. These people are asking for a delegation of experts to go over there and help them learn how to cope with these unfamiliar conditions. The council has debated about this most unexpected demand, and we have come to the conclusion that it would be an honour to accept, especially under the present conditions."

"Which are?" inquired Brentford. As far as he knew, Peterswarden had never been a dedicated Francophile, nor especially bothered with humanitarian concerns.

"France, as you know, is a close ally of Russia. Given the recent movements in the Russian part of the Arctic, the council deems, and I agree, that by ingratiating ourselves with France, we may deflect the interests of Russia in our zone of influence. That would be, if you prefer, the price of our expertise."

"And then, if I may say so, there are the natural ties that link our city to France," added Élisée Bulot, a diminutive, balding, moustachioed man who served as senator for Nouvelle-Ys, the French sector of New Venice.

"Yes, well, of course,"said Peterswarden, with a sigh. "There's that."

"There are two things I'm still struggling to understand," Brentford insisted. "The first one is why France would call us, rather than, well, their Russian allies, whom, I suppose, have a little firsthand experience of wintry life themselves. Or for that matter, rather than anyone who can put on snowshoes without tripping every two steps."

"I can read neither French nor minds, Mr. Orsini, so it would be presumptuous for me to think that I can read French minds. And meanwhile Mr. de Lanternois has not expatiated on that point. There is of course our natural superiority in dealing with the most extreme conditions, but besides that, I suppose that they do not want to look too dependent on other major nations. Comparatively, we can go unnoticed. Secrecy is also one of our specialties. This will be, in Polaris Guild parlance, a Canadian passport operation."

"A secret embassy, then . . ." Brentford said to himself, as if tasting the words like wine, for texture and body. He added aloud, "The second point I fail to grasp is why nothing can be done without my cooperation."

"Because, Mr. Orsini, as former Regent-Doge you would be the most honourable and prestigious ambassador we could send to France, and as a former Elite Engineer from the Arctic Administration as well as Gestionnary-General of the Greenhouses and Glass Gardens, you are the most efficient expert we can think of. I would hate to offend your well-known modesty, but you should know that the council is unanimous on this point. As a matter of fact, we have just voted."

Brentford looked in disbelief at the senators he had thought faithful to him, but none, it seemed, wished to meet his *et tu* eyes. Bloody turncoats. Could they possibly think they were protecting him? The very idea that Peterswarden had won them over to his side filled Brentford with bitter contempt.

"So, what is left to me is to accept or refuse, I suppose."

"Actually, your alternative is between accepting gracefully or accepting reluctantly. You know as well as I do that refusing a diplomatic assignment is cause for imprisonment. And knowing you as I have the honour to do, I am sure you will easily find nobler reasons for accepting. Helping suffering people in need of your talents, for instance, or respecting a dying man's last will," Peterswarden added, pointing to the litter. "A man who has risked and probably lost his life to ask for our help."

Brentford sighed. Not only was he in a corner, but he had his foot in a trap. Let the bastard be, a voice whispered in his head. Well, but not blindly.

"Had he any document on him that could precisely describe the extent of this mission?" he asked, not even bothering to hide his suspicion. The council was following this dialogue with a certain tense expectation, exchanging looks and whispers whose meaning Brentford could not quite decipher, except as a general confirmation that he was being set up one way or another.

"No, but this may be useful," Peterswarden said, flourishing a large horseshoe-shaped piece of metal fitted with leather straps and looking somewhat like a crown.

"I'm impressed," said Brentford, with barely suppressed irony. "But what is it, pray tell?"

"We are not sure, but de Lanternois *clung* to it, and he claims it contains all the necessary information. We are not certain of how it works, but we think it is some mind-reading technology. Rather less sophisticated than our own Psychomotives, as you will soon be in a position to appreciate."

Brentford was immediately distracted from the weird headpiece. "You mean I'm supposed to go there by *Psychomotive*?"

Brentford, decidedly, was going from surprise to surprise. The Psychomotive was an incredibly sophisticated, expensive, and risky means of transportation that had been almost totally abandoned twenty years earlier, but Peterswarden talked about it as if it were a child's sled.

The new Regent-Doge smiled unpleasantly.

"It is true that we keep them for great occasions, but I doubt there is a greater one than our first embassy abroad. I have just been in touch with the Drome-Director of the Arctic Committee for City Access on that matter, and he informs me that it is the fastest and safest way, for the first part of the trip at least, whatever the weather might be. It is still too early in the year for a ship to break the ice, and an airship would be too conspicuous."

"So this means I can't take many people with me."

While Brentford's inner poletician was disturbed by his assignment, the engineer in him was moving full stride into the challenge, planning, measuring, calculating.

"Six, plus you and the pilot, from what I have heard. As there is no time to lose, we have spared you the trouble of making a list. We chose the best experts in their fields—people whose talents we are sure you will appreciate having on hand. Here they are."

Brentford felt wary as the list was passed down the row of senators towards him, from one trembling hand to another.

"This has been voted on too, I suppose?" he asked, trying to brace himself before unfolding it.

"Of course. We are a very efficient democracy, Mr. Orsini. You deserve our greatest gratitude for that."

III

A Farewell Ceremony

Located at the tip of a foggy spit of black rock, Nouvelle-Ys was not the most welcoming part of the city. Except for the bright, half-timbered boutiques of the Rue Dahut, it was a small enclosed area of narrow canals and austere grey houses. Its inhabitants were mostly *Terre-Neuvas* who had drifted here after the demise of the "French shore" of Newfoundland and of the St. Pierre colony: tough and taciturn people who lived by whaling and sometimes by smuggling alcohol and did not mingle easily with the rest of the city. It wasn't unusual that when a stranger entered one of the public houses, the other customers switched not even to French but to their native Breton and Basque. But to Gabriel d'Allier, who was himself half a Frenchman (the lower half, he suspected) and whose peculiar lifestyle demanded a strictly disciplined secrecy, this isolation was rather welcome. Especially on the nights when he planned to take the Twins "going Haroun" as discreetly as he could, so as to better acquaint them with the city they were destined to rule.

Located along the d'Argent canal, the Maison Malgven was a favourite staple on these nocturnal expeditions. A warm, candle-lit, fuzzy place hung with fishnets and harpoons, it hid behind casement windows of thick yellow bubble glass. One could have a snug driftwood booth to oneself and by far the best buckwheat crêpes in the city. It had been the natural choice for this last evening together.

They had been waiting for Brentford for an hour or so when he finally slumped in to the sound of a rusty bell, a snow-sprinkled allegory of despair and every inch the harbinger of bad news.

"Sorry for being so late," he apologized as he joined them at their table.

"We thought you had chickened out of our little tearjerking party," said Gabriel.

"Quite the contrary. What were you crying about, so that I can join you?"

He wanted to wait a little before he broke the news that he and Gabriel would have to abandon the Twins altogether. He could sense, more than he could see, Lieutenant Lemminkainen, their personal bodyguard, half-hidden in the shadow in a nearby box: at least, thank God, this dependable man wasn't on the list. But for the rest, the Dauphin-Doges would have to take care of themselves in the most hostile surroundings. And although they were well-mannered enough to hide their fear, it showed through their nervousness and eagerness to talk.

"We were discussing our new Prime Preceptor, Ms. Frekker," said Geraldine, as the Fort Gradlon foghorn blew in the distance. "We met her today after the ceremony, and on the whole we found her a remarkably unpleasant person."

"And it appears that Valkyrie is *really* her middle name," added Reginald. "Regina Valkyrie Frekker."

Brentford had noticed her in the airship among Peterswarden's close circle of courtiers, a steely-eyed, athletic woman with a braided crown of blond hair. He'd heard that she was the former Headmistress of the Eleven Thousand Virgins, a Christian boarding school for poor girls that boasted a long tradition of corporal punishment, as well as sufficient friends in high places to stifle the occasional scandal.

"They may have thought you needed to be disciplined," said Brentford with a mock-severe frown—an awkward attempt at clowning to disguise his concern.

"I don't see why you'd say that," Gabriel remarked, quickly picking up the mood. "I've spared no spanking, have I?"

The Twins laughed, and it was hard to tell whether they were blushing or glowing. Once again, Brentford was amazed by their easy complicity. It was surprising to see how the notoriously unsociable Gabriel had dedicated himself to Reginald and Geraldine, even beyond his not-so-secret role as Prince-Consort, as some had nicknamed him—that or, with typically tiresome New-Ven wit, the Prince-Consortionist. Exquisitely bred though they had been by their arcticocrat grandmother, and somehow endowed with all the memories of their closest ancestors, the Dauphin-Doges had received only a patchy education in the humanities. Although Gabriel's so-called "serendipedia" methods were not always the most orthodox, he had painstakingly corrected and completed it, while adding his firsthand knowledge of the city's backstage, so that—at least for wonders of nature who had grown up in a crystal castle on an imaginary island—the Twins were now relatively conversant with the real world, if New Venice could be called that. Of course, Brentford reflected, Peterswarden was aware of this privileged relationship. Cutting off the Twins from their mentor would leave them clueless and, if Brentford could judge Peterswarden's intentions from his choice of a new preceptor, easier to intimidate.

Still, he could not bring himself to tell them the truth. He vaguely heard Gabriel amusing the Twins with his upcoming audition to become Playwright-in-Partibus at the Circus of Carnal Knowledge, and his plans to smuggle them into the audience, underage as they were. Brentford found it hard to interrupt that reverie. It was only when he heard Reginald say, with an almost imperceptible trembling in his voice, "It's a good thing for us to know you'll be around," that he suddenly launched himself into what felt like barely thawed water.

"Except that we will not be, unfortunately."

A pained silence followed this outburst. Nice start as a diplomat, thought Brentford.

"Are you trying to trick us into believing you have something interesting to tell us?" asked Gabriel.

"No, but I am sure you have, Gabriel. Tell us how you liked your stay in Paris?"

"That was in another country, and besides, the wench is dead," Gabriel answered, with a wink that turned to a wince. "Well, to speak frankly, it's sort of hazy."

He had left four years ago and remained there for almost two years. Officially, he had studied French literature at the Sorbonne and officiously, or so Brentford had gathered, for it was the usual deal when you were granted a scholarship abroad, he had worked as a Polestar guide for the Polaris Guild, a city agency locally known as the Press Gang that examined, contacted, and sometimes recruited new citizens for New Venice. The city was not keen on expanding, for its resources were limited, but given its mediocre life expectancy and its low birth and high suicide rates, fresh blood was needed from time to time. All of which made Gabriel the perfect candidate for the New Venetian Embassy in Paris, and provided the best excuse to complete the isolation of the Dauphin-Doges. "How would you like to go back?" Brentford asked him, trying to hide his anxiety.

Gabriel shrugged his shoulders.

"I haven't even thought about it. There's little chance I'll get another opportunity."

"You're leaving in three days, as a matter of fact. By special order of the Regent-Doge and the Council of the Seven Sectors."

Reginald and Geraldine exchanged a panicked glance.

"Can we come with you, Gabriel?" they chimed.

"I'm going to Paris, then?" Gabriel asked. He was puzzled, but, Brentford noted with relief, at least his curiosity was piqued. "And can I ask you why?"

"Because you wouldn't leave a good friend in the lurch, would you?"

"So you're going, too?" asked Reginald. "Oh, please, take us with you!" Geraldine added.

"I am afraid we cannot." Brentford sighed, as, with perfect symmetry, the Twins' faces twisted into a lopsided pout. Sensing tears were near, Gabriel tried to enliven the conversation a little.

"Are you taking me on a honeymoon at last?"

"Sorry to disappoint you, but it looks more like winter sports to me. Officially, they have had dreadfully cold conditions there and they need experts to shovel them out of the avalanche. Or so said a dying explorer whom they sent to ask us for help. You'll be the interpreter, I gather, and pretty much whatever else you want."

Gabriel remained silent for a moment, trying to make sense of the news.

"And unofficially? Something tells me there's a stone in this snowball."

"And a rather big, pointy one, yes. It's Peterswarden's way of tell-ing me that this town ain't big enough for the both of us. And to be frank, we haven't much of a choice. There's a law that sends you to prison when you refuse appointment to an embassy."

"I know," said Reginald. "It's an old law of the Republic of Ven-ice. They used to send former doges away, so that they wouldn't be a threat to the new doges." He had a passion for old Venetian history—just like Peterswarden, apparently.

"Maybe nobody wanted to leave Venice at all, and they were obliged to pass a law," said Geraldine thoughtfully, although she was more into Catherine the Great and Queen Christina of Sweden.

"So, if I understand correctly, it took him about four hours to get rid of you," Gabriel concluded.

Brentford grimaced. As usual with Gabriel's remarks, it was a suction-cup arrow; he felt this one stick right to his forehead.

"To get rid of us *all*. Have a look at this list," he said, handing his friend an official paper that by the look of it had recently been crumpled in a fit of rage.

The list was written in the unmistakable local style:

After a unanimous vote by the City Council of the Seven Sectors, The City of New Venice and the Northwasteland Commonwealth is honoured to be represented in Paris by the following delegation to the New Venetian Embassy:

> His Excellency Mr. Brentford Orsini, Envoy Extraordinary, Economy & Engineering Expert
>
> Mr. Gabriel Lancelot d'Allier, Chief Counselor for Culture and Communication
>
> Mr. Jean-Klein Lavis, M.D., High Commissioner for Health & Hygiene in Cold Climates
>
> Ms. Lilian "Lenton" Lake, Special Secretary for Suffrage & the Social Situation of the Sexes
>
> Mr. Alan Blankbate, Special Secretary for Sewage & Scavenging
>
> Mr. Thomas Paynes-Grey, Ensign-Explorer, Army Assistant-Attaché
>
> Mr. Tuluk, Envoy-Expert on Eskimo Economy

"Well, it's crystal clear, isn't it?" said Gabriel, folding the paper and giving it back to Brentford.

"Yes. All of the people who took part in last year's coup. Except Jean-Klein Lavis, that is."

"But he is French. And he helped us two years ago in that Faber business. The Forty Friends have not forgotten, obviously."

"I suppose, if you don't mind helping me getting everyone aboard and out of jail, that you could talk to him about this. And to Tuluk as well, whom you know better than I do. I'll take care of Blankbate and Paynes-Grey myself."

"And then there's Lilian."

"And then there's Lilian, yes," admitted Brentford.

They looked at each other for a while and then spoke at the same time.

"Well . . ."

"But . . ."

"Go ahead, Gabriel."

"No, please."

"Well, I have to take care of the the logistics. I'd better leave Lilian to you."

"But if she is to come with us, I suppose you'll have to face her sooner or later."

It was a draw.

"Okay, we'll do it together," Brentford said, and sighed.

"When will you be back?" asked Reginald, who, Brenford noticed with sadness, had passed his arm around his sister's shoulders as if to offer her the protection their friends were withdrawing from them. If these two needed to get closer than they already were, things were really looking grim.

Brentford hesitated.

"I don't know. Not before next spring, I'm afraid."

"That's almost a year," said Geraldine, sounding sorry and reproachful.

Brentford nodded. He could sense, nay, share, their apprehension. He dropped his last bomb, while he still had the nerve.

"Ah, and another thing," he said, turning towards Gabriel. "We are travelling by Psychomotive."

Gabriel gaped, thinking of all the ghastly stories he had heard.

"Isn't that dangerous?" Reginald asked.

"Our mother saw a pilot *dissolve* while driving one," Geraldine added in a tone halfway between adult concern and childish boasting.

"Well, we won't be driving it, at least . . ." said Brentford, for lack of a better answer.

"And what if you don't come back?" the Twins said in perfectly timed unison.

There was a moment of silence, except for a buzz of ultrasonic unease. Brentford racked his brain for a way to reassure them. And himself.

"You know what we'll do? I've noticed you like pledges. We are going to take a pledge."

He got up and, after a few whispers in the dark, came back with Lieutenant Lemminkainen, who sat uneasily at their table, hunched like a shy giant, his taut cheekbones shining from *chouchen*, the local eau-de-vie, but his eyes glinting with attention.

"Lieutenant," Brentford said in a low voice, "we have something to ask you. We are, Mr. d'Allier and I, under an obligation to go abroad in the service of the Regent-Doge. Delicate as it is, it would be very reassuring to us, knowing you as we do, to be certain that *whatever your orders might be* you will always make the Dauphin-Doges' freedom and safety your first concern. In exchange, you would have our word of honour that were any problems to arise, we would, Mr. d'Allier and I, defend you and bear full responsibility for your acts."

Lemminkainen looked at them all, very slowly.

"Your Excellency," he finally said, fumbling for his best English, "I know you do not mean to insult me, but I am not in the habit of letting others take responsibility for my actions. So, I will simply swear to protect the Dauphin-Doges from any threat, as is now my mission. In return, I will simply ask you to do anything in your power to come back as quicky as possible, in case we . . . need your help."

"I swear," said Brentford, a lump in his throat. But he realized, a little too late, that the solemnity of all this had upset the Dauphin-Doges more than it had appeased their fear. He saw, with regret and sadness, their smiles twist back into pouts.

"Don't you cry," said Gabriel to the Twins, "or I'll call Frau Frekker."

But, as the foghorn blew in the distance again, he took them in his arms.

To be continued . . .

EPISODE II

THE MOST SERENE SEVEN

I

The Wizard of Od

The following nightfall, Brentford disembarked at the Njörn Marina in Niflheim, the northernmost part of the city. Walking past the towering dome of the Gladsheim greenhouse, he reached a row of warehouses and took a left, towards a manor that—to its very gables—was a replica of Tycho Brahe's Uraniborg castle, except it was made entirely of cast iron. As if he were in any danger of being mistaken, a copper plate in Gothic letters read, W. B. SSON, WIZARD, above a coat of arms showing a hammer and pliers. If Brentford wasn't the right man, at least this was the right place.

Above the plaque, a knocker that looked like a small, grotesque gnome's head protruded from the door. Brentford had barely taken his hand from it when the plaque pivoted on itself and the bold antique script suddenly read ENTER; the door clanged open on its own.

Electric lamps switched on automatically as Brentford went inside. Before he had time to react, the square of the tiled floor he stood upon began moving gently downward, and he soon found himself gliding along four iron rails that grated and shot sparks and smelled faintly of rust. At times, he thought he could hear a distant music, like whistles or a chime, but he could not be sure of it.

Looking up, he could see the glare of the electric light dwindling in the distance. The dank darkness deepened around him, heavy and chilling like a soggy mantle. After what seemed like long minutes of nauseating descent, the platform eventually slowed and came to a stop with a little bump that made his heart hop in his ribcage. An open doorway pivoted in front of him, inviting him into a stone-walled room.

The first thing he saw when he entered was the huge fire that roared in the hearth built into the opposite wall. The intermediate space, propped with iron girders and beams, was occupied by long trestle tables covered with books, alembics, crucibles, metal coils, and machines in various stages of construction or dismantling.

Meanwhile, swollen waves of eerie sounds echoed around the stone walls, at times like the whistle of a departing steamer, at times like the hollow wails of Pan's pipes. An old man dressed in a crimson smoking jacket, his white hair carefully combed, sat with his back to Brentford, playing an organ whose glass pipes throbbed with a leaping blue glow—it was a gas-powered pyrophone, if Brentford's memory served, drawing its sound from the vibrations of two diverging flames. As the door clicked shut behind his visitor, the old man finally turned to him, revealing a swollen eyelid that gave his face a constant mischievous wink.

"Ah, Mr. Orsini. Welcome to my humble laboratory," he said, getting up with the help of a cane, a severe limp in his left leg. "I've been looking forward to this." His deep-etched face seemed never to have been young; he looked exactly to Brentford like a mad scientist in a play who has a beautiful daughter, living with him contentedly, happily cut off from the world and dedicated to his work—and bound to fall in love with the hero.

"Mr. Sson, I presume?" Brentford said, shaking himself from his reverie. "I didn't know my visit was expected."

"What sort of wizard would I be if I had not expected it?" answered the man, with more than a hint of a Scandinavian accent.

"The wizardry I have seen here so far is rather technical," observed Brentford without malice.

"Oh. There is no difference, really. Machine-building used to be a part of magic. It is just another way to make nature work beyond its . . . usual inclinations, is it not? What is it that I can do for you, Mr. Orsini?"

"I am supposed to borrow one of your Psychomotive vehicles in the service of the City."

"I have been informed of that, yes . . . It is purely a matter of money, as you know. I find money is an interesting energy. So full of magic . . ."

"Is it, really?" said Brentford. "It seems rather stubborn and down-to-earth to me."

"No, no. You are wrong, young man! After all, most of our sense of magic comes from it nowadays: it keeps alive in us the noble and ancient belief that the possible can come true. But it is a powerful and volatile spirit, and I grant you that when it is invoked by fools, money can replace imagination instead of enhancing it."

"You will just have to name your price. I have reason to think you will not find the Council thrifty in this matter," said Brentford sombrely. He wondered how much the Regent-Doge would pay to get rid of him. The sky was the limit, probably, but strive as he might he could not find that flattering.

"Very well, then. But I must warn you that Psychomotion is a powerful technology. Some would even call it dangerous. It is not to be used lightly."

It had already crossed Brentford's mind that the danger could be another reason behind Peterswarden's choice of transport for him. He tried to shrug off the idea—right or wrong, it would get him nowhere, and especially not to Paris.

"I've heard little about these machines, outside of rumours."

"Ah. But some rumours can be true. If you want to follow me."

Another, more comfortable elevator took them up to the berths of the Psychomotives. To Brentford's surprise, this area was much more luxurious than the laboratory. The walls were decorated with a mustard-coloured wallpaper in an Arts and Crafts pattern that blended stems and cogs, leaves and lightbulbs. Thick carpets lined the platform beside a long, shiny, black machine. Its design was surprisingly simple: two cylinders, one slightly larger, fitted together like the parts of a telescope. Two little portholes at the front of the wider, shorter cylinder indicated it as the cockpit; the longer, slimmer tube looked like the tank of a compressed-air locomotive. The whole contraption rested on rail tracks, and in the pit below, Brentford could see something like a reversed fin, obliquely pointing forward and almost as sharp as a knife.

"It looks quite comfortable here," said Brentford.

"Ah, Mr. Orsini. Imagine yourself sleeping peacefully in the earth and one day being taken out of the darkness to be burnt, beaten, chained to strangers and forced to work at full speed under extreme conditions of pressure and temperature. Even if you're a bit dimwitted and of a retiring nature, as metal mostly is, believe me, you will cruelly resent it. The elements of a machine are often unhappy together, the way whipped slaves are bound to be. A well-constructed machine, on the contrary, will be a smooth machine, where all the parts are kept in harmony according to the most natural bonds, a machine whose components bathe in the surroundings that are the most *sympathetic* for them, in terms of temperature, hygrometry, light, magnetism and so on . . ."

"And how do these things work?" Brentford asked, eager to get to the point.

"Oh! Very well. A little too well for human beings, perhaps."

"I meant, the principles. I have never quite understood."

"I seem to remember you are an engineer by trade. And if you are as good as your father was, the principles should not be difficult for you to grasp. Up to a certain point, that is," Sson said, affectionately patting the black graphite body of the tank, where the name *Voda* was etched in rune-like roman letters.

"Try me, please," said Brentford, who had wondered for a while when his father would be evoked. He himself remembered clearly, more from his father's point of view than from his own, the time when Afnor Orsini had talked to him about the legendary Woland Brokker Sson, the exile from the short-lived Boreal Republic of Spitzberg, and about his machines that challenged all known laws—and, it seemed, a few unknown ones as well.

"You may have heard about Odic Force?"

Brentford rummaged in vain in a dusty drawer at the back of his brain that he hadn't opened since his years as a Poletechnician at the Septentrional School of Extreme Engineering. His father's transphered memories yielded no better results, dim and uncertain as they were.

"I don't think it was part of my curriculum."

"Ah, schools nowadays . . . Well, maybe you've seen an Aurora Borealis, then?" the wizard said, with a touch of irony that slightly vexed Brentford. "This is where Von Reichenbach mostly got the idea from. In the 1850s, he observed that some sensitive subjects could perceive aurora-like coloured lights at the ends of magnets, crystals, and fingers. Actually what Reichenbach had found was a pervasive force that is present in the whole universe and resonates within our nervous system. Now, this force has certain kinetic powers, which can be projected from the body under certain circumstances. So, I said to myself, why not use it to power a vehicle? A vehicle whose fuel and motor are produced by the pilot himself?"

"That force—of will or whatever—would have to be very powerful to move such big vehicles," Brentford said doubtfully.

"Bah, nothing in nature is weak when it is properly invoked. Od is very strong at the poles. The auroras crackle with it, as ice crystals do. It can be slowly but easily accumulated and stored—I use pure ice crystals—and it is slow to discharge. Once the pilot is charged with Od, it is but a matter of channelling the force efficiently. For one thing, Od, as I said, is diamagnetic and can be used for easy levitation. Then, because the two hands of the body are differently Od-polarized, they can rotate two disks in different directions, hence furnishing electromagnetic power, which in turn operates contra-rotating turbines with mobile rotor blades for steering. It's as simple as that, really."

Brentford was unconvinced, but after all, this was New Venice. He had seen Helen stop Time and a kangaroo with a wolf's head emit telepathic messages: if he willed it, he could make his disbelief diamagnetic and let it float on thin air.

"Would you like to have a look inside?" asked the wizard. He touched some unseeable zone on the hull, a door slid open, and the bars of an iron ladder seemingly sprang from nowhere.

The circular interior of the Psychomotive was comfortable, with golden padded walls and black upholstered seats, zircon lamps on ebony tables, and small round copper portholes. But it was to the steering room that W. B. Sson led Brentford.

Two seats were installed there, facing the front portholes. One of them was topped with a helmet on a swivel, which was in turn connected to a complex system of batteries, dials, and wiring fixed at the back. In front of the other seat were a curious double steering wheel covered in runes, a brass gyroscope, and an instrument board with an array of paper-recorders.

"I still don't get the psychic part of it," Brentford said.

"It is all about receptivity. Alas, we are not all equal in regard to Od. Very few people are sensitive enough to it to perceive its emanations in themselves or in others, but it is nevertheless the last of the series of physical phenomena, and the closest to what we could call the world of the spirits—or, not to trouble you with that idea, the world of the mind. It is exactly what people used to call—misguidedly, for lack of a better word—animal magnetism. And like animal magnetism, it is quite simply the vehicle of Vision. The Psychomotive pilot, once equipped with this solenoid Odic Helmet—I call it the Tarnhelm—which is nothing but an Od accumulator, becomes somewhat clairvoyant and foresees obstacles in the darkness, hidden paths, possible accidents, and many other phenomena that demand, shall we say, a certain training: ghosts of past travellers, for instance. Here lies the rub. This machine can have unpleasant side effects, to say the least."

Brentford immediately thought of the story he had been told by the Twins, of the pilot Jeremy Salmon, who had literally dissolved on arrival.

"So, if I follow you, the difficulty is in finding a pilot."

"What about my mysterious daughter?" asked W. B. Sson with a mischievous smile.

Brentford was flabbergasted. "Do you read minds, too?"

"Ah! At my age, only the large print."

II

The Magical Crown

"It's called a *couronne magnétique,* or *magique*—a magnetical or magical crown, and I never thought I'd ever see one again," said Jean-Klein Lavis, in his unapologetically thick French accent, as he examined the curious object that Gabriel had brought him. Brentford and Gabriel, who had little inclination to put it on their heads, had been right in supposing that the Paris-born doctor would know what it was.

"They were invented in the early 1890s, I think, during the Suggestion Craze," the elegant French exile went on, in his exquisitely affable style. "If I remember correctly, the idea was that you could hypnotize a subject while he wore the *couronne magique.* The device would record and retain the command, so that when someone else put the crown on, they would act according to the first suggestion, as if it were contagious, so to speak. But I was certain it had been forgotten."

"So why would the explorer have been wearing it, then?"

"Maybe they have made progress on it, though I don't see how. Perhaps it was storing information. It would be interesting to find out."

The Magnetic Crown had proven good bait: Lavis was hooked. Of course, there was every reason for him to be interested. His first visit to New Venice had been as part of an invited delegation of doctors from the famous La Salpêtrière Hospital in Paris. Gabriel had first met him when Lavis had taken care of him after a drug-fueled duel, and Gabriel still remembered this with gratitude. A few years later, Lavis had come back to New Venice with a contingent from the crackpot Société des Polaires, which wanted to promote world

awareness through telepathy, and he had been instrumental in estab-
lishing contact with the Polar Kangaroo at a time when the city badly
needed to be defended from Delwit Faber and the Lobster Girls.

Fascinated by the city, Lavis had decided not to go back to Paris
with the Polaires, and had remained behind to settle in New Venice.
The House of Health & Hygiene had never formally granted him a
license to open a medical practice, but through cunning or vision he
had managed to bypass this obstacle by launching into a venture that
it had never occurred to the authorities to forbid: noticing, much to
his hand-rubbing surprise, that nobody had ever thought to system-
atically fight the depressive effect of the city's long winter months, he
had established the first phototherapy and chromotherapy institute
in the city, Lavis's Colour and Light Clinic, which soon attracted to
Barents Boulevard a numerous and wealthy clientele.

Behind the office in which he had received Gabriel was a large,
elegant room furnished with tables where people could casually use
the hand-held condenser lamps. Along the walls, a few ecstatic heads
bobbed above photo-bath cabinets, their owners' light-starved bodies basking in the warmth from dozens of colour-filtered bulbs. At
the back, an "operating room" boasted reclining chairs and beds
topped with the telescopic tubes of ultraviolet lamps (and, Gabriel
had noticed, a rather cute team of nurses); other snug private spaces
were equipped with red or blue coloured glass screens for tanning
and "edenic" relaxation. Neurasthenia, neuralgia, skin diseases, and
tuberculosis were treated there and sometimes cured, though Lavis
was honest enough to recognize the part that autosuggestion played
in the process. But then, it was still something of an accomplishment
in itself to create an environment that was conducive to it.

"Well, what would you think of the suggestion that you could
very easily go back to the source of the *couronne magique*?" Gabriel
offered tentatively. For all his loyalty to Brentford, he still felt annoyed
by the situation that loyalty had landed him in. It reminded him of
his days in the Press Gang, when he'd had to convince unsuspecting
people that life in New Venice would be a bed of hothouse roses. Even
if he was less pained by his bad conscience than by the disappointing
revelation that he in fact *had* something so common and cheap as a

guilty conscience, he nonetheless had qualms about selling a subzero Paris to Jean-Klein.

The Frenchman, fortunately, looked interested, and a smile dawned on his rosy, perfectly shaved cheeks.

"How could I do that, Monsieur d'Allier?"

"By joining the delegation to the New Venetian Embassy in Paris, for a year or so, under Brentford Orsini's direction."

For a moment, he thought about telling Lavis the truth about the high stakes involved in this operation. But given the doctor's cheerful reaction, he decided, well, who was he to ruin it for others? And after all, Gabriel thought, however much the Frenchman liked New Venice, it was an isolated and at times dreary place, and there could be little doubt that as the years went on, Lavis had grown nostalgic about Paris.

"The City of Light," the doctor murmured, as if to himself.

Gabriel reeled in the line.

"It appears that the City of Light urgently needs *our* lights after a few extremely cold months. You would be the Embassy's specialist for matters regarding health." And without giving him more time to think, he added, "The only inconvenience is that our departure is scheduled for Sunday."

"Are you going, too?"

"Well, you know Brentford. He would be lost without me."

Lavis nodded, like a man who tries to think things out, but Gabriel could see in his eyes that his mind was already prowling the streets of some dream Paris, half remembered, half made up. He knew it all the more because it was in this vapourous image that he himself had been living for most of the two previous days.

"Of course, I would have to get things organized for my absence," Lavis continued to muse. "But I suppose that can be arranged in the allotted time. The clinic is really slow in the spring, anyway. It could even be closed for a while . . . So, how do we get there?"

"By Psychomotive, it would seem," Gabriel replied as casually as he could. Much to his surprise, Lavis's enthusiasm increased.

"Really?" he said, glowing with anticipation. "I've never taken one, but from what I have heard about the way they work, I wouldn't want to miss this. Count me in, by all means."

It was early evening when Gabriel, his mission accomplished, returned to the dusky, misty streets, where here and there the openings of the boulevards and the angles of the buildings already seemed to have something faintly Parisian about them.

"Well, that was an easy catch," he thought, almost ashamed of his own satisfaction. "The master will be happy."

III

The Duel

The Northwestern Naval Armoury & Academy was a long white building along Parry Canal, with a massive square dungeon in the middle and a domed tower at each end. Brentford took the winding staircase up one of the towers, absorbing the vista as he passed the arched openings. The skyline was graceful, perhaps because there were more domes than spires, as befitted a self-contained city in a godforsaken place. It floated in a soft golden haze, more like a cloud of coloured light particles than a definite set of lines and angles. Brentford breathed in its beauty along with the bracing air, until a stinging in his eye warned him that he'd better look away. He was now an exile, and should not forget it, let alone forgive it.

As he ascended he could hear, closer and closer, the familiar clanging from the fencing hall on the top floor under the roof. For Brentford, that apparent chaos resolved into a melodious cadence of well-timed thrusts and parries, over a rumbling bass of rapid foot-work. But it was the smell, a subtle blend of warm rust and subdued sweat, that took him years backwards to the days when he was one of these fencing cadets, padded and yet exposed, the world reduced to a grey grid of mesh and two moving straight lines. He found himself missing the way the formalities and coded attitudes, the masks and protections, rendered one's opponent slightly unreal, reducing him to a mere target, a moving geometry of weak points. With a faint thrill of pleasure, he remembered precisely the way the ritual and its rules disciplined the murderous impulse that ran along his nerves and the faint thirst for blood that hardened his muscles.

Today the small hall was crammed with fencers, gliding on different planes like tin ducks in a shooting gallery. Brentford immediately saw that the meticulous pinpoint style he had painstakingly learned when he was a cadet had been replaced by a kind of happy-go-lucky carelessness: These cadets fenced with their arms instead of their wrists, and with their wrists instead of their fingers. To a purist like him, they looked like blind men waving white canes at each other.

As he expected, Thomas Paynes-Grey was there, sitting on one of the wooden benches that ran along the room, red and sweaty, a shock of curly blond hair sprouting from around the mask cocked open on his forehead. He was flexing his foible back to some lawful angle, after a thrust that must have been ferocious. In spite of his blond pencil moustache, his long, fine face looked very young, but having seen him lead the cadets against the Council one year before, Brentford knew that there was more to him than his healthy, cheerful mien. What that "more" was Brentford intended to find out as soon as possible.

"Ensign Paynes-Grey?"

"Oh, Your Most . . . er . . . Mr. Orsini," said the ensign, rising and saluting, "Glad to see you again, sir. I must say I was just gutted by the results of the election."

Well, at least he was spontaneous and frank.

So was Brentford. "Not as badly as I was," he answered, sitting beside him. "I still have to let off some steam. Would you care for a little bout with me?"

"I would be honoured. Foil, sabre, or épée?"

"Foil or épée, whichever you like, as long as it's not sabre. I never got the point of it. So to speak."

"Épée, then. Best of five?"

"Certainly."

"I'll get you some gear." And before Brentford could say thank you, he had sprung to a cabinet and come back with plastron, jacket, mask, and glove.

"I'll give you one of my épées."

"It's superb," said Brentford, weighing the weapon and squinting down at its dark-bluish blade. He noticed that the épée was slightly unbalanced, but decided to say nothing about it.

He put on the whites, and catching himself in a mirror, realized once again how much better they made you look—straightening the spine, cocking up the head, strengthening the hand; all of this turning you into an armoured angel who would face a dragon with cold-blooded aplomb. The mask was different but equally magical: it changed your head into the faceted eye of a fly, slowing time all around you, cutting your adversary's swiftest moves into a Muybridge series of laughably clumsy swats.

They soaked their points in the ink pots, saluted, and ten minutes later there was little that a short-winded but victorious Brentford hadn't had a chance to observe about the ink-smeared Paynes-Grey. He could blame his opponent's swashbuckling style on the training the cadets now received, no doubt, but the young man's relentless dynamism and recklessness seemed to be entirely his own. A certain stubborness too—it had taken Thomas three failures to renounce the cut-over feint and low lunge that got him parried in septime and touched in the knee every time—could be understood, Brentford supposed generously, as the sort of bravura with which he felt a certain sympathy. But the young man was no killer; after catching up and moving one touch ahead, he had left himself open for two touches by Brentford in the wink of an eye. What's more, in his salute afterwards he revealed no inbred hatred of defeat. Besides, from the way Thomas adjusted his uniform afterwards and slanted his cap back on his carefully recombed hair, one could deduce a touch of vanity and a sound consciousness of his effect on the fair sex (but here Brentford cheated, for he had other sources of information on that). All in all a good soldier, perhaps, but not a warrior.

Instead, Thomas Paynes-Grey was, in a sense, the quintessential New Venetian officer who spends his life waiting for an attack that never comes. Brentford himself had almost become one of these idle Hectors, and it was to escape the gnawing feeling of purposelessness that he had chosen administration as a career: In that, at least, there was something to be done. He supposed that it was the same desperate need for action that had made this "young noble of the poop" a leader in the mutiny against the Council of Seven—that, along with the pleasure of casting himself as a romantic hero. Reasons, Brentford felt, as good as his own had been, and perhaps even not all that different.

He took Thomas to the Map Room, a perfect place for a quiet conversation, mostly because it was always empty. Brentford liked its uncertain light, its subtle smell of dust, and the austerity of its meshed casings along the whitewashed walls. The cadet's St. Jude banner hung folded in a corner, rusty red as a dried bloodstain, its crossed anchor and quarterstaff crumpled into near invisibility.

"I don't come here often," Thomas confessed. "It looks too much like a classroom." He had the vulpine smile of the bad pupil who knows his charm will get him through.

"I think it's more like a museum," Brentford answered. "Or some enchanted place out of time. Very New Venner in that respect. But tell me, Ensign, don't you ever wish that you could see more action? Besides brawls in Venustown, I mean."

Thomas smiled again at this.

"There was a revolution last year, remember . . ."

"I remember it very well," Brentford sighed. "And it was a lot of fun. But I'm afraid it's over now . . . or, at least, it is *here*. The front lines seem to have moved somewhat."

"I'm not sure that I see what you mean," Thomas said, with a frown.

"Let's say that, as far as I'm concerned, New Venice is not in New Venice anymore. I'll serve it abroad and do my best to save it from there."

"Abroad?" There was a sparkle in Thomas's blue eyes. They had spent too much time watching the icepack through frosted field glasses, these eyes, and they clearly wanted a revenge.

"I have been posted to Paris to run the New Venetian Embassy. And I need a military attaché. For about a year. You seem the perfect choice to me."

"We have embassies now?" Thomas asked, not even trying to hide how much the compliment had flattered him.

"A shadow embassy, if you prefer. On a secret mission."

That sparkle again. Brentford watched Thomas as the scenes of his present life danced through his mind. A life of parades, pub crawls, unfocussed fights, and blurry girls in darkened gondolas. Thomas would miss it, no doubt, but after the rush of excitement that he had felt while leading the Cadets to revolution last year, boredom had taken its toll. *Paris* had a ring to it. It seemed synonymous with possibility. With adventure. With pride. With more blurry women.

"I'd serve New Venice anywhere," he announced grandly.

Brentford felt not only relieved but also moved by Thomas's loyalty, to the city and to him.

"New Venice is anywhere we are, now. Welcome aboard, Ensign."

IV

The Metis

It would be stretching the truth to say that Gabriel was on familiar terms with Tuluk. Sure, they had once shared an icy *iglerk*, smelly furs, and a seal full of half-rotten birds, but to Gabriel that was something that he would rather forget than celebrate. True, Tuluk had saved his life when he was dying out in the cold, and that was a bit harder to obliterate from memory, but—blame it on Gabriel's innate modesty regarding the value of that life, or on an ungrateful nature at the core of his soul—he was not one to dwell on this, either.

The present visit made his situation still more embarrassing. The previous day's mission with Jean-Klein Lavis had been to talk an expatriate into doing something that, after all, most exiles want to do eventually—return home. Gabriel doubted that the Inuk would show the same enthusiasm at the prospect of leaving his Arctic homeland.

And so it was rather reluctantly that Gabriel walked into the drab Blithedale neighbourhood towards the pink-granite gate of the Technical Teams Workshops & Warehouses. His maternal grandfather had worked there for a while, and Gabriel remembered that on one of his first visits to New Venice, as a six- or seven-year-old boy, he had been totally awed by this gate, as if it were the entrance to the abode of Tubal-Cain. To his sober adult eye, the place looked more like run-down barracks, or even, if it had not been for the odd clang or echoed call, like some abandoned boomtown mine. A man muffled up to the eyes in a small office full of clocks reluctantly gave him the information that he requested, and—after a few misses—he found the workshop where Tuluk worked as a sled mechanic. The place had an acrid smell of welded metal and cold grease, and Gabriel found himself liking it. He came on his mother's side from a family of jewelers, locksmiths, and wrought-iron craftsmen, so in a sense, he was at home here, even if it was a home he seldom thought about.

Tuluk was there with his back turned, amidst a shower of golden sparks, fixing the bent runner of a Coanda turbine sledge. Gabriel thought he had better wait before calling out to him, and so observed him for a while, thinking about the eeriness of seeing among these metal scraps and tools a man he had first met in the most unmerciful Arctic wilderness.

Tuluk was a half-blood, and even in this respect he was the pure product of Inuk common sense: it was customary for Inuk women to get pregnant from passing sailors so as to avoid too much inbreeding among their small population. The babies were felt to be no less Inuit than the other children, and Tuluk, when Gabriel met him, was an unusually tall but otherwise typical bulky, black-haired Eskimo hunter, with bear claws protruding from the toes of his fur *kamiks*. The father, nameless and apparently faceless, did not appear on the surface of his son. Lighter eyes, perhaps, were the only clue.

Last year's events, however, had turned the tide of his life. Tuluk, who had always lived outside New Venice, had not gone back to Flagler Fjord with his friends Tiblit and Sybil Springfield. He had, instead, discovered in himself a fascination for the clockwork and engines of the *qallunaat*. There were certainly many things for which you could reproach the white men. They were full of themselves, and everything they did on a big scale was bound to be either frightful or a ridiculous failure, or any bizarre blend of the two. But when it came to building machines, they were as clever as Inuit, but with many more resources and the freedom to make errors. Propelled or turbine sleds, among other things, had mesmerized Tuluk, and he would pester the mechanics who tended them until they explained to him how they worked. Brentford had heard about this, and, always willing to oblige the Inuit in any way he could, had managed to get Tuluk an apprenticeship in the Technical Team of the Arctic Administration. Not only had Tuluk proved himself priceless when it came to repairing runners, but he had also quickly shown an innate sense of mechanics, and was currently taking night classes towards a Technician's degree. He did not enjoy the math, but when it came to fixing things, he was reported to be something of a genius.

"Hello, Tuluk," Gabriel finally called out once the ringing noise had stopped.

The Inuk, in coveralls and *kamiks*, turned around and lifted his brass goggles to reveal a big, warm smile that took Gabriel by surprise. He could have done without the long greasy handshake, though.

"Gabiriliq. Good to see you. What brings you here?"

Gabriel hemmed.

"Well, you know me, I need a favour."

Tuluk laughed.

"Yes. The *qallunaat* always needs something. He owns everything and he begs for the rest."

It was a bitter remark, Gabriel thought, but Tuluk had delivered it with more philosophy than aggression. The Inuk was after all half-*qallunaat* himself, and grew a little more so every day that he spent in New Venice. To some New Venetians, like Peterswarden, such cases represented a sad corruption of the native purity of the Inuit. To Gabriel, who was rather wary of purity-mongers, it was interesting to try to imagine what was going on in this doubly irrigated brain. Not that he had a clue. He continued, tentatively, "In fact, the favour goes both ways. Mr. Orsini and I would like to invite you on a trip, and we would be very happy if you accepted."

"A trip out there, on the ice? A hunting trip?"

"Ah, you know we do not hunt."

"You mean you eat someone else's hunt. Someone has to hunt, no? You want me to hunt for you?" Tuluk squinted. It had taken him some time to adjust to the idea that you did not have to hunt to be a man, and in fact it seemed to Gabriel that he was still not quite convinced.

"No. It's not that sort of trip. We are going much farther. Much, much farther. To the south. Among the *qavaat*," Gabriel added, using the word that he thought meant both southerners and idiots—and which, for Tuluk, probably included Gabriel as well.

"Why do you want me there?" Tuluk's frown was one that all New Venetians who dealt with the Inuit came to know: a bizarre blend of curiosity and ironic distrust.

"People need our help. Their country became too cold. They think that an Inuk could teach them a lot."

"But why this Inuk?"

Gabriel had agreed with Brentford that it would be better not to use the jail as an argument. The threat would do little to convince Tuluk— quite the contrary. He would simply go back to living in the wilderness with the other Inuit and never be seen again in New Venice.

"Because you know the *qallunaat* very well, for one thing. And because you can help them with their machines in the cold. They have a lot of machines there, even machines we do not have here."

Tuluk looked at Gabriel, his hunter's eyes in slits, as if trying to spy where the trap was hidden.

"We have enough machines here. And I don't want to miss the classes."

Gabriel detected a hint of nervousness, the discomfort of a man waiting to enter a world where he does not quite belong, a man who fears that the slightest mistake will make him an outsider again, this time forever.

"You will miss the classes, true. But your boss and tutors have agreed that you will get a lot of experience that people here won't have and—" Gabriel had a sudden inspiration "—Mr. Orsini promised he will help you with the math. Once you're back, you can pass the test as soon as you're ready."

Tuluk pondered this. For the Inuit, the name Orsini was something of a gold-standard guarantee. Gabriel guessed that Tuluk did not know how far it had been devalued three days ago, and it certainly wasn't the moment to disabuse him.

"What is this place we are going to? Is it America?"

"It's farther than that. And on the other side of the ocean."

Tuluk nodded, obviously worried.

"I am curious to see the world, but I do not want to be like these Inuit Mr. Peary took to America. They were shown like animals everywhere, got sick and saw the skeletons of their forefathers in a glass box."

"There will be no such things, Tuluk. We'll work together. And I promise you that you will see things no Inuk has seen."

That triggered something. Tuluk bit his lip. "How long?"

"About one year."

The Inuk looked around him, at this workshop that had become a home and the school where he learned the *qallunaaq* mind by dismantling and rebuilding its noisy, crazy, but crafty machines. But the curiosity that had brought him here was not so easily quenched, and Gabriel had been counting on that.

"Do they have motorcycles there?" Tuluk finally asked.

"Of course they have! And cars. And planes. And we will travel by Psychomotive, which may interest you."

Tuluk stood silent for a while. Not quite a white man yet, he did not seem bothered to be seen thinking deeply and at length before opening his mouth. As he smiled, Gabriel knew that he had made up his mind.

"This Inuk will go with you, then."

Gabriel returned the smile. But beneath it, though he was glad that Tuluk would be around, he felt bitter, as if he had just conned the Inuk, like some vulgar fur trader. Whether he liked it or not, Tuluk had saved his life the year before, and now he could only cross his fingers and hope that he hadn't offered him death as a payback.

V

Lady Franklin's Friday

It was two in the morning, and Brentford was waiting in the shadows that the shy moonlight could not reach. From where he stood he could discern under the arches on the other side of the Lady Franklin Plaza a covey of elegant women in black veils waiting for the passage of the Scavengers along the Rae Canal. The ritual brought back bitter memories of his brief stint as a garbage collector, and of the night he had found his first love, Seraphine Le Serf, among these women. In these days of Peterswarden, the place seemed shadier and the night more menacing, as if it were Brentford being observed. But if he wanted to find Blankbate on a Friday night, this was about his only chance.

A barge soon hit the embankment, and a few masked black shapes glided under the arches and immediately began rummaging among the fur and warm silks that were offered to them. Anonymous as the Scavengers were, Brentford could easily tell Blankbate from the others. Less from his bulk, maybe, than from his poise: as if he were being careful not to hurt others, he moved his hefty body in a thoughtful way that made him look even more dangerous. Brentford averted his eyes, trying to block out the hasty rustles and the muted moans that the wind carried raggedly to his side of the plaza. He tried to think of what he had done so far about that damned Embassy and what remained to be done. His very anger had made him fast and efficient. The Psychomotive was checked up and loaded and the false Canadian papers printed. The only quantity still unknown was the pilot, about whom the long-winded W. B. Sson had remained, for once, secretive. Meanwhile the news from Gabriel was good: in two days he had successfully enlisted such diverse characters as Tuluk and Jean-Klein Lavis. As for his own recruiting drive, besides a few bruises in the ribs, the mission to Paynes-Grey had been a pleasure and a breeze. Convincing Blankbate, however, would be a different kettle of rotten fish. And to speak frankly, Brentford would rather have the head Scavenger remain in the city to keep an eye on the new Regent-Doge instead of showing his ominous silhouette around Paris.

As soon as the Lady Franklin's Friday seemed to be over, Brentford hurried under the arches and swerved towards the embankment, hailing the garbage gondola just as it was unmoored.

"Hey, would you pick me up?" he shouted from above.

The beaked masks looked up at him. There were not many people who would dare to approach the Scavengers, but Brentford was one of them, and they recognized him at once.

"Jump in," said one.

"Can I see Blankbate?" asked Brentford as soon as he hit the deck.

"Go ask him yourself," said another, spooling back the hawser.

They were not there for small talk, and neither was Brentford: he walked up to the wheelhouse cabin and knocked.

"Good evening. Sorry for dropping in this way," he apologized, as he lowered his head through the door.

"Good evening. You're always welcome. There's coffee in that Dewar flask," said Blankbate curtly, not exactly happy to see Brentford, but knowing there must be good reason for his appearance.

Pretending to enjoy the bitter, oily brew that the Scavengers called coffee, Brentford explained the situation, although all he could see of his interlocutor in the darkened cabin was the back of his oilcloth longcoat as he steered the craft down the canal. The Scavenger listened sullenly but patiently.

"Paris, you said?" he suddenly interjected, before falling back into silence.

They were now gliding into the dead of night with a single light at the prow, the only sounds the faint humming of the Trouvé electric motor and the cracking of spring ice. All around them, along the deserted Rae Canal, the mansions added their shadows to the darkness, so that Brentford could hardly see the other two Scavengers crouching on the deck, except when a moonbeam fell aslant their long, curved white beaks.

"Paris, France, yes."

The beaked figure nodded slowly, as if to himself, while his large gloved hands steered the barge towards a fork in the canal.

"I may have a reason to go there," Blankbate finally said, after another long while. "There is a condition, though."

Brentford was relieved to hear of Blankbate's interest, for he had little power to convince him otherwise. To a City Scavenger, prison would have been totally useless as a threat. Whatever they really were at base—untouchable criminals doing penance behind masks or righteous judges scourging the city of unavenged wrongs—Scavengers were beyond, or perhaps *below*, the law.

"I'm listening."

"That you do not ask me what that reason is, and you let me take care of it as I please when we're there. I won't bother you about it, and you won't bother me about it."

"Oh, I've bothered you enough these past few years, I suppose," said Brentford, sensing that it was not the time to be fastidious. "I simply hope you don't plan to get into trouble there."

"Maybe I will, but I plan to get out of it, too. And on my own. So no need to trouble yourself on my account."

"It's a deal, then," said Brentford, trying not to look too worried either for the mission or for the Scavenger.

Blankbate nodded, and they both fell silent again, each one absorbed in his own uncertain future, as the barge took the fork that led away from the gold-specked mansions, and deeper into the night.

VI

A Musical Evening with Kinky & Stinky, the Aristoskunks

"Iτ's the last time I'm doing this," said Brentford moodily as he drew the skunk mask down over his face. He had always tried not to be snobbish about having been the Regent-Doge and all that, but the idea of going onstage disguised as a skunk now struck him as a blow to his self-respect. It may have been a hoot when he was twenty, but at forty, it was a bloody disgrace. He'd had a hunch that the election was the beginning of the end, but he had never thought he would roll downhill so fast.

"Come on!" said Gabriel, who was dressed in the same way but who, judging by the tone of his voice, seemed to be enjoying himself. "We agreed that it was the only way, didn't we?"

Brentford shrugged his furry shoulders

"It's been so long since we did this. I'd forgotten how awfully hot it was inside this costume. And it reeks of mothballs."

"Don't worry, it's just for one song, right?"

"Yes, a song that we barely had time to rehearse."

"Are you people ready?" asked Bodicea Lovelace, knocking on the dressing room door.

The two skunks left the cramped dressing room and found themselves facing the Mistress of Ceremonies, with her face mask and black corset, not to mention the leather lightning of a long whip that shone as black as the arm-length glove that held it. She passed her tongue over her scarlet lips.

"You two look juicy," she said.

"Please, Bee, spare us your remarks," said Brentford. "Does she know we're here?"

"She knows that one of the acts wants to meet her after the show. Just as you asked."

"Great, then," Brentford sighed. "Thanks a lot for arranging this, anyway. I owe you."

"Seeing you like that, I feel repaid for my efforts. Are you ready to go?"

"Hmm . . ." muttered Brentford.

Bodicea strode back to the little stage, lashed the floor with her whip, raising a cloud of floodlit dust, and announced "Ladies and Gentlewomen, coming from the woods and dusk, with their hind glands full of musk, here are . . . KINKY AND STINKY, THE ARISTOSKUNKS!"

Brentford "Stinky" Orsini shook his head in despair and walked to the upright piano, blinded by the light, while Gabriel "Kinky" d'Allier seized the carbon microphone with a trembling hand and squinted through his mask to see something of the darkened room. But there was little he could make out save for the glinting of the bronze shields decorating the walls, and the vague arabesque shadows of paper rose garlands festooned around them. He could feel stage fright gnawing at his stomach, and it didn't help that there were only women and girls in the audience, men being forbidden at the Penthousilea, except as costumed entertainers.

"Hello, Ladies," he heard himself saying in a quavering voice, "Here is a song to our favourite goddess."

"One, two, three, four," Brentford muttered before banging on the keys a devilishly vaudevillesque chord sequence of G-D-G-D-C, which Gabriel took up with a slowly growing assurance, shaking his tail as he sang:

Well I happened to see Venus
And I don't understand the fuss
She's just another beach belle
Surfing the swell
On a seashell

Well I happened to see Juno
She's powerful, useful to know
But looks too much like my mother
It's another
That I prefer

She's got a Minerva brace
It gives her haughtiness
And grace
Something wise
In her pale blue eyes
She's got the face
of a goddess

Yes, I have met Persephone
Well, she's not what you'd call funny
And if you take her for your wife
She'll make your life
Trouble and strife
I had a glimpse of Artemis
She's a sure shot and she can't miss
But I'd rather not have antlers
Me, it's another
I prefer

She's got a Minerva brace
It gives her haughtiness
And grace
Something wise
In her pale blue eyes
She's got the face
of a goddess . . .

Then, slowing down for the dramatic coda—

But all her former lovers
Have signed their monikers

Have drawn hearts and boners
All over her plaster . . .

Out of breath, he saluted to stray handclaps and a few boos, while
Brentford tried in vain to mop his brow through his mask. They must
have earned a meeting with Lilian by now.

Bodicea came up to the stage and signalled to them to follow her
down the few steps that separated them from the dining room. They
slalomed though the tables, their masked heads down, while some of
the women amused themselves by stepping on the dragging tails of
their costumes. Finally they spotted Lilian quietly smoking by herself
in one of the curious semicircular booths, where both seats and tables
recalled the coiled shape of a snail.

"Here they are, Lilian," said Bodicea. Then, turning to the skunks
with a veiled wink, "Be brave," before quickly walking off.

"Well, thank you, Bee," answered Lilian.

She smiled a little forced smile and gracefully indicated the empty
seats before her, but the skunks found it hard to sit on their cumbersome tails without making fools of themselves.

"I always thought such appendages would be embarrassing. You
can take off your masks, gentlemen," she said. "I knew who you were
the moment you walked onstage."

The skunks obeyed.

"I suppose you are Stinky," she said to Brentford, as he awk-
wardly put his head on the table.

"Well, right now, very probably," he said, and winced. His sense
of humour suffered strange lapses at times. This was when Gabriel
found him the funniest.

"To what do I owe the honour of your visit, your Most Serene
Highness?"

Lilian sounded sarcastic but Gabriel could see she was more
amused than angry at their desperate stratagem to meet her, now that
she and Brentford were no longer on speaking terms.

Shortly after the revolution, they had been lovers, and passionate
ones, but their affair had not lasted long. She'd reproached Brentford
for his poletical timidity, and he had found himself unable to cope
with her philanderings involving "friends" of the fair sex. Gabriel had

been at a loss to understand why that was a problem, until Brentford explained that he simply did not want to share, adding grimly that neither did she.

But now they would have to find a way to make up. Brentford had calculated that putting his pride on the table was probably the best gambit he could play. If she was still wary, she seemed willing at least to listen.

"State affairs, so to speak."

"I can see that. Are you campaigning against hunting quotas again?"

"Tell me, Lilian. When you toured the world, did you go to Paris?"

"No. It was planned, but as you remember, it was in my suffragette days, and I got arrested for arson. So I was punished like the naughty girl I had been, and much to my regret, I've never seen gay Paree. But that's hardly a state affair over here, I'd guess."

"And what if I asked you to take your revenge and go back there with me now?"

"Do you want to propose to me, Mr. Orsini?" she asked, smiling through a wisp of peppermint smoke. "It is true you are not married to the Frozen Sea anymore . . . I heard she gave you the cold shoulder."

"Sorry to disappoint you, but I'm afraid it's strictly business," Brentford parried and riposted. Gabriel could almost see the sparks between them. And they seemed to be enjoying it as much as he did.

"You've been assigned to the New Venetian Embassy in Paris as 'Special Secretary for Suffrage and Social Situations of the Sexes.' "

"And 'Stinky Skunks,' no? Is this one of your bright ideas, Brent?"

"Not really. It is Peterswarden's. He wants to get rid of us."

"Does he? And I want to get rid of him."

"So everyone agrees, then," Gabriel said, tucking his head under his arm.

Lilian cast him a look as if she wanted to will him into invisibility, or at least into silence.

"What if I refuse?" she asked, turning back to Brentford.

"There's a prison sentence."

"I am not afraid of jail," she answered proudly. "I have been on a hunger strike, remember. Maybe I could do with another one," she added, pinching a cheek that was nowhere near plump.

"I'd rather see you in Paris than in prison," said Brentford.

"So that you can do your master's bidding, eh? Without even putting up a fight."

"Helen seems to think that it's better this way."

Lilian said nothing. It had been Helen who, through vivid dreams, had led her back to New Venice. It had been she who, in a way, had brought Lilian and Brentford together. Helen was no joking matter for Lilian. Her eyes flashed a sputtering "You'd better be sincere on this one"; the look and its meaning flickered between them as plainly as lightbulb letters.

"So there's nothing personal about this on your part?" she eventually said aloud, with a frown of thoughtful distrust.

"Oh, no. Not at all."

"I mean you don't imply that we could go to Paris together, and have fun, and maybe, well, start again."

"Not in the least, I assure you," said Brentford, mirroring her nascent smile.

"Be frank, Brent: You would be *horribly* annoyed if I came."

"Oh! Terribly so."

"And I'll be free to roam the cabarets and go to every *café-concert* show I like, without giving a damn about you?"

"Just as you always have. You'll be free to go onstage and dance the can-can, if that's what you want."

She turned away from him to better savour, Gabriel supposed, the Paris that now rose in her mind. Slowly her smile froze as she returned to the here and now.

"Forget it. I can't go. I have little inclination to obey Peterswarden, and besides, I have this place to run."

As Brentford began to protest, someone tapped him on the shoulder and, startled, he looked up to see the monocled Ms. Regina Valkyrie Frekker, looming over him with a cruel grin on her large, flushed face.

"Ach, Mr. Orsini," she cooed mockingly. "I liked your show very much. It's a shame that His Highness could not see it . . ."

He blushed, but saw a lifeline in her famous crown of chain-like braids.

"Frau Frekker," he howled, trying to be heard over the sudden blare from the stage of a neighing saxophone. "The new Prime-Preceptor of the Dauphin-Doges!"

At this, she cast a smug look towards Gabriel, who bitterly regretted—not for the first time in his life—his lack of real musk glands.

"And this is Lilian Lenton . . ." Brentford continued.

"Whom there is no need to introduce," Frau Frekker interrupted, dismissing his courtesies. "I am very attentive to her *advanced ideas* . . ."

Lilian's and Frau Frekker's eyes clashed with the instant cold magic of mutual antipathy, metal against crystal. Lilian held her gaze until the Prime-Preceptor raised her chin with a little yelp of contempt, clicked her heels and stalked off. Lilian stared at her empty glass in silence.

Brentford glanced towards Gabriel and rose from his chair, careful not to trip over his own tail, which he wrapped around his arm like an imperial cape.

"Well, if that's so, Lilian, we'll leave you among your new friends."

Rather risky to be insolent to a woman when you're dressed in animal furs, Gabriel thought, like one who knew from bitter experience. But Brentford, at least, had gotten his point across.

"Sure, scurry off on your little rodent legs, Brent," Lilian answered inscrutably. "And please tell me where I shouldn't find myself under any circumstances, if I want to be spared the sight of so-called old friends."

"W. B. Sson's Uraniborg Castle, tomorrow night. Seven."

✳

"*She did this!*"

"How can you be sure?"

"Lilian runs the place. She ordered someone to do it while we were talking. I'm sure Bodicea told her about us ahead of time, and this is exactly the kind of thing she would find amusing."

"Bah!" said Gabriel. "If that's the case, she'll send our stuff back tomorrow."

They walked along Barents Boulevard, still in their skunk furs since their clothes had been stolen in the Penthousilea. At first, every time a propelled sled passed by, heralded by its headlights, they hid in the shadows of the pillars that upheld the pneumatic train track. But they soon stopped caring. After all, they were leaving in two days.

"The good thing is that we'll be ready in time," Gabriel said as they walked on side by side towards the end of the Boulevard, the tips of their tails tracing two parallel tracks in a fine layer of spring snow. "And without having to force anyone."

"Yes. It seems everyone has a good reason to go to Paris. Except me, that is."

"Are you sure you don't have one now, *Brent?*"

VII

The Entertaining of a Noble Head

"Is everybody here?" asked W. B. Sson, rubbing his hands, as the guests stepped one by one from the magnetic "elevatory" into his library. This was a circular, domed room; its severe cast-iron structure was softened by scarlet drapes and warm wooden parquetry, and decorated with binding runes. There were so many books lining the walls that Gabriel could almost feel the itch and burn from the Humots book-demon tattooed on his arm, relentlessly tugging him towards the stacks.

The wizard had been adamant that everyone should meet the pilot at the same time. Brentford had taken the mad scientist's hint that the pilot would be his daughter and thought that he must have determined that it would be improper or imprudent to introduce the young woman to him alone, and so was waiting instead for a less intimate, more formal occasion. Maybe he had wanted her to make some sort of social debut: it crossed Brentford's mind that W. B. Sson's daughter could well be an automaton, a gold-plated girl with reason in her heart, waiting for an occasion like this to be unveiled to the public.

Tonight was the first meeting of the Most Serene Seven, as Gabriel had recently dubbed them. It was an occasion meant to break the ice and give them a common aim. Not that, judging by the first contact in the hall, it would have otherwise gone altogether wrong. Lavis, always a perfect gentleman and professionally used to all kinds of people, had quickly put everyone at ease with his relaxed yet impeccable manners. Lilian and Thomas had struck up their conversation right where they had left it after the coup, even if, as Brentford suspected (or hoped), they would not have much to say to each other in

the long run. Blankbate and Tuluk, of course, were the most circum-
spect: Tuluk, because he was entirely absorbed by all that he was seeing all around him; Blankbate, because it was most unusual for him
to socialize outside the completely closed circle of the City Scavengers. But somehow, all of them were now united by the show Woland
Brokker Sson intended to stage about his mysterious pilot.

Sson cleared his throat and began his remarks with his trademark
elfin smile. "First, I must apologize to Mr. Orsini. Actually, and much
as I regret it, I do not have a daughter. I do, however, have a pilot. The
best that ever was and, in fact, the very last there is. But I have to warn
you that you may not appreciate, shall we say, his . . . *condition.*"

"To be honest with you, Mr. Sson," said Brentford, a little vexed
by his own naïveté and the wizard's ability to read the large print of
his mind, "I didn't exactly volunteer for this mission. So there are
many things I am prepared not to appreciate."

"Very well, then. Still, there is something I have decided to spare
you, and that is making you explain the pilot's, er, *situation* to your
colleagues."

"Is there some kind of problem with the pilot?" Brentford
inquired.

"Well, yes and no," said Sson. "There certainly was a problem,
you could say, but it has been solved and, I dare to think, very satisfactorily. Nevertheless, it has been brought to my attention that the
solution may take some time to be fully appreciated. But you shall see
for yourselves. If you will follow me . . ."

He led the Most Serene Seven across the library to a double door
of solid oak and opened it with a broad gesture, only to reveal a
sweet-scented darkness.

"Benedict?" whispered the old man. "Are you awake?"

"Yes," answered a coarse voice that seemed to spring from the
pavilion of a rusty phonograph. "What is it you want, you old fool?
How could anyone get any rest with that bloody Pyrophone of yours?"

"There is a group of persons here who have a mission for you,"
answered Sson, who did not seem to mind the blatant lack of respect,
and even, or so Brentford thought, sounded slightly apologetic.

"It's jolly well time. I was starting to feel ants in my legs."

"May I turn on the light?"

"Well, it's their choice!" the voice said, and made a noise that was halfway between hoarse laughter and a very bad cough.

"Please," Brentford said, bracing himself for the worst.

Sson clapped his hands and the wall sconces slowly began to bathe the room in a warm, subdued light. The Seven found themselves to be standing in an orthogon covered in a muted green wallpaper and set with stained-glass panels, all decorated with stylized flowers and intricate Celtic knotwork. Potted ferns slowly swayed to some invisible birdsong, and they even heard a brook or a fountain babbling somewhere. But what knocked the wind out of Brentford and drenched him in cold sweat was the object on the round oak table in the middle of the room.

It was a human head, bald and generously moustachioed, and seemingly sprouting from the top of a wooden box sitting on the table that was studded with buttons and dials.

"Good evening, ladies and gentlemen," said the head, in a croaking voice. "Forgive me if I don't shake your hand."

"Oh my god!" exclaimed Lilian, who briefly regretted not being the kind of woman who fainted easily.

The Most Serene Seven now felt anything but serene, although they were not all struck in the same way. Gabriel was fascinated by any freakish atrocity; professional interest kept Lavis's eyes riveted on the head; Blankbate had seen more horrors than he would care to remember and so looked on calmly enough; Thomas worked hard to seem undaunted and even amused, especially when the pale Lilian looked towards him; and Tuluk, after sprinting for the elevator, decided he would not like to pass for a coward in front of the whites and shuffled back to face the head, trying not to look straight at it.

Brentford, his heart in his mouth, faintly hoped this was some parlour trick, but his own eyes could see that what was below the table was wholly different from what a wedged mirror should have reflected.

"Good evening, sir," he managed to mutter, trying to get a grip on his nerves and his stomach. He turned towards Sson.

"Mr. Orsini, it is my . . . er . . . pleasure to introduce you to Colonel Benedict Oberon Branwell, formerly Lord Lieutenant of the Lancaster Sound Lancers, and honourary . . . er . . . head of the Septentrional Geological and Geographical Society."

"Colonel Branwell?" asked Brentford, almost as incredulous about the name as about its owner. The man was a legend in New Venice. A veteran of the Eskimo Wars, he had also practically mapped the whole of Ellesmere Island on his own, backed by a small detachment of lancers mounted on their famous white Bactrian camels. But that was in the very early days of New Venice, and by any calendar, forward or backwards, he should have not been living—well, if you could call that living.

"Yes, this deserves a few explanations," conceded the wizard. "Strange as it may seem today, New Venice used to be a hotbed of advanced science and daring technology. Thanks to the Seven Sleepers, a lot of research that was frowned upon elsewhere was here funded and encouraged, with results that would have not been attained by, shall we say, more conservative methods. I suppose that you've heard about the amazing feats that Douglas Norton-Amantidine's work on germinative plasma accomplished in the field of animal hybridization, for instance?"

"Amazing, indeed," Brentford said approvingly, thinking how instrumental the Polar Kangaroo had been in his victory over the Council. But that, alas, was already history. The Polar Kangaroo had remained mute since then.

"Or you are perhaps familiar with Nixon-Knox's work on biogalvanism, for instance."

"More than I ever wished to be." Brentford shivered as he thought of his meeting with the dreadful Phantom Patrol, which prowled the icefield to defend the North Pole from any intruders. He had thought he would never see anything worse, but the head now smirking in front of him was looking like a strong contender.

"Well, my friend Colonel Branwell happens to be the victim of one of Nixon-Knox's first misdirected attempts. Those attempts sprang from the same need as Transpherence—namely, the concern of the Seven Sleepers to not only keep themselves alive, but to also preserve the intelligence and skills of their entourage. There were many paths to explore, but Nixon-Knox was especially fascinated by the works of a Frenchman who had allegedly connected the head of a guillotined man to the arteries of a large dog and had obtained a few signs of consciousness."

"I have heard about that," Lavis whispered to Gabriel, with a trace of disgust. "Laborde, in the late 1880s." He shook his head in disbelief.

"It was very unfortunate that the Colonel, who as a man of duty had bequeathed his body to science, fell into the hands of Nixon-Knox at this very moment."

"Aye. That fellow was seriously cobwebbed in the upper story," mumbled the Colonel. "This was a rude awakening, I must say."

"Nixon-Knox's methods worked rather well, as you can see, but they were extremely crude and painful. He was already on the slippery path that would lead him to the conception of the Phantom Patrol, and then to the Haslam asylum. The Seven Sleepers would not hear of unplugging the Colonel, so they asked me if I could take care of him and alleviate his pain. Now, if you will allow me, Benedict . . ."

"I don't see how I could stop you, you bloody quack," said the Colonel in a gruff tone that was the vocal equivalent of a shrug.

Sson walked up to the Colonel and unlocked the panels of the wooden box, which was about as big as a phonograph and as complicated inside as the workings of a watch. Brentford could see things moving, turning, clicking, heaving as the wizard pointed to them, while Tuluk timidly peeped over his shoulder.

"The basis of it is a thermomagnetic gadolinium motor, which is triggered by the normal temperature of blood and has about the working cycle of the human heart. What you see here, these rubber tubes and brass pumps, are this gentleman's vascular system, constantly irrigating the brain, thanks to these rotating disc oxygenators, with refreshed blood. The pumps also operate the bellows on each side, which, linked to these artificial rubber flaps, allow the Colonel to display the full extent of his biting wit. From time to time, a clock triggers the pistons of these little brass syringes, which are filled with nutrients. Of course, you'll have to refill them daily, and, equally importantly, you must trim the Colonel's moustache. The only little defect of the machine is that the Colonel, as his body has virtually no vital organs, is largely invulnerable to natural death as we understand it. Thank you for your cooperation, Benedict."

"You're welcome, old chap," said the Colonel coldly, as Sson latched the panels.

"Now, I must say the adventure has given the Colonel something of a short temper, especially when I beat him at chess, but, on the whole, we get along nicely."

"Bloody hell! When did you last beat me at chess without cheating, you halfpenny wizard?"

Brentford was starting to relax a little, warming to their duet. He still tried not to look at the head, but he felt he was getting used to its presence. And this was, after all, Colonel Branwell, someone whose name had been a byword for reliability. You could have a worse associate than a man who could not die.

"For a man of action, he is not in the ideal situation, and it is important to keep him busy," Sson went on. "As he is very knowledgeable about the Arctic, I thought that he could help me with mapping the area, all the more since I learned that he had undergone shamanic initiation during his trips. Indeed, he turned out to be a very gifted Od-receiver and an outstanding Psychomotive pilot. It seems that his unfortunate condition makes him impervious to the side effects that for some reason plagued many of the best pilots: spontaneous combustion, decomposition, dematerialization, and so on. Apparently having a ghost body is exactly what it takes to drive a Psychomotive—with a few prosthetic devices, that is."

"Well, enough about me, I say!" the Colonel protested. "You'd better have a good reason for disturbing a helpless old man."

This time Brentford could not avoid facing the head. He cleared his throat.

"Colonel, I must lead a diplomatic delegation to Paris, and I would be honoured if you agreed to take us there."

"Paris!" croaked the Colonel. "Chase me, ladies! I'm in the cavalry! *Les petits femmes,* eh?"

"Oh, yes, Benedict," said the wizard, "They'll be dying to see you . . ."

And now, thought Brentford, just as the three musketeers became four, the Most Serene Seven were Eight. Well, Seven-Point-Something . . .

To be continued . . .

EPISODE III

THE LOST EMBASSY

I

A Psychomotive Trip

On May 1, everything was ready for their departure. The Colonel was strapped to a wooden platform on the pilot's seat, the Tarnhelm on his head, and rotating rods ending in sugar tong–like prongs connecting his box to the concentric steering wheels. Sson explained that the Psychomotive would find its way to Paris "just like an old horse trotting back to its stable." Brentford knew it was but a figure of speech. Psychomotives, both because they were a secret and because they needed low temperatures to work properly, were not allowed to travel beyond the borders of the Northwasteland Territory. Thus, their party would have to disembark from the Psychomotive on Kolbeinsey Island, a secret maintenance station off the coast of Iceland, where Argonaut-class "submarine locomotives" would be waiting to take them on the rest of their trip. This meant that however fast they went, and even if the Psychomotive spared them weeks of uncertain sailing, the Most Serene Seven were still a long way from France.

No stands, no pennants, no brass bands, no cheering or booing crowds awaited the Seven as they stepped upon the berth, burdened with their luggage, just a few smug bureaucrats from the Regency and a fistful of embarrassed Sector Senators. Everyone had agreed that the departure should remain a low-key affair: the new Regent-Doge didn't want to it to turn into a rally for disgruntled Orsinites, any more than Brentford wanted to make a show of his being, after all, given a nice, swift kick in the rump. As Lilian cruelly reminded him, it looked uncannily like the Council of Seven's own inglorious retreat, and he tried not to think of how that had ended as he went on with the perfunctory salutations. Gabriel, meanwhile, not even bothering to shake hands, felt both relieved and worried that his double darlings Reginald and Geraldine had not been allowed to attend.

Still, once inside the craft, they were happy to discover that it was both cosy and surprisingly spacious, with rows of comfortable armchairs facing each other along the tubular cabin and a little washroom at the back, which even boasted a bathtub. And while some were faintly nervous about the rumoured side effects of Psychomotion, the *Voda* had glided off its berth and was underway before they even realized it, leaving behind a fallen zodiac of city lights as it headed smoothly towards the frozen ocean and the ghastly auroras.

And what quickly dawned on them was that neither privacy nor sociability were to be major issues, that the New Venetian tarot deck would remain unpacked and their books forlornly closed—for, as soon as the Colonel had steered the Psychomotive onto its course, the particular vibration of the engines and the low-frequency sound they produced, just below the threshold of hearing (and of nausea) turned the darkened cabin into a kind of dream-incubator. By and by, conversations trailed off and were replaced by contagious yawns, limbs and eyelids grew heavy, and the passengers, after tucking their boneless bodies into plaid blankets, felt themselves powerless to resist the avalanche of images and voices that tumbled through their minds, faintly but persistently. At some point, Gabriel, fighting to shake off the drowsiness, half-opened his eyelids in the dim light. His head was buzzing, and he clearly felt his blood pressure blowing his brain up like a toy balloon, pushing on his eyeballs, as precisely as a finger. Silhouettes of the others appeared to him, bathed in a blue and red auroral halo, a ragged fringe of silent little flames. It also seemed to him that hazy pictures dimly flickered around their heads in ever-changing scenes, but perhaps they were his own hypnagogic illusions, he thought, as his eyelids fell again, heavy as theatre curtains. Bathing in that fluid medium, blending blurred memories with dim futures, they all remained for hours half-consciously out of time until . . .

❋

. . . they sensed rather than felt the Psychomotive slow down and stop. A bell rang, calling Brentford back to his senses and then to the cockpit.

He struggled to get up, his mind foggy with sleep. He had just had a dream in which he was high above a ravine on a bridge that stopped right in the middle of its arc. Ghosts were lined along the bridge, luminous as a swarm of floodlit moths, watching him silently as he passed: "Students from a school of Night Architecture," his own voice informed him. When he reached the end of the bridge, Brentford closed his eyes and went on gliding over the abyss as a faint bell tolled in the distance. The images had barely faded and the thrill of falling remained intact as he entered the cabin, still wrapped in his tartan blanket.

"We have a problem, young man," the Psycholonel announced.

"Aren't we at the Kolbeinsey station?"

"Aye. We are. Except there is no maintenance station. And no submarine base."

Brentford frowned, trying to dispel the fumes in his brain. All he could see through the front porthole was a ragged black skerry barely outlined in the ash-grey dawn, covered with something white that could be snow or eiderdown.

"What do you mean, there is no station?"

"Well, it seems rather clear to me," the Colonel answered, trying to turn his eyes towards Brentford. "It's gone. Unless it was never there. This islet has a rather long history of being somewhat diabolical, after all."

Brentford closed his eyes and pinched the bridge of his nose.

"You've been here before, haven't you?"

"Aye. Many times."

The Colonel remained silent for a while and then said:

"Maybe it's not there *yet*, if you prefer."

"Meaning?" Brentford asked, slumping into the copilot's chair.

"Hmm . . . you're not going to like this, I'm afraid. It happens very rarely, and it's never happened to me before, but Sson warned me that Psychomotives sometimes have a certain side effect that can make them, erm . . . travel in time."

Brentford turned pale.

"What? What the pole are you talking about?"

"Black Auroras, or so Sson says. You know, those dark spots between the auroras. Every characteristic of the Northern Lights reversed. Including temporal ones."

"When was the station created?"

"In the late Twenties After Backwards."

"So, you're telling me we've jumped back in time twenty years?"

"Aye. At best."

"Is there a way to know for sure?"

The Colonel sounded calm, but Brentford noticed he was biting his moustache. "We could land on Grimsey, I'd say," he eventually proposed. "It's only forty-five miles south, but still in the Arctic Circle. New Venice laws forbid us to interact with the islanders, but I suppose we could make an exception, since technically these laws have not been passed *yet*. At least, the natives may give us the time of day."

"And what about going back? Couldn't we retrace our own steps, both in space and . . . time?"

"Well. For one thing, the Psychomotive needs to be serviced, which, without a station, is not going to be easy, eh? And even then, there is no guarantee we'd return to the right time."

Brentford nodded, thinking hard. "What I am going to say to the others?" he asked.

"That's your job, young man. Not mine," replied the Psycholonel.

Brentford staggered back to the cabin, nervously scratching a one-night stubble he could have struck matches on. Alerted by the absence of motion and the growing cold, the rest of the Most Serene Seven were slowly waking up, some stretching, some yawning, some looking around as if trying to remember where they were. As if *where* were the problem, thought Brentford. He tried to imagine a way to break the news gently, and decided there was none. He cleared his throat.

"My dear friends, I have news for you."

"Good morning. Are we at the station yet?" asked Lavis, who was already immaculately shaved and carefully combing his shiny fringe into place.

"In a sense, yes," Brentford answered and took a deep breath. "But things did not turn out precisely as planned, apparently. It's very possible that we have strayed a little out of our path. Time-wise, that is."

"What do you mean, *time-wise*? That we are late? Or too early?" Lilian asked, wrapping herself in her blanket.

"We're early," replied Brentford. "Very early . . . So much so, I'm told, that the station hasn't been built yet, and no submarine locomotive waits for us."

The Most Serene Seven looked at each other as if for a quick reality check.

"You must be kidding," Lilian finally said.

"How funny would that be?" Brentford asked. "And what's more, according to the Colonel, there's no possibility of returning to our starting point."

"What happened?" Thomas inquired.

"We don't know. Apparently, there's always a risk that a Psychomotive will take a wrong turn in time."

"No wonder they don't use them any more," Gabriel blurted dejectedly. "Peterswarden must have known."

"And the Colonel," Lilian added between clenched teeth. "And that wizard."

Brentford cut her off. "Please. It's vital that we stick together. We're all in the same lifeboat here. Now, we're going to go to the nearest island to try to find out more. Then we'll decide on the next step."

But the only answer he got was a leaden silence.

II

The Chessboard Island

Branwell steered them into a hidden cove at the north end of Grimsey Island, powered down, and then warned them that the Psychomotive was in condition to go back to Kolbeinsey but no farther. Receiving the news grimly, Brentford and Thomas, who happened to speak a little Icelandic, wrapped themselves in fur clothing, jumped out of the vehicle, and started to grope their way to the top of the surrounding ridge. Then, in the nibbling cold, they walked over grass and moss towards a small settlement whose church spire could just be made out in the hazy, bluish dawn. The church itself was good news: it meant that it was still sometime A.D. At least they wouldn't be chased around by pterosaurs.

In front of them, twenty-five miles beyond the town, they could see the dim coast of Iceland. Behind them was the frozen ocean, an icepack spread under blue-grey skies as far as the eye could squint.

"You've noticed, haven't you?" Thomas asked Brentford.

"What?"

"The daylight. And the icefield. There's no way it's spring here."

Brentford shrugged his shoulders.

"If we've changed years, we could have changed seasons, I suppose."

Whoever put the Grim in Grimsey had probably found it here in the first place. Waving away a flock of aggressive terns, Brentford and Thomas eventually reached a crude path and descended among the sparse, sod-covered huts of the village. It was early in the morning, but a few sturdy, weatherbeaten fishermen were already busy in the tiny stone harbour, ogling in disbelief these well-dressed foreigners looking as if they had just landed from the future, not quite without reason, Brentford had to admit. The word was already out, and the vicar waited for them in front of the small driftwood church, which was built, if they were to believe Colonel Branwell, just across the Arctic Circle.

Thanks to Thomas's high school Icelandic and the vicar's English, which sounded like hammered boilerplate, Brentford could explain the situation, and in a way that differed only a little from the truth. Deeming it wise not to ask the natives what year it was, he told them that he was a Canadian millionaire on a cruise with a few friends in a new-prototype ship that had, unfortunately, broken down. With no hope of repairing it, here, he would be most grateful if the islanders would allow them passage to Iceland.

The islanders, the vicar reassured them, would be very happy to help. But there was one condition, he added. A little custom to which all foreigners must submit. Brentford had a sudden vision of their heads stuck on poles againts the horizon while terns pecked out their eyes. However, the vicar's proposition turned out to be nothing more than a game of chess. Chess was the islanders' driving passion, he explained, and their only entertainment. Might they invite their friends over for a little game tonight? A win would ensure them any help they could get.

Hazily, Brentford recalled Gabriel's gabbling once about a lost island of renowned chess enthusiasts. It was in line with the Seven's current streak of luck, obviously, that they would beach precisely among these monomaniacal wood-pushers. He fumed at the unnecessary delay, but had little choice but to submit to the local rules of hospitality.

"And if we lose?" he inquired.

"Then you play again until you win," the vicar explained with a smile.

And so that very night Brentford found himself in a smoky, stifling room, entertaining a sweating vicar above a marble chessboard, while his parishioners, huddled around them, observed their champion with evident anxiety. Brentford had even less enthusiastic support from the No-Longer-So-Serene Seven, except for the attentive Tuluk, who was trying to make sense of what seemed to him to be strange hunting strategies. The rest of the Seven—*sans* Branwell, of course—sat gloomily in the background, their eyes repeatedly swerving back, furiously, to the calendar page on the wall: September 18, 1895.

At first, Brentford himself could think about little other than this date—a date when neither New Venice itself nor any of the New Venetians in the room were supposed to even exist. He looked at the chessboard with a mix of anger and bewilderment, but then, sensing the Seven at his back and the dark vibrations of their mood, he knew that he could not lose. He must win this game if only to win back their trust. But luckily, as soon as he touched the white pawn, something lit up in him: a flame from the days when chess had been all the rage in New Venice and an integral part of the school curriculum. Brentford discovered that he was still at home in this pattern of darkness and light, as familiar as the grid of a well-known city—of his own well-known city, in fact, for when he was Doge, the chessboard had inspired his distribution of nighttime illuminations, so that everyone in the streets was always at walking distance from the light. In his mind the pieces now exploded and shot in and out at full speed, in ribbons of crisscrossing transparent paths, forking out according to his opponent's possible parries. The first pawn's move was as fatal as the start of an avalanche. The vicar was a competent player, but not a match for a man who had played three-dimensional fairy chess daily as a schoolboy.

"Checkmate!" Brentford announced half an hour later, with more relief than triumph.

But as the vicar gently laid out his king, Brentford reflected that if there ever was a fallen shah, it was nobody but himself.

❋

"You have to pity people whose idea of fun in such a forlorn place is a goddamn chess party," Lilian said moodily, as the Seven trudged back to the Psychomotive in the crisp, crunching darkness.

"Nice game, by the way," Gabriel interjected. "Quite a *blitz* you played there."

"Sure," Lilian added mercilessly as she stalked along beside them. "But it's not as if he didn't have the *time*."

"Do you know what it made me think of?" Gabriel went on hurriedly, trying to deflect the conversation. "This article by Thibaut Traymore. Remember him? 'Retrograde Analysis in Four-Dimensional Reflecting Chess: a Metaphysical Meditation,' I think it was called."

Of course Brentford remembered the article. In the days when chess had become the fashionable metaphor for just about everything, their longtime college friend Thibaut Traymore had postulated an "hypnothesis," as he called it, that had enjoyed a certain success among students and Boreemians. The alternation of nights and days, he had offered, followed the alternation of black squares and white squares on an infinite chessboard. As the pawns of creation, we experience them successively, one at a time, but who was to know whether we could not move according to different rules, as queens or knights can? This, Traymore claimed, is what we do psychically when we dream or daydream, replaying or rehearsing in our heads the moves we have made or plan to make and testing different outcomes. Going even further, he proposed that what can be accomplished psychically could also be accomplished physically.

"I thought about that, too, during the game," Brentford said. Then he shrugged. "It's just another metaphor."

"And what's wrong with metaphors?" Gabriel asked, sounding personally offended.

"Nothing. They just won't take us home, will they?"

"No," Gabriel conceded. "But perhaps they'll show us the way."

September 1895, then. It could have been worse, Brentford told himself. But even if the previous millisecond is closer to us than the birth of the universe, it is equally out of reach.

Back inside the treacherous Psychomotive, Thomas was the first to broach the topic.

"Correct me if I'm wrong, but 1895 was sometime before New Venice's foundation."

"Indeed," said Brentford. "At this very moment, even if we could get back, we would have nowhere to get back to."

The news took a moment to sink in, probably because there was no bottom for it to alight upon.

"So, what do you suggest?" Lilian finally asked, in a tone that suggested she had just licked a grindstone. "That we wait until we are once again citizens of an existing city?"

"The only chance we have is to get to Paris," the Colonel announced from the tabletop.

"The Paris of 1895?" asked Thomas.

"Aye, my boy. Unless you know of another one that is available at the moment. Could be that the Magical Crown we carry has got us into this jam. Some magnetic effect that I can't fathom. But we know it comes from Paris, so that seems the only place to solve our little problem, what?"

Gabriel intervened.

"What did you tell me about it, Dr. Lavis? That those crowns were made in Paris in the nineties, right?"

"Exactly, Monsieur d'Allier. We could find the people who made them and we could ask them in what way it might be linked to our predicament. If indeed it is."

"And how do we get to Paris without the submarine?" asked Lilian, adding for good measure, "I'm afraid I haven't packed a swimsuit."

"Simple," said Brentford, sensing that this was not the time for the "Don't-Worry-Neither-Did-I" joke. "We'll do what everybody else does. We'll go by boat and train. Let's vote. Who agrees to go to Paris?"

Blankbate, who hadn't said a word so far, was the first to raise his hand. Lavis was a close second. Then Gabriel. All the people, then, who had originally manifested a desire to see Paris. Then Thomas. Then Lilian, although exasperatedly. Tuluk watched the others for a while, not sure that he understood what the problem was, but seeing Brentford raise his arm, he chose to trust him and cast the vote that made it unanimous, or almost.

"You don't expect me to raise my hand, do you?" the Colonel asked.

III

Exiles from Nowhere

As if going back in time was not enough, the trip forward in time to Paris seemed to render seconds into minutes and minutes into hours. It was days before the Most Serene Seven (and their multiple trunks) were able to board a trawler, which then sailed ever so slowly towards the mainland of Iceland, finally landing at Akureyri, a jumble of wooden houses sloping up towards farmlands, with a thriving little harbour full of Danish merchant steamers. Brentford negotiated with various captains and eventually got the party booked into cramped cabins on the *Fortuna*, which brought back part-load traffic to Denmark with a stop at Reykjavik. But it was only once they were at sea, seated at the captain's table having dinner with Captain Hjulsen, that it was explained to them that travelling overland to Paris through northernmost Europe in the latening fall was not a good idea, as the weather was unusually bad for the season: roads and railway lines would probably be blocked by the time they arrived. Perhaps, Hjulsen suggested, they would have a better chance of getting to France by sea. There would be ships going from Reykjavik to either Ireland or Britain— from there they could catch another to Normandy. Brentford sighed and thanked him.

And so to Reykjavik, a quiet, monotonous haven with irregular houses sprawling all over the lava-plain, and one very poor hotel. Except for ponies trotting everywhere, it wasn't very lively. But by chance, a German ship with a crew of scientists—unimaginatively baptized the *Poseidon*—had been delayed there on its way to Galway by bad weather, and had room to take on the "Canadian" passengers.

By October 5, after going trough serious swells that tossed everyone about in their bunks, the *Poseidon* had safely arrived in Galway. The Most Serene Seven, still reeling from the voyage, took up quarters at an inn near the Spanish Arch, and then scattered all over the city, eager to breathe some fresh air. But that air proved somewhat wet, with a local wind that was rumoured to drive people mad—the very last thing they needed.

Paris seemed very far away, and New Venice even more so.

Yet as the last few days had revealed to them, living in the past was not the problem it could have been. New Venice, cut off from the world as it was, lived in a time of its own, largely indifferent to outside history or progress. As a matter of fact, it had been built for exactly that purpose, a dream answer to History's nightmare. Whatever happened beyond its limits was perceived rather dimly, and certainly, for New Venetians, with their quaint clothes and manners, there was nothing particularly shocking about the Iceland and Ireland of 1895. More than a sense of belonging, though, it only made them each feel a gnawing nostalgia.

Brentford found Gabriel in front of a pint of Guinness in the taproom of Green's, a small narrow pub full of boatmen, just across the Claddagh.

"A better model of the universe than your chessboard," Gabriel commented, pointing to his pint, as Brentford sat. "A little foam over a cold, bitter darkness. And this place . . . Remind me never to call New Venice boring and drab again. It's a trademark here: Boring and Drab, established 1124."

"I would have thought it was some sort of homecoming for you," said Brentford.

"You mean, me being of Irish stock and all? It is, indeed. Like that fellow from *The Voyage of Bran*. Falling to dust as soon as he landed on the ould sod of Ireland, for he did not know that he had travelled a hundred years from island to island."

"Was that when d'Alliers were still Daleys?"

"That was when the Daleys were still the O'Dalaighs—a great family of seers and bards about as old as the country," Gabriel said, with a self-mocking pride that was Irish enough. "Knowledgeable, sharp-tongued fellows whose poetry could cause boils . . ."

"Oh! that's where you get your sharp tongue from, then?"

"Shh . . . Do you want to get me hanged? The story goes that when the English invaded, they cut down every tree in the O'Dalaighs' domain but one, to hang their descendents on if they came back. I suppose that, unconsciously, might be the reason that the family ended up in the treeless Arctic."

"And your father thought calling himself d'Allier would erase all traces?" Brentford joked.

"No. My mother made him do that when he was picked for Transpherence. As you know, she was a Newfoundland French Shore girl with Bourbonnais roots. She persuaded herself that she was of noble blood, because her own mother was called 'de' something. The French have this huge problem with nobility, as you will notice if we ever make it to Paris. But haven't I told you this story a hundred times?"

"I suppose so. I wasn't sure. I seem to have a hard time remembering things, these days. I've been . . . forgetting things about New Venice. Well, actually, it's more as if I'm not forgetting them so much as growing unsure about whether they really happened or not."

"I've noticed that, too," Gabriel said, nodding with concern. "Things don't come out very clearly. More like fantasies than memories. But after all, I suppose it is hard to remember something that doesn't exist yet. And you know the theory, anyway: memories are but a constant process of forgetting, which we patch up with imagination as well or poorly as we can."

"We'll have to work hard on that, Gabriel. Memories or fantasies, we mustn't let them disappear or blur. It's all we have right now. This is, as of today, the only place where the city lives," he added, tapping his forehead.

"I have no intention of forgetting it. For example, do you remember that place where we went to see that girl together, what was her name again? We drank a whole bottle of Belovodie vodka and . . ."

Brentford winced, then hissed, "Well, maybe there are some things we should forget, after all."

❊

In the morning Brentford, in full no-nonsense mode, had gathered information and proposed his plan, schedules in hand, to the rest of the Seven. The Great Western Railway Company operated a line between Galway and Dublin. From there, it branched out to Waterford, where you could catch a boat to Milford Haven, from which you could take a train to Weymouth, before sailing towards the Anglo-Norman islands, where a ferry line ran to Granville, France. They voted in favour of it unanimously, with weary hands, as nobody had the strength for further discussion.

It proved a long and arduous trip in cramped compartments, and the glum mood among the Most Serene Seven only made it longer. In quiet, rubeous Dublin, the sulking Gabriel had bought from the Hodges-Figgis bookstore a copy of H. G. Wells's recently published *Time Machine* to read on the train to Waterford. He faintly hoped that it would give him an idea about how to get back home, although the sphinx on the cloth cover did not look very encouraging. It proved interesting, indeed, on the notion that time travel is modeled not so much on physics as on the way the mind works, just as Thibaut Traymore had postulated in his chessboard theory, but on the subject of returning to a past that had become the future, neither Traymore nor Wells offered any insight. For the time being, no amount of nostalgia or hope could bring the Seven back to their home.

A ship ominously called the *Vulture* ferried them from the busy quays of rustic Waterford to Milford Haven, a grim, steep Welsh village that tried to pass as a port—and if that weren't a bad enough portent, Brentford noticed that a trawler called *Sybil* was nearby moored in the brand-new docks. From there, they boarded another GWR train, chugging and panting across a greyish stretch of country that seemed to be tacked to the windows.

In Weymouth, the train stopped right on the harbour, next to a pavilion that, Brentford thought with a pang, would have looked great on one of the endless New Venetian embankments. From there, the steamer *Lynx* took them to Jersey and the quiet, if somewhat dull, town of St. Hélier, huddling under the severe frown of its fort.

Somehow this place felt familiar, with its blend of French and English names, as if it were some prototype for New Venice. Was their home city scattered everywhere, now that it was nowhere?

Finally, on October 20, the Seven, crumpled and dingy, boarded another small steamer to Granville. An Arctic cold blew across the deck, where a few passengers shivered, and as the ship approached the Normandy coast, its hull began cracking through brittle, wrinkled pancakes of ice.

"It looks like we're coming home," Brentford joked about the vista, although he was worried to see ice covering the sea so early in the year. He wasn't surprised that he didn't get the laugh he only half-expected.

The Seven could have been excused, after weeks and weeks of a harrowing trip, for seeing in Granville nothing more than yet another nondescript port. A small, whitish city, sloping around cliffs, it could at least claim a decent hotel and a seaside casino—where, after Brentford had changed some gold at the bank, Thomas, drunk with military abandon, lost at the roulette table the first francs he had ever seen.

IV

The Phantom Train to Paris

They woke the next day to a drizzle of stingy snow under a smudge of steel-blue clouds. It was probably sunnier in New Venice now. "Now," "New Venice"—these words made Brentford chuckle a bit desperately as he thought of them. What language could describe the situation they were in, exiles from nowhere, banished from the future?

At the train station, it was explained to them, with typical Gallic bad grace, that due to storms the train service to Paris had been badly disrupted. Out of the four daily trains to Paris, only one would run: the express 56 had come in the night before and would try to go back in the early afternoon. But the reservations they had purchased in Jersey, they were warned, might not be the open-sesame they hoped, as a lot of people would now be taking the train by storm, Bastille-style.

So, the Seven walked around Granville at loose ends until the time of the train's scheduled departure . . . only to learn that it would be delayed by another two hours. Since leaving Grimsey Island, they had been crammed or shoved into one cramped compartment, cabin, or waiting room after another, and this had started to gnaw at what little sense of time they had managed to retain. They felt like puppets attached to the wires of the transport network, their articulations aching from redirections, their minds sloshing between frustration, impatience, useless anger, resigned exhaustion, and plain old bad moods. Peterswarden, Brentford thought, would be glad to see that his punishment had gone beyond exile to torture. If this hadn't been Peterswarden's plan all along, that is.

They returned to the station to overhear a rumour that this might well be the last train for a long while, as more snowstorms were on their way. As a result, the platform, hazy with damp breath and cigarette smoke, was even more crowded than the agent had forecast. The driver, M. Pellerin, and his fireman were hailed with the fervour bestowed on heroes and pioneers, while controllers were begged by ladies and insulted by their husbands. People with and without tickets rushed the doors with a riotous haste and a marked preference for first class. It took nothing less than Blankbate's peculiar powers of persuasion to clear the seats and bunks of their reserved sleeper compartment.

But barely twenty miles out of Granville, the train began to slow down. Its chugging turned to dispirited sighing as it groped its way though narrow banks of snow nearly two feet high and, as the evening fell, it was all topped by an increasingly dense bank of fog.

Meanwhile, the towns they passed were smothered in snow like villages in Christmas tales, their lights unpredictable and dim as will-o'-the-wisps. Brentford wondered whether the driver could see the signals on the track, and decided he didn't really want to know. Then darkness fell, and all they could see was their own sullen, sunken, gaslit faces suspended in the glass panes.

Coming to some difficult hills, the train began to climb, reluc-tantly. Even in the compartment, the Seven could feel the resistance of the snow as the snowplow coupled to the front of the engine tried to clear the way, even as the overpiled snowbanks beside the rails began to crumble and block the tracks still more. Somewhere in the valley, the locomotive stopped and then suddenly lurched, trying to force its way through a wall of snow. This seemed to work for a while, but did not get them very far. Eventually the steam-engine stopped and the train came to a standstill. After a moment of hushed silence, several passengers rolled down their windows to look outside, inquiring of one another about the situation in scandalized tones, as if the snow were a personal offence. What was the government doing? An Ameri-can voice resounded, claiming that in the United States everybody would take a shovel and clear the way, a piece of information the French passengers found to be a hoot.

Gabriel and Brentford stepped outside and took a few steps along the narrow strip that separated the ballast and the crumbling snow-banks, their feet making a crunching sound that each knew the other was happy to hear, even if it made them a bit melancholy, too. From time to time a filmy, unconvinced moon appeared through the fog, revealing all around them the waves of an ocean of snow that seemed to go on forever. Strangely, it reminded Gabriel, even down to the most minute details, of a similar scene in a novel. But, after all, it was a good scene, and Reality had simply copied it, the way drooling tod-dlers scribble arabesques to mimic their parents' handwriting.

Other passengers who had ventured outside exchanged ominous rumours through their mufflers. The controller, whose uniform now officially designated him as scapegoat, struggled through the crowd, and after placating a woman who threatened to write to the authori-ties to complain, announced a delay of about four or five hours, the time it would take for workers to arrive from the nearest station at L'Aigle, three miles away. An employee had been sent running there to get help.

Brentford and Gabriel walked back to the compartment in despair, their bodies now shaking with cold, while the shrill screams of the distress whistle got lost in the indifferent fog. The feeling of being nowhere, cut off from any existing world—so typical of train travel by night—seemed now to be a reality. For people who were already *nowhen*, it was all the more painful. New Venice seemed more and more like a fading dream.

So, tucked in their bunks, their faces barely outlined in the dark, the Seven talked about their city, and what it meant to them, trying to rebuild that dream with words, which by and by, turning to blur on the windows, further erased the surrounding landscape.

To Brentford, New Venice was an adventure of sublime pro-portions. It was all about *numbers*. He had governed the city for a year, and the demands of that job had been nothing compared with the pressure of bringing heat, water, and food to one hundred thou-sand persons every day, as hc had done while working for the Arctic Administration. In those days, every time he went to bed he felt that he had fought a battle and won it, and when he woke up, what he saw looking through the window was that the dream was still alive, because of his and others' loyalty to it.

To Gabriel, too, their city was a dream, but of a different kind: a fantasy come alive in which he could live out his own. His New Venice was a labyrinth of lit boulevards and dark alleys, and he sleepwalked through it, searching for his own Northwest Passage, his heart aching with desire and his mind in a coloured haze.

Lilian had known that lifestyle, too. But since coming back from her travels she had inhabited a different city—one that did not quite exist yet but that she thought she could see at the turn of the street and whose portents she collected and advertised, a bohemian city where women and men would be free and equal, where work would not prevail over leisure and art, where men could love men and women love women.

"I see this, too," Brentford commented, in the hope, she thought, of impressing her. "I mean, that the city either was, or will be, very close to what it could be, without ever actually being it. At times it seems hopeful, but at other times, it's like that crock of gold at the end of the rainbow; you think you'll never reach it. And, though I hate to admit it, the revolution that we staged changed very little. We were just struggling with different imperfections, and, I suspect, equally hopeless ones."

"It seemed quite perfect to me," said Dr. Lavis, the outsider. "I could not believe the place when I first laid eyes on it. When I went back to Paris after my first visit, I thought about it all the time, and I doubted that it was real. And not being allowed to say anything about it because of the Polaris Pledge only made it seem more uncertain. This is why I came back and stayed: to make sure that I had not been dreaming. In a sense, the dream came to define the truth—and how extensive truth *is*. It taught me that many things can be real that I did not think possible."

Thomas Paynes-Grey did not understand what was dreamy about it. The place was so cold, you couldn't doubt that it was real; the people were struggling in a very real sense; it was a city where things happened, and happened in a big way. Its pleasures and its pains were intense. It was both affluent and miserable, ecstatic and really boring. Severed from history and with a dubious future, New Venice was all about the present. You could live in it to the full, and follow life to its extremities.

Blankbate nodded at that, and for once expressed himself through other means than the cracking of his phalanges and upper vertebrae. "It's a real city," he agreed in his deep drawl. "Like every other city, it's dirty and dangerous, and the more beautiful it is, the more something ugly is likely to lurk beneath. It's like a law." He grinned, as if to indicate that he did not wish to be taken as seriously as his tone implied. "Every beauty is built with hard work and suffering. You don't want to know how many workers' corpses are embedded in the ice pillars that support the artificial islands, nor how many were found by simply dragging the canals. I see the beauty and I understand the pride, but believe me, it's got a dark side."

The Colonel interrupted through the holes punched in his Gladstone.

"I was there when the city was about to be finished. What this gentleman says is, I must say, a little truer that I'd care to admit. It is a harsh city, quite certainly. But when one looks at what the Seven Sleepers achieved, in such unmerciful surroundings, one can't help being in awe, eh? It is a very monument to those who sacrificed themselves to build it"—here Lilian could not hold back a snigger—"and it is our duty to protect their legacy. That's what the bloody place is about for me. Now, all this babble has made me thirsty. Has anyone out there anything to drink? A brandy?"

"Brandy, Colonel?" Brentford said. "Are you sure that's allowed?"

"Of course, young man! It's good for the gears."

Brentford shrugged.

"I'll do it," volunteered Tuluk, who was more and more fascinated by the clockwork Colonel, and who for once forgot to speak of himself in the third person. He fiddled for a while with the flask and the bag—not an easy task in a cramped cabin—and finally sat down. The silence reminded him that it was his turn to speak. He blushed, hesitated, and then began.

"For this Inuk, New Venice is two things. One is the city this Inuk saw from the outside. The lights in the night, the big round roofs, like igloos on the buildings, the arrows towards the skies, the warmth from the Fire-Maidens. And this city is like a dream, but not a good dream. A dream that is too big for the mind. It looks dangerous, as if it fell from the skies. But then, this Inuk came in and knew the city, and this Inuk saw you *qallunaat* live like us. You make things, you fix them, you build things, you get food and keep yourselves warm, one small thing after another, and this Inuk understands. He doesn't think you do it the right way, but he likes the way you're doing things, all these little clever things. So now this Inuk knows what the dream is made of and he is less afraid of it, because it's only made of people and work, like the Inuit's own dream."

And Brentford smiled because, without knowing it, Tuluk had almost uttered the motto of New Venice: *Somnia et Labor*. Dream and Strife.

The train seemed now to have fallen asleep, as if lulled by the Seven's fairy tale, but a restless and foul-breathed sleep it was. After four hours of waiting in doubt and despair, the good news eventually came that three platoons of soldiers, on reserve in Argentan for possible accidents, had been dispatched to shovel the express out of the snow, but that it would take a long time.

And a long time it took.

It was dawn when the track was cleared, if one can call a slight change of light in the fog "dawn." And there were eight hours to go before they would reach the city, through a land that seemed enchanted in the true sense of the term: held under a thrall of paralysis and silence. Only a few crows dotted the snowy fields, like commas and semicolons on an otherwise white page. The train went as fast as possible to try and reduce its twelve-hour delay, an attempt both ridiculous and brave. Maybe the driver was simply eager to get home; at least, Brentford thought, he had one.

What Brentford did not know yet was that, in the cab, the driver had died from cold and exhaustion, and the fireman had slipped on an ice puddle and knocked himself out while trying to remove his rigid colleague from the levers. The phantom train rushed through stations where it should have stopped, and by and by, telegraph signals were sent to announce it, but nothing else could be done, either to stop the train or to warn the passengers.

As they entered the western suburbs of Paris near Issy, a blur of drab greyish houses, the passengers began to notice that the train gave no sign of slowing down. On the contrary, the landscape tore by; the telegraph poles that stapled it together seemed ripped away one after another. The Seven gaped out the window as their stomachs tightened and sweat broke out on their backs, while screams of panic were heard in the other compartments.

And suddenly they were in the city itself, a colourless, twisted smudge, just as if a hand had wiped across a foggy mirror. Echoing between the buildings, the rumble of the wheels got louder and louder. In the dwindling distance, the twin glass arches of the Montparnasse station roofs were already visible, wide-eyed, as if not believing what they were seeing coming towards them.

The controller ran towards the back of the train, perhaps to pull the emergency brake at the back of the last car. But it was too late. They were already zooming into the station, and it became a striped, grating blur. In the Seven's cabin, fists grasped wrists, wild eyes locked, and for a brief moment, their heads were flooded with bright, blindingly white memories of New Venice: it was where the city lived now, in the fleeting, fatal interval between life and certain death.

With a crash of scraped metal that seemed to be a scream of pain, the locomotive hit the giant buffers at the end of the line. The train was slowed a little but not stopped. It screeched through the space that separated the track and the glass wall of the building's outer façade and, shaking off its dead drivers, smashed through it in a burst of smithereens. With a sound as if the whole world were being crumpled by an iron fist, the locomotive leapt from the platform down to the Place de Rennes, yanking the coal tender with it and crushing a woman in her streetside newspaper stall.

The Seven felt themselves torn as if from their own bones, and then violently slapped back in, their minds buzzing, their skins tingling with fear. They opened their eyes on the afterlife only to find they were still in the station. Indeed, gingerly climbing to their feet from where they'd been thrown, they could see out the window that their car was still in the station, almost where it was supposed to be: only the locomotive and the tender were hanging askew beyond the platform in midair. The passenger cars, by miracle, had not smashed into each other.

"I am afraid my arm is broken," Thomas finally said, with well-rehearsed military coolness.

"My back hurts," Lilian muttered, grimacing, while Lavis examined the ensign.

Gabriel massaged his bruised, swollen temple with a hateful glare in which shone his resentment at the very existence of Matter.

Brentford had no injuries, though the crash had done nothing to soothe a backache that had started days ago. Tuluk was also unhurt, wrapped in his cocoon of furs. Blankbate sat motionless, his arms folded, keeping any pain he felt to himself. The Colonel, too, was miraculously intact within his Gladstone, lucky for once that he had no limbs to break.

"What? Are we there yet?" they heard him asking. "I told you to wake me when we got there."

People started to gather around the wreck, more curious than helpful, indeed mostly incredulous about what they had just witnessed. It was a miracle, someone who wasn't the newspaper woman said. But, yes, it was a miracle that there weren't dead passengers everywhere. And it was another miracle that the engine hadn't caught fire—but sighed dejectedly on the sidewalk like a wounded rhino—or that its snowplow, buried three feet into the sidewalk, had not pierced the sewers nor crashed through the catacombs.

The Seven cautiously stepped down onto the platform, where the hubbub had reached its peak. Stunned survivors were groping their own limbs with wonder, as if seeing them for the first time, or crouching, overwhelmed, among forests of legs, sometimes sobbing into their hands. Women were being given smelling salts and led away away to the buffet, where they could try to regain their senses away from the crowd. Eventually a doctor approached the Seven.

"Anyone hurt here?"

"Ah, dear colleague," Lavis said, glowing at the opportunity to speak French again. "A broken arm and maybe a case of railway spine. Can you take us to La Salpêtrière for an examination?"

"There are some ambulances coming. I think you will soon be taken in charge. Let me see this broken arm."

Still uncertain on his feet, like a newborn foal, Brentford walked up to Gabriel, who was ferociously rubbing his temple.

"That was some journey, wasn't it?" he said.

Gabriel looked daggers at him and did not bother to answer.

"Well, I guess I'll take care of the luggage, then . . ." Brentford said with a sigh, shuffling off towards the baggage cars.

To be continued . . .

EPISODE IV

IN MORPHINE MISTS

I

The Double Doctor

The Seven had split up for a while, not without relief after so many weeks of forced coexistence. Brentford, Blankbate, and Tuluk—who was toting the Colonel in his satchel—took the luggage off in search of a hotel, while a horse ambulance took Lavis and his wounded cohorts down to the Salpêtrière Hospital.

Paris was indeed going through a dreadfully wintry October. Gabriel observed that the traffic on the way to the hospital was, if not frozen, seriously slowed by the snow, and if the drive had not been downhill, the two miles' distance would have taken maddening hours to complete—more than his nerves could have borne. Through the portholes in the back of the ambulance, he could see slanting carriages and improvised sleds crawling higgledy-piggledy over the snow like panicked insects. Here and there, hooded workers desperately tried to clear the way with shovels, while carriage drivers in box coats swore in cumuli of alcoholized breath. For a while, the ambulance fell behind a horse-drawn snowplough—a simple wooden frame bristling with twigs like a broom—which made progress slower rather than quicker.

The boulevards that they tried to trot along were wide gashes of greyish slush, while the buildings on each side, banked with snow almost to the first story, seemed suspended in midair. Under the leaden sky weighing over their zinc roofs, the long rows of houses stood moodily monotonous, as if careful to align their typically striped shutters. Only the black curlicues and arabesques of the cast-iron balconies gave the dulled eye something to dance upon.

Passers-by were muffled and stooped, indifferent to the news of the crash slowly reaching them through the steamy flourishes of newspaper urchins. It looked a lot like the Paris Gabriel had known on his previous visit, and whatever he did not recognize looked exactly like the Paris he had read about. But then, that was his reality, a curious blend of things and print.

The Salpêtrière, a former gunpowder depot topped by a hydrocephalic dome, was now one of the most famous hospitals in Paris, Lavis explained to the others in the back of the ambulence as they arrived in the main yard. For centuries, it had been a circle of hell, home to thousands of miserable madwomen with minds as ragged and torn as their clothes. But the great and now late Doctor Charcot had turned it into the Mecca of Mental Illness, thanks to his studies on female hysteria. Charcot had been a magician who could at will create and displace symptoms instead of simply curing them, as more vulgar minds would have done. People flocked from around the world to attend his Tuesday lessons, in which scantily clad patients, wearing peacock feathers upon their heads (the better to register their tremors), were mesmerized into compliant puppets and led through a series of tricks that would have made Barnum catatonic with envy. Actresses, singers, and dancers went to observe the patients' epileptic and demented movements, then adapted them for their own cabaret acts. It was where it happened.

As Lavis and the others exited the ambulance and walked past endless barracks and across wide squares where female patients stood still under leafless trees, he explained that in 1895 one of the house specialities had been "Railway Spine"—the traumatic shock that results from train disasters. It would have been an exaggeration to talk about luck that day, but in their present battered condition, the staggering members of the Most Serene Seven felt themselves fortunate to have among their number someone who knew about this place.

The waiting room at La Salpêtrière was long and dark, and thanks to the accident extremely busy, the people huddling on the wooden benches that ran along the walls, blurred amidst a cloud of vapour that smelled of garlic and wet wool. From time to time, as the doors swished open or closed, a faint whiff of ether floated in, fresh and soothing. The New Venetians struggled to find seats for themselves, and after having passed days in their own train compartments, the lack of privacy was irksome. It seemed a nightmare that would never end. Gabriel sulked on a chair, his face buried in his hands, feeling so exhausted that he suspected his head would stay stuck to his palms when he attempted to raise it.

"Don't worry," Lavis said, "I may know some people here." He had worked as a young doctor in the Charcoterie, as he called it, and he knew the whole staff—well, *had known*.

"They might find you changed," Lilian remarked.

"Oh yes. You're right," he answered, lowering his voice. "I keep forgetting. It's all so familiar. I remember clearly the day of the Montparnasse accident . . ." A light flashed in his eyes as he realized the implications. ". . . *Which means I may be still be here!*"

Thomas and Lilian looked at him quizzically. "You were here when the wounded passengers arrived?" she asked.

"More or less, yes. I was working in the photographic laboratory, and I checked in quite a few times to lend a hand. Not that there were that many victims, fortunately."

"So you should remember us, then?" Lilian persisted.

The doctor sighed and became visibly perplexed. "But I don't," he said. "I also don't remember the snow everywhere, nor such a devilishly cold October. I don't remember that the train driver died before the crash—I thought I remembered it had been a brake failure. There are other changes to what I remember that I can't fathom. A fork in the future, that's something I can understand, but a fork in the past—a different past is something that's beyond me, I'm afraid."

He sat pensively for a few moments, staring at the floor. Then he said, "I'd better see if someone can help us."

"That wouldn't be very fair to the other people," said Lilian, pointing her chin at the crowd.

"In Rome, do as the Romans do, or as we say in French, *We must howl with the wolves*," Lavis said as he got up, shrugging his shoulders before shuffling towards the glass door that separated the waiting room from the corridor.

"He's troubled, isn't he?" It was typical of Thomas to propose his psychological observations in the form of questions, perhaps because of his lack of self-confidence when it came to serious conversation.

"You would be, too, in his place, I guess. Coming back to a past you don't recognize," Lilian observed.

"I think so, yes," Thomas answered with a grimace.

"You arm hurts badly, doesn't it?"

He stretched his pale face into a defiant smile. It was impossible for him to whine in front of a woman, especially in front of a woman he was in awe of. He found Lilian deeply impressive, compared with the girls he had known. She was older, with a sharp sort of beauty, a quick mind, and a quicker tongue, and so far she had managed to parry effortlessly what he thought were his best moves. He was too young to remember her heyday as a singer, but he remembered vividly the day when, on the Cabot Canal, he saw her standing straight up in a gondola full of Sophragettes, a white feather stuck in her hat and a six-shooter in her kid-gloved hand. She had been a vision. That she showed any interest in him at all filled him with a kind of warm pride. But he also knew enough of her now to know that she would quickly cut him down to size if he behaved improperly.

"Oh! Nothing I can't handle, I guess," he said as convincingly as he could.

Suddenly, a nurse ran up to them, clutching her dress and apron.

"*Vous étiez avec le grand monsieur, là? Quelque chose est arrivé!*"

Lilian and Thomas looked at each other. Gabriel raised his head.

"Something's happened to Jean-Klein," he translated.

They rose from their seats and hurried after the nurse, who led them through a labyrinth of corridors and stairs until they reached a small side room, where a camera on a tripod was aimed at a hospital bed.

Lavis lay on the bed, his eyes wide open, while an intern with an apron and black felt skullcap checked his pupils and pulse. A woman with long black hair, in a black dress, stood curiously motionless in a corner of the room, her hands joined as if in prayer, her eyes raised to the ceiling and empty, as if her spirit, too, had skipped out of time. The intern turned to them.

It was Jean-Klein Lavis. But a much younger one.

"Is this your friend?" he asked in French.

Gabriel felt a chill run down his spine, and stood gaping for a while, before finally finding the words to confirm.

"I'm afraid he has passed away," the intern went on. He looked at the corpse, visibly ill at ease, and clearly not really knowing why. "I had my back to him but heard him drop as soon as he entered the room. I can only conclude that he suffered a heart attack."

Gabriel looked at Lilian. "Say nothing," her eyes pleaded. She was right. It was, after all, a mental hospital, not quite the place where you want to discuss time-travelling with the doppelganger of a dead man. Gabriel could see that the younger, already dapper Jean-Klein Lavis suspected something but simply couldn't recognize the corpse as himself. Reasonably so, Gabriel thought.

"I'm sorry," Gabriel said. "He was in the Montparnasse crash. That may explain the shock."

"Ah. Of course, the crash." The intern nodded. "I've heard about it. Have you any idea why he came up here?"

"He had gone searching for a doctor. You see, we, too, were in the crash. Madame has a backache and this young man a broken arm. We're in dire need of attention."

"I see. You will be taken care of. The nurse will escort you to the examination room, while we take care of the body. What was his name?"

Gabriel panicked, but then realized that, by chance, Lavis's passport wasn't in his pocket, Brentford having kept it for the hotel formalities.

"Jean-Charles Leclou," said Lilian, in a flash of inspiration. "From Quebec."

The intern nodded and scratched his head under his felt cap, unable to loosen his frown. "My condolences," he said eventually.

Gabriel had liked Lavis but was too exhausted to feel anything but a deep-seated sense of persecution about the way his day was going. Lilian seemed to be a little more affected, or maybe she was simply pretending to be sad, because after all, technically speaking, Jean-Klein Lavis was very much alive, in fact younger and better-looking, with a whole existence ahead of him. What she wanted, probably, was to give the intern a big hug and tell him not to worry about the whole affair. Thomas, holding his arm, had already digested the whole incident and looked fascinated by the praying woman still motionless in the corner.

"What happened to her?" he asked in English.

Gabriel was about to translate, but it proved unnecessary.

"Oh, routine hypnosis for some photographic project," the young doctor answered in English with a strong French accent that was pure Jean-Klein Lavis. It made Lilian smile.

"Now, if you please, go down and we will take care of your woes. We'll let you know about the body."

Gabriel thanked him as warmly as he could, and so did the others, leaving the young man to wonder why they felt they owed him such unexpected and deeply felt sympathy.

"Well," he said to the motionless lady, after the New Venetians had followed the nurse out of the room, "I'd better get this body out of here before I wake you up."

But he stood there awhile longer, his eyes going from the woman in prayer to the corpse that was himself.

*

It was about ten o'clock when they left the hospital to enter a cold, wet night. Their shadows fanning out beneath the blurry glare of gas lamps, they crossed an endless square whose black naked trees looked like charred nervous systems. Gabriel, who had spent the evening filling out maddening miles of official forms regarding the death and prospective obsequies of one Jean-Charles Leclou, had a bandage around his head, keeping in place a big swab of cotton on his right temple. It was, he thought, romantic and virile, even if the nurse to whom he had boasted of this had looked rather sceptical. "You think so?" she had asked, mercilessly.

More virility, no doubt, could be attributed to Thomas, who, arm in a sling, crossed the square with his typical cloak-and-dagger gait, as if returning wounded but victorious from a duel. But in fact he'd had a shot of morphine and felt quite elated by the peppermint draught that circled in his head and pulsed out along his bones. Lilian, with nothing more than a benign pain in the back, had cajoled the doctor into giving her a shot as well, and the persistent smile on her face made Gabriel faintly jealous. For people who had just undergone a tragic loss, they looked rather jolly. But as a matter of fact, they were all having trouble coming to terms with their bereavement. After all, if dying simply meant being replaced by a younger version of oneself, well, death, where is thy sting? There was more cause to celebrate than to mourn.

"There's something strange in all this," Gabriel said, as if to himself.

Lilian looked at him with a smile that was either benevolent or ironic.

"You don't say."

Ironic, he decided.

He persisted. "It's not only Jean-Klein, you see. I mean, we were sent to a Paris that was undergoing a cruel winter, although this Paris here—which wasn't the one we were sent to—is certainly suffering from a severe winter. And one, at that, that Jean-Klein did not remember, though he was, as we have seen with our own eyes, present on this very day."

Lilian stopped. Thomas did, too, but, as in all serious conversations, he kept his distance, a frozen smile on his face.

"What do you mean?" Lilian asked. "That this is a different Paris from the *real* Paris of 1895?"

"I don't know," he said. "There were, indeed, some serious winters in the nineties. But if there had been such weather on such a memorable day as that of the Montparnasse train wreck, the young Jean-Klein would probably have remembered it all his life. So there is a chance that the young Jean-Klein is experiencing a different present than the Jean-Klein that we knew did."

"I admit it's puzzling," said Lilian, sucking in her cheeks. "Something else strikes me: he had two bodies. I do not understand how the same man could have two bodies."

"Well, precisely—I'd say he can't have two bodies," Gabriel mused. "After all, one of them died as soon as it encountered the other. And just think, if the younger one had not been under the hood of the photographic apparatus at that very moment, perhaps he would have been struck dead as well. It reminds me of the superstition that seeing your double is an omen of death. Maybe that idea sprang from similar experiences of time travel."

Lilian shrugged her shoulders, dubious but clearly disturbed.

They were now nearing the curbside where they'd been told *fiacres* awaited passengers. Given the harsh cold, however, demand was such that they were few and far between. A dark-skinned, dark-haired woman wearing a fur-collared coat and high-heeled shoes was waiting there, shivering with cold. It was Lilian who recognized her. She hurried towards her, a broad smile on her face, and by the time the men joined them, they had already exchanged names. Gabriel and Thomas looked at each other, thinking the same thing: Lilian had a way with girls that they both envied.

"This is Morgane Roth," she announced to Gabriel and Thomas. "And she speaks English."

"Oh. My mother was English," she explained. "If gypsies are anything but gypsies, that is."

"We saw . . . your work at the photographic lab," Thomas said, meaning it as a compliment.

The woman chuckled. Her voice was hoarse from too much smoking, and it vibrated with cleverness.

"You are closer to the truth than you think. It is *work*. There's a bit more acting involved than the doctors would like to believe, though at the same time, that's precisely what makes them happy and famous. So maybe they know and let it go."

"You didn't see anything of what happened in the lab while you were mesmerized, did you?" Gabriel asked her.

"Oh, I've seen things. But I don't think you would believe me."

"Try us!" Lilian said pleasantly.

"A kind of luminous cloud, or aura, went from the dead man to the intern, just after he died. But, probably, that's only because auras are what is *suggested* to us nowadays."

The three exiles looked at each other in perplexity, not for the first time that day.

"You are a medium, then?" Gabriel asked, as a jingling cab approached.

"Oh, yes. Who isn't nowadays? And a lot of us go through these photographic séances. I wish I didn't have to do these somnambulist tricks to make ends meet . . . Listen," she said, smiling, "I really have to take this cab. Why don't you come to one of my séances tomorrow, meet a few friends? They're very *spiritual*."

A bundle of clothes with a red nose, emitting a blur of breath that could have caught fire at the first match, bent down from its bench to open the door and let her in.

"Here is my card," Morgane said, giving it to Lilian before the coachman slammed the door.

They watched the squealing cab carve its tracks into the snow.

"Now, anyone care for a drink?" Thomas proposed.

"Are you sure you don't want to sleep?" Gabriel muttered. Which was not what the young Gabriel would have said. But, Gabriel realized, the young Gabriel was as dead as the old Jean-Klein.

II

A Night on Mount Parnassus

On the advice of Gabriel, who had lodged there previously during a stay in Paris that, technically, had not yet happened, the New Venetian diaspora had settled in the Grand Hôtel des Écoles on the rue Delambre. It was a slightly presumptuous place, its façade studded with lion heads and crescent-crowned Dianas, and Brentford wasn't surprised that it had appealed to Gabriel's unerringly New Venetian taste. Except for a few Englishmen, who relished the opportunity to see Paris going to the dogs under all this snow, tourists were rather rare at the moment, and there had been no difficulty in lodging their entire party. The rooms were tasteful and comfortable enough, some with a view onto a small courtyard. There was even running water, and therefore no need to spend three sous for the carriers to bring it hot to your room. However, the taps had to be left on at all times so they wouldn't freeze, and the pipes gurgled constantly. Not exactly the conditions an ambassador and his retinue might expect, but then . . . an ambassador of what?

While Lilian and Thomas went for a drink together at the nearby Eden-Parnasse, in the busy, flickering rue de la Gaîté, Gabriel had gone back to the hotel, staggering with exhaustion, his temple throbbing relentlessly. At the desk he found a message confirming the presence of the others, as well as their room numbers. He climbed the stairs, and noticing light spilling under the door of Brentford's suite on the fifth floor, he allowed himself to knock.

Brentford was propped on his pillow, counting money from a small chest open on the striped bedspread. At least they wouldn't want for anything. Gabriel cleared his throat and sat at the foot of the bed.

"Well, that was quite a trip," he said.

Brentford smiled a weary smile. "If you thought that was hard, wait for the journey home. Travelling backwards in time is one thing, but travelling forward to a city that doesn't exist yet . . . ?" He shook his head, then noticed Gabriel's bandages. "How's your head?"

"It still holds most of my brain, I suppose. Everyone all right here?"

"Given the situation, not too bad. Blankbate is already out, prowling for God knows what. He's quite the night creature, as you can imagine. And resourceful, too—for all my reluctance, his idea of scraping the real dates off our Canadian papers and replacing them with something more credible not only got us out of Iceland but has worked wonders getting us into this hotel. I suppose a little forgery on an already false passport isn't too terrible a crime, is it? As for Tuluk, he's cleaning and feeding the Colonel. He's become practically Branwell's right-hand man now. They get along famously and joke in Inuktitut all the time. How did it go at the hospital?"

"Oh, it was nothing special, really. Lilian and Thomas were pumped full of morphine and Jean-Klein Lavis is dead, except that he's alive."

Brentford turned pale.

"Take me through that last bit a tad more slowly, will you?" he asked.

Once Gabriel had finished his tale, Brentford carried on nodding for a while. Then he said, "Did you try to explain things to the young Jean-Klein?"

"Well, you know, explaining something I don't understand wouldn't normally scare me. Hell, I used to teach literature in college! But, this time, I was tired before I began, and not feeling especially willing to end up in a straitjacket."

Brentford pursed his lips. "It's troubling what you say about Jean-Klein—that is, *our* Jean-Klein—not remembering the weather being like this. It sounds as if we're in some alternate past, but the circumstances are curiously similar to the ones we were supposed to deal with in the present."

"You mean that Peterswarden knew this would happen and sent us back in time on purpose?"

"I have no proof of that—and anyway, I don't see how he could have planned it," Brentford admitted. "We don't have much choice, in any event. If we want to understand what's happening, we've got to start at the beginning and get in touch with Jean-Klein Lavis, Jr., again. At least, we should see if he can give us the lowdown on the *couronne magnétique*, since the old Jean-Klein had heard about it. I agree with the Colonel that it might play a part in this adventure of ours. Let's go first thing tomorrow."

"You sound as if you're enjoying this," Gabriel said, between two gaping yawns.

Brentford looked surprised, but realized that it was true: the more trouble he was in, the more excited he became. Getting everyone back home—well, everyone but Jean-Klein, alas—was a challenge that made governing New Venice look like a breeze, and after a brief bout of despondency, he had discovered that he was not only ready but willing to take it up.

"Let's say I find it . . . interesting."

By the time he got to his diminutive but charmingly red-furnished room, Gabriel discovered that his nagging throb had bloomed into a full-grown migraine. The first thing he unpacked from his trunk was a wooden music box, offered to him by the Twins on the day of his departure from office. Their effigies stood under the lid, two little Dresden dolls dressed as Tamino and Pamina that slowly, jerkily danced to a melody from *The Magic Flute*. He looked away from the figurines, for fear they would make him miss their originals even more than he did. Instead, he opened a drawer hidden in the side, took out a flask of Armstrong Black Drop, and made sure that he still had everything else he'd packed to get through these months of exile.

The sandpackets were there—precious, small white squares labelled with serif fonts: the One Midsummer Night Stand, a reputed metaphrodisiac; the Fly Fantasia Flint, for simulated dream flights; the Princess Charlotte's Pinch, which caused déjà vu; the Giant Gravel Galore, which changed the size of objects; the Supreme Selenium

Standard, which triggered the eeriest out-of-body experiences; and then the most recent concoction, which Gabriel had not tried yet: the Diviner's Diamond Dust, a pinch of greenish-white crystals, and a powerful morphetamine that was rumoured to enhance lucid dreams until they turned into full-fledged hallucinations.

But this physically harrowing trip had for the time being drained him of any curiosity for metaphysics. He simply took a glass of the laudanum Black Drop and went to bed, his temple now pounding as if his brain were trying to ram its way out of his skull. A click of the electric light and it was dark.

And darkness felt like home.

III

The Blackamoor

For Blankbate, darkness wasn't home—it was a kingdom, a land of adventures and quests, full of trials and treasures. As soon as he had shaken off the mist of a short, solid nap, he donned his cape, muffler, and large-brimmed hat, concealed a few weapons on himself, and hurried towards the south, where the lights were dim and few and far between.

Walking in the black slush, he soon left behind him the dazzle of Montparnasse, and after passing the cemetery he turned to his left, where a green copper lion dared him to come closer. He ignored the warning, and brushing by the well that marked the entrance to the catacombs, spent long minutes walking down a deserted boulevard whining with icy winds.

He finally turned to the right, southward again, and followed a narrow frozen brook. The city grew darker, poorer, muddier. The sour reek of leatherwork wafted from the cankerous, cracked walls that crouched along its course. It always struck him that you only had to cross a street to stumble on a parallel world, a new reality, where the very stone seems to be different. From time to time human silhouettes sprouted from the moist walls, assessed Blankbate's bulk, and shrank back into nothingness. He was getting nearer.

He could hunt by instinct alone, but this time he knew what he wanted and he had come to Paris to get it. This thing, if he found it, would be his ultimate triumph, and a glorious addition to the Scavengers' Arcaves, even if materially it was worth next to nothing. Its value was not to be measured in gold: it was a symbol, without the likes of which no line of royalty could be complete. Such a talisman would make the Scavengers the last heirs and defenders of the dark, noble tradition of the Pariahs, the Untouchables who night after night saved the world from choking on its own waste, and got nothing in return but disgust and contempt. For these penitents, who emptied the garbage bins, sluiced the cesspools, scraped the sewers, and dragged the rivers for corpses, Civilization was a bit of a joke. Yet in many ways, they were its last defenders—and, Blankbate liked to think, its most likely survivors. They were, he thought, the coming race. He would take the *Little Black Father* and the *Blackamoor* back to New Venice and make them the jewels of the Scavengers' scrap crown. That was his mission.

He met the first ragpicker at the top of the rue Croulebarbe, a wide paved street just above the river. He was an old man, though probably younger than he seemed, and carried strapped upon his back a wicker basket that made him look like a mad, wretched St. Nick. The lantern in his left hand sent across the street the dreadful shadow of the hook he held in the right one. But formidable as the shadow looked, the hook was but a modest tool, splashing through the slushy sidewalk.

"Does it bite, comrade?" Blankbate asked, using the solid French he had learned in the Foreign Legion, more years ago than he would care to count.

The ragpicker looked at him from under his single bushy brow, suspicious and perhaps scared. That, too, was a part of their life, Blankbate thought. In Paris, as everywhere, their caste stuck together—had their own restaurants, their own cafés, their own slums, their own rituals, and their own justice. It was beyond their ken why anyone would meddle with them, and they knew too much about "real" people's real habits to be curious for more.

"Don't be afraid," Blankbate said, holding his hands well apart. "It's a lonely night, and I just felt like having a little chat."

"I'm working," the man answered gruffly.

"Such ungrateful work, eh?" Blankbate said gently, coming closer. "Especially with this snow. And so few who appreciate it."

The man stood silent for a while. Even from his position, Blankbate could smell the whiff of cheap wine that floated on his breath.

On closer inspection, he wasn't quite the ruin Blankbate had first sur-mised. His hair, though disheveled, was silvery white, and under his beard—which could have been cleaner—his wrinkled face retained a certain wounded dignity that years of running the gutters had not managed to erase. For one second Blankbate suspected the rags, the beard, the basket were a disguise, but the scarred, chilblained, dirty hands, barely protected by torn, woolen half-mitts, could not be faked.

"Even I, I'm not sure I appreciate it, y'know?" His accent too, as far as Blankbate could judge, was not quite as coarse as expected.

"I wasn't talking about liking it. I was talking about understand-ing it."

The man's eyes glinted. "Now, that's different. Nobody under-stands it."

Blankbate went down on one knee, reaching with his thick glove into the gutter, and picking up a little faded ribbon. He delicately wiped the dirty snow off it and handed it to the man. "Well, I'd like to understand it. My name's Alan Blankbate."

"My name is . . . Amédée." And after a moment of hesitation, he added: "Baron Amédée de Bramentombes."

Blankbate stood up. "Baron?"

Amédée gave a sad smile that revealed missing incisors. "You see me claiming it now? I had what you'd call a reversal of fortune. But that's history," he added, his eyes on the gutter, in a tone that made Blankbate think that he wouldn't need much pressing to tell his story. Perfect, then. That would make his own tale easier to spool off.

"Listen," Blankbate proposed, "why don't you let me accompany you through your round, and then we'll go and eat somewhere. What do you think?"

"But why?"

Blankbate looked around and, finally, shrugged. "It'll get us out of the cold for a while."

"We're almost done," Amédée confided, after they had circled a few streets. He walked quickly, with determination, his head constantly bobbing like a clockwork toy, and Blankbate struggled to match his stride. He had guessed correctly, though: the ragpicker had now overcome his wariness, and seemed badly in need of hearing his own voice.

"It's one o'clock and I've been at it for five hours. Even though I won't get more than fifty sous for all this. There are two sides to that damned snow, really . . . It covers the trash, but sometimes it also protects it from other pickers . . . Not that I wish them harm, y'know, but I have to make a living, especially with all these Belgians, Italians, Germans, and whatnot who come to steal our bread. You know what the problem is? We don't have a strong government."

Suddenly the man stopped, as if realizing that this stranger could well be one of these foreigners he was complaining about.

"You said the snow protects the trash, right?" Blankbate asked, to steer Amédée's thoughts back to where he needed them.

"Yes. If you want to find anything, you have to watch the snow to see if it's been tampered with, the footsteps around it, the shape of the lump, whether the dogs go near it . . . though there are fewer dogs now. A lot of them have been eaten this last winter."

"But then you find dog bones."

Amédée croaked, like someone who only vaguely remembered having read a manual about how to laugh.

"Yes. Yes." He nodded constantly, nervously, and every now and then forgot Blankbate and talked to himself.

"Fifty sous. It doesn't sound like a lot," Blankbate tried again, after a pause.

"Depends for whom, I guess," Amédée said, nodding.

All this while the man kept on walking, swerving suddenly when a rival's lantern appeared at the end of a street, heading always towards a hill, which he called the Butte-aux-Cailles (Quail Hill? Blankbate tried to translate). As they started to climb its steep, curved, narrow streets, Blankbate felt he had been spirited away from Paris. Only the main street seemed to have been imported from that nearby capital, and even that main artery seemed to end in midair, in a wasteland from which rose a kind of wooden derrick. For the rest, the old houses huddling up and around the hill and the limestone quarries looked more like a mountain village, if not a shanty town. That was where the metropolis decomposed into smelly atoms.

"You know the story of this *arrondissement*?" Amédée asked. "Last time the city was extended beyond its walls, the rich people in the west refused to live in what was supposed to become the thirteenth arrondissement, simply out of superstition over the number. So the order of the boroughs was reversed clockwise, and the poorest of the poor inherited number thirteen."

"Nice," Blankbate said with a frown.

"It's a good place, though," his guide went on, with a faint but unmistakable enthusiasm. "A lot of mattress-makers live here. You always find some merinos"—which Blankbate understood was what pickers called the wasted wool and fabric off-cuts—"sometimes as much as one pound. The problem is that a lot of us pickers live just down the road."

Then Blankbate saw Amédée cautiously lift on his hook not a scrap of fabric but a wet crust of bread that had fallen in the snow.

"Taking that too?" he asked, curious to know.

"Sure. Why not? If it's clean, we eat it. If it's not, the bourgeois will."

"What do you mean?"

"Nothing is ever really lost here, monsieur. Nothing, not a single fallen hair, not a single chicken bone. It will become a wig, a brush, a button, a china plate, a candle, a bar of soap, or a cream. There is nothing that a chic woman puts on her face that doesn't come from my basket, you see. When I think of my former life," Amédée sighed, "I see all of its luxuries as they really are, and believe it or not, I never regret them."

He turned towards Blankbate, suddenly very moved.

"I have visions, you see. I see these salons, and everything they wear and hold in their hands is made of filth and smells of death. And for some reason, these things disgust me less where I find them now."

He stood silent for a while.

"And what about the crust, then?" Blankbate asked. He wasn't surprised by what he had heard. After all, he was in the same trade, and things were not that different in New Venice. This was something all luminous, glorious cities had in common: they were built on, and lived upon, the vilest trash. Though why say vilest, Blankbate wondered. What could be more human than trash?

Amédée shook himself from his dream.

"The same. With the clean crusts, you can make baby mush, for instance. This is often what the country nannies, in the villages around, feed to the city children they are supposed to mind. The dirty crusts you can sell to people who raise animals. But sometimes they're so disgusting, even the beasts won't touch them. So people burn them to a powder, like coffee, and that's where breadcrumbs come from in certain restaurants. The really charred crumbs are sold as chicory or used to make toothpaste. This is why I stopped brushing my teeth a long time ago. I'd rather eat the crust while it's fresh."

Blankbate chuckled. "I guess there's some justice in all of this. Everybody's eating someone else's dirt."

"There's no justice, monsieur," Amédée said in a low, lugubrious voice, giving his pronouncement the weight of a universal truth. "It is simply the bourgeois feeding each other. It's a business, you see. People make millions out of what we collect and sell to them." He nodded solemnly at the thought.

"I'm done," he finally said. "Just let me put my cashmere"—he tapped his basket—"at my place, round the corner, and we'll go to eat."

"I'm not sure I'm that hungry any more." Blankbate joked pleasantly, as they took the stairs of rue de la Colonie, a wasteland where wooden shacks and trailers were scattered on each side of the winding, slippery steps. In the distance the city shone, but it didn't fool anyone here. On the other side, beyond the dark, mangy rim of the fortifications, spread the mysterious "zone," a no-man's-land peopled with shadows and distant fires. Under the snow, it looked about as welcoming as the frozen ocean seen from New Venice.

"It depends where we go. I know the good places. But it'll have to be on you."

"Will Le Pot Tricolore do?" Blankbate risked. Amédée looked at him, narrowing his eyes.

"Maybe yes, maybe no," he answered.

They eventually ate a sinewy beef stew at a restaurant just at the corner of the rue de la Butte-aux-Cailles, for the simple reason that the Pot Tricolore did not exist anymore. The quarter was undergoing rapid, ugly changes, and the old inn, which had stood just at the gates of the city not very far away, had been destroyed some years before.

"It is strange that you used the name, though," Amédée commented, with his perpetual nod. Obviously, the mention of the Pot Tricolore had reignited his wariness.

"Strange? I used an old Baedeker guide, that's all. Why don't you tell me your story, Monsieur Amédée," Blankbate proposed, trying to think of another way to win his confidence.

It was the kind of story that starts with a long sigh.

"I don't know how well you know Paris," Amédée began, "but, with all due respect, most people don't understand what it really is. It is a battlefield, it is a mass grave, it is a charnel house. Twice in the past fifty years, the people have been massacred in revolutions and civil wars. Dig a hole almost anywhere, under the St. Jacques Square or the new Opera, and you'll find limestone-eaten corpses. You've heard about the Bloody Week, I suppose."

"Let's pretend I haven't," Blankbate essayed.

"That's where my story begins. It was in the last days of May, twenty-four years ago, at the end of the Commune. I was a young officer, then, a ship-of-the-line lieutenant in the Second Regiment of Marine Infantry—you know, the famous Porpoises. I came from a good Breton Catholic family and I had no qualms about fighting for the Versailles troops that had the Commune under siege. I had no qualms about fighting at all, I must say. I was a part of that Blue Division that fought at Bazeilles, one of the worst battles of the Franco-Prussian wars. But a civil war, that's something else. For one thing, I didn't like it that the Prussians were helping us. But that was nothing compared to the rest. For a while, it did indeed look like a war. We charged, took the fort at Courbevoie, entered the city. And that is where the horror began. I was at Belleville, a workers' neighbourhood, over there, just at the other side of Paris," he pointed to the northeast, "and the platoon I was in charge of was given one of those de Reffye machine guns that can shoot twenty-five bullets in very short bursts. Prisoners, soldiers, and civilians, old and young, were brought in by the dozen, some captured at the barricades and some, even more numerous, denounced anonymously by their neighbours.

They were lined up against a garden wall, and it was my duty to command the firing squad."

He paused for a while, his eyes blinking. Blankbate did not know whether he was trying to summon or block out the memories.

"I did this for three days, night and day, a few steps away from the St. Jean-Baptiste church. The machine gun cut them in half, so that we had trouble getting the corpses back together. We put them in cheap coffins, and sometimes people came to take photographs; I still do not understand why. My men were tough men, but I could see they recognized themselves in the people they shot, poor people like them, who only wanted the bread and justice everyone is hungry for, and who sometimes even died shouting 'Vive la France.' My Porpoises reacted like soldiers; that is, they became more cruel, as if they were gunning down their own misery and shame. But I did not react that way. I discovered I simply could not take it. I felt ill. I trembled. I ordered, 'Fire!' with a voice that trailed off more than once. I had to sneak out to vomit. The few naps I managed to snatch ended up in nightmares. I tried to shake them off by walking, walking, walking in the city, but everywhere I went, it was the same: grinning corpses heaped or thrown in pits and covered in limestone. Paris itself was ruins and ashes, lit by fires and devoured by shadows. I walked and walked, and without even noticing, I started to run away. One dawn, I came to completely lost, not remembering what I had done. I was found and brought back to my post, but I couldn't stay there and ran away again. This time I was tried as a deserter, but a doctor diagnosed me with some traumatic disorder. Today they call this 'ambulatory automatism,' and it seems that they try to cure it, but at the time it made me a lunatic, plain and simple. I found myself in Bicêtre, the mental hospital for men, and it was arranged for me to leave the Navy."

He ran his dirty hands through his greasy silver mane.

"I spent years walking around the courtyard, sometimes managing to escape, but only to walk in circles in the city that was rebuilding itself. The tourists visited it as if it were Troy or Pompeii."

"Every city is a Pompeii," Blankbate said, thinking of the Scavengers' Arcaves, "and rag-picking the archaeology of the poor."

But Amédée was not listening. He went on, his accent by and by losing its *faubourg* edge. Even his face was changing, Blankbate noticed, as if some former self were trying to work his way up to the surface, filling up a cheek here, pushing out some bone there.

"I was eventually discharged and I became a tramp, and then a ragpicker, because after all, this was the only sensible way I could live in my condition. I could not kick the habit of walking around for hours and hours, going nowhere in particular and sometimes very far away. I had gone from a Breton baronet to the Wandering Jew. In my milieu, as you can imagine, that was hardly a promotion. For my family, not only was I as good as dead—I would have been better dead. My wife orchestrated a plot with her notary. They found the mangled body of a tramp, declared it was mine, and I lost all my money. There's nothing in France that a notary cannot do, you know, and what a notary has done is certainly not for a tramp to undo. Besides, they hired someone to find me and explain the situation, and under threat, I gave my word of honour that I would never try to claim anything of my former position, nor even to reveal my own identity. So far I have kept my promise. I don't need my honour for anything else, I guess."

"But you told me your name."

"I shouldn't have, it's true. But, then, it's my name. I can be excused for feeling the need to pronounce it from time to time. Especially to a stranger who understands the way I live."

Blankbate acknowledged the compliment with a brief nod. He could tell that Amédée had not told the full story.

"Why did you accept?"

"Fear. Shame. Helplessness. Lucidity, too. What kind of figure would I cut in a salon with these hands and this face? I do not wish to be an embarrassment to anyone. And as I told you, now that I know that this upper-class world is built from bones and trash, I'd rather forget about it. I don't miss any of it, believe me." But still, the note of regret was unmistakable.

"There's something you're not saying," Blankbate insisted.

"We all have our little secrets, don't we?"

Amédée drank from his glass of rotgut. Blankbate thought the conversation was over, but he could still feel its embers glowing in the ragpicker's eyes. He blew a little on them. "Why stay in Paris?"

"Ah," Amédée raised his grubby finger. "You've got me there."

If this was a smile, Blankbate did not wish to see another.

"My wife got pregnant during one of my spells of leave. I was already in trouble when I heard I had a daughter. Given the situation, I could not even dream of meeting her, you understand. But there is more. It was part of my wife's bargain that my money went to my young daughter—to make her own motives less suspect, I suppose. She can still administer it until my daughter gets married, and perhaps after that, for who would like to marry a girl whose father was a certified madman who used to walk around like an automaton and then made a career of prodding dung heaps?"

"I'm sorry to hear that. I still don't understand why you stay in Paris."

"So I can see my daughter, of course. Sometimes. Going out of her house and jumping into a carriage. Or walking in the streets. From afar, even. It doesn't always do me much good, but . . ." He struggled for words, like a man who knows he is going to say too much but cannot help himself. "It is what keeps me alive. And if remaining hidden is the only thing that can ensure my daughter's happiness, I'll do it gladly and to the end."

The wounded dignity Blankbate had noticed now crystallized in Amédée's face as it fought to resist the distortion of coming tears. The workings of pride never ceased to amaze Blankbate—such as in this man who ate off the pavement but would rather die than be seen crying. Blankbate thought of offering his help, but decided against it. He was of those people who think that the world would be a better place if everyone stuck to their own business.

"Now that I have made a fool of myself," Amédée was saying bitterly, "tell me what business you have with the Pot Tricolore."

It was Blankbate's turn to be honest. Somehow he resented this, but there was no other way to make progress with his search. He began, "There are things I cannot say. But let us say I am, like you, a Scavenger." He let the news sink in, but Amédée did not look surprised.

"I search for things, and I find things. Things that may not look valuable and are in fact deemed quite useless. But, like your crust of bread, these things have a hidden value."

Amédée nodded, his gaze now focussed and attentive.

"Now, what more could a Scavenger's heart desire but some object that at the end of his quest would represent for him not money, but instead the sacred value of his own thankless task? Something that were he to find it, would be like finding himself?"

"Like the Holy Grail," said a Breton child somewhere inside Amédée.

Blankbate spread his hands apart. It was not for nothing that the Fisher King was the Scavengers' patron saint.

"There. So now tell me what you know about the Pot Tricolore."

"It was still there when I started in the trade. It was before all these foreigners came, before we had to fight against the garbage cans. We were still a family, the twenty thousand of us. Now, it was, in certain ways, a very hierarchical society. There were three levels, depending on the quality of your sack and hook: the Union of the true proletarians, who had only sackcloths, instead of baskets; the Chamber of Deputies, who were slightly better off; and above them the Chamber of the Peers, who had good wicker cashmeres, six-franc lanterns, and copper on their hooks. The Pot Tricolore was where we congregated for our assemblies, especially for the grand banquet on the first day of summer"—Blankbate smiled at this, for the Scavengers held a banquet on the very same day—"where all of these differences collapsed for a while. On such days, it was toast after toast, and wine was brought in an enormous vessel called the *Moricaud*—the Blackamoor—and poured out into a little earthen pot that we called the *Petit Père Noir*—the Little Black Father. Those days are over, but I assume that's what you are after."

"Exactly. I came a long way for them. A very long way."

"Just for them?"

"We're talking about the Holy Grail."

"Then, Monsieur, with all due respect, I would strongly advise that you go back to wherever you came from. The Little Black Father is, I'm afraid, broken. But I know where the Blackamoor is and I wouldn't like to put you in danger on account of it."

"I pick garbage, too, Monsieur de Bramentombes"—Amédée flinched at the name—"and am not afraid of gettting my hands dirty. And I need your help."

Amédée considered the notion of someone needing his help, then looked as if he had found a five-franc *pièce* on the sidewalk.

"You have been warned," he answered, "but you called me Monsieur and bought me a meal. That's the best thing one man can do for another. I'll tell you what I know . . ."

To be continued . . .

EPISODE V

THE MECHANICAL MEDIUM

I

The Marvellous

The following morning, the compassionate Brentford did not dare disturb the oversleeping Gabriel. He left the hotel on his own, a tad dispirited by the feeling that he was supposed to solve everyone's problems by himself. It had always been his scourge to be deemed a man of action, although at heart, he was a thoughtful, contemplative fellow. Still, he had played the part assigned him, and most of the time he had cut a decent figure, so much so that it had caused his name to become a byword for dependability—in New Venetian families, the words "Go get Orsini" had become a catchphrase, used anytime for any problem, however trivial. And now: *You're lost in time? In a foreign country? Under Arctic conditions? Need to get back posthaste to save your city from turmoil?* "Go get Orsini."

Now, though, it was Orsini who was going to get someone.

The Salpêtrière was a city, really, with its streets and squares, its church and, well, its hospital. It took a good half hour of wandering before the Man Who Solved All Problems found the building where he might stumble on Lavis—that is, if he had understood what the grumpy concierge had muttered through his shrubby moustache.

The Intern Ward, or Charcoterie, was a small house that recalled a country inn tastefully coated with patches of verdigris-coloured moss. In compliance with the universal law that dictates that every young doctor must be a lubricious prankster with a drinking problem, its inside was decorated with smutty frescoes, including a door redesigned as female pudenda framed by enormous thighs. Brentford had sensed a strange tingle on his neck when he stepped through it, and now he looked back at this bold representation with a certain puzzlement.

"The origin of the world," someone behind him said pleasantly enough. Brentford turned to see a black-capped intern sitting at a long table, drinking coffee from a glass. "It all goes downhill from there, I'm afraid."

Brentford was startled to recognize Lavis. At least there was one of the Seven to whom the journey had done some good. He looked fresh and smooth, in impeccably ironed and creased elegant clothes visible through his unbuttoned smock. He even wore the sempeternal spats that the old Lavis had never been without. Brentford tried to kick into gear the rusty, leaky, smoking contraption that was his secondary-school French. He heard his accent coming out with slight Italian overtones and suddenly felt like Pulcinello on a stage.

"Would you be Jean-Klein Lavis?"

The intern hesitated, perhaps thinking about the strange corpse he had seen the day before.

"I am, yes. In what way can I help you?"

"I am Brentford Orsini, a friend of Gabriel d'Allier and Lilian Lake, whom you met yesterday under particularly painful circumstances."

"Oh, this . . . Monsieur Leclou was a friend of yours too, then? Please accept my most sincere condolences. And do sit down, I beg you. Would you like a taste of our famous sock juice?"

"Well, I don't think . . ."

"Ah! Sorry!" Jean-Klein chuckled. "I mean coffee."

"Oh! That would be nice. Thank you," Brentford said with relief, as the young doctor filled a small, bulbous glass.

Brentford sat down, still trying to come to terms with the fact that his interlocutor's body was presently lying in a morgue somewhere, that it was a dead man who now put a hot glass before him on a table carved with obscenities. Some Italian part of Brentford's taste buds revolted against the brown, watery decoction that he was now supposed to drink. His Scottish stomach told him it had known worse, and at least the stuff was hot.

"Hmm . . . Monsieur d'Allier and my other friends have spoken very highly of you. And we think that you might be able to help us with a little problem that we have."

"You have a problem *besides* losing your friend? I am sorry to hear that. I would be very pleased to help you, but you'll have to forgive me the fact that my competencies are few and exclusively medical."

"And sartorial, perhaps," Brentford said, intending to flatter, though he quickly noticed that he had vexed Jean-Klein Lavis. "It is said that true elegance is never noticed. So I may not be as competent as it pleases you to see me. Besides," he said, trying to sound more pleasant, "I suppose you did not come to la Salpêtrière for a tailored suit, unless it is a straitjacket that you need."

I may need one soon, thought Brentford. Size forty-two. Herringbone. Double-breasted, seventeen-inch velvet straight collar, with Russian-leather straps and silver buckles—an awful lot of buckles . . .

"No. It's about a little headpiece, actually," he said, unfastening the bag that held the *couronne magnétique.*

"It's quite strange," Jean-Klein remarked out of the blue. "I have the oddest feeling I've seen you somewhere."

"I do, too, I must say," Brentford said evasively. But it bothered him. What if the old Jean-Klein's memories had contaminated his younger self? Like a kind of reverse self-Transpherence? Would he remember New Venice, then? Could they talk about it? Brentford was tempted to find out, if only to keep the city alive in his mind. But no, not yet. Gabriel was right. Not to a man who cracks jokes about straitjackets.

Brentford put the *couronne magique* on the table. "Here it is. Do you have any idea what it is or how it works?" he asked, overplaying his ignorance.

Jean-Klein's laugh had the ring and pitch of rationalism: mirthless and slightly contemptuous. Brentford knew it well, for he had once had the same laugh himself. In his case, years in New Venice had added more than a little self-directed irony to it.

"I suppose I could explain to you what it is and how it does *not* work."

"That would be a start. I'd appreciate it."

"It's called a *couronne magique*—a magical or, to be precise, a *magnetic* crown. You could say it started here, like so many things, with the study of hysteria. A doctor named Luys was interested in the way magnets can be used to provoke, displace, or, he discovered, suppress the painful muscular contractions that plague our epileptico-hysterical patients. He was also very adept at hypnosis, with which he obtained similar results, especially using rotating mirrors. Unfortunately for him, I think, or at least for his reputation, he worked with the wrong person, namely Dr. Encausse, who under the name of Papus practically rules the Parisian Masonic occultist underworld. Luys apparently bought into the notion that the mind, like a magnet, emits a certain field, an effluvium that can be captured and transmitted."

"Something like . . . Odic force?" Brentford risked.

"Ah! Od, neuric fluid, radiant matter—never mind the bottle, as long as you get drunk. My chief at the photographic lab, Baraduc, even tries to photograph these so-called auras, and he seems especially happy if he obtains a blurry, spotty cliché instead of a decent shot. The crown is quite simply an application of this. You suggest a patient while he wears this crown, and once he's hypnotized, the effluvia charge the crown with the suggested instructions."

"And it does not work?"

"Well, what do you think? Luys and Encausse say it does, of course. But there is very little you can prove or disprove when you're working with suggested subjects, and I should know because this is my field of work. And as for effluvia, quite frankly it's all codswallop."

Brentford nodded and thought he'd better withhold the information that he had travelled through Time, from a city not yet built, using a codswallop-powered vehicle.

"I shouldn't tell you this here, but I tend to side with Charcot's archrivals, like Bernheim, who thinks that hypnosis is but a balance of power. Put a rich, educated, authoritative man in front of a poor, scared, sick girl and there is likely to be a lot of suggestion going on. But really, I'm one-sided about it. You should meet Encausse, who works at the Charité Hospital. And if you're interested in effluvia, I think you should try to meet his good friend Colonel de Rochas. He runs the École Polytechnique, and he is now part of the Comité de Salut National, which is supposed to deal with weather conditions. Can you imagine that the man appointed to get us out of this chaos is actually persuaded that you have blue flames coming out of your skull? How improbable is that? Welcome to France, Monsieur Orsini."

Brentford gave the polite smile of a man who talks daily with a living mechanical head about a city in the Arctic Circle governed by hermaphrodite Siamese twins born from a dead woman, and refrained from further comments about the probable and the improbable. Getting up, he thanked Jean-Klein profusely.

A small, balding man suddenly interrupted, bursting into the room red with anger to howl something at Jean-Klein before storming away, all too quickly for Brentford to understand.

"You just met Gilles de la Tourette, our chief," Jean-Klein explained, "who is a member of the National Health Committee, too. We were just talking about the fantasies regarding hypnosis. Just imagine that less than two years ago, de la Tourette was shot three times at close range in the head by a woman who was persuaded that the doctors of the Salpêtrière had mesmerized her—remotely—against her will. She had also, it seems, written threatening letters to Rochas, who had probably sent her way some of his powerful male effluvia. It is a small otherworld, apparently."

"Well, nothing like a gun to reverse the balance of power."

Lavis smiled.

"Indeed. Since then, and especially since Charcot's death, de la Tourette has become very irritable, very rude—practically a case study for his own theory. I even suspect him of having *a little bike in the head*, as we say here. In any event, much to my regret I have to end this interesting conversation to get back to work."

They shook hands. "Have you been informed that Monsieur Leclou's funeral is tomorrow at nine a.m at the Parisian Cemetery in Ivry?" Jean-Klein asked.

"Thank you. We'll be there. I suppose . . . you won't."

Jean-Klein stared at Brentford in a thoughtful way. "I'll be there more than I think, perhaps," he finally muttered.

Brentford was startled by the comment, but said no more before exiting.

On his way out of the building, however, he was surprised to meet Thomas coming in. Thomas, in turn, looked rather embarrassed. "Hello," he said, blushing.

"You're going back to the hospital?"

"Yes, to check the plaster. It does hurt a bit," he said with a wince, clowning a little.

Brentford had never heard Thomas complain before, even in jest. It wasn't his style. There was something fishy behind this. A girl? A nurse? A patient? He sighed, but he wasn't Thomas's father. Years of friendship with Gabriel d'Allier had taught Brentford that giving moral advice to friends often yielded results opposite to what was intended. Still, it was nevertheless with a worried brow that he headed towards the Seine.

In spite of all that he needed to do, Brentford found himself loitering like a tourist. It was not yet November, and the Seine was already frozen solid, its bed cluttered with a jumble of bezeled ice blocks that shone in the pale, blurry sun like a miniature Arctic Sea. Muffled to the ears, he followed its banks, passing a few other stray strollers and watching children play among the blocks.

The Jardin des Plantes, on his left, seemed eerily quiet, and he remembered having read in some English newspaper that the animals in its menagerie had been devoured by starving Parisians the previous winter. As this year's winter was already even worse, Brentford worried about what on earth the people would eat this time, before realizing that, whether he liked it or not, he was now one of those people.

Enormous pyramids of snow towered beside the bridge piles like so many shards of glaciers, and after a few puzzled seconds, he spotted the workers emptying their barrows of shoveled snow over the parapets. Other passers-by were engrossed in this spectacle, too, with the common male fascination with work that's hard and that's not one's own. To Brentford it seemed a brave but futile labour, like trying to bail out a boat with a thimble. He remembered that he had been sent to help Paris learn not to fight the snow, necessarily, but to live with it, and he almost regretted having other worries on his mind. Maybe he should kill two birds with one stone before the cold killed them all and go to see Dr. "Papus" Encausse at the Charité Hospital to find out about the crown; or to the École Polytechnique to speak

with Colonel de Rochas, the man Lavis said dealt with "weather conditions" and dabbled in effluvia.

Deciding to decide on the way, he set off and soon noticed that
the cold felt colder there than it did in New Venice. Maybe it's not so
much the cold you feel as the way a place copes with it, he mused.
Maybe it was seeing an army of old women trying to clear snow heaps
with brooms that sent shivers down his spine, he thought as he passed
the wine market and crossed the rue des Fossés St. Bernard. And as to
Gabriel, Brentford surmised, it was the sight of the dark-green, flaking
bookstalls along the quay, shut down and with snow up to their rusty
locks, that would make him turn up his collar and lengthen his stride.

Then Notre-Dame flashed through dead branches to loom over
everything, flaunting its indifference to the catastrophe. Brentford
turned left to reach the Place St. Michel, and in a café on the corner,
the Soleil d'Or, he had the pleasure—forbidden in New Venice as a
"threat to literacy"—of using a telephone. He called the hotel and
asked Gabriel to meet him. Taking a hoarse mumble for a yes, he
sat down and ordered a croque-monsieur from a waiter whose atti-
tude made it very clear that serving people did not make him their
inferior—quite the contrary. Meanwhile, there on the Boul' Mich', as
the locals called it, there were still a few attempts at circulation: the
tramways were dead, of course, their rails buried under layers of off-
white snow, but a few brave horse omnibuses were still hoofing it up
and down.

Gabriel appeared sooner than Brentford had expected. In accordance with the very New Venetian idea that extreme weather conditions were not an excuse for sloppy grooming, he was dressed to the
nines-below-zero, in sixteen-holed boots, black velvet jodhpurs, a grey
double-breasted jacket with a fur collar and a matching cap with its
earflaps tied up on the top, showing a simple dressing on his wound
instead of yesterday's bigger bandage. Brentford noticed that he also
carried a cane with a carved knob depicting the Polar Kangaroo.

The sight of Gabriel attired like that warmed him for a moment—it
was the closest thing to being in New Venice, except that they were
still separated from it by an abyss of time.

"Trekking back home, Gabriel?"

"Going to get Orsini. The plumbing's not right in my room."

"Before that, if you don't mind, we're going to the Charité Hospital to meet the inventor of the magical crown. You may have heard of him—Papus. A doctor, a high-ranking Mason, and one of the leading occultists in Paris."

"As you know, I'm more into the Widow's daughters than into her sons," Gabriel said with a grimace. "And what did our new friend the late Jean-Klein have to say about the crown?"

His answer pleased Brentford twofold: first because Gabriel appeared to be in a more congenial mood, and second because his friend was finally showing some concern about their situation.

"He was very dismissive about it. I didn't dare tell him that I was probably talking to him because of one."

"He'll change his mind when he gets to New Venice in twenty years or so. Imagine his life: he goes to New Venice, comes back to Paris in a time slip back to his youth, only to become the Jean-Klein who will go to New Venice . . . and then it starts all over again!"

"If he ever gets back to New Venice, I'm not going to feel sorry for him," Brentford said with a sigh—then added sombrely, "and if we ever make it back, I'd hate to have to go through this all over again."

Having paid (or, Brentford having paid), they left and crossed the square, stopping to observe for a moment the enormous fountain depicting the archangel Michaël trampling a winged, tailed Lucifer and plunging his lance into his accursed side. The basin was frozen and the chimeras on each side were spouting icicle oriflammes, as if, here too, time had stopped.

"Pretty weird monument," Brentford commented.

"As a matter of fact," Gabriel answered, pedantic in his good-natured way, "it was conceived as a reminder for the working class of the failed revolution of 1848. It reads something along the lines of 'See what happens when you revolt.' "

"The allusion was too subtle for the Communards, apparently."

"Ah, that's the problem with the Great Unwashed, you see. They can't even read tacky allegories. But they've been punished for their ignorance. They now get a big cream cake called the Sacré-Cœur hovering over their slums—as if France were begging forgiveness of God for letting the poor play with matches."

"I thought the French were rational," Brentford said, although Jean-Klein's pithy explanations had somewhat diminished his certainty.

"Reason is just their excuse for their pettiness and their total lack of imagination. But to generalize is to be an idiot, and I'm sure that your witch doctor at la Charité will prove himself a *very* imaginative fellow."

❊

La Charité, they discovered, was a lugubriously grey neoclassical hospital on the rue des St. Pères on St. Germain-des-Près, and it gave Brentford a brief spell of déjà vu. If the Salpêtrière looked like an army barracks, this hospital looked more like a prison.

They told the concierge that they had found an object of value belonging to Dr. Encausse and that they wished to hand it over to him personally. This must have been a typical gambit to see the doctor, because the concierge barely reacted, simply pointing them to the room where Encausse gave consultations to outpatients.

"All right," Gabriel instructed Brentford as they entered, "the man deals with arcana. He is, at heart, a gullible fellow. We'll just have to look dark, intense, evil—frowning over some intense metaphysical pain, our eyes burning with the fires of hell, crackling with magic—and he'll be eating from our hands."

He took one look at Brentford.

"No, not like that. You look like you've just eaten Eskimo food. Perhaps we should stick to the Masonic handshake."

From a distance, Encausse, a fat man in his thirties with a fuzzy, double-pointed beard, appeared affable and seemingly devoted to his patients, some of whom were gazing at him with moist eyes as if he were a holy man. Well, as long as the doctor did his job correctly, Brentford thought, it hurt no one that he spent his evenings chanting nonsense in a pentacle. And after all, who was he to mock people who believe in magic? He thought of Helen, what he had seen her doing, and what she had done to him. Back home, he and Gabriel had been exposed—no doubt more than "Papus" himself—to a more-than-healthy dose of the supernatural. The difference was that he and Gabriel at least had the decency to admit that they didn't understand it. He respected mystics, but occultists, he reckoned, were like people who would draw a map of a place where they'd never been.

Working hard to look secretive and deep, the New Venetians wedged themselves between the other patients to get in front of the doctor, and taking his palm in what they hoped was the proper handshake, introduced themselves as Brother De Kink and Brother Stinkson from Polaris Lodge number 186 in Fort Smith, Northwest Territories. They mentioned that they had found a kind of crown that, they thought, worked in mysterious ways . . .

Encausse looked very interested, and he explained earnestly, "I do not insist on separating my medical work from my other interests; quite the contrary, they are one and the same thing. It is my conviction that most diseases come from the disjunctions of the astral, which is the sole concern of occultists."

Brentford and Gabriel approved in unison, trying to look profoundly touched by the truth that had just been revealed.

"However, as Ecclesiastes says, there is a time for everything. Allow me to finish my work here, and if you please, I will seek you out to discuss these matters as soon as possible in a small bookstore a few streets from here, Five rue de Savoie. It's called Le Merveilleux. I truly hope I'll see you there."

✳

The Marvelous Bookstore was located in a knot of little narrow streets just off the Seine, nearer to the Latin Quarter. Gabriel had browsed about half of the shelves when the shop bell finally rang and Encausse appeared. After exchanging a few whispers with the owner Mauchel, a defiant man who had been staring at Brentford and Gabriel since their arrival as if they were going to cast a death spell on him from behind the stacks, the doctor took them into a little back room hung with black drapes and decorated with letters and symbols, two winged sphinxes, and a cardboard cutout of John Dee's

Hieroglyphic Monad. It looked like the set for the first act of a high school production of *Faust*.

"This is our Martinist temple," Papus explained, glowing at his own satisfaction. "It is becoming very successful. We will soon be opening an occultist school just across the street."

Brentford and Gabriel did their best to look impressed and interested.

"So, you told me you had a certain object . . ." said Papus, with a sudden intense look that he supposed impressive.

"Oh, yes, of course . . ." Brentford said, taking the crown out of his satchel and putting it on the desk between them.

"Just as I thought . . ." Papus began, with a frown. "Before we talk about this, I am sure you won't reproach me for expressing my curiosity about who you are, exactly."

Brentford had an inbred distaste for lying. Gabriel did, too. However, thanks to the complications of his amorous life, he had learned to live with it.

"We come from a place very far to the north, and regard ourselves as very modest seekers on the path of authentic learning," he said now. "Our Worshipful Master, the late Godfrey Daniel, 33°, 89°, has recently passed away, and we found him on his deathbed wearing the crown. He had told us shortly before that he had received some objects from Paris that would be his legacy to us, and his will made it clear that he was talking about the crown. But we do not know why he was wearing it when he died, nor what, exactly, it signifies."

"But you traced it back to me?"

"You are the most famous Master in Paris. We thought that if anyone knew, it would be you."

"It is quite a coincidence, if such a thing as coincidence exists, that you came to me, because—I say it with humility—I happen to have invented these devices, with Dr. Luys. Their proper name is the *couronne magnétique*. But what I do not remember is having sent any of them anywhere. These are very rare, you understand. Have you any idea of how your Master got it?"

"Much to our regret, we have no information for you on that," Brentford intervened. Technically, it wasn't a lie.

Encausse frowned and nodded. "I suppose it will have to remain a mystery, then. In any case, I can still explain to you how they work . . . We discovered, in the wake of Mesmer, that you can affect the nervous centres by putting them in a magnetic or electromagnetic field. When it comes to directly influencing the brain, a magnetic crown is the most efficient tool. It not only records the brain's activity; it also stores it and can transmit it, from the transferring subject to the receiving one, exactly like a phonograph."

Brentford started at the word *transferring*. Its connection to Transpherence, which he had thought about when meeting Lavis, came to him again, more strongly this time.

Encausse continued, unaware. "Using this, I could transmit any kind of neuropathic symptoms from one patient to another: headache, vertigo, fainting spells, memory loss. One of Luys' male patients, who unknowingly wore a crown charged two weeks earlier by a female subject, began walking and talking like a woman as soon as he put it on, and could barely be convinced that he wasn't one. As you can imagine, it opens amazing perspectives. For instance, the strength from a healthy subject could be transferred to a depressed or excited brain."

"Contagion as cure," Brentford said, as if to himself.

"And all the more since the neuric forces accumulated in the crown do not fade immediately, and could very well be used to influence even a third subject. They are so persistent, in fact, that you have to wash or sometimes even heat the crown red-hot to get rid of the influence. All this, of course, could be indefinitely furthered."

"But tell me," Brentford suddenly asked, "could the *couronne magnétique* affect temporality?"

Encausse looked puzzled. "In what way?"

"Hmm . . . Let us say that a *couronne magnétique* has been charged on a dying man, and then put on another person some days later. Does that second person's sense of time recede by two days? Does he feel that he has somehow gone back in time? Does he forget the present he lives in?"

Now Encausse looked surprised.

"It could, yes," he said, "technically speaking, though only until the effect wore off. But I must admit I've never thought of this. Is this what you were referring to when you said that the crown behaved in mysterious ways?"

Gabriel was improvising. "Positively," he said. "I must confess: I put our Master's crown on my head, and . . . I really felt I was dying."

"Can you describe that?" Encausse inquired, leaning across his desk with a sparkling glint in his eyes.

"Well . . . My body just disappeared, and I could see my whole life revolve around me, and then I realized that it wasn't mine," Gabriel elaborated from his memories of the Transpherence he had undergone.

"This is fascinating," Encausse said, his head bobbing in approbation. "Your master probably wanted to record some message for you to experience after his death. Maybe he put his most cherished memories in there. But the crown may also have recorded the very instant of his death, or the minutes that followed, when his astral self fought to leave his earthly body. I must admit, such possibilities never occurred to me. You see, what I call neuric forces I could just as well call vital fluid. I could call them life itself. Nothing could possibly be more powerful than this. I would like very much to examine this particular crown more closely, if you don't mind. May I take it with me?"

Brentford and Gabriel exchanged a quick look. "We're sorry," Gabriel said while Brentford quickly put the crown back in the bag, "but it's a personal legacy that has been entrusted to us. It was stipulated by the deceased in his will that we should not separate from it."

Encausse angered quickly. "If this how you are going to thank me for my time . . ."

"Our gratitude will be the greater for your understanding," Brentford countered. "We promise to keep you abreast of any further developments. Thank you very much, Doctor."

"I have in my turn one question, gentlemen," Encausse boomed as they got to the door.

"Certainly, Doctor," Gabriel said.

Their interlocutor sounded unpleasantly suspicious, as he said, "You are, you say, from a Canadian lodge called Polaris. Would that be near the Arctic Circle?"

Brentford and Gabriel looked at each other. *Uh*, thought one; *oh*, thought the other. "Sixty degrees north. The northernmost lodge in the world," Gabriel boasted.

"Would you by any chance have heard of any Palladian influence in your chapter?"

"Palladian influence? What would that be?" Brentford asked, sincerely puzzled.

"Never mind. I suppose that Fort Smith is far removed from the current concerns of European lodges. I envy you. There has been a lot of talk lately about a secret location in the Arctic where Palladian or Luciferian so-called Masons printed antichurch pamphlets. You have never heard of it, of course?"

"Never before," Brentford insisted.

"That is what I thought. Goodbye, gentlemen," Encausse said, with a knowing smile that Brentford read as contemptuous and Gabriel as malignant.

Once outside, back on the quays, Brentford took a deep breath, which felt like a razor blade to his lungs. The day was evaporating and the worn beige colour of Paris, which made it look like a seashell, now turned a severe stony grey. The mist was ascending around the dusky houses, and they began to look like memories.

"I thought that would never end," Brentford said. "By the way, that was a brilliant lie you came up with about how we got the crown."

"It wasn't a lie. It was a fiction. We just got more truth out of it than we first put in."

"It made me think of something I'd never thought of before. As Jean-Klein told us, the crown that de Lanternois wore would be a fairly recent invention here. Then there's the notion that it bears a message about a Paris smothered under snow, which is, indeed, the way things are *now*. . . And then your mention of our supposed Arctic location, precisely where de Lanternois was found with the crown, elicited a strong interest from Encausse . . . Are you starting to see a pattern?"

Gabriel shrugged. "I'm not that crazy," he said.

II

The Phantom Members' Club

Brentford still hadn't unraveled all the implications when he arrived at the hotel—alone, since Gabriel had decided he'd rather spend the evening walking around—and found the colony in turmoil, thanks to an accident that took him some time to piece together.

"This Inuk was with the Colonel," Tuluk explained in his room, trying hard to retain his seriousness. There were clothes all over the floor, and all kinds of strange Inuit objects, and the scene added powerfully to Brentford's ongoing sense of chaos.

"We talk about New Venice in your room," Tuluk explained, his barely contained smile threatening to split his face. "Miss Lilian knocks the door. She looks for you. The Colonel, he says, like this: 'What you need Brentford for?' he says, and the Colonel, he puts out his tongue, a very long tongue. He says like this, 'I can still pleasure a lady.' And then Miss Lilian she is very angry, very angry. She . . ." Tuluk made a wide sweep with his hand.

"Slapped him?" Brentford asked.

"Yes. She slaps him on the face. And she says, 'That pleasured *me*, thank you very much.' "

It certainly sounded like her. Brentford could almost hear her voice.

"How did the Colonel react?"

"Nothing. The Colonel says nothing. This Inuk is afraid that she breaks something in him. Miss Lilian, she walks away. She slaps the door . . ."

"Slams, you mean?"

"Yes. Slams. Very strong. Like a crazy bear woman."

"The Colonel is all right?"

"The Colonel, he is all red. Very not happy. But this Inuk, he looks in the box, and he finds it is all good."

Tears of suppressed laughter were now streaming from the corners of his eyes.

But although he would have liked to join in the chorus, Brentford felt it was his duty to intervene.

❊

"How are you, Colonel?" Brentford asked.

The Colonel, "seated" on the bedside, rolled his eyebrows so forcefully that Brentford deciphered it as, "If I had shoulders, I'd shrug."

"Tuluk told me about the the incident with Lilian," Brentford persisted in his best neutral voice.

The Colonel answered nothing, but stared ahead, as if watching an enemy line bristle on the horizon. "Never complain, never explain," his whole demeanour insisted.

"I'm sorry it happened," Brentford continued.

The Colonel emitted a clicking sound and heaved a rubbery sigh that Brentford thought painful to hear. "You're a man and a decent chap, Orsini," he said. "Maybe we can talk about these things, you know, between men."

"That's what I'm here for, Colonel."

The Colonel remained silent for a while, then harrumphed. "Well, I wouldn't wish anyone to be in my place, not for a second, old son. But you have to understand that even if I don't look like one, I am still a man, and men will be men. I may not have much in the way of body or appendages, but as long as there is a brain up there, I have sensations, and a rather awful lot of them, that I have few occasions and little means to satisfy."

"I understand." Brentford said. "Phantom, er, members."

"That's it, old son, there are but *phantom members* in my club." This was followed by a creaky attempt at laughter that Brentford's musical ear was not especially eager to hear again.

"Is there any way I can help?"

The Colonel thought for a while. "Well. Hmm . . . Paris is renowned for certain houses, as you know, and I wondered if one of you could take me to one."

Brentford let the words sink in. If there were anyplace in the whole wide world where a head mounted on gears would have a chance to get laid, surely it had to be Paris. But still . . .

"Colonel, please understand," he began cautiously, "I have nothing against this in principle and I am sure that Parisian professionals are very open-minded. But given our situation, it would be unwise, to say the least, to have you out womanizing around town. I do not doubt that you would be a success in your own way. But, by nature, prostitutes are linked to policemen, and I would not want one to snitch on you. I truly do not wish to find myself having to explain why I happen to be carrying a talking head in a Gladstone bag around to brothels under a false identity."

The Colonel took it in, straightening what remained of his neck. "Thank you for trying to help," he said curtly. "If you'd be kind enough to tell Tuluk that I'm hungry."

During the entire, harrowing trip that had taken them to Paris, Brentford had avoided Lilian as much as someone can be avoided in cramped compartments and dollhouse-sized cabins. Over that time they had exchanged only a few, noncommittal words, nothing that amounted to a real conversation. When they talked, it was indirectly, mostly through Lilian's merciless remarks on men, politics, or any other topic that could ricochet and hit Brentford in the eye. But now it was time for an actual dialogue.

Lilian was in her room getting ready for the evening, brushing her blond hair in front of the cheval glass, her taut body sheathed in a cream silk dress that outlined angles and curves that Brentford tried simultaneously to imagine and forget, being successful at neither. Had he been a head mounted on a box of clockwork gears, he couldn't have felt more inadequate than he did now.

"You could have killed the Colonel," he told her.

"Don't tell me that thingummy is *alive*," she replied savagely.

"It seems he is still too alive for you."

Lilian turned towards him, her eyes hard as gems. "What was I supposed to do, the Dance of the Seven Veils? His head is already on a plate anyway."

"Certainly not. I just wish that we all could keep up a minimal solidarity. Things are complicated enough as they are, without us going around slapping each other."

"Complicated, really? Who got us into this mire, Mr. Know-it-all? Why don't you *go and get Orsini?*"

"Come on, Lilian . . . It's not as though I'm not in this too. I'm truly sorry I brought you here, and now, I promise, I'm doing my best to get us home. Though it may seem impossible . . ."

"It does, indeed," Lilian interrupted, "and I'll bet it's actually even more difficult than that . . ."

For a moment Brentford thought she might be angry not only at the whole maddening situation, but also at his incapacity to please her. But that was probably wishful thinking.

"Okay, Lilian. Forgive me. Please," he said with a sigh.

"I promise I'll forgive you when we're home, *Stinky.*"

Dismissing him, she turned back towards her mirror, revealing a wedge of typical New Venetian pallor. It had always been Brentford's dream to spend the night drawing on it. He waited a few seconds for the storm to pass.

"How's your back?" he asked hesitantly.

"Not too bad, judging by the way you're looking at it," she said. "Once you've rolled your tongue back into your mouth, perhaps you could help me by fastening my necklace."

"You won't consider it bad form if I keep my mittens on?" It had been one of his best private jokes, but she ignored it.

"Are you planning to go out tonight?" he eventually asked, straining for the proper note of small talk, while his hands trembled slightly as he took the necklace from her nonchalant hand.

Goddamn fingers. Goddamn lock.

"Why not?" she asked him. "As long as we're stuck here, we might as well enjoy it a little. I'm going to a séance, led by the medium we met yesterday at the hospital. Do you want to come along? Maybe she'll tip us off about what the future holds in store."

"I've had my share of abracadabra today, thank you. Are you going with Thomas?"

"Don't tell me you're jealous of that oaf? You know I don't have that thing for uniforms women are supposed to have."

"That's why you're always hanging out with him?"

"More like he's always hanging on to me. And at least he's not the jealous type. Unlike with you, when he's talking nonsense, I can easily entertain myself with my own thoughts. I find it very relaxing."

"So, he's joining you?"

"If he hasn't forgotten. He is a bit of a scatterbrain, isn't he?"

"I met him at La Salpêtrière this morning. Trying to find his way to the right end of a morphine syringe, I suspect."

"And?"

"Nothing. Just pay attention to him. If you please."

"Do I really have to be responsible for all your filthy friends' vices? What a lovely mission. I'm not your baby brother's keeper, you know."

"Then ask the spirits for a solution," Brentford tried to joke.

"Only if they're high spirits, Brenty boy. Those are the only ones I'm interested in tonight."

III

The Spiritype

"How's your arm coming along this evening?" Lilian asked Thomas, as they tucked themselves into a cab, a plaid on their knees and their feet on a warm brick.

Thomas flexed his biceps as if he wanted Lilian to feel them. What she didn't ask was who had scribbled a heart onto his plaster. "The cast itches a bit, but I guess I'm all right." He chuckled.

"You're sure you don't want to stop here for a little refreshment?" she inquired, noting that they were trotting past the Salpêtrière.

Thomas blushed and hemmed. "No, thank you. I'm perfectly fine, thank you very much."

"I'm glad to hear that. So now be a good boy and stop sniffing all the time. It gets on a lady's nerves."

Thomas overplayed his difficulty in finding a handkerchief and blew his nose with a flourish that would have made trumpeter Land-frey green with jealousy.

"You're quite the hylic type, aren't you?"

"The what?"

"Nothing, darling."

They turned and looked out their individual windows, staring into the night in silence as the cab crossed the Austerlitz bridge under a drizzle of snow. On the right, the black shape of Notre-Dame crouched on its arches, like a malevolent spider. On the left, the icy Seine was a light-grey ribbon of rubble, meandering among ranges of snow-smothered sand heaps until it reached a backdrop of night sky that looked solid and thick as a wall. They trotted slowly towards the Place de La Bastille, passing along the Arsenal harbour, where barges wintered in the ice, some of them frozen aslant like wrecked ships, until suddenly Thomas thought he recognized the New Venice pennant on the mast of a small yacht. But even as he twisted in vain to catch sight of it again, it came to him that this was impossible. Still, he could have sworn . . . He didn't mention it to Lilian, who, he thought, had yet to get over her brush with the Colonel, or even more likely was lost in her own reveries about home.

A tall column rose at the centre of the Place, a golden genius on its top that looked like the dying flame of a wax candle. The cab, turning right into the rue de Charenton, was confronted by a maelstrom of carriages that were circling the famous square—for no other reason, Lilian suspected, than that people wanted to get high on noise and light. Parisians, evidently, had decided to behave as if their situation was normal and under control. And why not? After all, that was the way New Venice had been built—or *would be* built, she corrected herself.

The drivers exchanged Homeric insults, which were more like ritual spells for fluidifying traffic. The cab finally bounced free, moving eastward through streets that grew more and more featureless. It was as if the city was, mile after mile, simply losing interest in itself. The rue Montgallet, where they were headed, started under a railway arch and, as if disheartened by such modest beginnings, continued on uninspired between sad houses and farmyards. Number 42 was near its end.

Just as they arrived, Lilian saw a carriage stop in front of the house and a man in a cape and top hat step down from it. They joined him at the door, where a griffin served as a knocker. The man held it in his large gloved hand, looking at it intensely instead of banging it. He was over six feet tall, dapper but built like a heavyweight boxer, and the sparse gaslight revealed a long, haughty, angular face with strongly marked eye sockets but no brows to speak of, a nose both long and broad, and a jutting chin. He had, in short, the look of an Easter Island head carved in ivory. That, coupled with the slightly contemptuous pout of his thin lips, gave an overall impression that would have been threatening had it not been for his playful eyes, whose irises seemed to be speckled with gold dust.

He let go of the knocker to tip his hat.

"I suppose," he said, with an accent that deserved an O.B.E. for sheer, unflagging Britishness, "that we are going to the same event. Allow me to introduce myself. Lyonel Owain Savnock, at your service. You can call me Milord, if you prefer."

Thomas and Lilian prudently introduced themselves.

"I am truly enchanted," Savnock said with complete indifference. He turned abruptly to Thomas. "Excuse my mentioning it, sir, but this is a uniform I do not know."

"Royal Military College of Canada, Milord. The Navy," Thomas said, reciting his lesson.

"Oh. I see. Fairly recent institution, *Officer Cadet Smith*. Isn't that the nickname you cadets are given?"

Thomas looked at him and then at Lilian, puzzled and embarrassed, but Savnock, after a sidelong smile, turned back to the griffin head and gave the door a few slow, strong, solemn knocks.

A maid admitted them, and with a lamp in her hand preceded them up the winding stairs without speaking a word.

The apartment was on the third floor. The maid led them along a cluttered maze of narrow corridors until eventually they came to a small red salon, where she asked them to take a seat.

Morgane Roth soon joined them, wearing a black dress and a tight little black ribbon around her neck. Lilian could now observe her more closely than she had been able to so far: she was a dark, sinuous beauty in her thinnish thirties, with maliciously glinting black eyes that belied her world-weary smile.

"I'm glad to see you," she said to Thomas and Lilian. Lord Savnock got up and raised his hat again, this time revealing a head so closely shaved as to be as bald as his brow, and bowed for a *baise-main*.

"Dear Madame Roth. Your salon has been recommended to me by a very dear friend. He calls you a magician."

"I doubt any magicians would agree with that—they tend to look down on mediums. In any case, what I wanted to tell you is that the séance you are about to see is very unusual."

"In what way?" Lord Savnock asked genially. Lilian noticed that his suit, which had seemed to be pitch black, was actually midnight blue, as were his tie and silk hat. She thought this strangely enhanced the effect of his gold-speckled eyes. And she found the lion's-head knob of his cane strangely familiar without knowing exactly why.

"Since Mrs. Williams's unfortunate event last year here in Paris—oh." Seeing that Lilian and Thomas were at a loss, she explained, "Mrs. Williams is an American medium who came to Paris and was exposed when séance members caught hold of her and found a white rag doll, intended as a visiting spirit, concealed in a fold of her dress. As a result, people are now extremely wary of these sorts of apparitions. And, I must add"—and here Lilian saw that she was fighting to keep a straight face—"the spirits were themselves so scandalized they no longer wished to appear in such a dubious atmosphere. We genuine mediums have had to develop new protocols for communication with them that would reassure everyone. So I hope you will understand and forgive me if our séance does not look exactly as usual."

"Quite the contrary," Savnock reassured her. "This makes it all more the more interesting, I would say."

"If that's the case, then," said Mme. Roth, "I won't delay any longer, since other people are waiting for us to join them. Please . . ."

❋

"I'm afraid I can't touch other people's hands," said Thomas to the assembly at the table, pointing at his sling.

"And if you do not mind, I would like very much to keep my gloves on," Lord Savnock said, triggering in Lilian another faint reminiscence the origin of which, once again, eluded her.

Miss Roth was unfazed. "No matter. Mr Paynes-Grey, just put your good hand forward, and the persons on each side of you will come closer to you to connect to your thumb and auricular. And I'm sure that those gloves are no match for His Lordship's nervous fluid, Lord Savnock."

"I do not see the Magnetizer," remarked Mme. de Bramentombes, one of the two women who had joined them, the other being her daughter. The madame was a plump, heavily made-up but good-looking lady in her fifties, dressed in mourning clothes but with a peacock feather in her hat. She seemed miffed already by these lapses in the ritual. After all, the guidance of a Magnetizer—who talked the medium into her trance and conducted the event—was important. What if the medium started to go wild and rambled about improper things? A Magnetizer's presence was not only a common feature at a séance, it was good manners.

But this medium did not agree. "There is no Magnetizer, dear madame, nor is there any need for one," she answered politely but firmly, in a way that made Lilian thrill with approbation. "As you know, they are often little more than impresarios. And, if I may add, I do not think that by allowing ourselves to constantly surrender to the suggestion of men that we women will appear as the equal sex that we are. We are strong enough, I think, to entrance ourselves."

Mme. de Bramentombes pursed her lips, manifesting her defiance of such advanced ideas. Her daughter, however, sitting next to her with eyes hidden beneath a black veil, smiled so fetchingly at the explanation that Thomas regretted not being seated beside her. He advanced his foot under the table, trying to make contact. This was spiritualism as he understood it.

"I use a skylark mirror," Roth went on, uncovering a curious device on the table. It was a treelike assemblage of small rotating mirrors placed under the beam of an electric lamp suspended high above her. "It is electrical. When I fall asleep, I will automatically release the pressure on the switch. Do not forget to keep your eyes closed until the whirring has stopped. Then you may ask your questions."

Sitting down, she removed a black cloth from the sphere that it covered. A kind of black beetle appeared, its carapace studded with round alphabetic keys.

"But . . . it's a writing machine," Mme. de Bramentombes exclaimed.

"A Malling-Hansen 1892. Made for the blind," Lord Savnock commented appreciatively. "A good friend of mine had the same one. Are the spirits going to turn into secretaries?"

"I am the secretary."

"But all these machines . . ." Mme. de Bramentombes muttered with disgust.

"It's nothing new, dear madame. We have always used technical devices like Ouija boards and psychographs. Passive mediums, who write while unaware, as I do, are even called *mechanical* mediums. This is simply the next logical step in our commerce with the spirits."

"But, the spirits? Do they really appreciate it?" Lord Savnock inquired.

"As you know, Milord, the spirits take a keen interest in human development in all its forms, not merely those that enable their own communications. And I must add, some of them are very happy to play with new inventions."

"Ah, well, if it pleases the spirits . . ." Mme. de Bramentombes sighed, before forcing a smile, chin up, and passing it around as if it were a jewel on a cushion.

It began. The lights were turned off, hands (and fingers) joined in a circle. Lilian had never been to a séance, and she had the distinct feeling that something strange was happening. Nothing supernatural, no: just the effect of strangers, men and women, suddenly brought closer by the darkness around them. It was enough to create a palpable energy—the power, she thought, of possibilities. The mere act of agreeing to open themselves to uncanny sensations and emotions made them tingle and itch with something that was both embarrassment and a certain expectation; a fear, perhaps. And the fear, in its turn, summoned shapes, presences, shadows that seemed to be waiting in the wings of the world, behind the backcloth of the night.

The lamp above Miss Roth flashed on. Dots of light whirled across her face and her wide-open eyes until, with a jerk, she went into a catatonic trance. The swirling lights went out, the mirror stopped whirring, and her guests opened their eyes, some gazing at the medium, some meeting each other's looks.

Suddenly, with a low growl, Miss Roth extended her hands over the machine.

"Whose spirit is here?" asked Lord Savnock.

Roth's hands moved slowly over the black metal sphere, and then started to type very quickly. A sheet of paper crept out of the machine tray.

Lord Savnock bent and withdrew the paper, holding it with his gloved hand. He chuckled before he read,

What do you need my name for, you half-baked apes?

"Well, it seems we didn't pick the cream of the crop," Lord Savnock said with a laugh, before pocketing the sheet. "But at least he speaks English fluently."

"I have a question," said the plump Mme. de Bramentombes, half-raising her hand, as if she were in school. "I want to know," she said after a long sigh, "whether the spirit has met the soul of my late husband, Amédée de Bramentombes."

Her daughter translated in a charmingly wavering English for the others to understand.

Like a puppet, with her eyes rolled back in her head, Miss Roth banged at the keys. The lady withdrew the printed sheet and, noticing with disgust that it was in English, handed it to her daughter.

You two-faced old hag! As if you don't know where
he is!

Mme. de Bramentombes squealed at the translation and, breaking the circle, brought her handkerchief to the corner of her lips, as if she had been slapped. Once again Thomas thought he caught a smile under the girl's veil.

"It's my turn," he said. He was finding the séance rather funny. But as he opened his mouth, fumbling for a good joke, he suddenly thought of the pennant he'd seen in the Arsenal harbour. "It's a question about the future," he added. "I'd like to know whether the North Pole will be conquered one day, and whether a city will be built there."

Lilian felt a tremor in Savnock's hand and saw that his eyes had suddenly narrowed to slits.

It took a long time for Morgane Roth to begin typing again.

Lilian took the sheet and read:

Bugger me with the holy angels' golden horns!
Don't you ever again bother me with stupid
questions when the answer is sitting right beside
you! I've had enough of this dumbshow! It's
curtains for tonight, morons!

Lilian and Thomas looked at each other. Well, thought Lilian, spirit or not, it's right: we're sitting next to each other and we know that the city will be built. It may not have the most charming manners, but that spirit seems to know its trade.

Mme. de Bramentombes, still furious, huffed angrily while Miss Roth gradually regained consciousness. "It's scandalous," she said finally, bolting up from her chair and shaking her head like a loser at a roulette table.

Morgane Roth blinked and slowly found her bearings.

"I'm sorry," she said in a hoarse whisper after she had perused the *spiritypes*. "Some spirits are not as elevated as others. And some are little better than pranksters and tricksters. Please pay no attention to these answers."

"As far as I'm concerned," Savnock said, "the experience was conclusive, even if the answers were much less so. I do not know if you are a magician, madame, but you are a great artist."

✳

Later in the night, Thomas and Lilian were sitting on a leather couch in Morgane's bedroom—they were now on a first-name basis—smoking hashish cigarettes and drinking Mariani coca wine. A cranium, painted in lozenges, sat grinning on the chimney and, on the wall, a spider sketched in charcoal, with an enormous bulging eye, seemed to be crawling out of its frame. Morgane was reclining on her bed, constantly pulling at her cigarette holder, so that by and by she faded out under a wispy veil of smoke that made her look like an entranced sybil, albeit one whose oracles were always sharp and astute. She was the kind of woman, thought Lilian, whom darker ages would have gladly seen roasting at the stake.

"I liked what you said about the women," Lilian said, "you know, that they don't need Magnetizers."

Morgane smiled, basking for a moment in Lilian's admiration.

"Remember that it was young girls who invented spiritualism," she said. "And there's good reason for this: besides being, as in my case, an alternative to prostitution, it's one of the rare ways women are at liberty to express themselves without having to endure censorship from men. Ask yourselves, for instance, why it is that female mediums receive from the spirits so many communications about free love, the equality of the sexes, or universal suffrage? As to typewriters, believe me, they will eventually free young women from their domestic shackles. Even if it's to take dictation from that lowest form of spirit known as the businessman."

Enchanted and finding herself eager to make an impression, Lilian assayed, "I wonder why that curious man called you a great artist. I found that a bit offensive."

Morgane laughed. "Because, whoever he may be, he understands what it's all about. What we mediums do *is* a performance. We work ourselves and our audience into a state where anything *could* happen and, I have to say, often *does*."

"You mean it's all humbug?" Thomas asked, slumped on the couch.

"Now *you're* being offensive," Morgane said lightly, bending over the coffee table to roll another cigarette, her dress sliding silkily down to uncover her olive shoulder, much to both of her guests' appreciation. And, as Lilian remarked, when it came to rolling hashish cigarettes, she truly was an artist—they were as slender and appetizing as she was.

"Would you say that a painter or writer is a fraud because he uses fictive means to let us glimpse some truth?" she continued. "Or would you call a poet hysterical because he claims to be inspired? This is what I do in my modest way, in my little theatre, even if most of the time I must admit I don't know where it all comes from."

"So you really do hear voices?" Lilian inquired. "From a particular spirit?"

"From various spirits, if you can call them that. A lot of them. I'm what's called a *flexible medium*."

Then she bent towards Lilian and whispered through the cloud of hashish, "And I am, believe me, very *flexible*." She sat back, watching Lilian blush, then said, "And anyway, was anything that was said tonight false?"

"Madame de Bramentombes didn't look too convinced," Lilian remarked, her hands cupping her knees, trying to behave as if she had not heard Morgane's inviting murmur.

"She was angry. Which is different. And nothing angers like a truth you don't want to hear. But I think she got what she was asking for, though not in the sense she expected. But what about you? Was the answer you were given anything but true?"

"In a sense, it was true," Lilian said. "And I noticed that Thomas's question interested Lord Savnock *very* much."

"Oh," Thomas intervened. "He explained to me as we parted that not so long ago, he had been asked to fund a polar expedition, and that it was strange how the Arctic seems to obsess a lot of people these days—" As he tried to straighten up on the sofa he let out a cry.

"Your arm?" Lilian asked.

"Yes. I've had nothing for it today," he said, grimacing.

"You mean tonight." Lilian turned to Morgane. "You wouldn't have anything for pain?"

"Let me see," she said with a wink.

She came back from the bathroom with a little bottle full of a pellucid liquid. "Will the Grey Fairy do?" she asked.

Thomas looked at Lilian, as if to ask for her permission. Lilian suddenly got up and, taking the morphine bottle, gave it to Thomas and said, "A little of this and a good night's sleep on top of it will do wonders. Let me see you to the door, now. I'm sure you can find a cab back to the hotel."

"But—" Thomas stuttered; however, before he knew it he was capped, scarved, gloved, and already half out of the door. "But, Lilian—"

"I know, you're a hero. See you tomorrow."

The door closed on muffled laughter and a square halo of light, which quickly went out.

❊

"She called me *Brenty boy*," Brentford thought as he fell asleep.

To be continued . . .

EPISODE VI

ETHERAMA

I

A Turnip Field Funeral

On the list of Parisian things that gave Brentford the chills, following a hearse on a cold morning through a drab expanse of dead trees and crosses half-buried in the snow was quickly climbing to the top.

It resonated drearily with his growing sense of loneliness, and with a sense of being let down. Of the Seven only Gabriel had accompanied him to the Ivry Parisian cemetery, and only, he suspected, because they had run into each other at breakfast. Lilian, Brentford thought with a pang, had not spent the night at the hotel, and neither had Blankbate, who had not been seen since the day of their arrival. Wherever Lilian had been, it wasn't with Thomas, who was audibly snoring behind his closed door. Only the dependable Tuluk, at least, had a reasonable excuse: he had to look after and entertain the Colonel.

But the only slight relief Brentford felt was that Jean-Klein, Jr., had not showed up. The whole ceremony was absurd enough as it was.

"So, what did you do last night?" Brentford asked Gabriel, breaking both their reveries.

"I went to that famous ballroom, the Bal Bullier, at the end of Boulevard Montparnasse."

"Ah, perverse and peevish!" Brentford quoted mechanically.

"Not at all. I just watched the people dance."

"Not even a little flirtation?"

Gabriel shrugged his shoulders. "You know, I've realized something about women recently . . . They're *people*, Brentford, just like you and me. They are not *better* than we are."

"I'm surprised that it surprised you."

"Well, I've been nurturing suspicions for a while, to be honest. But still . . . it's so disappointing."

"Well, perhaps it makes them more accessible," Brentford offered in a comforting tone.

"I don't pander to real people, Brentford. Nor do I wish to impose my fancies on them."

Brentford was a bit surprised by his friend's philosophy. For a man who had spent the previous year cavorting with underage hermaphroditic twins, it seemed grimmer than necessary. Maybe Gabriel missed the Twins. Maybe he'd still got the blue devils over Stella. Maybe, like Brentford himself, he had racked his brain about the Nature of Time just a little too much these past days. A bit selfishly, Brentford thought that it would be better for the mission to have a Gabriel around who wasn't exclusively focussed on living *the inimitable life*, as he used to call it.

Not that you could predict what Gabriel would do or not do. For instance, he had stubbornly refused to talk to the priest of the Church of Saint Peter and Saint Paul about the details of the life of Leclou; it had fallen to Brentford, just before the ceremony, to prompt the priest's oration by expatiating inventively on the good Christian life that Jean-Charles Leclou had led until the end. Now, at the edge of the grave, the speech came back to him, preposterously useless. Yet it was not without great sadness that he watched the coffin hastily and clumsily lowered into the tomb and heard the wood grating on the granite. As a piece of New Venetian wisdom had it, "It is always silent when the goldfish die."

Not far from here, at the foot of the cemetery wall, another burial was taking place. There was something sneaky about it, especially in the way the people around the white wood coffin seemed hurried and nervous; but since most of these mourners were uniformed gendarmes with rifles in their hands, even their discretion looked rather conspicuous.

The little cortège around Jean-Klein's grave disbanded, and Brentford and Gabriel were walking back to the gate when a short, rotund figure detached itself from a tree and waddled towards them on fat but quick little legs.

"Excuse me, gentlemen," the man said, touching a finger to the brim of his bowler hat. He had a ruddy face with a stubby snout and a handlebar moustache. His dark, deep-set eyes were small but inquisitive and sparkling. "Would you be the friends of the late Jean-Charles Leclou?"

Brentford and Gabriel stopped in their tracks and looked at each other with a stern gaze saying, *Beware.*

"We are, yes," Brentford confirmed.

"Ah, then, perhaps you can help me. I am Commissaire Tripotte from the French Sûreté. It is my duty to make sure that the foreigners in our country see all their rights respected. And a decent burial is certainly one of the most sacred rights of man, don't you think?"

"I hope everything was done satisfactorily," Brentford answered.

"No doubt, no doubt. But you know that in France we have a passion for paperwork, and this is what worries me. Nowhere could our services find the slightest document belonging to Jean-Charles Leclou. And we have checked all the hotels in Paris. You are, unless I am mistaken, Canadians yourselves, and I thought that perhaps . . ."

"Certainly," Brentford said, summoning as much self-control as he could. "Did you check with the Canadian Embassy?"

"The Canadian Embassy? You are a true patriot. I don't think that Canada yet has an embassy," Tripotte said, his eyes narrowing. "There is, however, a Canadian *Commission*, and I have checked with them, but to no avail."

"You must allow them the time to search. Ours is a huge country."

"That is word for word what they told me! But if you ever have any ideas—such as, for instance, the name of the hotel where he resided—please do not hesitate to let me know. Here is my card."

Brentford took it and looked at the all-seeing eye that served as the symbol for the Sûreté.

"I'll contact you if I find anything," he said.

Tripotte saluted them and turned away, not towards the gates but towards the other ceremony, where he obviously knew people.

Watching him go, Brentford asked Gabriel, "Are you doing anything this afternoon?"

"Not that I know of. Weren't you supposed to try to see de Rochas?"

"It will have to wait, I'm afraid. We must go to the Canadian Commission—immediately."

✳

A man and a woman were leaning against the wall by the gate. The man wore one of the *casquettes* usually sported by Parisian proletarians, and he stood with his fists in his pockets; the woman, a freckled redhead, had wrapped herself in a flowered Alsatian shawl.

"Be careful," the man whispered to Brentford and Gabriel as they passed.

"Of?" Gabriel inquired.

"Tripotte," he said, indicating with his chin the other funeral, now drawing to a close. "Not a man you want to be in trouble with. By the way," he said, extending his hand, "I'm Raymond Bastiani, crafstman printer, and this is Lucie Blanchard, my good friend."

They all shook hands.

"Tripotte is in charge of the B Notebook," Lucie explained a little later, a prickly red wine before her in the incredibly narrow Taverne du Vieux Moulin. "It supposedly holds files on every foreigner in Paris. And, since the anarchists' bombings of recent years, a very close watch is kept on all of them."

"I thought bombings were a thing of the past," Gabriel said, struggling to recall a little French history.

"If you can call two years ago the past, you're right. Since they passed the Scoundrelly Laws, anarchism is practically extinct as a serious threat. Even the worst provocateurs seem to have lost interest. And, last year, with the Dreyfus case, it was the Jews who were increasingly designated as scapegoats," Raymond explained.

"They have some respite now," Lucie added, "since however hard you try, you cannot blame harsh winters on the Jews. But when food is scarce, foreigners are an easy target. So it starts all over again. The constant watching, and sometimes worse . . ."

"What do you mean by 'worse'?" Brentford inquired.

Raymond lowered his voice. "The other funeral, for instance. It took place in the plot reserved for guillotined convicts, in a spot we call 'the turnip field.' There have been no public executions lately—no official executions, that is. But beheaded bodies are still turning up regularly, and most of the time they're the bodies of foreigners. Such was the case with the burial you saw. And nobody seems to care."

"Did you know the victim?" Brentford asked.

"We did, yes. What you would call an anarchist. But now anarchists are like everyone else, more concerned with their next meal than with the world to come. He was innocent of any crime. We don't know if he was even tried before the 'sentence.' "

"Didn't the authorities react?" Brentford asked.

"Just enough to signal that they were not involved. Which doesn't mean they weren't," Raymond said. "You've seen the gendarmes— even at the burial today, for instance. Officially, they're there to prevent riots."

"But you're saying that Tripotte is involved?" Gabriel asked pointedly.

"We hear rumours," Lucie muttered. "And we hope they're nothing but that. But Tripotte was after our friend, and someone must be tipping off these mysterious executioners. For the rest, all we know is their name: they call themselves Les Loups des Bois de Justice."

"It's a pun," Gabriel explained to Brentford in English. "The Wolves of the Woods of Justice. *Bois de justice* means timbers or woods of Justice . . . which is also a name for the guillotine."

"Hilarious," said a straight-faced Brentford.

Lucie leaned forward. "What we mean to say is that, in our experience, it is not a good idea to attract Tripotte's interest."

"I'm afraid it's too late, unfortunately," Brentford said with a sigh.

II

Skating at the North Pole

hen he'd been in Morgane Roth's dark corridor the night before, it had taken approximately thirty seconds for Thomas to arrange a rendezvous with Blanche, the veiled daughter of Mme. de Bramentombes.

It was early in the following afternoon (not that one could judge the time by the colourless sky) when he stepped down from the slow brown omnibus that had brought him, with significant delay and discomfort, from St. Sulpice to Pigalle, a spacious ring of houses and bars around a miserable fenced circular garden. Tuluk stepped down in his wake, overplaying a backache by grimacing and stretching. The idea of horse locomotion on snowy sloping streets seemed to him one of those half-baked ideas that the *qallunaat* were liable to come up with.

"To the left, here, is rue de Clichy, number eighteen," Thomas said, his head bent over the brand-new Baedeker he held with his only working hand. "Now, you understand, Tuluk, if she is with her mother, you'll have to take care of her—the mum, that is. I'm sure she will be thrilled to meet an Eskimo. Especially dressed as you are."

On Thomas's urging, Tuluk had made an effort to adapt to a more Western look, but the result was a tentative, piecemeal outfit that left much to be desired. His upper half might pass muster, but he had retained his warm sealskin trousers and his *kamiks*, which were comfortable to walk in. Even by the blasé standards of Paris, he was a sight to behold: passers-by cast bewildered, disapproving looks, and the steely stare they got in return made them hurry on their way. Thomas wondered if taking him along had been such a bright idea. Not that he had had a choice. Tuluk, who so far had never walked further than the bird market a few yards up the rue Delambre, had come back from it curious about the city, and could not be persuaded to stay at the hotel. Besides, the Colonel had encouraged him to see the sights, if only so he could tell him about them later. Putting the Inuk to use in the best possible way—as an anti-chaperone weapon— had been Thomas's only choice.

Together they descended the Boulevard de Clichy, almost empty now because of the snow, and Thomas, noticing the posters plastered on the Morris columns, observed that the Parisians had not only embraced the cold weather, but turned their fascination into a sort of fashion: a singer called Polaire, who had an incredibly slim waist and beautiful almond eyes, was obviously the hottest thing in Paris, and an almost as widely advertised skating rink—the very one they were on their way to, in fact—was even called the Pôle Nord. It was funny, Thomas thought, to have to go to Paris to finally reach the North Pole. And it was still funnier that this was precisely the place Blanche de Bramentombes had suggested for their rendezvous. She was inspired, she'd said, by his question about the Pole during the séance.

Three francs later, they were inside the Pôle Nord, and Tuluk couldn't hold back a cry of surprise. Stretched out beneath a long iron-and-glass roof that was supported by thin iron pillars was a rink of smooth ice that was at least forty yards in diameter . . . and every square inch was busy with skaters, mostly women. The rink was encircled by a walkway, with tables behind it providing refreshments. A mezzanine loomed above, full of onlookers and *flâneurs*, and on a platform a brash brass orchestra was hammering brazen tunes in the slightly stale air. But what astonished Tuluk the most was the so-called Arctic panorama—there was even a little wooden chalet!—that surrounded the place, waves and waves of snowy hills and bluish peaks. He felt his eyes welling at the thought that it might not be possible to ever go home again.

Meanwhile, Thomas had already rented a pair of skates and was trying to put them on in spite of his sling.

"I suppose you don't want me to get you some," he said to Tuluk, who bent to help him. "I've always wondered why the Inuit can't skate."

"Where Inuit live, the ice is not smooth," Tuluk answered moodily. Actually, he felt like trying, but his pride forbade him from making a fool of himself in front of the *qallunaat*, especially on the ice. But it slightly vexed him, he realized, that the whites managed to look so elegant as they glided and swerved on it. Let's see them at the real North Pole, he thought.

"See if you can hunt for a seal here, then," Thomas joked. "Now, I'm going to look for that girl, or at least, I'm going to get her to see me. Watch me, and if you see me with the mother, come closer so I can introduce you."

Tuluk nodded and Thomas jumped onto the ice. Even with his broken arm, he managed to slalom at full speed between skaters without ever losing his balance, showing such virtuosity that many people stopped in their tracks to admire him as he passed, while scattered applause greeted him from the mezzanine. It did not take long, of course, for the still-veiled Blanche de Bramentombes to notice him from her table along the side, and to wave at him. Skidding up in a froth of crushed ice, Thomas grasped the fence with his good hand and suavely began the conversation. Mme. de Bramentombes was nowhere to be seen.

Not that Tuluk cared. Oblivious of his mission, what interested him now was how the *qallunaat* made the ice. You could actually see the machines through a window on the opposite side of the rink. He walked up and gaped in awe at the huge tank-like machines standing amidst a wilderness of pipes, belts, and wheels. A tall man with an aquiline nose and a long drooping blond moustache gave him a sidelong look.

"Excuse me, sir. You are Inuk, aren't you?" he asked in English, though his accent was unmistakably French.

Tuluk looked at him and for a while had the feeling that he had seen him before. But how could that be?

"This Inu . . . I am, yes," he said, feeling uneasy.

"From where? Greenland? Baffin Bay? Alaska?"

Hadn't Mr. Orsini said that they had to remain incognito? Tuluk didn't like to lie, and it didn't come easily to him.

"Greenland," he said, satisfied that it was the closest approximation.

"And you're in Paris for . . . ? If that's not too indiscreet, of course."

Tuluk blushed and realized he was sweating now.

"Machines . . ." he improvised. "I like machines."

"Oh . . . machines." The man looked surprised. "Machines to make ice. I suppose it surprises you that we give ourselves so much trouble over something that is so common for you? You must find it absurd."

Tuluk was not sure what *absurd* meant, except that it was a word that the whites often used to talk about their own endeavours.

"How do they work?" he asked.

"These? The Fixary machines? Well, you see, these on the left are steam engines. They pump ammonia gas into those big condensers over there, which turn it into liquid ammonia. From there, it's refrigerated in this big tank, and used as a coolant to refrigerate another liquid, calcium chloride, which is then pumped through very narrow tubes that run all under the ice. With enough horsepower and ammonia, you could even reproduce the Arctic—a bit like they've tried to do here," the man observed, as if lost in his own thoughts.

Though Tuluk only understood half of this, the half he understood fascinated him. Everywhere the whites were fighting the ice, but here in their free time, they made it, with mind-boggling machines, even though they had it elsewhere already for nothing. He wanted to know more about the machines, but did not dare ask, feeling ill at ease because of the man's own inquisitiveness. Taking advantage of his interlocutor's brief spell of reverie, Tuluk suddenly turned away and headed towards the exit, feeling the eyes of the man following him now, like two harpoon tips in his back.

III

The Dominions

On their way to the Canadian Commission, Gabriel and Brentford walked past that sturdy parthenon of the Chambres de Députés and swerved towards the bridge that led to La Place de la Concorde. As they crossed the frozen Seine, the Eiffel Tower loomed up on their left, brand-new in the blurry sun, the gilded skeleton of a chimera, a giraffe neck above elephant legs.

"*I fell*—that's an apt name for a tower that high, isn't it?" Brentford said as they stopped to look at it.

"What?"

"The *I fell* Tower. Get it?"

"That's exactly what I was afraid I'd heard," Gabriel said with a scowl.

"Okay, let's say that was an Interpherence," Brentford mumbled apologetically, referring to one of the aftereffects of Transpherence, which is when words or phrases used by one's dead father spring up directly into the transpheree's mouth. For some heretofore-unexplained reason, these bursts of speech were inevitably incongruous, or plain daft. If the plan of Transpherence had been to imbue the son with awe of his father, it was quite a failure. Rather, it was the kind of clowning that remained longest, perhaps because, Gabriel suspected, it constituted the true core of fatherhood.

"Well," Brentford said, in an effort to redirect the conversation. "This is certainly some bold statement of manhood. I wouldn't be surprised if Eiffel were one of those phallus-worshipping Masons."

"Oh, I think he is. Besides being a puny fellow," Gabriel confirmed. "That said, if you stand below the *I fell* tower, as you so wittily named it, you will see it looks as if you were standing under your mother's petticoat, as the French say. It is both God and Goddess, or the supreme Hermaphrodite. That's what makes it powerful, I guess, if it doesn't make it pretty." And he smiled a melancholy smile, which Brentford attributed to his pining for Reginald and Geraldine.

They were across the river now, at the foot of the Avenue des Champs-Élysées, passing a fountain overbrimming with frozen froth.

"Now look at how, from here, the obelisk seems just to penetrate the Triumphal Arch," Gabriel said, pointing at the culprit with his cane.

"It's like that fountain you showed me yesterday," Brentford said thoughtfully. "I suppose a city is ruled by such images." Then, he added longingly, "This is something the Seven Sleepers were good at." A picture of New Venice formed faintly behind his eyelids, a blur of white perspectives billowing back to nothingness, but sharp enough to pierce his heart.

As they moved away along the Champs-Élysées Gardens towards the Arc de Triomphe, a man who had also been looking at the Eiffel Tower suddenly turned to them, revealing a goatee and eyes that shone enthusiastically behind a pince-nez.

"A celestial castle!" he exclaimed in a thick Russian accent, with the unecessarily loud voice of a partially deaf man. "A tower so high—tens of thousands of meters high—and from there, a cable that would naturally be stretched by the earth's rotation and could support a celestial castle in geostationary orbit. Men could inhabit space, travelling by elevators. Would not that be great?"

"Certainly," Brentford said politely, though the man was evidently talking to himself. "But not before the entirety of the earth's surface is made inhabitable, I suppose."

But the man, now scribbling sketches in his notebook, was not listening.

They trudged on until the bulbous iron-and-glass roof of the Hall of Industry came into view, looking New Venetian enough to attract them like a lodestone. Built for a world's fair, as an answer to London's Crystal Palace, it was a titanic building, encased in arches of stone that seemed to go on forever, and its front gate—a rookery for allegories—rose as immodestly high as a triumphal arch. Inside, however, in the milky light that poured from the flyspecked roof, the endless, drafty, glassed gallery was nearly deserted, except for a few patrons at scattered tables, and a wheezing marching band whose brass looked like rusty machines and whose musicians gestured like demented automatons.

"Slated for destruction within a year, if I remember correctly," Gabriel informed Brentford.

"That's a bit sad, isn't it?" Brentford responded. "We should take it back home. It's a brave piece of masonry." He paused, lost in his own thoughts. After a while, he added, "I always wondered whether they were Masons, the Seven Sleepers."

"They probably were. Almost everyone involved in polar exploration was a Mason. Kane, Peary from the Kane Lodge, a lot of others. It must have something to do with the arcane that eludes us."

"So there may be something to those—what was it?—*Palladian* Masonic lodges that Encausse told us about. Where they were printing 'antichurch' pamphlets . . . We should look into that, don't you think?"

"Yes. Why not?" Gabriel said, unconvinced but willing to try anything that would take them back to where they belonged. "Before we freeze in here, preferably."

The upper stretch of the Champs-Élysées seemed to be better off than the rest of the city. At the end of the garden, near the circular Ice Palace—a name that triggered a conniving smile between them—Brentford and Gabriel observed an army of blue-clad street sweepers cleaning the road with military discipline, while behind them a dozen other workers pushed a huge wooden contraption designed, Brentford guessed, to plane and resurface the remaining layer of snow.

"They're taking care of appearances here, aren't they?" Gabriel remarked.

"Well, where images rule, they have to remain visible."

✷

The Canadian Commission was located just off the Champs-Élysées on rue Montaigne. It had been there little more than a decade, representing a Confederation not yet in its thirties and with little official

involvement yet in diplomacy or foreign affairs. Introducing themselves as Canadian citizens, Brentford and Gabriel were promptly
received by a French Canadian with red hair in an unruly cut, a long
face that was liberally freckled, and a clever but fiendish look.

"Alexandre Vialatte," he introduced himself. "Monsieur Fabre,
the General Agent, cannot receive you at the moment, but I am his
secretary. I'll do my best to be useful."

As happens via life's mysteries sometimes, there was an immediate and mutual sympathy between Vialatte and the New Venetians,
which did not stop the latter from some subterfuge.

"Brentford Orsini from Annapolis Royal," Brentford said, fumbling for his best Nova-Scotian brogue.

"Gabriel Daley, from St. Anthony," Gabriel added, overplaying
his Newfoundland accent.

Vialatte nodded, visibly amused.

"I'll get straight to the point." Brentford said. "We are in Paris for
what you might call a secret mission . . ."

"You're not going to tell me on whose behalf, I suppose."

"Oh. Friendly powers. Very friendly. That should not concern
you. You have my word of honour on this point."

"I understand. Please go on."

"We have recently been in contact with a local officer of the
Sûreté. Tripotte is the name. From what I understand, he's in charge
of some infamous 'B Notebook.' "

"And, for discretion's sake, you would rather not be in it? I understand, but I'm afraid there's nothing I can do for you," Vialatte said.

Brentford persevered. "Actually, we are perfectly happy to be in
the notebook. But as certified Canadian subjects, declared such by
yourselves. And it would be great if you could confirm as well that a
certain Jean-Charles Leclou is actually French Canadian."

"Oh, yes, Leclou. Buried this morning, right? Your friend Tripotte
was pestering me about him yesterday, but I did not want to give him
the impression I knew him when I have nothing on any Leclou what-
soever. But tell me, don't you have papers certifying that you are, as
you say, Canadian subjects?"

"More or less, yes," Brentford admitted. "But we think a word
from you would do more to placate Monsieur Tripotte and his ilk."

" 'More or less'? I suppose you could say that all Canadians are more or less Canadians, at the moment. But, pardon my frankness—" he insisted, tapping his pen impatiently on what Gabriel observed was a copy of Tardivel's *Pour la patrie*—"Are you, or are you not, compatriots of mine? I'd like very much to know the facts, before I decide whether or not to lie to the French police."

"I am, as I said, a Newfoundlander," Gabriel said. "I suppose it will be a couple of years before we join the Confederation. But I don't think the difference should matter to Monsieur Tripotte, and I do already see myself as Canadian."

"Oh, you'll be one eventually, I suppose. Perhaps more than I will ever be," Vialatte said with a smile, exaggerating his Québécois accent a little.

"Well. As I said, I was born in Nova Scotia," Brentford conceded, which was true, since it was customary for children of New Venetians to be raised under somewhat milder climates until they were seven. "But I admit that since then, I've lived a bit off the map."

Vialatte stared at them, puzzled but interested. "Off the map? You mean unexplored areas? Up north?"

Brentford and Gabriel looked at each other and decided to take the chance. "Farther than that," Brentford finally answered, feeling a thrill of expectation as he waited for Vialatte's reaction.

Vialatte tapped his pen against his desk, a half-smile on his face. "Interesting. There seems to be a lot going on up north these days. Strange dealings, indeed. Not that I am at liberty to say, really . . ."

"Would that be around Ellesmere Island?" Brentford tried.

"That's as good a guess as any other, I suppose," Vialatte answered, approvingly. "So you're part of *that*, are you?"

"Maybe we are," Brentford said, dying to actually be a part of whatever took place on Ellesmere Island circa 1895.

Vialatte leaned forward over his desk and whispered, "As a matter of fact, a certain gentleman was here but two days ago to discuss certain matters with us. Very delicate matters, I may add. But I suppose that's no news to you, who are familiar with *friendly powers*."

"Oh, we are but minor figures in all this," Gabriel assured him.

"I see," Vialatte answered, a bit sombrely, as if he regretted having said too much.

"So, regarding Tripotte . . . ?" Brentford pressed.

"To be frank with you, I'll gladly mislead Monsieur Tripotte for no other reason than that it would give me the greatest pleasure. I find him a thoroughly unsympathetic man. And what I know of him is not likely to make me change my mind."

"What do you mean?" Brentford asked, expecting more rumours about the Wolves of the Woods of Justice.

"He's one of those French coppers who put a little butter in their spinach, as they say here, by being on payroll of the Okhrana."

"The Russian secret police?" Gabriel asked.

"It is run here by a certain Rachkovsky, a very devious fellow. Rich and cunning. From what I gather, his policy is to encourage anarchist agitation here and in Britain so that they pass harsher laws against foreigners. To this end, he has recruited former or actual Sécurité officers to pass along files on political refugees, so as to infiltrate them with informers and provocateurs. We Canadians may be drifting away from the Crown, but there are still some aspects of British law that I am not willing to abandon. Respect for individual freedom and liberty of conscience are among them. So, actually, if you want me to tell Tripotte or any other Okhranist scum that you come from the moon, I'll gladly do that."

Brentford tried to suppress a smile of relief. "Canada will be enough, if you don't mind," he replied.

"Canada or what's left of it," Vialatte said, with a smile neither Gabriel nor Brentford was sure he understood.

IV

The Eskimo Explorer

As soon as he left the "North Pole," Tuluk walked down the rue de Clichy all the way to the boulevards. He breathed deeply, relishing his freedom. The trip to Paris had been pure *nuanangilaq*—no-fun time. It reminded him of the bleakest days of winter, when he was a young Inuk, forced to remain for days in a cramped, smelly igloo while a blizzard raged outside. It can drive people to murder, this absence of solitude and space. One of his cousins had stabbed another, just because he could not stand to stare at the other's big belly any more, just inches away from his eyes. "I couldn't help it," the cousin had explained. "He was *so* fat . . ." But the nightmare journey was over now, and Tuluk felt like walking for hours. No matter where he went, he would not lose himself. The whereabouts of the Grand Hôtel des Écoles remained constantly tugging in the back of his mind, and at any given time, he could easily spool his way back.

He had been told that the city had a problem with the snow and the cold, but he couldn't understand what it was. It looked solid and rich, this city, and so what was wrong with a little snow? It was the inhabitants who were the problem, Tuluk reckoned. They did everything wrong, from the clothes they wore to the vehicles they used. They were trying to fight snow and ice without realizing that these elements can be protective, easy to work with, even fun. They had to wait for their food to come from outside, like infants. Their helplessness was pathetic, when you thought about it.

But he understood as well that the Seven were also helpless in their own situation. He was not quite sure what that situation was, but neither were the others, it seemed. The idea of being trapped in time made no sense to him, perhaps because, after all, the Inuit had always lived secluded in a time of their own, and whatever history they had was endlessly recycled into tales for the too-long evenings. What had happened to him and his companions during the trip seemed one of those stupid things that would only concern the whites, with their way of always putting themselves in desperate muddles just for the hell of it. And it would be a white who would get them out of here, sooner or later. That was the kind of thing they were able to do, when they set their minds to it. Sometimes it seemed they could do anything. Except cope with a little snow.

For the time being, though, he found Paris a fascinating place. The boulevards, for example, were amazing. They were wide and deep and apparently endless, making the Marco Polo Midway or Barents Boulevard look puny by comparison. There were more people here than he had ever seen put together, busy like black flies on the long white backbone of the road. The houses were high, their ground floors a row of cosy restaurants and dazzling window displays. The whole place had the distinct sheen of money, Tuluk reflected, that mysterious white magic that enlarges buildings, sharpens angles, and refines details, that is warm to the eye and cold to the touch.

And he discovered that he liked being among so many people. At the beginning of his life in New Venice, the crowds had troubled and aggrieved him. They were so big, he simply could not get them inside his head. But now the lights and the noise were in his veins, and he could not imagine himself going back to a life that consisted simply of hunting, eating your hunt, and talking about your hunt. Maybe it was because he was half-white, even if he had never known his father, some burly Scottish sailor or, perhaps, seductive explorer. Other Inuit he knew had never gotten over meeting the *qallunaat*. Some fell for the life and drank until they were crazy. Some went back to the old ways and suddenly found them too harsh and senseless. And not a few had killed themselves. Tuluk would be as white as his survival demanded. It was as simple as that.

He ogled white women as he made his way along the avenue, and he blushed when his gaze was returned. Sometimes it was the man who walked with the lady who stared back, in anger, and Tuluk found it amusing to answer with his best murderous look until the man averted his eyes and lowered his head. But none of these women was as well-mannered or smelled as good as the ones he had visited in the red-lanterned house at 63 Boulevard Quinet yesterday, prompted and funded by the Colonel, in exchange for a report. They had been very nice, although it was a shame that they wore no tattoos on their faces.

He had walked a long way, effortlessly, as if the sidewalk were taking him along, vaguely looking for some more red-lanterned houses, thinking that more women might await him, and that he still had a few francs from the Colonel's purse, when a man stopped him in front of a fancy building, showing him the archway with insistence. Tuluk entered, passing through a lobby full of the frills and gilt that the whites were so fond of and that made their houses look like cakes, and found himself purchasing a ticket at a booth—for what, he was not sure, but his curiosity took over, and he climbed stairs that were pleasantly white and smooth as ice to the top.

His first reaction was terror.

Wax figures in the likeness of men stood still in the half-light. They were dressed in strange costumes and played out unclear scenes with outrageous gestures and the fixed stares of madmen. They reminded Tuluk of the effigies of the Seven Sleepers that were sometimes paraded in New Venice. But here these *inunnguait* were doing something, in their sick and clumsy way: someone was stabbed in a tub, some red-robed, dark-skinned men with spears fought against white soldiers with guns, someone was sitting in prison while men in uniform cut the collar of his shirt. It was the way the whites saw the world, all too rich and bloody, and it gave you the williwaws.

He passed among the figures cautiously, jumping in alarm at every corner, feeling the powerful magic that exists in such images, the way they seem about to wake when you look them in the eyes. He was sweating and wanted to leave, but at the same time, he felt compelled to go on. There was something familiar here, which he could sense was drawing him in. Maybe it was because the place looked like the Inuk afterlife, that underground place where the dead are said to relive their last moments for ever. And then he saw it.

It was a diorama, just like the one at the ice rink they called the Pôle Nord: an Arctic landscape so well imitated that Tuluk, for a brief spell, could almost see the hummocks dusted by light snow, hear the wind rustling his fur hood, feel the presence of a seal, like a faint grey liquid shadow, under a sheet of ice. The light was done just right—an agonizing golden haze, bathing the distant hills in a powdery halo. But that wasn't all. Tuluk moved closer to look at the dying man.

He wore furs yet was clearly not an Inuk, but rather an explorer. He was on all fours, like an animal, his feet probably frozen. His right hand was extended in front of him, as if to call for help from someone he had just seen.

Tuluk bent to read the plaque in front of it, thanking his days at the missionary school. But he did not speak French and so could not make sense of what he read after all—except for the word "Ellesmere."

Tuluk stood silent, listening to his senses. The stillness of the scene buzzed around him oppressively. There was something he still couldn't quite discern: what the man was looking at. Tuluk bent closer and looked the figure in the face, but couldn't see through its snow-goggles to its obscured eyes. He took a quick look around, then, with a deft gesture, took off the goggles and looked deep into the glass eyes. In one of them, he could make out a faint white shape. He drew closer. Wasn't it . . .

"Hey, you! What do you think you're doing?" a guard called out from behind him.

Tuluk stood up suddenly as the man seized his arm.

V

The Cabaret of Nothingness

By the time Thomas and Blanche de Bramentombes walked out of the North Pole, night had fallen. The sky had turned lilac blue and coloured the snow a tender mauve, and as the streelights came on they sent stooped, hurried shadows reeling across the rubbly sidewalks.

"It's still early. Would you like to accompany me for a drink?" Blanche asked Thomas, in her fumbling but delicate English. She had learned it, she said, from a friend.

"Won't your mother be worried?"

"She's supposed to be busy tonight. There's a nice place a little farther, back on the boulevard."

It was going very smoothly, Thomas thought. She was pleasant and easy, not to mention comely. Her talk was lively and witty, although sometimes interrupted by a cough that sounded like the tearing of silk, and he could hear a faint wheezing in her breath as they walked side by side up the street. She must have had a bad cold, or maybe a touch of asthma, he reckoned. Her mother must have thought that skating at the North Pole would be good for her health.

Regardless, it would have been the perfect evening, except for one thing: the gnawing feeling that someone was following them, hiding in shadows made even blacker by the snow and the sickly light. But every time he turned back, there was nothing suspicious, just a dark downhill stretch of street and indifferent passers-by. Maybe he was simply nervous. From the morphine—or lack of it.

"This is a strange place . . ." Thomas said as they took their seats in a cabaret on the Boulevard de Clichy. He was going to add "for lovers," but that seemed a tad premature.

"Tourists are supposed to love it. You're a kind of tourist, aren't you?" Blanche asked him teasingly, as she lifted her veil above her haloed eyes to take a Geraudel cough drop from a little heart-shaped, filigreed silver pillbox. She was not, perhaps, the aristocratic beauty that her name promised, but to Thomas there was something very French, very cheeky, in her open and almost mischievous face, and in her rouged cheekbones and little stub of an upturned nose, which allowed an easy passage to her lips—a journey that Thomas promised himself to take at the first opportunity.

He averted his eyes and looked around him again. There was a touch of New Venice about the place, in the way that nothing inside it hinted at its surroundings. The decor was mostly black, and the walls were covered with ghastly paintings, all the more spectral when seen through the blue fog of cigarettes. Overhead dangled an atrocious chandelier made of human arm bones holding candles in their skeletal hands. The long tables beneath were coffins on which a few tapers had been glued down. The obnoxious waiters were dressed as priests or undertakers and served a drink that they advertised in sepulchral voices as Death Germs.

"Our speciality, Maggot Juice and Tubercular Spit!" the waiter announced, dressed as a sinister priest, as he banged down two glasses on the table.

Blanche laughed and coughed again, with a wink at Thomas. A dark thought about her health crossed his mind, but he dispelled it with the brave cowardice of youth.

"Now, if I were your mother, I'd be worried," he said, struggling to be heard above the hellacious din.

"It's you that's worried about Mother. Since you're so concerned with peace in my family, you should know that I was brought to the Pôle Nord by my uncle, and when I go back, I'll simply tell my mother that I left him because he had business to do. And business he does have, believe me."

"Your uncle?"

"Mother's brother. He was just leaving when you arrived at the rink. He is a very busy man, very mysterious, very rich. He has gold mines in Australia and I don't know where else. And I am his only heir. She won't even dare to ask him whether what I say is true."

"So, you're quite the heiress, then," Thomas said, with a total lack of delicacy, which he had discovered women sometimes appreciated.

"Certainly. But you'd better make your move quickly," she said, with a curious smile that Thomas could not decipher. Was she referring to other suitors? "Is that what you're after? A good marriage?" she asked.

"Not yet, anyway."

She laughed at that. "We are going to have fun, you and I," she said, nodding at some dim view of the future. Before Thomas, slightly taken aback, could react to this . . . opening? . . . she said, "Why, for one thing, don't you come to one of Mother's salons? There's one next Thursday. There will be a lot of interesting people there. You could even bring the friends you told me about."

"Why, that's very generous," he answered, although he didn't know where or, well, *when* he would be next Thursday.

In another room, a ferocious organ boomed, and a monk came into the "Hall of Intoxication," waving a bell to announce the evening's show. Some patrons started to shuffle forward, and headed in a procession towards the "Vault of the Dead."

"Well," said Blanche suddenly, her mood darkening a bit, "If you want to see the show, please do so. I've seen it so many times, I know it *by heart*. I am afraid I have to go now. See you on Thursday, then? Eighty-seven Boulevard Denfert. Oh, no, I have a better idea! Why don't you come by tomorrow afternoon? We could do a little fencing together. If you fancy fencing, that is, and are not afraid of . . . pointy things."

Thomas stood gaping as she left, her black cape waving among the coffins. And one second after she disappeared, he already missed her.

The show bored him. A man lay in a coffin, was stripped of his flesh and then reincarnated. Nothing new and all done with mirrors. The show in the other vaulted room, where a troupe called the Gay Spectres revealed more flesh than bone, amused him a little more, although not to the point of being as aroused as his neighbours, if he properly understood the rustles and whispers in the darkness all around him. As the Sad Spectres entered the stage, he stood up and followed the long corridor back to the Hall of Intoxication. Somehow his exhilaration had deserted him. This godforsaken, taste-forsaken place was to blame, no doubt—unless it was Blanche's sudden departure. Or perhaps the weight on his chest was the thought of the little phial on his bedside table.

Then, for the first time since he had left him, he wondered where Tuluk was.

The Hall of Intoxication was almost empty when he stepped in. But at the table, where, he realized, he had imprudently left his coat, someone was waiting for him. For a moment, he thought this was somehow a part of the whole damn cabaret act.

The man wore a red uniform jacket under his fur-collared coat, and also, oddly, a pith helmet. He had a long, sad, equine face with the smallest of pencil moustaches. His left side looked normal, but the right was all prosthetics: glass eye, wax ear, black shiny sugar-tong hand, and even his leg, from what Thomas could see of it, crossed above the other at an unnatural angle, sticklike and stiff.

"India," said the man simply, by way of explanation, with an accent as British as his uniform. "Interesting place. Can I offer you a drink?"

Thomas accepted and sat down as if casually, but caught himself wiping clammy hands on his trousers.

"Allow me to introduce myself. Captain Ivanhoe Yronwoode, military attaché to the British Embassy in Paris."

"Thomas Paynes-Grey, I'm, er . . . a navy cadet. From Canada."

"Ah, Canada . . ." the captain said, sternly. "You'll miss us more than we'll miss you. But it is always sad to see an empire—if I may so put it—torn to pieces."

At this, he put his claw-hand in front of Thomas and clicked the tongs twice, with a long pause in between.

"Is there something you want from me?" Thomas asked. He was now weighing the possibility of a fight.

"No. But there is something you want from me. And that is advice."

"Not that I know of."

"Oh, you don't want advice on how to seduce Miss Blanche de Bramentombes, then? You are very brave. But very foolish."

Thomas suddenly recalled his feeling, earlier, of being shadowed. He had been right. "You know her?" he asked suspiciously.

"I have that honour. I suppose that now she refers to me as a friend."

"Where I come from, such an imputation could be taken as fighting words," Thomas said, trying to look straight into Yronwoode's eyes, both the monocled real one and the artificial one. Both were hard to meet and hardly encouraging.

"You don't want to fight a man you can't hurt," Yronwoode answered placidly. "And who, for some reason which now eludes even himself, wants to give you a little help. But if you're not curious, we may as well part now."

"I admit I'm curious. But I am not prepared to hear anything unpleasant about Miss de Bramentombes."

"Then, I won't say that Miss de Bramentombes is a nymphomaniac and a pervert, whose wretched life, thank God, is numbered in months rather than in years. I'll simply say that out of her good Catholic heart, she is dedicated to giving her life to the dispossessed, and has never been known to resist a man who was either a tramp or a cripple. She left me for a scrubby legless fellow who lived in the *zone*, outside the city. But apparently even a modest sling will do, these days."

Thomas felt sick rather than angry. "That was incredibly unpleasant," he said. "I have to go home now. I'll send you my witnesses, if you would be kind enough to give me your address . . ."

"Witness things for yourself, and then if I'm proved wrong, send me whomever you want. You can find me at the Embassy."

Thomas tried to get up, his head spinning. "Agreed," he said coldly.

It was only outside that he realized that he was still squeezing the entrance ticket to the Cabaret du Néant—a little tin tag, embossed with a skull and bones. *Une entrée à la Crêve*, it read. Thomas didn't know what that meant, only that it had cut a gash in the palm of his hand.

VI

Thulé-des-Brumes

Brentford stayed at the hotel that evening, busying himself with diagrams on which he drew and crossed out arrows between points labelled PALLADIAN, CANADA, MAGICAL CROWN, and NEW VENICE. Gabriel had quickly excused himself, arguing that in Paris, it was in cafés, among conversations and meetings, that the action was found and the problems were solved.

Not that Gabriel expected anyone to solve his own problems. Broken hearts are like beheaded chickens, he mused while walking along the Boulevard Montparnasse. They run furiously everywhere for a while, charging into nothingness, and once their blood is spent, they stumble miserably unto death. Such would be the case, he was convinced, with his phantom-hearted self. Where he had once had a heart, he now felt but a lump of rotten meat, and whatever stirred there was probably nothing but the crawling of maggots.

Well, there were the Elphinstone twins—praise to whatever crazy God made them. But with the Twins, and contrary to public opinion on this matter, he'd had mostly good clean fun. He felt a great affection for them, which for lack of a better word he would call avuncular. But beyond that, the Twins were too wonderful and sacred to be loved, and they were too selfish, too bound up in each other, to feel real love for anyone else. Whatever one did with them, and Gabriel had done an awful lot, one always felt like a servant or a pet.

So, for all Gabriel knew, his lost shadow was still crumpled and forgotten in the back of one of Stella's stocking drawers. These days, accordingly, if he were about to pass by a girl that he found attractive, he would change sidewalks. In a position to speak, he found himself blushing and tongue-tied, as if he were winding back at full steam towards puberty.

Imaginary girlfriends, he decided, were the best. They were loyal and lecherous. They were there when you needed them and they made you feel like a better lover than you actually were. They wouldn't leave you for another fellow, and they were not only not angry when you brought another imaginary girl home, they were pleased and playful. Gabriel liked to imagine such a companion at his side, veiled in black so her face might change according to his need. She was sharp and witty, had a voice that was either a little hoarse or maybe burdened with the slightest lisp, and eyes from which a promising glint scintillated through the lace of her veil.

Tonight, Gabriel had decided to take his imaginary girlfriend to a small *crèmerie*—or milk bar—on the rue de la Grande-Chaumière, just off the Boulevard Montparnasse. It held about ten people—usually, boisterous artists from the many studios in the neighbourhood—and you could eat fresh food there for a franc and a half.

It was already crammed when Gabriel arrived and ordered *gigot* with white beans. The place resounded with booming voices speaking French but with strong foreign accents, and Gabriel quickly lost track of what his imaginary girlfriend was talking about. One of the men seemed especially agitated, speaking loudly and wandering around with fork in hand and an energy that bordered on aggression. His face struck Gabriel as both handsome and crazy; his wild shock of hair and fiery steel-blue eyes gave him the look of someone perpetually sitting on an electric chair. His hands were red and scarred, as if they had been burned.

"What are you looking at?" the man said when he noticed Gabriel staring at him. He held tight to his fork and looked as if he were ready to lunge. The surrounding tables went silent, the diners' expectation not devoid of amusement, as if they were used to such scenes.

"You! Are you a Russian spy?" the man shouted. "Or one of those *electricians* building a machine on the roof of my pension?"

"I am neither of those things, sir," Gabriel said cautiously.

The man stared at him for a while, then sat back. At which point Gabriel suddenly recognized him. He was facing none other than the great August Strindberg. "May I say I am a great admirer of your work," Gabriel said, even as he realized that his favourite work by Strindberg—the demented diary that the dramatist had kept, or was keeping, during his stay in Paris—had not been written yet.

"Pshhah! That's all over with," Strindberg answered dismissively, almost angrily, though Gabriel could tell he had been flattered by the recognition. "No more literature. Now I am an alchemist!" He proudly brandished his sore hands.

Two hours later, as they sat in front of an absinthe at the cosy Closerie des Lilas, Strindberg's madness had ebbed somewhat, but the intensity of his presence still consumed his companions. Here was a man roasted alive on the gridiron of his own nerves, and he made Gabriel want to both strangle him and pray for his soul to find a little rest.

"I am sorry for my little scene at the *crèmerie*," Strindberg suddenly said, although with what still seemed a defiant look. "You know what drives us crazy? Our modernity. The trains, the telegraph, the letters, the photographs, the press. They hook us. They obsess us. They worm inside our brains. I was raised in the age of stagecoaches and books, I was used to seeing and digesting the world at a certain pace. And now, look! We get our brains beaten to a pulp in trains, our nerves wired and extending all over the Procrustean Bed of the world. How could we not be crazy when we have lost our sensations and gestures and let them be replaced with others that are totally deranged, totally degenerate? Unless we are at the dawn of a new mankind, developing new senses by the dozen and hundred. Take telepathy, for instance. Do you know how easy it is to impose your will on someone else's brain? To cast a spell through a photograph? Uncovering Nature's secrets is the only naturalism worthy of that name. The occult, I say, is the future of Literature."

"But the book will remain, don't you think?" someone ventured. "It will not be replaced by the phonograph."

This was standard table talk of the time.

"Oh! It will be," someone else said, leaning across from another table. "Writers will become tellers of tales, and will be liked less for their style than for the tone of their voice."

Now Gabriel launched himself, taking advantage of the fact that he knew the history of French literature and could get away with a prophetic flourish. After all, it's not every day that you know the future. He said, "I do not think the book will be replaced by the phonograph, but the phonograph will leave deep traces in it. Even Mallarmé himself, the most bookish of men, is very concerned by these questions: I hear that he now conceives of the poet as an 'Operator,' who not only writes but performs his Poem."

At this point, hearing the praise of a colleague, Strindberg lost all interest and turned away, but a man sitting at the next table suddenly turned towards Gabriel and looked at him closely. He had a greasy jet-black fringe over a flushed brow, clear, clever eyes, and long elegant fingers on the hand he extended towards Gabriel.

"Paul Vassily. Pleased to meet you. Can I offer you a drink?" the man asked.

✳

Gabriel's drink with Vassily—along with many others, to judge by the stack of saucers piled up before them on the marble-topped table—was not taken at the Closerie but at the Café d'Harcourt, down the Boulevard St. Michel, on Sorbonne Square. It was an incredible place, bright as if on fire, and noisy as hell with snatches of bawdy song and the clack of dominoes. But most of all, it was full of painted ladies whose long, coloured dresses swept the floor—a filthy melange of slush and sawdust—with clumsy, alcoholic grace.

"You pay me a bock, *chéri*?" one of them asked Gabriel, having picked up the scent of a foreigner. But if there was a moral principle left in Gabriel, it was that he would not pay for sex, not even with a glass of beer, no more than he would for the air he breathed. He dismissed the lady as politely as he could, and off she staggered to another client, majestically wrapping herself in her fleabitten boa.

"Ah, whores," Vassily said simply, with a kind of detached, appreciative look. "I should warn you that the ones here are especially naughty."

"You won't hear me speak ill of naughty girls," Gabriel said. "At the end of it all, they are the ones we remember."

"What you say is mostly true," Vassily agreed after a moment of reflection, "even if the memories left by the ones around here are often burning. Not that there is a shortage of fresher and somewhat saner flesh, especially in these unfortunate times. Our poets may be as much appreciated as our prostitutes, but these dreadful winters have dwindled one contingent and strengthened the other. I'll let you guess which, of poets and prostitutes, are more resistant to the cold."

"You're a poet yourself?"

"More than I am a whore, I should hope, even if our dear Baudelaire claimed it is one and the same thing," he said. He suddenly became serious again, and Gabriel knew that the time had come for some intense avant-garde poetry talk. "However much I revere the great Mallarmé," Vassily went on, "I think we can go still farther along the way he opened for us. Poetry is too delicate a thing to be passed through the muddy filters of language alone. It is a dialogue between eternal minds, between pure souls that have to remain unsoiled by the cumbersome, uncertain mediations of the printed word. Symbolism, Mr. D'Allier, is nearly dead—here comes Suggestism. Imagine, this—" he leaned closer to Gabriel "—a few carefully chosen formulas whispered to a hypnotized subject, opening a whole theatre of visions in the soft folds of his sleepy brain. The subject would live the poem like a mysterious dream coming from the astral plane."

"Would the subject remember the poem afterwards, then?" Gabriel asked, vaguely hoping that Magnetic Crowns would crop up in the conversation. He could already envision catatonic amateur poets wearing the magnetic laurel crowns of fashionable poets fastened above their empty eyes.

"No, that's the beauty of it, you see—the poem secretly etching itself in the deepest recess of the subconscious mind . . . always there but never quite there, like a half-remembered dream . . . a forgotten word pressing on the tip of your tongue, nameless still, but full of the essence of the Thing . . . Well, since you appreciate the delicacies of the art, I would be honoured to demonstrate for you my latest psychopoem *Pierrot Lotophage . . .*" But before Gabriel could think of an excuse to avoid the performance, Vassily admitted, "But I must confess that the method has yet to be perfected. For the time being it only seems to work with young persons of the fair sex—an audience, I must say, that I am perfectly content with. For now, though, perhaps you will enjoy this." He handed Gabriel a folded piece of paper.

"What is it?"

"A very precious coupon. I was supposed to give it to Strindberg, but I do not think he would cut a pleasant figure beside *le Maître*."

"The Master?"

"Well, Mallarmé, of course. This is an invitation to his reading of *The Book*, as he calls it. For connoisseurs only. Of which I noticed that you are one. Next Tuesday, at his place, rue de Rome."

"I had no idea he did this . . . for real." Gabriel was amazed.

"I don't know if it's really for real. You'll see for yourself," Vassily said with a sly smile.

❄

Vassily, typical of that class of Parisian bohemians who live on family money, resided rather comfortably in a little apartment on Sorbonne Square itself. The place was entirely hung with crimson velvet, so that, invited there later that night, Gabriel felt as if he were entering some inflamed internal organ. A stuffed Grand Duke owl was perched on a roost in the living room, eyeing visitors with glassy, unruffled disapproval.

The bookshelves immediately attracted Humots, the little book demon tattooed on Gabriel's arm. He knew it was bad form to scrutinize people's bookshelves, but his demon was stronger than he. When Humots was itching, Gabriel had merely to extend his hand to find the book that he needed, sometimes without knowing he did. How could he resist, for instance, the rough, smelly, musty Rosez edition of the *Songs of Maldoror*—the one that had slept fifteen years in a cave without ever being opened, biding its time and accumulating over the years a dark, malevolent power?

"A gift from a Belgian friend. It's very special to me," said Vassily, with understandable pride, not to mention a little wariness.

Gabriel flipped through it and read: "*She was known as the snow girl because of her extreme pallor.*" Good call, he thought. Humots was hot. There would be something for him on these shelves. *The Snow Girl*—wouldn't that be a great name for an imaginary girlfriend?

Next, a series of booklets attracted Humots. Diana Vaughan. *Mémoires d'une ex-palladiste*, read the cover. Ex-Palladian? A thrill ran up his spine.

"May I have a look?" he asked Vassily.

"Oh, this? It's just been released. Really strange book. The most bizarre feuilleton since the Sixth Song of Maldoror. If it is a feuilleton . . ."

"What do you mean, 'If it is a feuilleton'?" Gabriel flipped through the pages quickly, perusing them for any mention of the Arctic.

"It's about the Masons being worshippers of Lucifer, doing black masses, wanting to rule the world, and so forth. Some people take this idea very seriously. Huysmans does, for instance. I think on the whole it's a beastly read. For some reason I cannot fathom, if there's anything in the world that's more boring than Masonic literature, it's anti-Masonic literature; I don't know why. But if this is simply a feuilleton, then it's genius. The newspaper form, the false readers' letters, the games, the sense of detail, the mad erudition . . . very painstaking, very inventive."

"But this Diana Vaughan, does she exist?"

"Does Diana exist? Oh, there are portraits—not my kind of beauty, if I may say so—but also interviews, letters. She's supposed to live in a convent now. But what does that prove? Some years ago a journalist called Léo Taxil had everyone believing there was a drowned Roman city in the Leman Lake. Unfortunately, it was more poetic than true. And it is the same Taxil who is behind this series."

Prompted by Humots, Gabriel grasped another volume in the series. It was the same mind-boggling blend of Masonic gossip and ridiculous rituals. The next two booklets that he grabbed threatened to yield as little, and then suddenly he stumbled on an author with a name that rang a sleighbell: Vice-Admiral Albert Hastings Markham.

Every New Venetian knew that name. As a young officer, Markham had been a part of the 1875 Nares expedition to Ellesmere Island. It was on this occasion that he had reached the Farthest North, above 85°. His man-hauled sledge was christened the *Marco Polo*, and it was from that, or from a common inspiration, that he named his starting point Marco Polo Bay. And of course it was in Marco Polo Bay that New Venice was built, and, whether through coincidence or design, the standard of New Venice bore more than a passing resemblance to the Markham coat of arms—not to mention, of course, that the city's marina was named after him. He was rumoured to have been close to the Seven Sleepers.

Diana Vaughan's story about Markham was continued in the fifth feuilleton of the series, which had just been published. In it, she told how Markham, a Mason with the title of Grand Superintendent of the Royal Ark, was also an elected Grand Master of a Perfect Triangle located in Valletta, on the island of Malta. It was said that one day in 1893, for doubting reports of a magic arrow that wrote messages by itself, he had been instantly spirited away, to find himself in Charleston in the presence of the Eleven-Seven who ruled Palladism, and then, after an audience with them, he was sent back the same way to Malta. It wasn't much, but it was another link between the Palladium and the Arctic.

Vassily cleared his throat, probably impatient with Gabriel's bookshelf manners. "You'll have to excuse me," Gabriel said, putting back the booklet. "I have a severe addiction to ink."

"Don't we all?" Vassily nodded. "Thank God we have other addictions to assuage it a little."

❋

Even after a few glasses of Chartreuse, however, Humots remained restless, forcing Gabriel's gaze to return to the bookshelf. A thin pamphlet, its spine sticking out from the shelves, seemed to attract the book-demon to the point where the itch made Gabriel nervous.

Finally giving in and sliding it out, he asked Vassily, "What's this?"
Vassily was now drunk enough to oblige.

"*Thulé-des-Brumes*, by my friend Alphonse Rétté," he replied.
"Quite a little success, and, I dare say, a good candidate for Suggestism. In fact, it might give you some idea of how Suggestism would work."

"Well, I must admit a certain reluctance to be hypnotized."

"That might not be necessary," Vassily said with a knowing smile.
"There are alternative methods."

He started to read, in a vibrant, lyrical voice, stopping frequently to draw on his Uppman cigar, then exhaling his words in thin streamers of bluish haze.

> *O exquisite joys! To go thus very alone, for weeks on end, under the polar night that is set ablaze, here and there, the silent fireworks of the Boreal lights: to laugh at the snow, the oblique flight of dream butterflies that brush and caress and drape me in ermine. Then, to stop to mould white statues that will never melt . . . Yes, to the North, always, with no other aim but to go there . . .*

It was far from the best poetry Gabriel had ever heard, but certainly he could relate to its inspiration—more so than Vassily could suspect. His thoughts evaporated into dim images of snowscapes and, hardly discernible from them, the outlines of a white city, raising its domes into the weak light . . .

> *. . . Listen: there is an island so lost in the recess of the Boreal sea that one has to be us to know it. . .*

And then there was the drink Vassily had fixed for them both, explaining that it was the best accompaniment to his friend's poem. It was a cocktail of champagne and ether, in which from time to time Vassily advised him to dip a raspberry. It took only a few sips before Gabriel felt his brain had become padded with satin. Vassily's rendition of Rétté's poem floated in and out, the images billowing in Etherama like a breeze-blown curtain. And at some point, Gabriel felt his imaginary girlfriend softly take his hand in hers.

Helen . . . yes, this whiteness, when I close my eyes and exhale the syllables of your name, thus, amidst the opiate smoke of some eastern tobacco. And I feel so peaceful . . .

Helen . . . New Venice was everywhere now, it bathed Gabriel, sucked him into an undertow of visions and then spat him back out onto the shore, full of longing and hope, only to plunge him again into a whirl of frothy pictures:

The gondola glides under the bridge . . . a Thunder of yore wakes up; dusty flags are waved; bats whirl around.

The knights cry out: "Take us with you; we were in your retinue when, leaving the Unfortunate Islands where you reigned, you tried to conquer the Princess of the Pearls.

The prince is singing: The knights have died in the crusade.

At this, they all throw their shields in the river.

But the gondola is gone.

When dawn came, Gabriel had fallen asleep and was dreaming of New Venice.

To be continued . . .

EPISODE VII

THE ENIGMA OF THE SNOW-GLOBE EYE

I

The Wax Newspaper

Brentford was woken from a dream of New Venice by the bellboy banging on his door, announcing a telephone call. Still in his dressing gown, he went grumpily down to the lobby to learn that the Commissariat de Police of the rue du Faubourg Montmartre had detained a certain Mr. Tuluk for the night, and that the authorities would be grateful if Mr. Orsini could come and answer a few questions.

It took him almost a whole morning of plodding omnibus rides to get to the rue du Faubourg Montmartre. The street was an affluent tributary to the boulevards, yet the pavement outside its supposedly exclusive shops was festooned with long lines of shivering people. In Paris, Gabriel had explained, you never knew whether a queue meant scarcity or snobbery. Brentford's welcome at the commissariat was rather lukewarm, but he relaxed when he found Tuluk sitting on a chair in the middle of a room and the sergeants laughing their heads off at whatever gobbledygook he was spieling. The comic muse, Brentford recalled, was an integral part of the Inuit's survival skills.

In this jolly atmosphere, he was able to patiently reconstruct what had happened. A guard at the Musée Grévin had caught Tuluk standing in the middle of a diorama, trying to steal some of its precious objects; he had resisted with more petulance than was allowed; and it had quickly become a matter for the police instead. Unable to deliver any satisfactory explanation as to his identity or conduct, he had been invited to spend the night in the "Violin," as the police called their famous custody cells. Brentford, remembering a similar incident at the Inuit People's Ice Palace, wondered if dioramakleptomania was a deep-seated impulse among Inuits.

Eager to sort out the situation with Tuluk, he was called instead into a dismal office, furnished in the typical faded and lacklustre style of state bureaucracies, and found himself face to face with Tripotte—exactly the thing he had feared.

"Ah, we meet again, Mr. Orsini," said Tripotte, with a thin veneer of cordiality, weaving his plump fingers across his paunch.

Brentford's veneer was barely thicker. "I am sure that this time, the Canadian nationality of my friend cannot be doubted."

"I must admit, he looks the part," said Tripotte. "As to the answers he's given me, I'm afraid they're beyond my competency. Why in your opinion would an Eskimo want to steal something from an Arctic diorama? Hasn't he enough of these things back home?"

Brentford was totally at a loss. Arctic? That Tuluk's case had anything to do with the Arctic was news to him. But good news, somehow. He fumbled for a noncommittal answer. "Maybe he thought those objects didn't belong there. The Inuit are very respectful of their own culture. Things that may look like crude tools to us are immensely precious to them."

"He was trying to steal the goggles off the wax figure of a polar explorer, as a matter of fact. I don't doubt that those would be precious to an Inuit."

"Explorer?" Brentford whispered to himself, before noticing that Tripotte was closely observing his reaction and collecting himself.

"Maybe it was just the diorama," he said. "The feeling of being home. You know the Inuit are a simple people, and when they're exposed to our civilization they can easily go off their onions."

As he expected, the racial angle worked wonders with Tripotte, who said, "I can easily believe you on that point." Then, with a touch of regret, he added, "As I can also believe that, according to the Canadian Commission, Mr. Leclou hailed from Montréal."

"So, it's all clear, then," Brentford answered with relief. "Unless charges have been pressed against Mr. Tuluk?"

"By the Grévin Museum, no. That is about the only kind of publicity they don't go in for. And your friend had his wits about him enough not to resist the police for too long. Apparently, he thought clowning was his best defense, and we can hardly charge him with making a fool of himself. I just wonder what you'll turn up with tomorrow, Mr. Orsini."

"I assure you I have nothing to do with this Grévin affair," Brentford answered as emphatically as he could—even as he realized that, whatever the Grévin affair was, he was now totally involved in it.

✳

As soon as he had taken leave of Tripotte, Brentford snatched Tuluk away from his rapt audience and took him for a quick sausage lunch at the nearby Café Brébant. Tuluk ate voraciously, as waiters, visibly pained by his sloppy table manners, circled worriedly around. Brentford, meanwhile, barely touched his plate, gazing instead out the window and brooding over a tatterdemalion who was using a tack on the sole of his shoe to pick up cigar and cigarette butts, then carefully sorting them, probably to resell. But the snow made it difficult: either he had to dig holes through it in the hope of finding bounty, or else splash through wet slush when he spotted a recently discarded butt. Brentford's heart sank as he watched him.

Tired of waiting for the improbable moment when Tuluk would be sated, Brentford turned back to him and asked for his story again.

"So what is it that you saw in the eye of this explorer?"

"The last thing that he saw." Tuluk answered with his mouth full. "The spirit that took him, my mother would say."

"Which was?" Brentford bristled with interest.

Tuluk rummaged through a pocket, then another, and another, then the first one again, and, with a smile, he put something on the table.

It was a glass eye.

"So you *did* take it."

"This Inuk was too quick for the guard," Tuluk boasted, even if, in good Inuk fashion, he was still too modest to speak of himself in the first person.

"And they saw nothing?"

"No, this Inuk puts back the goggles. Very quickly. They think this Inuk want to steal the goggles. But the goggles they are on the eyes of the *inunnguaq*, and they don't look below."

The glass eye looked up at Brentford, and not kindly, he thought. He returned the stare.

"And you say there's something in that glass eye?" he asked. Not that he didn't trust Tuluk, but the Inuit, living in a barren, monotonous, nocturnal land, were well known for complementing their sharp but frustrated senses with the working of their imaginations. Their drawings, for instance, always showed imaginary beasts or spirits. At least, one hoped they were.

"Look," Tuluk encouraged him.

Scanning the room to make sure none of the waiters was watching, Brentford brought the glass eye close to his own and stared into its iris. At first, he saw nothing there, but when he tilted it towards the light, he thought he detected something deep in the heart of the sphere, something very faint and uncertain, like a defect in the glass: a kind of long, thin splatter. The outlines of a city . . . and its reflection on the ice?

Maybe it was only an optical illusion, or a pattern that was pure chance. He rolled the eye between his fingers to take another view, and when he turned it upside down, he thought he saw a shimmer, as if snow was falling slowly over the city.

Ten minutes later, Tuluk was in a cab on his way back to the hotel, and Brentford was hurrying towards the Grévin Museum, the snow-globe eye bulging in his watch pocket.

❄

At the museum, Brentford decided that it was best not to draw attention to himself. So, he forced himself to stop and look at each one of the repulsive wax pantomimes in the "three-dimensional newspaper," as they called it, that led to the diorama. Once there, he hardly dared draw close to the red velvet rope that surrounded it, and when he finally forced himself to read the descriptive plaque, he felt a shiver:

LA MORT DU COURAGEUX EXPLORATEUR AMADIS DE LANTERNOIS SUR L'ILE D'ELLESMERE MAI 1895

Although he'd suspected that the diorama would be about de Lanternois, Brentford was still taken aback—and then even more surprised by the plaque's revelation that de Lanternois had died before New Venice even existed. Peterswarden, it seemed, had fooled Brentford and probably the whole Senate of the Sectors with a heavily made-up mummy. But had Peterswarden known what would happen next? And if de Lanternois had died before New Venice was built, why had the artist depicted the city in his eyes?

Looking for clues, Brentford examined the diorama's landscape. It looked authentic—like a drifting chunk of the Arctic, down to its sickly light and nagging refractions. And for the figure of de Lanternois, the use of wax made perfect sense, Brentford reflected: the artist had been trying to seize the exact moment when the explorer's face, purple, almost blackened, had been frozen still and his last emotion expressed forever. But this emotion was more complex than it first seemed: seen from one angle, de Lanternois' taut features expressed exhaustion and pain, but viewing them from another angle, he appeared to be smiling ecstatically. That his extended arm and the open palm of his hand could be either a salute or a plea only strengthened the uncanny impression. His eyes, no doubt, would confirm the ecstasy, but it had been the artist's cleverness to hide them behind goggles, so as to keep the uncertainty intact. Brentford thought, a little uneasily, about the empty eye socket, and also wondered whether, beneath his hood, the de Lanternois figure was wearing the crown. But the hood was caked with false ice, and its shape told him nothing.

"Excuse me," Brentford said to the guard. "This diorama is beautifully executed. What's the name of the artist?"

"The artist?" asked the guard, as if he had just learned an entirely new word.

"The craftsman, or whomever produced this diorama."

"Oh, that. I don't know if I would call 'im an 'artist.' It's the first time I've been asked that."

While his astral double strangled that of the guard, Brentford remained smiling and patient. "I suppose he has a name?"

"Oh, sure. It's Edgar de Couard."

Brentford's heart skipped a beat. The de Couards were a dynasty of New Venetian painters, arch-rivals of the Elphinstones for the City's biggest commissions. Edgar was famous for his book *Le Bon usage de la Couleur* and for—*Damn!*—the dioramas of the Palace of Memory located inside the Blazing Building. It was his mad son, Edouard, who had nearly destroyed New Venice by pumping blue pigments into the Air Architecture shafts.

Brentford had found his first New Venetian citizen in Paris.

"Where can I find him? Are there workshops in the building?" he asked, trying to master his excitement.

"Him? He's way too crazy for that. Mad as a rabbit, I can tell you that. When he works here, he wants no one to look at him—he's always hiding behind screens or sheets. I've heard he has a studio in Montmartre, but I don't know where exactly. But I doubt he'd ever let you see him. He's so goddamn sensitive he can't even look at himself in the mirror."

Brentford thanked the guard and turned back to the room of displays. Now, in the dim rooms of the museum, the figures looked to him as if they were waiting for a city to be built, and for their life to start again, up there, in the lethal, ecstatic North.

II

The Little Red Heart

oulevard Denfert-Rochereau was a few minutes' walk from Montparnasse. Early in the afternoon, dressed in his best, his arm in a blindingly white sling, Thomas rang the bell at the dark-green carriage door of number 87, which looked more like the entrance to a bourgeois house than to a *hotel particulier*. Maybe Blanche de Bramentombes was not the rich heiress she claimed to be. But Paris is a folded city that, past certain frontiers, unfurls itself into manifold surprises. From the archway of the door, he could see, at the end of the paved lane carefully cleaned of its snow, a beautiful three-story house surrounded by a garden that, with its tough eucalypti and rhododendrons, had remained impervious to the wintry weather.

A fresh, plump, toothsome maid introduced Thomas into a drawing room where a fireplace diffused a lulling warmth. Bunches of white roses bloomed on every item of Louis XV furniture that could accommodate a vase, forming a continuous Arcadian landscape with the fuzzy, sparkling groves on the room's painted panels and in the mirrors that reflected them. There was a light, heady lushness to the whole snuggery, and the morphine coursing through Thomas's veins made it come alive, deepening the perspectives and gently swaying the foliage.

He heard nimble steps pattering down the stairs and Blanche entered, already dressed for fencing, wire mask and foil in hand. She wore a black knee-length dress tightly belted at the hips and embroidered with a little red heart, black satiny tights, and a pair of black leather elbow gloves. Her curly black hair was held in a fuzzy bun and haloes of mauve circled her eyes, bringing out her pallor and that shade of feverish Troubled Nymph's Thigh Pink on her cheeks.

"Sorry to keep you waiting, Mr. Paynes-Grey," she told him with a smile that seemed expectant, as if she were waiting for him to understand a joke she had just cracked. As she sat, he noticed that her black dress was lined with scarlet.

"To think I wanted to bring you flowers," Thomas said, vaguely pointing at the avalanche of flowers surrounding them.

"Mother believes they're good for my health and spends a fortune in the greenhouses. I think it looks like a funeral. What do you think?" she asked casually, as she beheaded a rosebud with a swift lash of her blade.

"I think . . . it's heady," Thomas admitted, taken aback by her poise.

"Don't get too heady with me. What about a little exercise?"

✳

The fencing "strip" was a stretch of creaking wooden floor in a garret above the third story that looked out over the gardens and domes of the Paris Observatory. A mirror ran along the wall, as if this had once been a dancing school. Various toys and baubles lay discarded in the corners collecting dust, a melancholy sight. Thomas realized that he did not know how old, or young, Blanche was, and, at this point, he didn't dare ask. Blanche gave him some whites and, as he slipped behind a screen to put them on, he wondered who they had belonged to. A fencing master? The sinister Major Yronwoode?

"Are you okay?" she asked through the screen.

"Well, now you come to mention it, not really. This sling is a real bore."

"Let me help you," she said, coming round the corner of the screen and helping him out of his jacket, with more delicacy than Tuluk usually managed. He relished the opportunity to expose his muscles to both her eyes and hands, and shivered at the brush of her leather gloves.

"Please, put my arm behind my back," he asked, as she softly replaced the sling. She hurt him as she did so, and for a moment he thought she was doing it on purpose, but he let her continue without so much as a groan. Still, he remembered Yronwoode's advice. He would have to sort some things out, he thought, while grasping his foil and swishing as if to sign his name in the air. He caught himself in the mirror. Bathed in the Apollonian halo of morphine, he thought that he looked quite good.

"I think that as a strong man in the flower of youth, you should have a little handicap against a feeble creature like me," she said, as he flexed his legs in front of the mirror.

"And what would that be?"

"You only win if you touch right in the middle of my heart, here."

"I suppose that is acceptable," he said with confidence, before saluting. "*En garde! Prête!*"

"*Prête!*"

She wasn't a bad fencer—far from it—except that after a heated passage of arms she had to stop for a while to catch her breath, or laugh with short, brittle trills that flushed her cheeks and made her eyes water.

"Who taught you to fence so well?"

"My uncle did. He is a fencing fiend. I think the clanging reminds him of money, but that's merely my personal theory. An English friend has recently added a few lessons. A man of unusual skills, I must say."

Thomas, for a while, had played the gentleman, parrying more than lunging and trying not to score easy hits, but the mention of Yronwoode stoked him up. The morphine started to play tricks on him, too, coaxing his pride into reckless moves, multiplying the point of her weapon into a swarm of bothersome bluish flies, or into blurred swipes that seemed to float in slow motion through the air. Her little red heart danced before him, like a will-o'-the-wisp above a fresh graveyard, always just out of his reach.

"I'm afraid you have too small a heart," he said during a pause, rivulets of sweat dripping down his brow.

"I think I've been told that before," she said, and he could sense her smile under her wire mask.

"Would Major Yronwoode be liable to say something like that?"

Blanche did not look surprised. "If you have met Major Yronwoode, I suppose you'll excuse him for being a bitter man."

"He was more than bitter. He was impudent. You would not believe the things he said to me."

"I take it that you didn't believe them, either, then."

"I even offered him to send him my witnesses," Thomas said proudly.

"Because you thought he was telling the truth, or because you thought he wasn't?"

Thomas hesitated. "I'd believe you if you told me he wasn't."

"Let's make a deal about this duel. If you hit my heart, I'll tell you the truth. But if you don't . . ."

"If I don't?"

"You'll have to believe me and do everything I say."

"I'm not sure that makes me want to win. But, as you wish: *en garde, mademoiselle. Prête!*"

He launched into a few wild flurries, and many times hit her close to her heart. The exertion started to make him feel anxious and nauseated, and he decided to strike once and for all. He attacked with a *flèche*, charging towards the heart, but the point passed under her arm and they got locked in a *corps-a-corps*. Their masks knocked and scraped and he caught her eyes shining behind their cage. He could hear her wheezing, too, and suddenly he felt afraid to hurt her. He started to retreat, but losing his balance, he tripped and stumbled onto his back, his arm sending a tidal wave of pain over his entire body.

He opened his eyes. She was bent over him, her mask still on her head, her point lightly pushing his Adam's apple.

"You are dead, Mr. Paynes-Grey."

"And I'm in heaven," he said, looking at her.

"That or something else. Does your arm hurt terribly?"

"Since you ask, yes."

She pretended to put her shoe on the arm, moving her heel as if about to press down. He watched her do this with more curiosity than fear.

"It must be terrible," she eventually said. "Your suffering for me certainly deserves a reward." She walked to the chimney and took a black velvet case off the mantel.

"Here is a little present for you," she said. "To seal our friendship."

He managed to sit up, and settling the case on his knees, he opened it with his good hand. Nested in purple silk and velvet was a glass and silver syringe, delicately detailed with curlicues. His initials were carved on the top of the plunger, and for a second, it was like reading his own name on a gravestone.

"This is a Pravaz syringe. And this," she said, waving a small phial, "is a sixty-percent solution, from Hornuch, rue de Rome. The best in town."

On her knees, she undid his jacket and found a spot on his chest. She stung the needle under his skin, letting it hang down. Taking out a spoon, she poured a little fluid from the phial, pumped it into the syringe, and then screwed the syringe back onto the needle. She wedged a small wooden board between the plunger and the syringe, to block the plunger once she deemed the injection sufficient. Then, she pushed the plunger, and he burned in heaven, as she glued her lips to his.

"*Touché*," he whispered.

III

The Anaglyph

Brentford discovered, from a telephone book, that Edgar de Couard's studio was not in Montmartre, but in Ménilmontant. Nobody, however, answered the phone, so Brentford had to walk all the way up the hill to the neighbourhood as the afternoon declined. He remembered a remark Gabriel had made a few days before about the unbelievable amount of walking done by the heroes of Parisian novels, and felt that on that score at least, he qualified for the position. Of course, when it came to snowy streets, he'd had a lifetime of training, and could surely teach those other heroes a thing or two.

He followed the boulevards and their triumphal arches, which stood like ancient ruins amidst the smoky, noisy hubbub of the neighbourhood, all the way to the Place de la République, a vast stretch of wilderness that the north wind made still less hospitable. A blackened bronze of Marianne, the sturdy female virago representing the Republic, stood in the middle of the square, her arm raised as if calling for help, while Liberty, Equality, and Fraternity, white against the snow that crept up to and over them, grew blurrier, threatening to disappear any day now. Nobody seemed to mind the allegory.

Brentford came closer to a long string of heavily wrapped-up people who were queueing, with typical world-weary jocularity, not at a newspaper kiosk, Morris column, or urinal (those minarets of the Parisian faith), but before an automated distributor of warm drinks—mulled wine, mostly—which also featured a warm-water tap for rinsing glasses. Brentford made a mental note to install some in New Venice, before remembering that he was not the Regent-Doge anymore and that there was no New Venice to regent anyway.

Another queue filed up to the cable car linking the Place de la République to the heights of Belleville. The car was tiny and cramped, damp with condensation, and reeking of mulled wine. With grating hiccups, it worked its way across a frozen canal that made Brentford homesick, and from there up a populous street. The workers who lived there had cleaned the street themselves, a man in the funicular explained, so as not to lose the benefits of their cable car when they got home from their harrowing work. Too bad the government wasn't so efficient, a woman remarked, triggering laughter that contained little mirth.

He got off at the rue Pyat intersection and walked past the modest shops and hotels until, suddenly, he found himself at the top of a hill, near a vertiginous path leading through snowy waste grounds into a knot of leprous streets. A panorama of Paris stretched across the snow-laden horizon, and for the first time Brentford saw the city as a whole.

Half-smothered in snow it spread before him, an ashen labyrinth that the first lights spangled with glowing embers. The sheer amount of human work that had been needed to build this insane, glorious heap of rubble struck Brentford as vaguely monstrous. The city seemed to have been built by Titans and djinns, not by poor men who had laid stone upon stone upon stone. Like many idealized places, Eden and New Venice included, it looked like a doomed promise of happiness. On the left, Notre-Dame raised her amputated hands to the leaden sky, cursing, it seemed, more than praising. At the other end of the scene, the *I fell* tower looked ridiculously small, a clockwork toy Babel for the spoiled children of progress.

He turned his back regretfully and went down the rue des Envierges, noticing louche figures passing by on the narrow sidewalks, though none approached him. Maybe this is where the shy ones go to live, Brentford reflected, thinking of de Couard. He could understand that a man of his antisocial nature would find refuge here, far from the fanfare of painter-infested Montmartre. He lost himself in a tangle of winding, humble streets, only managing to regain his bearings when he stumbled on the forlorn Ménilmontant station from the disused circular railroad. The rue des Cascades, where de Couard resided, was a little farther on, on the side of a barren slope, and with its blind walls and wooden fences it looked as lonely and rustic as a mountain village—nothing at all like the Pandemonium Brentford had just fantasized about. He found the artist's house at the corner of the rue de Savies, its large picture window betraying the presence of a studio. Crude faces, he noticed, were carved into the wall, in a modern version of prehistoric art.

Brentford suspected that de Couard would not answer the knocker, which bore the face of a woman. He played out a little war of nerves, letting a few seconds go by between each knock, so as to give the painter the impression that his unwelcome guest had almost given up, except that he hadn't, and wasn't going to. Eventually hearing somebody coming to the door—probably to take a peep through the *judas*, as the French called peepholes—Brentford pulled out the snow-globe eye from his pocket and held it in front of the hole. The door squeaked and a blind old woman, with eyes as dead as the one he flourished uselessly, invited Brentford inside.

"I want to speak to Monsieur de Couard," he said, and as he doubted that this alone would gain him entry, he added, "About the snow-globe eye in his figure of de Lanternois."

One minute later, she came back to let him in, her face creased in staunch disapproval. Located slightly below street level, the glass-roofed drawing room was tasteful and warm, with faded peach walls, indigo velvet draperies, and deep rosewood furniture, but it had a stilted, stifling atmosphere that made Brentford feel instantly ill at ease.

De Couard rose regretfully from the deep leather armchair—the only one in the room—in which he had been reading, and stared at Brentford over his tinted pince-nez with not the least hint of benevolence, but rather, Brentford thought, with a diffused gleam of madness, all very well for an artist but enough to get anyone else committed to an asylum. He looked nothing like the scruffy, absinthe-stoked *rapins* who crawled the Parisian art scene. Rather, he was tall and stooped, with steely blue eyes and hollow cheeks, blond hair that looked like a stork's nest, and a long double-pronged beard that gave him something of a regal air. Brentford could smell old money, an excellent if hard-and-fast upbringing by sadistic priests, and, judging by the unruly mob of tics that rioted on his face at any given time, a case of neurasthenia well above fashionable norms.

"Monsieur de Couard, I presume," said Brentford, at his most diplomatic. "I am truly sorry to disturb you and interrupt your work, but—" with a nod at the glass eye in his open hand, "—it is precisely the quality of your work that prompted me to call."

"The e-e-eye," stammered his host, pointing an accusing finger at the little snow globe.

Oh, God, thought Brentford. This is not going to be easy. "I find it a fascinating piece of art. Would you mind discussing it with me?"

Now, Brentford could see that de Couard's eyeglass lenses were of different colours, red and blue. But whether he looked through them or around them, the painter carefully avoided Brentford's eyes, even as he reluctantly steered him towards the rosewood sofa against the wall. The spectral, blind old maid reentered the room and Brentford watched her with growing unease as she tremblingly brought tea to the coffee table in a jangle of Sèvres china. The tea, however, proved to be Russian and first-class.

Brentford shook off his discomfort and looked for a firing angle. De Couard might be shy, but he was also, after all, an artist, and surely there was little risk in flattering his vanity.

"Monsieur de Couard, I am very grateful for your time and hospitality. It is the sad lot of artists, I know, to have to put up with their admirers. In my case, it is only your talent that you have to blame for your trouble."

"The eye belongs to the wax figure," de Couard stammered, reproachfully but so softly that Brentford had to lean forward to understand.

Brentford tried to appease him. "It will soon be put back in its place, don't worry." Maybe showing him the eye had not been such a good idea after all. It made de Couard seem even more strung-out than he clearly already was—and even, it seemed, more than a little scared. It might have been only the holy horror an artist feels at the desecration of his work, but Brentford sensed that there was something more in his discomfort—something that could bring him closer to New Venice.

"I have been, as I said, very impressed by your Arctic diorama at the Musée Grévin. I happen to come from just such a remote, distant place, in the Confederation of Canada. And when I saw your diorama I felt such a shock that for a while I felt that I had been carried back to the Arctic."

De Couard was listening; Brentford had him hooked. Now he began reeling him in, very cautiously.

"It was almost as if I could feel the brush of the wind, hear the crack of the ice," Brentford went on, embroidering his own impressions onto Tuluk's story. "I wondered how you achieved such exactness. It's almost—hallucinatory."

De Couard lifted up his eyes for a brief moment, but lowered them again before he spoke, his stammer almost under control. He said, "I suppose you're familiar with the latest theories of optical perception?"

"More or less," Brentford admitted, even as he wondered what the hell they could have been in the 1890s. "Simultaneous contrasts? Pointillism?"

The painter nodded, and confided slowly, "I have gone much further since then . . ."

Listening to a half-mad stutterer as he expounds the latest theories about the physiology of colour perception might not be everyone's idea of a good time, but one of Brentford's greatest qualities was that he considered himself never too old to learn. Besides, he remembered that Edgar de Couard had been—would be—among the first to live in New Venice, and surely for that alone the painter deserved his undivided attention.

What de Couard explained was roughly this: it had recently been proved by psychophysics that the sight of colours was *dynamogenic*—that is, colours stimulated not only the visual organs but the entire nervous system. Depending on the colours, this stimulation triggered reflex discharges or inhibitions, and corresponding emotions, positive or negative. "Believe me," he said in a confessional moment, "a sensitive man can find himself on the rack when two unmatched colours strike his senses, as if a cacophonic fanfare were playing right by his ear. The outer world as it is now can be a cruel place for such a man."

To a painter, he went on, this meant that painting had to go beyond the eyes; it had to reach the innermost recesses of the brain, had to change for itself "the ratio of the five senses," as the great William Blake had said. Pointillism—of which, de Couard insisted, he was a dedicated epigone, even if he loathed its well-known anarchist leanings—had systematized painting according to the laws of the perception of colour contrasts. Now, painting had to be systematized according to the very laws of the mind and its own sets of contrasts.

Brentford interrupted. "You mean painting can control the mind?"

De Couard said he believed it could, but added that he would rather use words such as *suggestion* rather than *control*. Painting, he maintained, could be hallucinatory. Panoramas and dioramas had proven it, when people were persuaded they saw moving figures, or were so disturbed they threw objects at the canvas. Such powerful visual stimuli can loosen our grasp on reality to the point where the other senses join in the illusion: that was why Brentford had heard the wind in the Musée Grévin, de Couard explained—even though he also insisted that the Grévin diorama was a miserable work.

"Like some sort of Synesthesia," Brentford—always the good pupil—proposed.

De Couard welcomed the word with the grave nod of an initiate. It would be the key to the Artwork of the Future that Wagner had predicted. It would not be a clumsy patchwork of mountebank arts, as philistines often misunderstood it, but it would immerse the spectator in a totally different atmosphere, in totally different situations, in a totally different reality. In that respect, any Montmartre cabaret was more advanced in painting than even the work of the pointillists.

It all reminded Brentford of the story of the Chinese painter who was paid by a rich patron to paint his masterpiece and seven years later delivered what looked like a banal landscape. As the patron's reproach was being leveled at him, the painter turned away, walked into his painting and was never seen again. De Couard, it seemed to Brentford, was a man whose dream was to walk into his own painting.

The painter, now clearly warmed by a sacred passion that he seldom had occasion to vent, asked Brentford to follow him into his studio—a long, large space, so immaculate one would never suspect it belonged to a painter if it hadn't been for the two palettes on display, one for the warm colours and one for the cool (he never mixed them, he said, as scornfully as a shy man could). The room was divided in the middle by a long black curtain, in front of which, set on a tripod, was a curious shiny machine made of superimposed colour disks and moveable rods.

With nervous yet precise, staccato gestures, de Couard now drew the curtains over the room's picture window, to shut out any spying eyes, and lit the Argand chandelier. Next, he handed Brentford a tinted pince-nez like his own, and set about rolling back the drape, apologizing for the poor quality of this work in progress. The floor should be painted, he said, and the ceiling too, so that the spectator could see nothing but pigment. But that would come later, he explained as, with a final tug on the curtain, he revealed a large, rectangular canvas.

At first Brentford saw nothing but a confused whirl of luminous dots that here and there seemed to suggest hazy shapes. Nonetheless, following a gesture from de Couard, he put on the spectacles and stepped in for a closer look—and suddenly found himself transported somewhere else, speechless and dizzy.

Under a grey snow-laden sky, a gigantic city jumped at his face and curled all around him, topped in the centre by a mammoth Parthenon. On the left, a gigantic but finely wrought steel cupola blocked a part of the horizon, and on the right, palatial buildings, grouped in closed squares and courts, rose for miles into the distance in mysterious ministerial rivalries. Between them, copper walkways and titanic iron bridges crossed the sky at precipitous heights. In the background, along endless canals, enormous snowy embankments teemed with marquees and pennants, as if a festival were taking place, and Brentford thought he heard bronzed slivers of music from a marching band. In the foreground, on a circular boulevard where the snow had turned to slush, arcades teemed with dots that seemed to move. A mail-coach shone as if covered with diamonds. Brentford thought he heard a bell ring, faintly, as if tolling under the water. It all disintegrated into a haze along the edges where, he realized, the painting was still unfinished, sketched in crayon or pastel, bringing evanescence to the dream.

Brentford plucked off the glasses and tried to dissipate it altogether. He stepped back, faintly nauseated. He was the one stuttering now.

"It . . . it's wonderful," he admitted.

"You are too kind," de Couard answered, giving a shadow of a bow. "It is inspired by Rimbaud's poem 'Villes.' "

Brentford took a breath and stepped in again under the anaglyphic painting to examine the canvas more closely, the city dissolving as he did. He saw it was actually transparent, multilayered, like a diorama, but also painstakingly dotted with nearly microscopic blue and red specks of paint, which, he supposed, gave the three-dimensional effect. Feeling he was being too inquisitive, he retreated.

"Oh, it's nothing," de Couard went on, and Brentford could not tell if he spoke out of a pathological modesty or because his real ambitions were still more megalomaniacal. "The subject dominates here, not the colours. The day will come," he predicted, "when an abstract array of pure colours will dictate feelings as precisely as a man can dictate words to a typist."

"The relief effect is truly striking," Brentford said. "How do you achieve it?"

"Anaglyphs have made much progress recently. I have heard that an Englishman, Mr. Friese-Green, has even recently adapted the technique to those despicable moving pictures that will soon be all the rage among Beotians. It works according to the same principle of colour contrast that made pointillism so far ahead of its time. Blending the two seemed only logical."

"It must be a great amount of work."

"Not so much, actually, since I have had this machine," he said, pointing at the black contraption Brentford had noticed.

"Yes, I was intrigued by that . . ."

"It was devised by the French poet and inventor Charles Cros, who was so unsuccessful with the phonograph, or as he called it, the paleophone. According to Cros's own *Principles of Cerebral Mechanism*, his machine simulates the effects of colour perception on the nervous system. For me, it's most helpful to systematize the use of colour contrasts."

"I've never heard of Cros. Such a machine must be rare, I would suppose."

"It is the only one that exists. I knew Cros's work, but I would never have known that the machine had been built had I not happened to meet his brother. He is as strange as Charles. He happens to be Keeper of the Seals of the small kingdom of Auracania and Patagonia."

"I have never heard of that, either."

There was no stopping de Couard now.

"It is quite famous here. About thirty years ago a certain De Tounens, a French adventurer from the Sixties, federated some Indian tribes to claim the independence of Patagonia. For a while he reigned over sixty square leagues of Chile as Orélie-Antoine the First, and even sent out a few ambassadors here and there. He was soon overthrown and expelled, though, and, after a few attempts at reclaiming his throne, came back to France to die. And when he was dying he remembered an old school friend, Achille Laviarde, and entrusted the crown to him. This Laviarde was really up to the task of kingship: he named a cabinet in exile that included Cros's brother, and His Majesty is still enjoying a certain popular prestige, at least in the cafés of Montmartre, where the kingdom supports itself by selling titles and medals. It was among them that I met a man who had bought this machine from Cros's brother and offered it to me as an advance payment for the painting you just saw. He had been, he explained to me, very impressed by the de Lanternois diorama."

Decidedly. So a man involved with a fanciful kingdom had commissioned this painting of a Northern city, with de Lanternois on his mind? Interesting, thought Brentford "So," he inquired, "this painting is not for sale?"

"As I told you, it's a commission," de Couard said, a bit suspiciously.

"Was adding the snow-globe eye to the figure part of the deal?" Brentford asked.

De Couard blushed violently and started to stammer again: "I . . . I . . . have a clause of con-con-fidentiality."

Brentford took this as a yes. What did the eye mean, then? Was it a test? A message? For a moment he imagined it rotating in the wax face, covering the city with snow at every turn. He dispelled the idea and found another one just underneath it.

"Would you accept another commission?" he heard himself ask.

IV

The Tail of Saint Mark's Lion

It was a dream that woke Lilian. She was facing the wax figures of the Seven Sleepers when one of them, tall and bald, came to life, showed her the knob of his cane, and said, "Didn't you recognize the tail of the Lion of Saint Mark?" She sat up. For the second day in a row, she found herself next to Morgane Roth, in her puffy, mellow white bed. Under a tangle of black hair, she could see Morgane's sinuous back slithering under the covers. She felt like softly putting her palm on it, but leaning over her she said only, "Morgane, I have to go."

When she came back from the bathroom, the heavy-lidded Morgane was already sitting cross-legged on the bed, rolling a cigarette from the excellent Maison Dausse hashish resin that helped her, she claimed, "go into the astral." Lilian took a few distracted puffs while collecting her scattered clothes. She didn't exactly feel remorse, but the trick she had played on Thomas didn't seem as funny as it had two nights ago. Not that she feared for him: he was a big slab of beef, after all, and could take care of himself. No, it was more a part of the overall feeling that for the past few days she had been oblivious of the desperate predicament of the Most Serene Seven. Her dream, which was still floating wavy and dim on the surface on her mind, had left her feeling, finally, compelled to do something.

But arriving back at the hotel around four o'clock, she found no one there except the Colonel, and she certainly didn't feel like talking to him. Going downstairs, she came across Gabriel, staggering back to his bed from God least of all knew where. This will have to do, she thought. Seeing that he would need a little rest before she could speak with him, she arranged to meet him for an early dinner—at seven at the Crémerie Darblay, on la rue de la Gaîté—an invitation at which he nodded absent-mindedly.

At seven p.m. sharp she was waiting impatiently at Darblay among the actors and musicians from the nearby theatres, excited by her discovery and sorry not to have seen Brentford first. But already Gabriel was there, throwing open the door of the clean little milk bar just as the clock finished striking the hour.

Lilian had to admit that she did not like him. Of course, that might be because of his friendship with Brentford. When she and Brentford had been lovers, she had always resented Gabriel's presence as slightly parasitic and somewhat suspect, though she could not say exactly why, as Gabriel had never been anything but courteous to her. But she still remembered—with mortification and anger—the day when she had been out driving with Brentford in his Albany sled and she had openly criticized Gabriel . . . and Brentford had invited her, politely but firmly, to cease or get out of the sled.

Maybe it was Gabriel himself who put her ill at ease. He was kind of a conundrum, and as a matter of fact, he intimidated her. He was slight of build and soft-spoken almost to the point of shyness, but wore faddish, highty-flighty clothes, and in conversation he was as sparkling as champagne and as bitter as absinthe. The upper half of his face was delicate and racy, with the ringed eyes of a tormented soul, but it ended up in a prognathous jaw and a shambles of jagged yellow teeth that would have got him classified as a potential criminal by all current standards of anthropometry. The sensitive poet that upper face promised finished below as a degenerate brute. Well, that was something you could call many men, including that ass Thomas, who had *corpora cavernosa* for brains. But it was Gabriel's fate and, she realized, misfortune, to wear the badge of duality stamped right on his face. That said, Lilian felt inclined to give him credit for having protected those cute, crazy freak twins in a way no one else would have dared to do. The thought of the Twins, and the danger they were in, brought Lilian back to her dream. Gabriel, for all his flaws, was loyal to Brentford and the Dauphin-Doges. He would have to do.

"Neat little place," he said as he sat down.

He was very tired, and mired in the unpleasant aftermath of the previous night's ether binge—a cold, bitter taste lingered in his mouth, and his cranium felt as if it had been stuffed with old, dirty rags dipped in crude oil. He didn't know what to say to Lilian. As a matter of fact, she intimidated him. The first time he had seen her was on stage with the Sandmovers, twenty years ago, and he couldn't help having a crush on her then, with her long Rapunzel hair braided with electric garlands. The new, metamorphosed Lilian who had sprung up last year, bony, brave, and sarcastic, was still more forbidding, and though he had nothing but sympathy for her gnostic take on the suffragette question, he had never found the nerve to say so, probably because he surmised that she wasn't interested in his opinion. She was, simply speaking, the kind of woman that did not belong with the girls in his lullaby league, and the fact that she had been Brentford's sweetheart only put her further off limits.

Lilian watched him eat garlic-buttered snails with a vague shiver of disgust.

"How's your head?" she asked, pointing to the patch on his temple.

"How's your back?" he asked in return. It was typical, she supposed, of his way of being polite.

"It's well taken care of," she said, remembering the long massage from Morgane that had made her lose all sense of time and place—maybe not the memory that she needed at the moment.

"And Brentford? How is he doing?" she asked, out of politeness, she thought, but as she mouthed the words, she found herself feeling genuine concern.

Gabriel stared at her incredulously. "You know Brentford. It's always hard to say. Duty goes before his personal feelings."

That is his problem, indeed, she thought, but did not say so. "I always wondered what made you so close," she mused, as if to herself.

Gabriel lifted his eyes from his plate, surprised again at her candour. "Let's say I'm the Dionysos to his Apollo," he answered, straight-faced, though Lilian assumed it was probably some kind of private joke he had with Brentford.

"I thought you were more the Sancho Panza to his Don Quixote," she quipped. "But have you gods made any advance on our homecoming?"

"Nothing to uncork the champagne about, I'm afraid," Gabriel answered. He was too tired to mention Markham and his link to a secret society working in the Arctic. It was too inconclusive to be worth the trouble.

Lilian hesitated. She would hate to make a fool of herself. She said, "I may have something, although I'm not sure it deserves champagne."

Gabriel lifted his eyes slowly back to her. "Who likes champagne anyway? It's for children and cronies."

"It's a dream I had, actually. You remember Morgane, the medium we met at the Salpêtrière? Two nights ago, Thomas and I went to one of her séances. There was another man there. A shaved, square-jawed brute in a dark blue suit. Lyonel Owain Savnock is his name. And I had the faintest feeling I had seen him somewhere, but I could not place him at all. However, I noticed that he had a curious lion's head for a cane knob. And last night I dreamed I was among wax figures, and I heard him asking me, "Didn't you recognize the tail of the lion of Saint Mark?" And then I knew who he was. One of the Seven Sleepers."

Gabriel goggled. "The tail of the Lion of Saint Mark? I had totally forgotten it. One of the most dubious relics in Saint Mark's Dream Cathedral in New Venice, even according to the rather expansive criteria of credibility in the Roman Catholic Church. My godfather, the archbishop, used to show it to me when I was a kid. You're sure he was one of the Sleepers, though?"

"I knew him from his wax effigy," Lilian went on. "Give or take a few years, it was the same bald head, the same shaved eyebrow, the same boxer's jawline."

"The one with the white sash, then. Lord Lodestone?"

"Lord Lodestone, yes."

It was too extraordinary to believe. "He was never called Lord Savnock, was he?" Gabriel asked, though he knew the answer.

"It could be an assumed identity. Or maybe his name in New Venice was the false one. Lord Lodestone. It did always seem too good to be true."

"You named your last band for it, though."

"I never made the connection, I must say," said Lilian, with genuine surprise.

"Now you've made it," Gabriel answered with a wry smile. "But didn't Thomas recognize him?"

"There was a French girl there—you can't possibly imagine that our True Thomas was attentive to anything else? Though now that you mention it, there was something strange in a question Thomas asked the medium, and in Lord Savnock's reaction to it. It was a question about a future city near the North Pole, and the answer didn't really mean anything, but I saw that Savnock was quite startled."

"No wonder, if he really is Lord Lodestone."

"He explained to Thomas that he was, or had been, asked to fund a polar expedition. Hence his interest."

"That would make sense." Gabriel nodded. He wished that he had a better brain tonight, instead of a ball of crumpled newspapers. He struggled to connect all this with Markham, but it was like trying to a put a square peg in a round hole. Nevertheless, as the news sank in, he considered the ramifications. The Seven Sleepers, or at least one of them, was in town. Timewise, it was plausible. New Venice had not yet been founded, but it wasn't far off. Perhaps Lord Lodestone was here precisely for that reason—to get a few things done, or to oversee them. Gabriel felt thrilled.

"You're a genius, Lilian," he said, blushing, which in turn made Lilian redden herself. An awkward silence fell.

"This deserves a celebration," Gabriel declared a moment later. "But we'll drink together once we're home. The Seven of us."

V

Beware of the Wolves!

When Brentford left Edgar de Couard's studio, night had already fallen—or had less fallen, perhaps, than risen from the ground, for its murk felt earthy and damp. Going down the rue Vilin—more a wasteland than a street—he passed shadowy groups of workers shivering in the cold. Too poor to take the cable car, they were wearily trudging up the hill towards homes that would not warm them much. Most of them, in fact, went no farther than Au Repos de la Montagne, the cabaret at the top of the street.

Taking advice from his Baedeker, Brentford reached the canal and then crossed the boulevard de Magenta—where a dead horse was lying in the middle of the snowy street—and soon found himself once again between the triumphal arches that saluted long-forgotten victories in total indifference. He followed the narrow, deserted rue d'Aboukir and was strolling around for a while, thinking about Helen, when he noticed the busts of Egyptian goddesses (was it Hathor?) on the Place du Caire, lining the façade of one of these glass-roofed arcades that were, in some respects, the blueprint for New Venice: a utopian world where you could live a life of leisure and abundance, forever protected from the wrath of the weather gods. This particular utopia looked rather dead, though, at this time of night, with its echoing tiles and closed printing shops.

Swerving westward, he walked towards the mute bulk of the Bourse, that most vulgar of temples, and then south down the rue Vivienne, with its closed fancy boutiques, which now, at barely eight o'clock and all the lamps out, looked frozen in time by the cold.

Suddenly, the rumble of cavorting steps drowned out the echoes of his own, and he was overtaken by a little girl of eight or ten years, who skipped along in front of him and sometimes stopped to look behind, as if to make sure that he was following. In the darkened street, all he could make out was the crude shawl around her shoulders, and her feet, sockless in sodden shoes.

He caught up to her and she hopped alongside him.

"Monsieur, wouldn't you like to see my—" and she ended with a word Brentford did not understand, in a voice that was musical in the way of a tuppenny flute, although a tuppenny flute playing a rather vulgar tune. "It's a nice little . . . My little sister has just . . . it clean."

Brentford did not understand every word, but grasping the general sense of the proposition, melted with horror.

"It's only two francs to see it," the little girl said with poise. Now, at the corner of the rue des Petits Champs, he could see her plump cheeks, red from the cold, her little upturned nose, and grey-blue eyes under her blond braided hair. But he could also see her red nose, caked with dried snot, and the circles round her eyes.

"And for five francs you can put your—"

"Shut up, will you," Brentford interrupted, frowning and waving his finger.

"Monsieur, please, don't be cruel to a poor little girl. Perhaps you'd rather see my little bum?"

"Certainly not. Now—"

"Maybe you like little boys better? If you want, I know a place—"

"*Tssk!* Not another word!" Brentford almost shouted.

"I see what it is. I'm too old for you," she said, making a little curtsey, her head aslant in a clumsy attempt at charm. But Brentford could see the goosebumps where her shawl met her neck and the sight filled him with compassion.

"I don't want to hear another word. Please," he said, taking off his scarf and placing it around her.

"Capital! Thank you, Monsieur," she said, clapping her reddened hands. "It'll be one franc for you, Monsieur."

"Please. I'm not the man you're looking for. And now I guess we'd better look for your mother."

"That's what I thought! You like them old, do you?"

"Keep quiet, now, will you?" he said, taking in his a little hand that felt icy right through his gloves. "Where do you live?"

The little girl struggled, looking sincerely scared. "Don't take me to my mother. She'll beat me if I come back without money."

Brentford sighed. He had to do something, but what? *Living in a wicked universe? Wanting to put it right? Go get Orsini.*

"I'll give you money, then. More money than you'll earn living like this."

He didn't know if it was an Interpherence or not, but his tone of voice struck a paternal note that felt a little scary. "So where do you live?"

The child hesitated. "If you give it to my mother, she will keep everything," she said, with a little sigh.

"Okay," he said. "I'll give you five francs right away." He fumbled in his *porte-monnaie* for a silvery full moon of a coin that she then put avidly into her dress pocket. "Now where do you live and what's your name?"

"I'm called Pirouette," she said joyously, spinning herself. "From rue Pirouette."

"And where that would be?"

"But Les Halles, of course," she said, shrugging her shoulders in disbelief at Brentford's ignorance.

✻

So to Les Halles they went, Pirouette's hands now warmed by hot water from a minaret-like automated fountain on the Place des Victoires. Passing a lonely, mysterious column, they entered Les Halles, the Central Market and its rows of massive square pavilions that were, at this time of night, only alive with fleeting shadows of sweepers and *persilleuses*, the local prostitutes. The other side of Les Halles was a maze of dark, narrow, dirty streets lined with slanting hovels whose ground floors bulged as if reaching to crush passers-by between their sodden, cankered walls. From time to time, a door opened, revealing the hellfire of a cabaret and a warm gust of roasted food, reminding Brentford that it was well past dinnertime. Not that the place was appetizing. One of Haussmann's Labours was supposed to have been cleaning these Augean stables, but thirty years later, some islets had obviously managed to resist the soapy flood of progress. Here, Brentford surmised, you could breathe the true air of Paris, as long as you were careful not to breathe too much of it.

The rue Pirouette was in the worst area of them all. Its little namesake indicated a house with a door barely held by its hinges. Inside, a smell of cabbage and cat's urine filled the winding staircase, which had a greasy rope for a banister. Brentford absorbed the shock and then, Pirouette in tow, went up the creaking steps to the third floor. He could feel, in the half-dark, the child nervously twisting her hand in his.

He banged on the door, feeling a little stage fright.

The blowsy, disheveled hag who opened the door was so true to type that she seemed to have sprung from Brentford's reading rather than from the dismal garret where she lived. The ceiling was low and its beams black with smoke. A table covered with a filthy waxed cloth, a few ill-assorted chairs, and a repulsive kelp mattress on a frame of white wood were the only furniture. A cast-iron stove, on which gurgled a stew that smelled vaguely of mutton, smoked the room more than heated it. Stuck to the ragged wallpaper, a yellowish picture cut from a journal showed General Boulanger, the addicted dandy who had almost become president a few years before but had shot himself upon his mistress's grave instead. It would have to do as a romantic touch, surmised Brentford.

"Yes, what is it?" the woman asked, a whiff of cheap absinthe on her breath. She had a flat, flushed face under the knot of snakes that was her hair, and looked a solid fifty but could well have been younger. Brentford felt faintly nervous, until he realized that he was less scared of the woman herself than of her misery.

She frowned at Pirouette's presence, but as soon as she had identified Brentford as a man with money, rather than a *julot*—a policeman from the vice squad—she warmed to him accordingly.

"What have you brought here?" she asked her daughter, revealing a few missing teeth in a forced attempt at a smile. Brentford tried to remember that she was a poor woman, with a life of hardships, and probably had as bad a start as her daughter was getting now, but still he found her repulsive.

"It was actually I who brought her here," Brentford explained, eager to put an end to any misunderstanding. "I do not think a child of this age should run the streets at night, and especially on such an errand."

The woman frowned.

"What business it is of yours?" she asked malevolently.

"The business that your daughter wanted very much from me."

"What!" the mother said, slapping the child before Pirouette could retreat behind Brentford's back. "Look at that dirty little strumpet! I told you not to pester men."

Brentford felt a surge of anger but managed to control it. He simply raised his hand. "Please. That's not necessary. We both know what the situation is."

"Why? Is she accusing me? You are so damn ungrateful!" she howled at Pirouette, before pointing at her. "She is a true bitch in heat. It's the blood of her father, that goddamn degenerate drunk."

"Listen!" Brentford insisted, flashing an imposing pink and blue hundred-franc banknote. On its back, an allegory showed Wisdom vainly trying to hold back Wanton Fortune—good luck to her, thought Brentford.

The mother's eyes widened as she were St. Bernadette, and Wanton Fortune was the Holy Virgin.

"This is yours if you promise me that you will take proper care of this child and not send her onto the streets again," Brentford explained, with the nagging feeling that he was at the fifth act of some awful melodrama. "May I have your word of honour?"

The mother sniggered at the word *honour*, but grasped the note.

"Sure," she said.

"You promise?"

"Whatever you want, Milord."

Pirouette was sobbing behind Brentford. He took her by the shoulders and placed her in front him. He could feel her trembling.

"Now, Pirouette. There's money in the house and no need for you to earn it as you did. If there are any problems, you can come and see me," he said, bending down to murmur in her ear the name of the hotel.

He patted her on the head, then lightly pushed her forward. His conscience did not feel as good as it should have, he thought. And as the curtain fell, nobody applauded.

He pretended to go down a few steps, but then, following his instinct, remained hidden in the smelly shadows. He did not have to wait very long before he could hear the first screams and blows, and Pirouette's yells and yelps of anguish and pain.

With a sigh, he climbed back to the landing, and without bothering to knock on the door, pushed it open with his foot. Since candour had failed, he thought he'd try the cloak-and-dagger approach.

The mother froze in the act of hitting the huddled-up Pirouette with her long-handled ladle. Brentford resisted smacking her, but instead pulled the little girl to her feet and dragged her to the door. As soon as he turned his back, the mother started to howl.

"Stop, thief! He's stealing my child!"

Brentford turned back with a sigh, and to his utter disbelief heard himself declaim, "Say as much as another word, and I'll push your double chin straight through to the back of your throat."

At this, the mother went berserk and, jumping on Brentford, started pummeling him. He parried the blows as best he could, but still found himself unable to return them. Then suddenly the air vibrated with a G-sharp *bong*. The mother crumpled to the floor, revealing Pirouette standing behind her on a chair with a greasy frying pan in her minuscule hands. The cloak-and-dagger drama had, it seemed, turned into a Guignol show.

"Great," Brentford whispered to his panting self, after checking to make sure that Madame was still breathing. She was, and poisonously so.

"I guess she'll be sleeping it off," he said to Pirouette, who, still standing on the chair, waited anxiously for his verdict. She nodded, reassured.

"Poor mummy," he heard her say, as she stepped down.

Brentford dragged the mother onto her kelp mattress, and Pirouette tucked her in beneath the dirty grey cover. He watched her kiss her mother's sweaty forehead, while he pondered the mysteries of love.

"Perhaps we should go," he said, with a dim view of his next step. "At least, Princess Pirouette, let me take you for a dinner."

Pirouette's face lit up, and she rose to put her hand on his extended forearm with a princely, haughty, clownish look. That hand, though, was still trembling from terror.

*

Brentford did not want to outstay his welcome in Les Halles, but he quickly realized that he would have trouble getting into any of the city's proper restaurants with a ragged, dirty little girl at his side, whereas it should not prove too much of a problem in these godforsaken surroundings. And if he had been looking for a sign about which course to follow, he quickly found it: the first cabaret they stumbled upon was called—if one was to believe the tin-plate angel that floated above the door—the Ange Gabriel. This will do, decreed Brentford. A little magical thinking never hurt anyone.

The *entresol* looked like an ordinary wine shop, but its sinister-looking patrons marked it out as something of a flash house. Ambushed behind the brambles of their sauce-drenched moustaches, they eyed the incoming pair with a knowing, mocking look that Brentford found especially unpleasant. After mumbling something about dinner, Brentford was directed to a spiral staircase on the left, and from there into a small room, narrow as a corridor, where, miraculously, a piano had been crammed. The marble tabletops were scribbled with graffitied names and hastily sketched profiles, and the decor, Brentford reflected, would have entertained Gabriel immensely. Painted with dubious taste on a dozen panels, it told the story of the archangel coming to Paris and being seduced by a legion of scantily clad, frivolous women.

Pirouette knew the place and reassured him as to the clientele. Most of them, she explained in the tone of a child who recites her *leçon de choses*, were just workers who were paid to pass as pimps or thugs—so as to provide the extra thrill to the bourgeoisie who came slumming to this place. The little scholar of Parisian low life was less encouraging, however, about a fellow who was sitting with a woman a few tables away from them. He was tall and well built, with curly black hair and a long hooked nose that was pegged on a strikingly noble face. He was the literal incarnation of the words "sublime" and "demigod" by which Parisian Workers often designated themselves, and seeing him made Brentford think of a fallen prince.

"It's Bath-au-Pieu," whispered Pirouette conspiratorially.

"What?" asked Brentford, whose French slang was limited to the few colourful words Gabriel had taught him.

"It means Swell-in-the-Sack, Good-in-Bed, you know," said Pirouette, patiently, as if talking to a child. "My mother says he is indeed. She loves him to death, like every other woman I know. He's been circling around me a lot recently," she explained, not without a little pride. "But I think my mother is jealous and won't let him do anything. Isn't he handsome?" she added dreamily.

As a waiter who looked fresh out of jail served them a piece of mutton that looked freshly dug from a limestone pit, he remembered that the little girl in front of him was not quite the little girl he would like to think she was. Moreso, since he had imprudently called her "princess," there was something faintly flirtatious in her behaviour, made all the more pathetic by her cute, cheeky face, so babyish and snow-chapped.

"I've got a joke for you," he announced, desperately trying to steer the conversation towards more wholesome topics. "Do you know why the Eskimos do this when they're watching something in the distance?" he asked, placing his hand above his eyes like a canopy. Thank God for Interpherence, he thought.

"No," she said with an instant smile. "I give my tongue to the cat." Probably another of those repulsive French expressions, thought Brentford with distaste.

"Because . . ." Brentford answered solemnly, flattening his palm against his eyes, "If they did this, they would see nothing."

She looked at him with a forgiving smile. "My turn," she said. She pinched her small chin between two fingers, till it bulged and showed a little cleft in the middle. "What's this?"

Brentford shook his head.

"My baby sister's slit."

Oh, God, he thought. But, laughing at his wince, she had already switched to another game.

"And do you know this?" she said, now very excited.

She had taken her napkin, and unfolding it, moved it up and down like a theatre curtain behind which her face appeared and disappeared in turn, with a new expression between each eclipse. Anger, Pity, Joy, Surprise, Despair, Pleading, Wonder followed each other on Pirouette's contorted face, as if on one of Charcot's mad models.

"The Faces of Paris," she said, with a laugh. "A game my dad used to play with me."

Suddenly, her look darkened. "My mother will kill me if I go back. Seriously, she will. I don't want to go back."

"Maybe you don't have to," Brentford reflected. "I can put you up somewhere, just long enough for things to calm down a little."

Pirouette looked at him dubiously. He could see her child's mind trying to think in the long term, but for her the long term, however she looked at it, didn't seem that long. And why would it be, in that den of iniquity, in that Parisian Babylon? Although Paris was no more Babylon than it was the New Jerusalem. All cities worthy of that name were both: they were one because they were the other, just as New Venice was—or would be. Blankbate may well be right on that account, Brentford mused—and promptly began to worry about the Scavenger's whereabouts . . .

Lost in his thoughts, he had vaguely noticed that Swell-in-the-Sack and his lady (probably of the peripatetic persuasion as well) had moved from their table, but he was surprised to find the tall fellow suddenly standing next to his table and talking to Pirouette.

"Well, well, look who's here," he was saying. "The little Pirouette in flesh and bones. Not much of either, though, eh?" He pinched her cheek, but it was her whole face that blushed at the compliment.

"Good evening, Monsieur," said Brentford, coldly.

"Congratulations. You found yourself quite a trump," the other said, speaking to Pirouette as if Brentford weren't even there. Swell-in-the-Sack turned to his companion, a buxom brunette with so much makeup on her face that she looked like a painted wooden saint. "Didn't I tell you, Marie-Honnête, that this child was a phenomenon of intelligence?" He patted Piroutte's head. "You don't have your two feet in the same clog, eh? You're truly your mother's daughter."

"Come on, Saturnin," the girl said. "Leave them alone. You're going to be late for the march."

"Sure. G'bye to the company," said Swell-in-the-Sack, with a smug smile that Brentford felt like ripping off his face.

Eventually, Brentford said to Pirouette, "Maybe it's getting late," wondering faintly whether he had kept his calm or simply chickened out. People were streaming into the room, and someone had even started banging on the piano. "Why don't you come with me? We'll find space at my hotel, or somewhere else, while your mother returns to her senses."

Pirouette nodded and finished her stew with a slurp that was reassuringly childish.

Brentford was happy to leave the rat-trap of Les Halles, even if the stew had proved excellent. But after the Ange Gabriel, even the damp, cold air felt bracing and healthy. Twenty seconds later, however, it just felt damp and cold, and Brentford hurried south towards the Seine, Pirouette in his wake. Just as they arrived at the Fountain of the Innocents, they came across a long convoy of carts watched over by a detachment of Alpine Hunters, the same kind of troops that Brentford had been seeing patrolling three by three everywhere in the city. Paris, without really admitting it, seemed to be living in a subtle state of exception, and was visibly bracing itself for the worst. The shadowy carts, he noticed, were all filled with vegetables: under the electric glare, the beets, leeks, and onions shone like rubies, emeralds, and gold, and, it seemed, had already become as precious. It was something that he could perfectly relate to as former head of the New Venice Greenhouses, but as an exile in ill-prepared Paris, it rather worried him.

Continuing south, they passed the black, ominous, secretive monolith that was the St. Jacques Tower, then crossed the frozen Seine. Brentford inhaled the scene: the slithering strip of rubbly ice, the polysyllabic bridges, measured like classical verse, and the jumble of steeples, columns, and chimneys that crushed and folded eras upon one another and pushed them towards the vanishing point where ice stopped and night began. The lights, diffused in the clouds above, shone over the city with the muted glow of a rusty Aurora, and suddenly, with a touch of vertigo, Brentford saw Cabot Canal, New Venice's Grand Canal, and the palaces that rose along it, with their bas-reliefs and caryatids suddenly made alive by the brush of the rosy lights. The Aurora played on the frozen canal, tinting it with the faintest ghostly hues, as if a rainbow had been trapped under the ice . . .

"Monsieur . . . Monsieur . . ."

Brentford shook off the vision and found himself back in Paris, a shiver from New Venice still twisting like ivy round his spine.

"Sorry," Brentford said to Pirouette, who, wearing his gloves, which were five sizes too big, held out her hand for him to hold.

It was only when they arrived on the other side of City Island that they saw the torchlight procession. There were perhaps forty men. The torches in their hands shed a furious, restless light on their long fur overcoats and revealed that they were wearing wolf or dog masks that recalled to Brentford the Egyptian god Anubis. Several of them drew a sledge, on which was mounted, as if on a throne, a white-bearded man in a wheelchair, and on its wheels, Brentford noticed, a spiral had been painted. Behind the throned man, a tall rectangular shape stood upright under a long dark drape. The whole parade was entirely silent, which made it still more awesome.

The Loups des Bois de Justice, Brentford understood.

Two *sergents de ville*, huddled in their cloaks, watched it from the parapet above the Seine. Brentford tried to draw closer.

"I thought the torchlight processions had been forbidden," said the first policeman.

"That goes to show the nerve they've got. And right under the Préfecture."

Brentford realized with sudden terror that, indeed, he stood just across from the Police Prefectorate, and this while holding the hand of a ragged nine-year-old girl who was obviously not his. He almost expected Tripotte to come out at any minute, with that drippy grin of his, but luckily, all of the policemen were busy trying to make sense of the procession. With the slightly exaggerated gait of someone who wants to prove to the world that his conscience is clean, he briskly took Pirouette across to the other bank, and back towards the Grand Hôtel des Écoles, on the rue Delambre.

✻

After another stop at a *chauffoir* on the rue Vaugirard, where paupers huddled to warm themselves at braziers, Brentford and Pirouette finally arrived at the hotel. Entering his suite with Pirouette in tow, Brentford was surprised to find Gabriel, Lilian, Tuluk, and the Colonel all in agitated consultation, while the silent Blankbate, still wearing his joke-shop disguise, remained seated in a corner. Brentford remembered their pact of silence and kept his questions to himself. For the time being, he felt contented enough just to see his flock gathered.

"Sorry I'm late," he said. "May I introduce you to Pirouette?"

The little girl made a comical curtsey to the crowd. As she lifted her eyes, Brentford could see that she had fallen for Lilian immediately.

"It really is an incredible story . . ." he started to say, not knowing where to begin the tale of his day.

Gabriel interrupted him gently.

"The Seven Sleepers are in Paris, Brentford."

To be continued . . .

EPISODE VIII

THE CITY OF BLOOD

I

The Vampires of La Villette

Thomas Paynes-Grey and Blanche de Bramentombes stepped down from the cab and joined the dozens of people waiting in line at the gate of the Villette abattoir. Dawn had just broken somewhere behind a pearl-grey sky, and the morning air felt like a dip in icy water.

Thomas yawned and stretched.

"You mean you have to do this every morning?" he asked, vaguely regretting his offer to escort her.

"Twice a week, on killing days," she answered. "Or so the doctor says. But it is rare that I have someone to accompany me. You are so kind." She rested her gloved hand lightly on his good arm.

Thomas nodded and sighed. He watched the people in the queue, some anaemic, some feverish. They would have been much better off if they had stayed in bed, he thought, rather than standing there shivering on the wide, wind-blown avenue that led to the slaughterhouse. Behind the gates, a platoon of Republican foot guards, or *cipaux*, as Blanche called them, were watching the place as if it were the Bank of France, scrupulously checking the little medals that the Villette workers carried on their blouses before letting them in. With the oncoming winter, this might well become a more important place than any bank in the country, Thomas reflected.

Blanche's hand gripped Thomas's suddenly, and then immediately relaxed. She smiled through her veil, but looked nervous and worried.

"Something wrong?" he asked.

"No. Nothing. It's just the cold."

He left it at that, but eventually catching one of her glances he turned in the same direction, and suddenly saw—was that Blankbate, standing on the opposite sidewalk, with a scruffy old bum at his side?

"Don't look," Blanche hissed.

"I know that man," Thomas said. "Excuse me a moment."

"Hello!" he called, striding across the avenue to shake hands with Blankbate. "What are you doing here?"

Blankbate pointed his false beard towards the old man, who was watching Thomas with a look that was both fearful and angry.

"Helping someone," Blankbate said curtly.

"Nice to meet you," Thomas answered good-naturedly, extending his hand to the man, who looked at it with a curious blend of shyness and disdain.

"I'm trying to be discreet," Blankbate said between clenched teeth.

"Oh! Ah! Sorry," Thomas said. "Then good day to you, gentlemen." But Blankbate whispered to him before he could retreat, "Careful with that girl."

Thomas smiled. "Oh, it's worse than you can even imagine," he answered, before moving on. Still, it was the second time he had been warned about Blanche, and it was starting to worry him more than a little. He found her in an atrocious mood when he returned.

"Do you know that old man?" he asked.

"No, I don't," she said coldly. "Let's go. They're opening the gates."

Thomas said nothing, but felt miffed. After he had gotten up in the middle of the night, undergone the torture of cab transportation through impassable streets, and frozen his family jewels—as the French tastefully refer to them—in that no-man's-land at the other end of Paris, well, perhaps he deserved a little more kindness.

With minimal fuss from the *cipaux*, the queue eventually entered the City of Blood through the wrought-iron gate, crossed a wide snow-covered esplanade where stood a lonely clock, and swerved towards the walled slaughter yard. A long row of wooden doors under a glass and iron roof, it was filled with blaring moos of terror and the stench of panic dung.

A brigade of five or six butchers was waiting there, watching the women from the queue with hungry looks that were sometimes returned, and commenting on them in a strange language nobody understood, Blanche excepted.

"It's *louchebem*," she explained, "The Butcher-Boys' lingo."

A *baladeur* brought a red heifer to the gate, and the butchers, ignoring her trembling struggle, attached her halter to a ring on the ground. Thomas could see that they turned the slaughter into a spectacle of pitiless but careful craftsmanship, perhaps less out of respect for the victim than out of the pride they felt in their trade.

A Herculean man wearing an apron and carrying a spiked sledgehammer that Blanche called a "merlin" stepped up and quickly swung his godlike weapon. They heard a dull crunch as it struck the skull; the cow fell to her knees with a dejected *moo* that sounded like a sigh. Almost instantly, one of the boys plunged a poignard into her backbone and the *patron-boucher* deftly slit her throat from end to end. As the blood spurted onto the greasy, dirty floor, Blanche clenched Thomas's arm with such strength that he could feel her nails digging into his flesh.

One of the Butcher-Boys had put a pan under the throbbing gash and collected the blood. In a moment, the "blood-drinkers" began to produce their glasses and cups and hand them to the boy, who filled them and gave them back. Blanche took out of her purse an ornate pewter tumbler carved with her initials, explaining to Thomas that it was a present from her first communion, handed it to the boy, and got it back full of thick, frothy blood. Fascinated, Thomas watched Blanche lift her veil and drink from her tumbler. She noticed his stare, and her gory lips blew him a kiss. "You should try it," she said, adding playfully, "It's very good for men."

"Thank you. I won't need it with you," Thomas answered, with his best boorish gallantry.

By and by, the satiated queue disbanded. Blanche lingered a little while, ogling the scene, trembling, as the butchers started to eviscerate the dead animal. She even exchanged a few garbled words with a tall, well-built, hook-nosed fellow, who called her "Lanche-bluche." Thomas observed him with jealous zeal, as the man went on to whisper something to the *patron-boucher*, before leaving him with a curious sign of the hand, a zero or circle traced with index finger and thumb.

"We should be heading back," Thomas said sombrely. The whole morning, and his strange meeting with Blankbate, had left him ill at ease; nothing that a good shot of morphine wouldn't fix, though.

"Hmm . . . Yes . . . You'll take me home, of course?" Blanche asked with an inviting smile as she let down her veil.

II

New Venice Revisited

That morning, Brentford had remained at the hotel. Sitting at his desk wrapped in a quilt, he scribbled and sketched in his pink and blue notebooks, jotting down his memories of New Venice, drawing a few buildings, and carefully notating his dreams, because he had realized that they were more vivid than his recollections. The Colonel, on the table, twisted his neck to read what Brentford was writing ("Me, glasses? That would be the last straw!") and commented freely. These were usually Brentford's favourite mornings, and today, with the news that the Seven Sleepers, or at least one of them, might be in town, thrills of excitement ran through his pen, and the pale ghosts of New Venice rose around the room with more substance than usual.

Well into the previous night, the Seven had spoken about New Venice, and Brentford had noticed how little they all knew—himself included—about its foundation. It was one of the Sleepers' most eccentric claims that the city had been built with the help of "supernatural powers"—including stone levitation by Tibetan monks—and, accordingly, the few historical facts surrounding the construction were laced with legends, most of them conflicting, as yesterday's conversation had shown. The chronology of these events was the most difficult thing to reconstruct and, thanks to the Sleepers' intemperate tampering with calendars, nearly impossible to correlate precisely with historical time outside New Venice. If the Sleepers had wanted to make the city as mythical as possible, they had been remarkably successful.

Likewise, an oath of secrecy had been enforced among the first generation of the Two Hundred and Ten Hyperboreans who had "built" and run the fledgling city. The two arcticocratic scions among

235

the Most Serene Seven, Duke Brentford Orsini and Earl Gabriel d'Allier, remembered the oratorical precautions their fathers had used in telling foggy anecdotes about the foundation, and how they had laughed off their own tales afterwards, always insisting that they were probably legend. Brentford's and Gabriel's respective Transpherences had done little to enlighten them, for their fathers—who had lost their own fathers before Transpherence was perfected—had been told the same stories, and their memories remained for their sons fleeting and dim, like half-forgotten dreams. All that could be inferred from these few glimpses was that the city had been born fully formed and had not changed much, insulated from time as it was.

Here, the Colonel's presence became a treasure for Brentford. He had been around for a long time, had actually been one of the Two Hundred and Ten as Baron Branwell, and of course he was now the last of them. His memories had remained relatively intact (perhaps, Brentford thought, because they were from a nearer future) and he was only too happy to tell the story of his coming to New Venice.

"I was not involved in the first stages of the construction," he told Brentford now, "though I arrived early enough to see it before it was finished. It was built in less than ten years, which, given the conditions, was rather amazing."

"And when was that?"

"In 1902 A.D., I think. But given the different calendars, one lost track rather quickly."

"How did you find yourself there?"

"It's a long story. I was serving as a captain in the Second Dragoons, the Queen's Bays, you know, in India and then in Egypt, until 1897—which means I'm not likely to meet my double, like that poor Dr. Lavis—and then in the Second Boer War. I'll spare you the details, but I was wounded, discharged, and given a job in the War Office when I returned to England. I quickly got bored, but then one night I met a woman named Lucy, and got into, shall we say, an intimate relationship with her. It quickly struck me that she seemed to know a lot about me, and by and by, she revealed to me that she was an Ice Nymph."

"A what?" Brentford asked.

"Ah, the Ice Nymphs, young man . . . half-courtesans and half-spies, all beautiful, and well versed in the ways of the flesh. They travelled the whole wide world on behalf of the Polaris Guild to press-gang disaffected young men into going to New Venice. They were very persuasive, believe me. Once you had been chosen, it was more than bad form to refuse—it was also, or so they hinted, a bad idea. If you rejected the offer, your memory of it would have to be erased. They had hairpins that were long and poisonous, and could leave permanent damage in your spine: a life-long palsy that would leave you control only of your eyelids. You would become, in their own term, a snowman.

"But mostly they presented the city in a way that made it *desirable*, see? You discovered that you had always wanted to go there and start anew. And the money was good, too, except that it came from their own mint and couldn't be spent outside New Venice. Of course, they could have told us all that beforehand. But I'm getting ahead of myself here . . .

"The contract was signed in blood. I resigned from the War Office and wrote a few letters to relatives and friends, invoking secret missions to explain my impending silence. It was time to go. 'Will I ever see you again?' I asked Lucy the last time I saw her. 'Of course,' she answered. '*You have a memory, haven't you?*' You will think me a sissy, young chap, but I must say, my heart shrank in my breast like bollocks in a cold bath.

"For the trip, I was allowed a metal canteen and nothing else. We sailed in the early summer while the frozen sea remained mostly open. It was amazingly well organized: the Night Navy, a flotilla of nondescript little icebreakers, looking battered but proving to be rock-solid, shuttled back and forth from different American and European ports. They carried only moderate quantities of goods or citizens, so that the inevitable losses would remain reasonable, and they always sailed by night to keep the whole operation secret.

"Once aboard, officers from the Polaris Guild, in midnight-blue uniforms, gave us our first fur outfits and drilled us on survival tactics—and our understanding of the basic tenets of the New Venetian philosophy. Some dissenters, mostly desperate workers who were in it for the money, had second thoughts about the adventure, and sometimes protested, threatening to tear up their contracts. 'No problem, gentlemen,' the officers said, with polite smiles, 'Once we're there, you'll be free to come back by your own means.' And we, the dreamers and adventurers, already proud of being New Venetians, cackled like schoolboys because the location of 'there' hadn't even been disclosed.

"At first, the trip seemed to go on forever, the hum of the steam engines vibrating through your bones. But as we drew closer, the night disappeared altogether, and cautiously but doggedly, we sailed blinking through the ice, spotting cities at every turn before realizing they were icebergs or mirages. The travelling season was drawing to a cracking close, but at last we arrived, wherever it was we were arriving at.

"An immense ice harbour was built a few yards from the coast, probably carved from a gigantic iceberg, its front shaped like a liner's, its rear ending in pronged piers. A swarm of ships, bobbing like gulls among the floes, were moored and discharged, checked and refilled, and hastily sent back to where they came from, before the sea turned back once more into rugged, infrangible crystal.

"New Venice itself, seen from the ship, seemed to fulfil its improbable promise. It was not entirely finished, but the missing parts were modelled in ice, blending almost seamlessly with the actual buildings. It was inside these immense halls of ice that the new buildings were to be assembled or reconstructed according to the blueprints, before the next batch of material arrived the following summer.

"Up close from the landing pier, though, the city still looked rough and uncertain, the way a boomtown would. The embankments, covered in slush and mud, were scarred with dirty tracks and cluttered with crates and half-assembled machinery. Instead of bridges, wobbling metal sheets crossed empty canals. Work was going on with a sullen, dull clatter that echoed in the leaden sky. I realized for the first time in my life that a city was, above all, hours of merciless labour, one stone upon another.

"For the length of the summer, the harbour throve, thronged with ships carrying building materials, canned food or seeds, together with "Arctic Arks" filled with plants and animals, all selected for their resistance to the cold. Horses were never a big success in New Venice, except to draw the odd sleigh, and I soon found myself leading a company of lancers atop Bactrian camels. We were doing some exploration, some guerrilla fighting with the Inuit—The War with the Eskimos, as it is now grandly called—and not seldom, we chased fugitives or searched for the bodies of the Banished and carefully erased all their traces.

"Because, you see, young man, it was a harsh life. There is no question that the Seven Sleepers, who at that time were still called the Seven Seers, pampered us to the best of their awesome abilities. When I arrived, there were already theatres, concerts, museums, and, most of all, a lot of festivals, parades, and games, celebrating the city or its guilds. Everything was done to give the New Venetians a sense of pride and belonging, and on the whole it was rather successful. But remember that, at that time, the Air Architecture was not yet working, and the winters still took a dreadful toll on us all.

"To tell the truth, in the night season, the ideal city looked more like one of the concentration camps we English had built in South Africa. We were kept warm and entertained, but the lack of women who were not prostitutes, the exhaustion, the low rations, the general ill will that spread between people during the Wintering Weeks . . . it all went to your head. The workers from the Builders' Brigade—for the most part poor people who would have done anything for sixpence—not only brawled among themselves but also, a few times, revolted. And I must add that more than once we lancers were called on to quell that kind of trouble. There were also thefts and murders, but at that stage the Seven Seers were strict disciplinarians. The Gentlemen of the Night had not yet been formed, but there was a secret police force with informers in every nook and cranny. They were totally invisible, and their methods rather expeditious. The Ravens, they were called. A lot of 'accidents' happened, heads broken on slippery embankments, people falling through cracks in the ice and drowning . . . Felons who could not be disposed of in that way were punished with banishment, which simply meant death. Another alternative was to join the dustmen of the city, the Scavengers, who were then beginning to become

Untouchables. But once again, you have to understand it what was the situation needed. It was a city that was no more solid than a mirage."

"Perhaps," suggested Brentford, "you happened to meet the Sleepers? Lord Lodestone, for instance."

"I could have at that time, because when I arrived he was Lord Sunday, the Archon in charge of army and police matters. But in the beginning not all the Seven Sleepers were in New Venice. There were probably one or two at any given time, the rest being busy, I suppose, organizing things from the outer world. I say 'probably' because it was impossible to know. They were hidden away most of the time, and when they appeared, it was always out of the blue, and commanding a hushed awe I've never seen the like of. Even for the Two Hundred and Ten, like me or your grandfather Felice, who were supposedly closer to them, they were almost impossible to see, and only the Council, I suppose, had direct access to them. Even when they were alive, there was already this mystic aura about them, you know.

"However, I did get the chance to meet Lord Lodestone years later, when I became Commander of the Order of the Winged Sea-Lion. He was old then, and one of the last three remaining Seers, but as I remember it, he was still very charismatic and had something very *mischievous* in his eyes. If he ever suspects that there are people in the know, as Mr. Paynes-Grey's ill-considered question at the séance may have led him to believe, I am afraid that we are in a bit of fix as a result. I have seen his ways and he is a brilliant, but also quite dangerous, man. Only a dangerous man, a *very* dangerous man, could accomplish what he did, or, er, will. Never trust his kindness. I am sure he has some for mankind, but not for the part of it that stands in his way."

"I'm not standing in his way. Lord knows I want nothing but his success," Brentford protested.

"I know, young chap. But at this very moment, he is guarding a secret. And he may not like to find out that you know it even better than he does."

III

Magnetophosphenes

After a night of struggle with the Angel of Migraine, Gabriel was in no mood for the Colonel's creaking ramblings, and decided to go back to the Salpêtrière to get his bruised temple examined. It had throbbed for the whole sleepless night, and in the mirror looked swollen and purple, as if a new embryonic brain were trying to grow out of the side of his head. It would be an occasion to see the new Jean-Klein.

"It's not great, but it doesn't seem too bad, either," Jean-Klein reassured him. "Avoid alcohol and drugs, perhaps."

Gabriel pretended that he had not heard. "Is there no way to alleviate the pain? I don't think laudanum is helping much. It's not that painful, but it's so constant that it's driving me mad. Especially above my eye."

"Do you want me to give you morphine, too, like that friend of yours who I see hanging around here every day? Charming as he is, I'll soon have to kick him out of the place if he doesn't kick the habit himself."

"No, thanks. I prefer short-lived habits."

Jean-Klein thought about it for a while, then said at last, "I may have something for you. It's a new therapy, which I find very promising but which is still in the testing stage. They're looking for volunteers."

"And that would be?"

"Magnetotherapy. Magnetic fields that are applied to the body, directly or indirectly, and seem to be efficient against various types of ailments. I hear it's especially spectacular against muscular aches and neuralgias."

"It sounds a lot like suggestion, doesn't it?" Gabriel teased Jean-Klein.

"Except suggestion has nothing to do with it!" the intern protested pleasantly. "Our body is electrical by nature, so isn't it only logical that it would react to electrical or magnetic stimulation? It's happening in the Collège de France. The laboratory of Dr. Jacques-Arsène d'Arsonval. In fact, if you like, I'll take my afternoon off and take you there. D'Arsonval is giving his *leçon*, and we can speak with him afterwards. That said, it may be more interesting for me than it is for you."

✳

The Collège de France was located opposite the Sorbonne, midway up the rue St. Jacques.

In a bare, yellowish classroom occupied by thirty or so happy few, d'Arsonval, half hidden behind a drooping moustache that made him look like an ancient Gaul, delivered a densely technical lecture involving the use of a "telephonic muscle"—or *myophone*—from a frog's leg and used to transmit the human voice. Oh, those ingenious Frenchmen, thought Gabriel. Never a dull moment.

The audience, though sparse, was elite, Jean-Klein explained. "That man over there is Étienne-Jules Marey, the inventor of the chronophotographic gun."

Brentford looked at him. "The . . . ?"

"Chronophotographic gun. A rifle to shoot not birds but pictures of them—it's a camera with a revolving cylinder. He's one of our greatest geniuses, in my humble opinion. And there, that's Berthelot, a great chemist. He's slated to be part of the next government, too."

Recognizing Jean-Klein as one of his warmest supporters, d'Arsonval was—as predicted—kind enough to receive him after the class, together with his protégé, taking them to his laboratory: a large, whitewashed, orderly place, full of generators, accumulators, resonators, and Leyden jars. A coil, looking like a cage, was suspended by pulleys from the roof—a device that would have made a mad scientist jealous. Somewhere near the laboratory, cats were howling desperately as they were taken from their cages for experiments, Gabriel supposed. "Personally, I use rabbits," d'Arsonval said, with a wince. "Much less noisy."

He examined Gabriel and checked his blood pressure. "Ah, migraine . . ." he sighed, scratching his scalp under his not very academic casquette. "One of the biggest mysteries . . ."

He motioned Gabriel towards a chair set in a wooden frame placed directly beneath the coiled cage, which was then lowered down around his head. Gabriel wasn't too keen on the sensation. He thought of the howling cats.

"It is a new method I am developing, which I hope will be less cumbersome than electrotherapy and equally efficient," d'Arsonval explained, as he toggled a lever on a white panel full of dials. "The subject is exposed to a strong alternative electromagnetic field. Unlike electricity, the magnetic flow is not attenuated in the body, which is, so to speak, transparent to it. As for the use of low frequency, it causes no sensation of heat nor even muscular contractions, and it is really analgesic and quite sedative."

From time to time as he spoke, d'Arsonval checked the various meters and adjusted the dials by minuscule increments. "Now, the problem," he said, "is that organs and nerves react to very specific frequencies, just as the retina or the eardrum do not respond to vibrations that are either too slow or too fast. So we always have to twiddle a little before we get the right setting, but there's hardly a place in the body that we can't reach this way."

Gabriel felt himself reddening, as if ashamed, and his face started to sweat. Whatever was happening was not painful, but neither was it comfortable. He could feel something like a tugging or a crawling on the top of his scalp, and a slight pressure on his left eye, as if someone were holding the ocular globe between grubby fingers. He closed his eyes.

Then, suddenly, before he could say anything to d'Arsonval, his eyelids were filled with sparks. Fireworks of luminous dots and filaments, gold and green, exploded in his retinas, eddying into ever-changing, three-dimensional figures. The surrounding blackness heaved and deepened as they did, forming a fluctuating space, where the dots and lines aligned themselves, scattered, and regrouped again, sketching different patterns that remained abstract, but, if Gabriel focussed, turned into more concrete visions. Fountains. Mountains in the old Chinese style. Terraced fields. Trees in the breeze. The outline of a city.

Vertigo seized him.

"I see light," Gabriel announced.

"Ah, magnetophosphenes!" d'Arsonval explained with enthusiasm. "The magnetic flow excites your retinal neurons. It enhances what Helmholtz calls *luminous chaos*, the spontaneous lights that your retina produces. Very interesting. Perhaps it enters in resonance with the frequency of your eyeballs. Let me check the numbers; I'll have to remember them. Thirty amperes, forty-two cycles per second," he said, jotting down the figures on the page. "How are you, Mr. d'Allier? Stay with us . . ."

But Gabriel said nothing. He watched the city that had just etched itself right under his eyelids like a engraving made of black and bright light.

"Home," he whispered, before fainting.

IV

The Astral Plane

In the dreary, skyless afternoon, Brentford went back to visit Edgar de Couard in Ménilmontant. He had to knock for a long time before he was let in.

"Forgive me," whined the painter, stooping and casting furtive looks towards his guest while leading him inside the house. "I was doing my exercises."

"Exercises?"

"Yes. Vision has to be exercised. It is a muscle like any other."

"Vision? As in eyesight or . . . second sight?"

"Clairvoyance, if you prefer," de Couard muttered almost inaudibly. "The art of the future will be visionary or it will be nothing. You see, Impressionism has been a wonderful step forward, but it was totally pledged to the here and now. The same was more or less true of Pointillism, with all its dreary social concerns. But there's more to Man than reality, don't you think? Now Painting has to win back the realms of Unreality. Do you know Moreau? Redon?"

"Vaguely," Brentford admitted. "But what you showed me yesterday was rather realistic. I mean in the way it was painted."

"Imagination deserves to be expressed as acutely as any other reality. It has to become reality, and not only for the sight, but for all the senses," de Couard said, blushing at his own ambition as if he were confessing some shameful sin.

They entered his studio. In the middle of the room, wide canvases hung side by side, wired from a roofbeam, each one bearing a different, simple symbol: a black reversed egg on a white backdrop; a blue circle on red; a silver crescent on a black ground; a yellow square on a shade of indigo; and a triangle, red on green. They were painted with such pure tones that they vibrated in the space and made Brentford blink—the figures seemed to hover above the background and their fringes pulsed as if the colours might run in the air. The blue circle, especially, sucked Brentford in, and he felt he could almost hear the static crackling of its wavelength. He closed his eyes, and the after-image exploded in red, like a flaming sunset.

"My," Brentford said. "These are certainly potent. What are they?"

"These symbols are *tattvas*," de Couard whispered. "Ether winds that make matter vibrate according to their waves. Each one of them is connected to an element or sense, and can enhance its powers."

Brentford remained dubious.

"So you're an initiate of the Eastern mysteries? A theosophist?"

De Couard timidly shrugged his shoulders.

"Madame Blavatsky has left rather mixed memories here, but I think that in spite of the theosophists the Eastern tradition has been less muddled and abused than the Western one. So far, that is. I'm not exactly a theosophist, but I am . . ." he hesitated, but saw no reason not to go on, "an *adeptus minor* of the Hermetic Order of the Golden Dawn, a British organization that has recently founded its first lodge in Paris. They were the ones who introduced me to Tattvic Vision. It is part of their curriculum."

"Golden Dawn. It reminds me of something."

"Ah, it is successful at the moment, I must say. Paris is a city of Isis and seems to remember it," he answered, seeming reluctant to say more. "To go back to the *tattvas*, they function as doors to the astral plane. What attracted me to them is that they work according to the very same principles of complementary colours that rule modern painting. You concentrate on one of these symbols until the complementary colours flash on your retinas, allowing the vision. Just as in pointillism or in anaglyphs, truth emerges from the coincidence of opposites."

"Amazing," Brentford mumbled politely. It always surprised him to realize that his immediate distaste for this kind of nonsense was more like a protective reflex against his own fascination with it.

"The symbol becomes a door, through which you can project yourself into the astral plane."

"Astral plane? That's a phrase I hear often, these days. Dr. Encausse—Papus—whom I met recently, seemed to use it a lot."

"Oh, sorry. I forgot you were not an initiate," de Couard answered, as haughtily as his shyness allowed. "Though I suppose knowing Papus is an initiation in itself. There's not a single lodge he is not part of, I guess. Even the Golden Dawn, though it is my belief he is only there to check on the concurrence. I suppose having him around is part of the deal if you want to be a part of the occultist scene in Paris."

"And the astral plane would be . . . ?"

De Couard was surprised by the candid ignorance of the question. "It is the intermediate plane between our sublunar world and pure Divinity. It is filled with all things future and past, angels, demons, elementals, and spirits of the dead, but also with the images we produce, our dreams, our fantasies. Your astral body, or plastic mediator, can access this plane, just as it does in dreams. But the visions are limited, as if seen through a microscope, and purely symbolic, and to be interpreted as such. Only the trained yogi can find himself at will among its actual events, living them with all his senses."

"Is the astral plane . . . a real space?" Brentford asked, trying to understand.

"Ah. Space, like time, is a form of our sensibility, and strictly pertains to matter. Let us say that these planes are spaces removed from time and place. The space of the images is itself but an image of Space. It's only logical."

Is it really? Brentford wondered. Still, he found himself wanting to know more. "Is the technique difficult to master?"

"It is the simplest and the most efficient of techniques. If you are disciplined, that is, and respect the order of the *tattvas* during the day," the painter answered, indicating on the wall a round calendar full of sibylline-like symbols.

"And this Rimbaud City? You saw it by using this method?"

"It is, I believe, what Rimbaud himself saw. I simply retrieved it from that huge emporium of images recorded in the astral plane," de Couard explained, with what he evidently thought was modesty.

Brentford mulled it over for a while, then said, "If you remember, I spoke to you yesterday about a commission. That commission is also about a city. I've made a few sketches." He flashed his notebook and the drawings he had done there in brown ink. Perspectives, buildings, vistas of New Venice, as well as he could remember them now. "These are a few ideas I jotted down. It's imaginary, of course," he reassured de Couard.

"Imagination, memory, premonitions—these differences do not exist on the astral plane."

"I'm glad to hear that. But, let's say I want to 'see' more of that city. Could I use those techniques?"

"That is what they are meant for."

"Would the Golden Dawn teach them to me?"

"If you're initiated as a neophyte, yes. I do not think there would be any problem," de Couard said, before falling silent for an embarrassing while.

"And you mentioned . . . Isis?" Brentford went on to break the spell.

"It is the cult they celebrate. The lodge is called Ahathoor, which is sometimes but another name for Isis. But the name doesn't matter. It's all symbols, isn't it?"

Brentford agreed, remembering the three heads of Hathor he had seen at Place du Caire. There was a strange method to the madness of Paris.

"So, would you be so kind as to introduce me there?"

"I . . . I seldom go out now. My nerves do not allow it. It is the curse of the aesthete, these days. As I said, I'll send you there with a recommendation, yes. But . . ." he fumbled for words, ". . . I would recommend that you maintain a certain prudence. The Golden Dawn claims that it has established contact with one of the Three Secret Chiefs. The Secret Chiefs, Mr. Orsini . . . Do you realize? The most powerful people on Earth, ruling secretly over the destinies of Mankind. This could be very dangerous."

V

The Operator

L ater that evening, at 87 rue de Rome, a veiled lamp and cigarette smoke gave the living room a cosy but other-worldly atmosphere. The guests moved against the light in indefinite silhouettes, sometimes stilted, sometimes vapourous. A conversation was going on, muffled and solemn, its hum almost a chant.

The master stood near the chimney, a small man simply but elegantly dressed in a black jacket and a floppy tie, holding high a grizzled head with the pointy ears and beard of a faun. Gabriel, although a bit hungover from his magnetic revelation, couldn't help feeling a thrill as Paul introduced him and he shook hands with Stéphane Mallarmé.

"Mr. d'Allier? There is the sweetest French ring to it. You come to us from Canada?" the poet inquired.

"From Newfoundland. We are our own people."

"Newfoundland . . . Canada . . . these are beautiful names for an equally beautiful idea. It is my theory, you see, that English is the perfect alchemical blend of Anglo-Saxon and the *langue d'oïl*. It was the French of the Normans that, grafting itself onto the barbaric Saxon tongue, gave it its most magnificent blossoming. And, in these new countries, where both English and French are intertwined again, it is as if English were bathing itself in the fountain of its own youth, and as if French were remembering the buried treasures it had thought forgotten. If I were you, I would be grateful to live in a land where they could be restituted and shared anew."

Gabriel was interested, but still tongue-tied, so contented himself with nodding. After all, Mallarmé probably preferred to hear himself talk and, visibly, was used to the fawning wonder that greeted the least of his utterances. The Poet's demeanour was cordial, but it was that kind of facile cordiality that seemed to raise a barrier between beings, rather than open one, and there was an unmistakable touch of haughtiness in the way it offered itself. He was exactly as his legend had it, no doubt because he had been chiselling himself relentlessly into his own statue. His presence was powerful, but Gabriel sensed that this, too, was a well-rehearsed act. The man had constructed himself like an obscure, tricky poem. And though Gabriel was impressed, his feelings before the poet were nothing compared to what he felt when, turning away, he recognized among the crowd the tall, thin figure and drooping moustache of Louis d'Ussonville.

What on Earth—if that was where they still were—was the Sleeper doing here? He had been brought by an equally tall, sharp-featured, clever-looking fellow whom Vassily identified as the famous anarchist art-critic and writer Félix Fénéon, in whose office at the Ministry of War detonators had once been found. Thanks to the testimony of Mallarmé, among others, at the resultant trial, he had been freed, but a whiff of black powder still hung about him.

At the time Fénéon was one of the most ardent defenders of the avant-garde, and, as Paul explained, he often brought patrons ready to invest in Mallarmé's plan to reintroduce poetry into the "political economy," not so much as a commodity but as a lay religion or popular cult. The idea was that rich patrons would pay Mallarmé a nominal sum in recognition of his "moral right" to offer his books cheaply to the masses, thus reconciling elitist tastes and the democratic public.

It all sounded very New Venetian to Gabriel, and things slowly began to click. He knew d'Ussonville's reputation as a fanatical hunter, as an expert on the fur trade, forestry, and mining, and, most of all, as a wizard of real estate—but not as a connoisseur of poetry or art. There had to be another explanation for his presence here. He had to be scouting for ideas to experiment with in the north of nowhere: how to blend art, politics, and economy into the total work of art that would be New Venice. And suddenly it dawned on Gabriel that nothing was sure yet, that nothing about New Venice had been decided, and his thrill turned to full-blown excitement. Right now, New Venice was nothing but possibility. Maybe there was a way for them, the

Most Serene Seven, to help—not only to make sure the city came to exist, but that it would become the New Venice they were dreaming about. And for a vertiginous moment, he thought: What if that's how it actually *did* happen? What if the New Venice we know is the one we suggested ourselves . . . ?

"I think the lecture will be starting momentarily," Vassily reminded Gabriel, as he stood there gaping.

The party moved into another room, where chairs had been arranged in rows, and Gabriel manoeuvred to keep d'Ussonville in his sight without being too conspicuous. Mallarmé, now styling himself "the Operator," sidled in between the chairs and the wall and stood behind a large Empire table that was set before a lacquered bookcase. With the unctuous, thoughtful movements of a Catholic priest, the Operator removed from the bookcase some large sheets of paper, which he then arranged in a different order—the "Book," if Gabriel had understood correctly, was the sum of all possible permutations—before reading them aloud in a high-pitched but otherwise neutral voice that let every word ring for itself in the expectant air.

What the Book was about, however, Gabriel hardly knew. Figures on a beach, feasts . . . He wished he could concentrate more. After all, he was living an event that was thought never to have occurred, and instead of sucking out its very marrow, he was distracted by the presence of d'Ussonville, trying to read on his face which passages were of interest to him. He was especially attentive, Gabriel noticed, as Mallarmé read:

"Vision, magnificent and sad! The Ruins of a great palace—wide as a city—or a city made of one single palace.

This is what the echo answers—double and deceptive—when asked by the travelling spirit of the wind.

All that we know is that—the tenebrous past lies there—and indeed, the desert took it back—unless it lies in the future, closed to human eyes, down there, at the bottom.

The façade—a double fountain—where the sleeping, doomed People—do not come to mirror themselves anymore."

And then again, a little later, when the poet declaimed about hunting *"the two most untameable beasts, the Polar Bear and the Black Panther,"* Gabriel saw d'Ussonville focussing his eyes with renewed energy.

Gabriel had to wait an excruciatingly long time to get closer to him. Later, there was another lecture—or "séance" as Mallarmé called them—meant as a commentary on the first, though it did not seem much clearer, notwithstanding the dazzling fulgurations of his words.

This was all followed by excessive homage being paid to the Operator, during which, seeing the poet surrounded, Gabriel considered stealing a page or two of his abandoned text, finally thinking better of it.

At last he was able to approach d'Ussonville as people were beginning to leave. Gabriel was searching his mind for the right introduction when he noticed the knob of d'Ussonville's cane: a golden kangaroo.

"Excuse me, sir," Gabriel said. "I can but be amazed at the likeness of our canes." And he displayed the Polar Kangaroo that topped his own stick.

D'Ussonville seemed surprised, then interested. He took a long look at Gabriel's cane.

"If I'm not mistaken, your kangaroo has a wolf head, doesn't it?"

"Something I saw in a dream."

"Ah. In my case it's simply something I saw in Australia, a place I remember with fondness. In a dream, you say? A bit like what we've been put through here," he added in a low voice.

There was a general bustle, and they found themselves out in the cold mineral canyons of Northern Haussmania.

"A very beautiful dream. I found it personally very enlightening," Gabriel said when he got the chance. "This city that *'lies in the future, closed to human eyes, down there, at the bottom.'* Are we not all dreaming of such a city?"

"Kangaroos. Cities. You dream a lot, Monsieur."

"Perhaps every city started as a dream. I would like to see this one built."

"I think I understand what you mean," d'Ussonville said. "I am currently part of the board that oversees proposals for the 1900

World's Fair. It's certainly an exciting time to make such dreams come true."

"Founding a city, even an ephemeral one, from a dream or a poet's vision . . . Could there be a greater adventure?"

D'Ussonville stopped and looked at Gabriel.

"I don't believe I caught your name . . ."

"Gabriel d'Allier. From Newfoundland, Monsieur."

"Do you happen to know a man called Vialatte at the Canadian Commission?"

"I do indeed. At least, I met him once."

"He may have a job offer for a dreamer. Now if you'll excuse me, I have other appointments."

Gabriel saluted him. But after a few steps, d'Ussonville turned back and, coming closer, told him: "Forgive my indiscretion, but I couldn't help but notice the amethyst ring you wear on your right hand. I find it tastefully done. Where does it come from?"

"From my family. My grandfather on my French mother's side, Joseph Montméroux, was a silversmith."

"Montméroux? Interesting name," d'Ussonville said with a nod. He seemed lost in thought for a while, then eventually said, "One last thing, perhaps. Kangaroos, besides being the exact opposite of the giraffe, as Châteaubriand once remarked rather stupidly, are benign enough creatures. But beware of anything that carries a wolf's head. Goodbye, Mr. d'Allier. Maybe we'll meet in a dream."

VI

Thelema

ours later it was Brentford, not Gabriel, who was to meet Alexandre Vialatte. Their appointment was at nine o'clock at the Abbaye de Thélème, a two-story redbrick house on the Place Pigalle with stained-glass windows that shimmered in the foggy night.

The inside was decorated in Renaissance style, sparing no stucco, and was staffed by homely monks and comely nuns. Tables lined the walls, leaving open a space for dancers, but even though a consort of pluderhosed musicians strummed mandolins in a corner, it was still too early in the night to see much action. The real Pigalle came alive at two, Vialatte explained.

Brentford looked at the lacy arches above his head and felt there was something New Venetian about the place, a defiant challenge to the here and now. No wonder, he reflected, that the Seven Sleepers came here to develop their master plan for a city that would be nowhere and out of time. This was the delicate topic that he wanted to broach.

"So, how is our dominion catching on in Paris?" he began.

"Not so badly. We're trying to make it fashionable. That's the surest way to a Parisian's heart, it seems. We even managed to create a little ice hockey league last year. You remember Meagher, of course—our world champion?"

"Meagher? Certainly," said Brentford, averting his eyes to hide his total ignorance, but not quickly enough for Vialatte to miss it.

"It must be a long time since you've been home?" he asked, managing to make this sound more like curiosity than suspicion.

"Too long, yes."

"But you'll be going back soon? Even if it will be a slightly different country?"

Now, that was going straight to the point. Brentford felt relieved. "There's not much to say about that yet."

"I'd be curious to exchange information, though," Vialatte said in a lower tone. "To speak frankly, I've been offered a part in this adventure, but I would be very, very happy to know more."

"You mean about the Polaris Guild?" Brentford asked haphazardly.

Vialatte nodded. "That could be the name. I'm supposed to recruit people. Maybe you are, too."

"Not exactly. I'm more—*we're* more, like . . . pathfinders . . . looking for ideas." This was as much as he could say without feeling like a liar.

"That was what Lord Savnock gave me the impression of doing."

"Lord Savnock?" Brentford couldn't hide his dismay.

"I am surprised you don't know his name. Or maybe you were a bit disingenuous with me?"

"Oh, I know him all right. What surprises me is his presence in Paris. I am not so highly placed that I was informed of it. I'd be curious to exchange information with you as well."

There was a moment of silence while a supercilious monk served them tournedos Rossini. After he left, Vialatte resumed in a still lower voice.

"Lord Savnock doesn't seem like a man who likes to have his affairs discussed."

"He also goes by the name of Lord Lodestone, by the way."

Vialatte smiled appreciatively. "I knew that much. Lyonel Owain Savnock, Lord Lodestone. What do you know about his background?"

"Nothing. He goes to great lengths to make sure of that."

"He does indeed. But there are public records about his family, including some going back to 1578. It was the time when, in accordance with a fantasy held by John Dee that the English should claim the 'Northern Iles and Septentrional parts' in the name of King Arthur, Martin Frobisher was sent to build a mining colony on Baffin Island, then called Meta Incognita. It was the greatest Arctic expedition in history up to that point—no fewer than fifteen ships. And in the great English style of the Hudsons and Franklins, it failed miserably. Desertions, wrecks, dissension, trouble with aggressive Inuits, the promised gold ore turning out to be vulgar iron, the funders bankrupted . . . Frobisher returned to England, leaving only one single man behind him. Convincing someone to stay had been no easy matter, but Captain Samuel Savnock, one of his wounded lieutenants, eventually accepted, on condition that he would be granted a peerage and title to the yet undiscovered lands between there and the Lodestone that was then thought to be at the North Pole. It may have been little more than a desperate joke by a man who thought he was about to die, but, as a matter of fact, in 1580 Samuel Savnock was posthumously made Lord Lodestone. It was, of course, something of a hoax, or a kind of homage, perhaps, but it did help secure the Northern Isles for the Crown, and it was official enough so that when some years ago one of Savnock's direct heirs claimed the peerage that had been in abeyance until then, the experts could find no fault in his documents. That's how Lyonel Owain Savnock became Lord Lodestone, four hundred years after the death of his ancestor."

"His actual ancestor?"

"You'll have to ask him," Vialatte said with a wink. "Apparently, he turned up out of nowhere—as you noted, not much is known about his own background. He's rumoured to have spent years in Tibet and India and made a fortune there, some say in the opium business. Others think he was in the service of the Crown—secret service, that is. Since opium traffic and Her Majesty's interests tend to go hand in hand, the two hypotheses are hardly contradictory. In any case, his identification paperwork was impeccable, and apparently he had some very high-placed supporters in the British Committee for Privileges and Conduct. Maybe it was not so much the man as his projects that endeared him to them."

"Which were?"

"You know that better than I. You see, even if the English have the knack of making defeats seem heroic, it was almost impossible to do that with their Arctic endeavours. Despite Markham's Farthest North, the Nares expedition of 1875 was rather disappointing.

In 1882, during the International Polar Year, it was the Americans, the Germans, and the Scandinavians who were topping the bill. At that time, there was a lot of talk about a permanent settlement in the North, according to the so-called Howgate Colonization Plan of 1879. It seemed that the horrendous job done by Greeley in Fort Conger had somehow frozen the idea for the Americans, but in England it was seen as the right moment to counteract the growing U.S. influence in the area. The British did not want to appear too directly implicated, and they counted on us, their fledgling dominion, to take care of that barely thawed backwater of their empire. That was why, among other things, they transferred the so-called Franklin District to us last year."

"The Franklin District. What an auspicious name."

Vialatte laughed. "Isn't it? It's a very delicate mission that we inherited. The Arctic, as you know, is not fully explored and is regarded more as an international zone, and every claim upon it has to be handled very carefully in a tense diplomatic environment. Even with the place technically ours, there is little we can do to protect it, because we're still busy drawing our own inner frontiers, and it's no secret to you that we are sadly lacking in both funds and inhabitants. The Far North, for us, is barely a reality, and certainly not a priority. But now, the Crown has discovered someone who could claim the land and, in a way, minister it for them until they can reap its rewards, if there are any, or rid them of it, if not. So, Lodestone was redirected to us, here in Paris, to negotiate farther away from the spotlight."

"Negotiate what?"

"He has some title to the land, of course, but so do we. So we had to reach a gentlemen's agreement—whatever he is, he is certainly a gentleman. So the agreement is that he and his successors were given claim on the Queen Elizabeth Islands for a hundred years, like a tenant. And in a century, we can claim it for ourselves, if we think it's worth the trouble. In exchange, we're offering timber and ore as well as naval facilities. We'll be spared the rest of the costs of exploration and colonization, but when the time comes, it will be ours. Of course, it may be a long time before the Arctic makes sense economically and militarily, but when it does, it is my intuition that it will be *very* precious."

Brentford was wide-eyed. "Fascinating," he said. "I didn't know any of this. What would be the official relationship of the settlement with the Crown?"

"Northwestland, as it is now called, will have a secret status close to that of the dominion of Newfoundland, or a 'dukedominion,' as Lord Lodestone insists on saying, except that the link with the Crown, or Canada, is supposed to remain strictly classified. To the rest of the world, or more exactly to the *very few* who will ever be in the know, it's simply some kind of scientific settlement with volunteers and private money from all over the world."

Brentford nodded, slowly taking it in. It was enlightening—the version of New Venetian history he'd been taught was, like everything else about New Venice, bathed in the mists of myth. Now, he found himself wondering, for example, if the Backwards calendar, or the legend of the Return from Sleep, had anything to do with this hundred-year clause . . .

He asked, "And do you know what Lord Lodestone expects from such a deal?"

"Not really. I used to think it was simply a crackpot's dream that we were trying to use to our own ends. But Lord Lodestone, in the two or three meetings I've had with him, does not appear to be a crackpot *at all*. Eccentric, certainly, but with one of the sanest, soundest minds I've ever encountered. But then, he's English. They all seem sane at first."

"But at least you have a good notion of what his plans are, I suppose?"

"Not really. Even the plans are still very much in the planning stage. From what I gather, his idea is a small settlement, like a town, which would be autonomous for most of its needs. It's his theory that all the previous attempts at settling the Arctic have been thwarted because the first group of settlers was always too small. Lodestone believes you have to start on a certain scale if you want to make things happen—you need all kinds of craftsmen, peasants, workers. Women, of course. Living like humans instead of like animals. It is a rather convincing argument, I think."

Brentford couldn't help wondering if he should he tell Vialatte what Lodestone really had in mind. Vialatte seemed to know nothing about the Seven Seers or even the name New Venice. There was a definite sense that Lodestone was trying to double-cross the world's biggest empire, as well as all the other nations while he was at it. But Brentford, who wanted Lodestone to succeed at any cost, was desperate not to reveal anything that would put the project in jeopardy. True, he felt a little dishonest to withhold anything from the helpful Vialatte, but truth, as Gabriel was fond of saying, is too precious a thing to waste on people who are not ready to appreciate it at its fair value.

"And you?" Vialatte asked. "How did you find yourself involved in all this?"

Brentford mulled it over carefully.

"As I told you, we are doing research."

"But my question was, how did you get involved? You've never met Lord Lodestone yourself, have you?"

Brentford had a sudden inspiration. "I got involved through a man called Felice Rossini, a guide with the Duke of Abbruzes on his mountain-climbing expeditions. He should be on the Guild's list, and if not, you should make sure that he is."

"And how was he informed?" asked Vialatte, noting the name down in his notebook. Brentford felt a chill run down the nape of his neck. Had he just secured his future life in New Venice? It was like watching oneself being born.

"Through the Duke himself, no doubt. He's the kind of character who would be in league with Lord Lodestone."

"That's possible, I suppose," Vialatte answered thoughtfully. Something, it seemed, had not quite convinced him, or maybe he'd noticed the resemblance between the names Rossini and Orsini. "And is your . . . research giving you satisfaction?" he went on.

"There are so many things happening here, it's hard to absorb it all, but, yes, I feel we're making progress. Look at this very place, for instance—the Abbaye de Thélème. It's both extremely realistic, down to the last detail, and at the same time, it's not a real place at all, either in time or space. Maybe this is the kind of things Lord Lodestone is after."

"Perhaps, but the notion doesn't seem particularly suited to polar conditions."

"On the contrary, I would say. The psychological element always played a major part in the downfall of the previous settlements—it was always too many bored, frustrated men, jumping at each other's throats. Mixing men together with an environment that is something more than just ice would be a breakthrough in polar exploration. The lack of beauty or comfort is what drives human beings crazy after a while. The real victory of the human spirit over the coldest, darkest landscape on Earth will be obtained not merely through toil, hardships, and sacrifice, though obviously there will be plenty of those, but also through culture, spirituality, and celebration. These are essential to any human community, and no settlement can go far without them—except back to wilderness and cannibalism, as the Franklin and Greeley expeditions unfortunately proved."

"Though I know Lord Lodestone little, there is something of that in him, very certainly. The aesthete . . . Maybe that is what he wants to create, some sort of ideal city."

"A Thelema," Brentford approved, with a smile.

"Speak of the devil and he doth appear," Vialatte suddenly said, *sotto voce*, while pointing his chin towards the door.

It was Lord Lodestone.

He looked abominably drunk, saluting the columns and squinting as he scanned the room. Waiters nearby tensed, ready to either help or restrain him. Then he saw Brentford and Vialatte and tottered towards them, lifting his cane when he got to their table to point it at Vialatte. He kept it a few inches from Vialatte's nose for an uncomfortable while, staring through eyes half closed, the silver tip of his cane remaining surprisingly steady.

"Sir . . ." Vialatte started, in a tone that seemed pleading. Brentford was transfixed, almost shocked by the way the drunken Sleeper nonetheless radiated strength. The colour of his dark-blue suit seemed to throb off his clothes and pulse in the air.

Then, without saying a word, Lord Lodestone suddenly pivoted and strode from the room.

VII

The Red Castle

Only a few yards away from the splendour of Notre-Dame, the St. Séverin quarter was a knot of narrow medieval streets that even in cold weather smelled like a cesspool. The activity in the greasy ravines zigzagging between the slanting, dark, and cracked houses was on a par with the dereliction of the surroundings: the miserable flea markets were filled with tottering ragpickers, the four-sous restaurants were filled with rejects from Les Halles, and dangerous pimps were making the rounds of the streets around them as calmly as prosperous bourgeoisie out on an evening stroll, while stooped shadows hurried from lushing ken to lushing ken.

Here Crime held its court.

And here, Amédée de Bramentombes was finally keeping his promise to lead Blankbate to the source of the Blackamoor: a café in the meandrous rue Galande called the Château-Rouge, the Red Castle—a red house indeed, also known, invitingly, as "The Guillotine."

It was the temple of *la pente*—the slope, as the French called their low life. And as Blankbate and Amédée stepped from the cold into the large timbered room of the ground floor, Blankbate felt that he was entering an outer circle of hell: an enormous stove puffed turgid heat, its smoke blackening the walls and carrying in its eddies a reek of musk, vomit, and bleach. The thirty or so patrons didn't seem all that dangerous: sleepy old ragged crones; drunkards staring through an absinthe haze; exhausted, sick girls, more or less nude under their coats, one of them, her head on the table, begging her neighbour for the bottom of his drink . . . The dregs of humanity, thought Blankbate, although not without pity. To the right, an opening led to a room that Amédée told him was nicknamed the "Hall of the Dead." In the trembling glimmer from a single-wick lamp hanging from the ceiling, Blankbate could just make out a glimpse of bodies piled up on the clay floor; he could hear them snoring and, occasionally, retching.

But it was another room, visible at the back of the place, that, at Amédée's direction, they headed for. Blankbate could see that, all things being relative, part of this forty thieves' den was somewhat more cosy, with its walls covered with clumsy frescoes depicting a wedding party passing over a bridge. Inside, however, were figures playing cards and drinking spirits. They raised their heads and cast meaningful glances at Blankbate and Amédée as they entered, all of them looking so spectacularly mean that one might have been forgiven for thinking they had been dressed up and paid to look ferocious. Even the Parisian underworld was part of the tourist trail, and Blankbate could see that these thugs had taken their parts to heart.

And so did he. He moved with composure and did his best to look dangerous. Those still staring at him now did so with more interest than menace—they could sense a business proposition in the air.

Among so many unattractive faces, Blankbate could not but be struck by the beauty of one man, sitting at a table with his heavily made-up girlfriend. Amédée noticed Blankbate's stare. "That's the man we're looking for," he said. "Bath-au-Pieu."

They walked to his table, where Swell-in-the-Sack signalled with an elegant gesture that they were welcome to sit down.

"This is the man I told you about," Amédée said to Swell-in-the-Sack, with a nervousness that Blankbate chose to blame on the situation.

Swell-in-the-Sack ignored the ragpicker and turned towards Blankbate, displaying what he considered his best manners. At his side, the girl remained silent, almost motionless, like a doll on a pillow.

"You are new to this place, I suppose, Monsieur."

"Let us say that I am."

"You are lucky to have a man such as our Amédée to show you the sights . . . he knows the city down to the last detail. I also take it that you share his passion for collecting objects."

"That's true. One in particular is of special interest to me."

Swell-in-the-Sack looked straight into Blankbate's eyes, which did not flinch behind his tinted lenses. "Would that be a comb for your false beard?" he asked suavely.

"I'd rather have a false beard than a false front," Blankbate said quietly but confidently.

Swell-in-the-Sack remained silent for a while. "Everyone has his reason to hide what he hides, I suppose," he mused. "Of which particular object do you speak?"

"I think the ragpickers here call it the Blackamoor."

His interlocutor nodded, as if deep in thought. "And do you wish to buy it? Or . . . steal it, maybe?" he eventually asked.

"Whatever it takes."

"I see. Would you . . . kill for it?"

"Are we talking about striking a deal here?"

"We could well be. So?"

"Let's say I'm willing to discuss the price."

"That is reasonable," Swell-in-the-Sack said. "But in a more discreet place. I'll take you to the man in charge, and we'll see what he has to say."

Blankbate hesitated. But he felt he was closing in, and in the end, determination prevailed over prudence. He had come here to do a job, and by the Fisher King, he would do it. "That sounds reasonable," he conceded.

Swell-in-the-Sack stood up and invited Blankbate to follow him.

"Now, Marie-Honnête, you keep this gentleman company," he said to the woman while pointing a long finger towards Amédée. "I think he has a crush on you. And once you're done, don't forget to run a few errands for me. On the sidewalk."

Sniggering, Swell-in-the-Sack entered the first room with Blankbate in tow, then motioned him to the other back room.

"Now, we'll just have to drop in at the Hall of the Dead."

"Is this where the man in charge is?"

Swell-in-the-Sack grimaced, as if he were not at liberty to find the joke funny. "A friend of mine. He's got a key I need. *Stay here.*"

There's something fishy in all this, Blankbate thought as he waited. He decided not to lose sight of his guide, and followed him into the Hall of the Dead. In a split second, he knew he had fallen into a trap.

The light went off, but not before he glimpsed a wolf's head. Five or so people fell on him, striking him with what felt like blackjacks made of bull's pizzle. He threw blows haphazardly and felt some land convincingly, but then he was caught on the temple, and he felt his body go liquid, spilling his mind in the oily shadows, over the sleeping drunkards who now whined in their nightmares.

"You can look back. It's done," Marie-Honnête said to Amédée, once a distant rumble had receded in the backyard that ran along the first room.

The ragpicker trembled in front of her, biting his thin, parched lips.

"I never wanted to . . ."

"But this you will want. Here are your thirty francs," she said, handing him a little purse. "So go hang yourself."

He took the purse and pocketed it. "It was not for the money, it was for my daughter. They told me I wouldn't see her again if . . ."

Marie-Honnête blew the smoke of her cigarette into the old rag-picker's face. "Fathers," she said, mechanically shaking her head with disgust.

Amédée remained silent for a while, and then, without saying another word to Marie-Honnête, got up and walked out. He was sur-prised to find that a conscience still twitched in him after all these years of hardship and humiliation, and he was not sure that the dis-covery was good news.

Just as he passed in front of the rue des Anglais, something that felt like a fire tong grasped him and dragged him into the shadows.

"Monsieur de Bramentombes?" said an English voice.

Trembling with fear, Amédée hardly dared to look up, but did not have much of a choice, as the metal hand now seized his collar. He met a shiny eye between a waxed moustache and a pith helmet. The mouth opened on ceramic teeth and spoke.

"Sorry. We haven't been introduced. But I think we should have a little conversation."

VIII
The Influence Machine

hen Brentford arrived back at the Hôtel des Écoles, the first thing he heard in the corridor leading to his room was the Colonel's creaking laughter cranked up to an alarming volume. Bursting into the room he found Pirouette up on her tiptoes, tickling the Colonel's neck and behind his ears. Branwell's usual creaks sounded more and more like those of some overloaded engine about to explode. Brentford hurried to bring the game to an end.

"Pirouette, please, you're going to damage him!"

"Ah! For once I was having fun," the Colonel complained between gasps, his face flushed to a redcoat hue, his wrinkled cheeks streaked with tears. The laughter turned to such a grating cough that Brentford wouldn't have been surprised to see the Colonel spit out a loose cog.

"Weren't you supposed to stay with Lilian?" he asked Pirouette, trying to look stern. She glanced down as if ashamed, but he could detect the trace of a mischievous smile—that of a little girl who knows she will be forgiven no matter what she has done.

"I spent the day with her, and she bought me a new dress at the Bon Marché!" she said, twirling her skirts around herself with a radiant pleasure that disarmed the disciplinarian in Brentford.

"Lilian asked me to take care of her," the Colonel explained. "She had an appointment somewhere. This child has kept me good company. Very bright for her age, isn't she?"

"Oh, yes. Quite advanced," Brentford mumbled. "Forgive me, but I think it's bedtime for little girls and clockwork colonels."

He saluted the muttering head and, taking Pirouette's hand, took her back to Lilian's room, where again he knocked to no avail.

"What did Lilian tell you?" he asked her. "Was it an appointment or a date?"

Pirouette bit her lips, making her cheeks look like those of a little animal keeping food in its jowls. "I'm not saying."

"You're just the recruit I needed, Corporal," he sighed, patting her on the head and leading her off towards his room.

But hearing some din behind Gabriel's door as he passed, he deposited her safely in his room and walked back to investigate. He entered to find Gabriel sitting on a chair mounted on a low wooden table and holding a metal rod in his hand, like some demented fisherman, while Tuluk busied himself noisily with what seemed to be a Wimshurst influence machine. Where the two of them had gotten it and what they intended to do it with it was beyond imagining. Brentford decided he'd rather not know, as a matter of fact.

"Doesn't anybody ever sleep around here?" he inquired.

"Can you help us with this, Brentford?" Gabriel asked. "It's an old static bath machine that Jean-Klein sent me from his lab this afternoon. It's for my headache. I tried magnetism but it did strange things to me, so I was prescribed electrotherapy instead. Jean-Klein didn't have the time to do it himself, but he thought I could handle it."

Brentford sighed, tried to smile, and looked at the machine. It was nothing very complicated: eight ebonite disks inside a glass case, rotating counterclockwise, producing a polarized high-frequency current. Gabriel, holding one of the rods, was to be one of the poles, while the operator, holding the other rod, would be the other. When the operator's magic wand approached Gabriel's charged body, the current would flow, more or less powerfully according to the distance between the two rods. Whether it would do any good to anyone was another question.

"What's the problem?"

"We got lost between poles," explained a perplexed Tuluk. "Mr. d'Allier is to be the negative one."

"You don't say. Please, Tuluk, turn the crank," Brentford directed. "And, you, Gabriel, move your wand closer so I can check the polarity." Brentford took up the rod that was directly connected to the machine and lit a match. As he held the match closer to Gabriel's rod, nervous threads of violet light trembled and jumped between the discharge rods.

"That's the positive one. You're all set, I guess," Brentford confirmed. "And oh, before you get fried, did you catch anything today?"

"I just met Stéphane Mallarmé," Gabriel answered.

"The poet?"

"With a capital P, if you don't mind. He read some poems about a future palatial city. Quite interesting. Even the bits I didn't get. Which was most of it. Well, all of it."

"Future palatial city? I thought that was Rimbaud?"

"It seems the topic is fashionable. Although I did look at Rimbaud's *Illuminations* this afternoon. There are a lot of Arctic references, indeed. Including, if you can believe it, '*The Splendide-Hôtel, built in the chaos of the ice and the polar night.*' Rummage through your fading memory and tell me if it reminds you of anything."

"My wedding," Brentford said sombrely. "I wish I had forgotten that. The chaos still haunts the place, if you want my opinion. So, seriously, you're telling me that the first and best New Venetian hotel d'Ussonville built is actually something out of Rimbaud?"

"Quite literally."

"It's amazing."

"I wonder if the fact that I saw d'Ussonville at the lecture tonight would diminish your amazement or, on the contrary, increase it."

Brentford stood enraptured. "You *saw* d'Ussonville? At Mallarmé's?"

"I even spoke to the man. Meet thy maker, I told myself."

"And?"

"He pointed me back to Vialatte, for some reason."

"Vialatte belongs to the Polaris Guild, as I have just learned."

Gabriel nodded at this smooth clicking of the universe. "And interestingly," he went on, "d'Ussonville gave as the alibi for his presence the fact that he was on the selection board for the 1900 World's Fair."

"A future city again."

"I'd go so far as to say that the mysterious man behind de Couard's painting was not Lord Lodestone but Louis d'Ussonville,

who, it seems, is in league with art critics of vaguely anarchist leanings. Who knows how many of the Seven are here?"

"And did you tell him that you will some day turn his grandchil-
dren into *debauchés*?"

"*They* debauched *me*, Brentford. But no, of course not. I would
hate the man to give up building New Venice just because of my little
quirks."

Suddenly an enormous violet spark flickered in the room, and
Tuluk was catapulted back a yard and landed on the floor.

"Are you all right?" Brentford asked, as the Eskimo, when he
came to, tried with great difficulty to get up. The hair on his fur pants
bristled with static.

"I am. Thank you," Tuluk eventually said, between deep, uneasy
breaths. "I think this stupid Inuk has made a little mistake."

"You may want to ground the machine, after all . . ." Brentford
suggested, looking doubtfully at the wiring that sprouted out of the
Wimshurst. "Just pass this chain round the pipes. Well, maybe not the
gas pipe, Tuluk . . ." Then he turned towards Gabriel. "Do you really
expect to accomplish anything by this method, besides blowing the
hotel to bits?"

"Jean-Klein told me it was safe. And do you know you can also
absorb drugs this way, directly through the skin? I may try that someday. For now, I wondered if one could see better visions this way. I'd
like to take a stroll in New Venice. I came really close today."

Brentford disapproved of the method, but he understood the
motive.

"I am probably going to use an Indian technique called *tattvas*
that de Couard told me about, for exactly the same purpose," he told
Gabriel. "We'll share the results and see who does best. Be reasonable
with the drugs, though. I don't feel like going to the Ivry cemetery
every other day."

"Don't worry, Brentford. It's under control."

"That is, in my experience, exactly what every addict says . . .
Sorry, Gabriel, I'm a bit overwrought. But I see we have every reason
to be excited. One of these days, we'll stroll in New Venice again."

IX

The Dead Rat

It was almost two in the morning when Morgane and Lilian entered the Rat Mort—the Dead Rat—on the Place Pigalle. To Lilian, the ground floor looked like a normal enough restaurant, but upstairs, Morgane told her, was where the action was. And when they topped the stairs, Lilian saw it was true: amidst panels that represented anthropomorphized rats at weddings, revels, and funerals, a wavering crowd sparkled under greenish gaslight—mostly women, as Morgane had promised. Befurred, behatted, bejewelled, entramelled in the leashes of impudent poodles, they moved in a heady fog of cigarettes and perfume and addressed each other with laughter and nicknames. A gypsy band racked the air with shrill guitars and yelps. *Champagne flooded*, as the French say.

"So this is the place," Lilian said to Morgane.

"*The* place, yes." She stopped a girl carrying a basket of flowers and bought a nosegay of violets, which she offered to Lilian with a little curtsey.

"Well, thank you. You're such a gentlewoman." Lilian smiled, radiant, and sniffed the flowers.

"Just don't snort too hard, Lily. The *coco* is in the middle."

"Cocaïne! Is that how it's done here?"

"Sweet, isn't it?"

Lilian had thought herself a worldy sophisticate who had seen it all, but since meeting Morgane, she'd felt like a debutante. And Morgane, she suspected, liked it that way. They circled, looking for a table.

"Hey, look who's here," Lilian said suddenly.

It was the long figure of Lord Lodestone, reclining on a red plush seat, his eyes half closed, a moribund smile on his flushed, sweaty face as he nodded approvingly at the women passing before him. His eyes met Lilian's, and in the half-light she thought she detected a wink.

Then he sprang to his feet and, two strides later, was holding her hand for a *baise-main*. His breath reeked of spirits as he spoke.

"Ah, I was waiting for you."

Lilian and Morgane looked at each other.

"You mean . . . *us*?" Lilian managed to ask.

"I meant it more generally, perhaps—you or someone like you. But I could not have found better. There's a cabinet reserved in my name upstairs. Would you care to join me for a very informal supper?"

"We are not interested in private cabinets with men, I'm afraid," Morgane said quietly.

"Clearly. Nevertheless, I believe you'll enjoy yourselves, and you are exactly the women I am looking for. So, no offence taken and none intended, and the invitation stands."

Morgane was about to refuse again, when she felt an elbow in the ribs and heard Lilian say, "We'd be delighted, sir. Just give us a moment to freshen up."

"I'm glad to hear that. I'll be at the bar. Freshening up."

"Is my nose clean?" Lilian asked, turning from the powder room mirror.

"Yes. And pretty."

Morgane kissed Lilian's nose, but then frowned as she asked, "Why did you accept his invitation?"

"I'd like to get to know him better, although not in the sense you mean—"

"I mean nothing, Lily, and any sense would be all right with me. I would be a poor medium if I were not a little open-minded. It is just that I can feel that this man is dangerous. But maybe that's what you like . . . ?"

"Not especially. I'd like to think of myself as the dangerous one tonight."

"That's the *coco*. Dance with it, but don't listen to it."

They left the powder room and asked a waiter for Lord Lode-stone's private cabinet.

"Ah, Lord Lushington, you mean. I'll escort you there."

"The waiter called you Lord Lushington," Lilian observed as she sipped champagne. "You're known by many names, aren't you, Milord?" She trembled slightly as she spoke, for, after all, she had been a New Venetian child raised in awe of the Seven Sleepers. But the cocaine, she hoped, would make a lucid, confident woman out of that little girl.

Lodestone snorted. "Lushington! It's just a joke. The most effi-cient way for an Englishman to stay invisible in Paris is to play the role of *Milord l'Arsouille*. They expect it—the rich, kinky rounder, who throws banknotes around like ticker tape, snorts drugs, canes little girls or boys, and suffers from a severe case of nostalgia for the mud. Or nostalgia for the slush, more appropriately, these days."

"If I may say so, you play the part perfectly," Lilian cracked. Morgane glanced at her with a flash of concern, preparing herself to intervene, in case Lilian went too far, and so didn't expect what came next.

"Not as perfectly as Miss Roth plays hers," he riposted. "That was a very thrilling séance that I had the good fortune to attend."

"I am glad you appreciated it," Morgane answered cautiously.

"Yet you seemed to be troubled by my friend's question that night, Milord," Lilian interjected.

"Both you and your friend seemed to have been troubled by my trouble. Should I put this down to the compassionate nature of that somewhat primitive but warm-hearted creature known as the Canadian?"

This was delivered with an imperceptible chill that Lilian under-stood as a formal invitation to dispense with further sarcasm.

"I fail to see what is wrong with compassion," she answered, more cautious than chastened.

"I must confess myself not quite familiar with it," Lodestone answered, this time with the obvious intention of appearing intimidat-ing, although a bit too obviously to be taken too seriously. Perhaps,

Lilian considered, it was meant as more of a warning—the kind of warning a man of his sort would surely call "benevolent advice."

He leaned forward on the table, and she noticed that the slur had evaporated from his speech. "To get back to the topic at hand," he said, "there is something that did strike me about the séance: that you proposed, and proved, that men are unnecessary to hypnotism. I wonder how much further you would be ready to push that argument."

"With all due respect, further than you might think, Milord," Morgane replied.

"I may think further than you realize, Miss Roth. Let us go all the way, then, and get straight to the point: in what ways would a society ruled by women, a gynocracy, if you prefer, be better for humankind than a society ruled by men?"

They both thought about it for a moment, and then it was Lilian who said, "It simply makes more sense."

"In what ways? I'm afraid I've forgotten your name."

"Lilian Lake. It makes more sense both in terms of religion and of society."

"A religion, really? Please explain this to me." His query dissolved in an ironical tinge that displeased Lilian but did not deter her.

"Very well, Milord. But you'll have to concede first that religion can be defined as what regulates the relationship of what is ephemeral with what is permanent."

That *coco* must have been good, thought Morgane.

"That's probably the best definition I've ever heard," Lodestone admitted, sounding genuinely impressed.

"Then," Lilian went on somewhat impishly, "you will recognize that the masculine principle, for some physiological reasons that are well documented, cannot claim to be such a permanent principle, cursed as it is with its sorry state of impermanence."

"I'm surprised that this impermanence could be a concern for such a beautiful woman as you are," Lord Lodestone answered with what men sometimes consider gallantry, and women plain vulgarity.

Lilian shrugged off this interruption. "It would be more logical to have a ruling principle that wouldn't be subject to such accidents.

Hence I would choose the feminine principle as the permanent ever-lasting source of all being."

"I have no objection to this," Lodestone said, pleasantly enough. "But how would that apply to social matters?"

"Would you have no objection either, Milord, to defining society as what regulates the relationships between men and, chiefly, the relationships between men and women?"

"You are a true little Socrates, Miss Lake. The perfect intellectual midwife for such great dunderheads as your servant. I still have no objection."

"By social regulation of the relationships between men and women, I mean family bonds, marriages, births, inheritance, and so on—am I still correct in describing these rules as the cornerstone of any society?"

"Certainly, you are correct," Lodestone said, growing visibly amused.

"Now, central to family bonds is the notion that sons are the children of their fathers. But, alas, it is a well-known fact that it's not always possible to prove such a claim, and that patriarchy, by insisting on ascertaining fatherhood, actually undermines its own legitimacy. Only the mother knows who its father is. Accordingly, a matriarchy seems to me the safest and most sensible way to found family, and hence society, on a stable, certain principle. Especially as it's consistent with the Mother religion we talked about earlier."

Lord Lodestone applauded quietly.

"Very convincing, and I fully agree with your reasoning," he said. "I may not come to the same conclusions, however. Regarding religion, I would rather bypass the two principles you describe as a slightly vulgar Punch and Judy show and go a little farther towards the source: Light and Darkness, these are good principles to start with, considerably more far-reaching when it comes to the universe as a whole than the masculine and feminine, which so far only exist on our very parochial planet. Now, regarding society, your reasoning, once again, perfectly satisfies me. But history, I'm afraid, has decided otherwise, and however notoriously poor are Reality's arguments, they are not to be easily contested. I doubt very much that men, as long they refuse to be enlightened by these truths you imparted to us with such zest, would be ready to relinquish their powers to Mother Nature, for Mother Nature, you know, has not been as loving towards her sons as she imagined. She is known to have been squint, cruel, and more than a little obsessed with death. '*Can mercy be found in the heart of her who was born of the stone?*' as the Indians say of Kali. We have had to grow up alone. We have had to invent our own permanence, find our own path into the light, build our own world."

"Like building *cities*. . ." Lilian murmured.

Very softly, Lodestone took Lilian's wrist, and then squeezed it so that she felt he could break it like a twig. He leaned towards her, a broad smile on his broad face, and whispered gently, "I like games, Miss Lake. But this one you are playing, it has to be played very well, you understand?"

She pulled her hand away with a swift tug. "Have I played it well so far, Milord?" she asked, trying to withstand his glare.

"Almost perfectly, Miss Lake. *Almost* perfectly . . ."

If Lilian doubted Lodestone was dangerous, she soon had proof of it.

They walked out of the Dead Rat at about four o'clock in something that by no means looked like the morning. They all needed a little stroll in the fresh air, and Lodestone offered to escort them down to the rue Pigalle. But as they started down the street, the shadows became alive with ominous silhouettes, and by and by, a group of thugs gathered around them, intent on blocking their way.

But before the ruffians could make the move that would turn harassment into assault, Lodestone seized a whip from a sleeping coachman, and kept on walking straight down the middle of the street, his arms slightly apart, flicking the whip around like a lion tamer entering a cage. Lilian and Morgane followed in his shadow, and, from the corners of their eyes, could see that the silhouettes, though they muttered slurred insults, were not advancing anymore. One by one, they stepped back reluctantly, waiting for some easier prey.

Lilian had to remind herself that she despised such shows of strength—because for a moment, this one had rather impressed her.

X

An Invisible Visitor

Once alone in his room, Gabriel discovered that he could not use the influence machine on his own simply by holding an end of each wand. It left him exhausted, his temple pulsing barbed waves through his head. Still, after long minutes of useless exertions and much twisting of the sheets, he discovered that something in him adamantly refused to consider sleep an option. And as he well knew, struggling would only make his insomnia worse.

After a long moment of immobile brooding, he decided it was time for some action. He turned on the bedside light and fetched the Music Box. Rummaging through its secret drawers, he picked out a random packet of Psylicates. The Diviner. It would have to do.

Opening the drawers had immediately triggered the music box, and its tiny twin figures started dancing to "The Magic Flute." The little buggers, Gabriel thought with nostalgia. Through his tears, their dance became a blurry whirl. That was the trouble with these synthetic sands—they always made your eyes sting and water.

But they hit quickly. Gabriel closed his eyes, and already had the feeling he was retreating—or advancing?—into his mind, like a phantascopic camera gliding on a gondola. His *luminous chaos*—since that was, apparently, the name for it—shimmered and sparkled, the dots crowding madly, like the stars on a very clear summer night. Meanwhile, he began to feel the first bodily effects, which were not especially pleasant: it was like being kneaded, pressured, elongated, and softly disarticulated as if to be fit into a mechanism of which he was to become a cog. Then air began to whistle through his bones in gusts of unbearable pleasure, and bolts of silent black lightning flashed through his brain to the point at which he thought it would split in half.

His eyes still closed, Gabriel watched his luminous chaos grow brighter and still more primeval. It had expanded into a universe, deepening immensely and perpetually gushing from some invisible well. Storms of scintillating dots whirled like mad galaxies amongst explosions of pure darkness fringed by bristling diamond haloes. Dim waves of light pulsed nervously, as if heaving to bloom into recognizable shapes. Clusters of shadows flocked into grotesque profiles and grimacing faces as wide as the night sky.

Gabriel, or some better part of him that was being moulded anew, floated for a while, then started to tremble, feeling cold to the bone, as the vision seemed to get darker. A picture slowly slid into view, varnished and neatly delineated, like a miniature, meticulous oil painting. It was a depiction of a white city on the seaside, frothy specks of slanting light gleaming on its angles and domes. It seemed motionless at first, but from what seemed an embankment or pier, a white shape hurtled towards him at full speed, though it never came any closer, as if it were running in place.

But then it was in his brain, as if a cloud of white butterflies had been violently sucked down a black plughole. His mind sank down in a pool of slimy black water. Only his temple, still throbbing painfully, gave him a vague sense of time receding farther and farther away, until he forgot about it and about himself.

Hours passed unnoticed.

He woke with a terrible headache, and whiplashed by icy shivers.

Something had just touched his foot.

He remained on his belly, motionless, half-conscious, a small maelstrom of fear swirling in his stomach. It must have been a dream, he thought. He tried to calm down, and, with difficulty, found within himself the levers to raise his limbs, and slowly extended his foot. With a flash of horror he experienced the same feeling of cold contact. It wasn't a dream—but perhaps he'd left something between the sheets? He didn't have the courage to check again. He turned sideways, knees up, trying to curl into a ball of oblivion, but fear had taken hold of him now, and he was trembling in chilly electric bursts, while a cold sweat drenched his back.

Then, something moved at his side, almost imperceptibly, giving off the faintest whiff of ether. Gabriel nearly jumped out of his skin, when what felt like a cold hand lightly touched his shoulder. Trembling like a leaf, barely holding back an urge to scream, he told himself that this was just an hallucination, from too much drugs or electricity or pain, but the thought changed nothing; he sensed that the presence was still there, like a barely perceptible draught of chilly air, turning the marrow of his bones into a solid core of ice. Face it, he thought. That will dispel it. And abruptly, he flipped onto his back with wide-open eyes. It was dark in the room, and no thing—or no one—was immediately visible. But still, there was the strong sense of something—a darker shade of dark, a slow breath in the air, the slightest weight upon the bed.

Then he heard a voice very near to his throbbing temple.

"Be still," said the voice—a woman's.

Something strange and confusing was happening in his soul. He had never wanted anything as much as he wanted to obey—no, to *please*, the voice. It felt full of tenderness, and he could feel a sense of love building up inside him. But, equally violently, his mind protested. No, he shouldn't listen to the voice. This voice didn't exist. And if it did, it was dangerously seductive, like the voice of a siren.

And yet he loved this voice. The thought of refusing her anything made him miserable. He despised himself for this, but there was no way that he could go to her. He had to stay with the others, find a path back to New Venice. That was his life.

"Sorry," he sobbed, "I'm so sorry."

The voice sighed, as if disappointed, and the sigh pierced Gabriel's heart. But his fear was stronger than love. He closed his eyes again, blocked his ears. He desperately wanted to get up but knew his muscles would mutiny. Thrills of anguish ran like blue flames along his nerves. There was a motion close to him, and, very distinctly, he felt a kiss falling like a petal upon his forehead. He sat up

then with a jerk, icy sweat pouring off him like water from a melting snowman. He turned and grasped a notebook: writing down
the dream would prove that it was nothing more than that. Still
trembling with fear, he wrote illegibly, tracing signs that were not so
much letters as the curve of his panicked heartbeat.

XI

The Steam Guillotine

It was the cold that brought Blankbate back to his senses. He realized he was outside, blindfolded amidst what sounded like a bustle of people, his breath reeking of chloroform, his hands tied so tightly together that his wrists hurt, and with the dull, cold pressure of a gun's muzzle pressed hard against the nape of his neck. His could feel that his false beard and tinted glasses had been torn away, and he found that painful and humiliating, after all these years—to have his real face exposed, even to strangers. The scene at the Red Castle came back to his mind in hazy flashes. He could not believe he had been so naïve.

The pressure of the gun muzzle relaxed a little, long enough for someone to unknot the blindfold. Blankbate flexed his muscles, ready to react, but what he saw stopped him dead. He found himself standing amidst the roofless, charred ruins of some immense palace, the night visible above him and through the rows of chipped arches that circled the building at every level. Through one of the arches the moon shone, bulbous and pale, like a blind man's eye. The ground was snow-covered, scattered with broken stones, weeds, and dry shrubs, and dark, snakelike ivy crept up along the remains of the walls. About twenty men surrounded him, all of them wearing wolf masks and fur coats with carnations in their lapels, some carrying torches that sent bulky shadows slowly pulsing across the ruins. A rectangular shape that seemed two stories tall, covered with a black drape, stood on a flat stone. In front of Blankbate, a fat man with a long white beard, his face unmasked, sat in a spiral-wheeled chair, a fur blanket on his knees. He spoke softly, but with an ominous hiss.

"It has come to my attention that you were interested in meeting the owner of the Blackamoor. At the moment, that happens to be me. What is it I can do for you?"

"Let me go," Blankbate answered, straightening his aching spine. He had been beaten, and now his body effloresced with vivid patches of pain.

"Ah, this I cannot do, unfortunately. Neither can I offer you the Blackamoor, of which I am only the keeper, and which it is my duty to protect. But I can assure you that you will see it tonight."

"Where are we? What are you going to do to me?" Blankbate shouted, his voice laden with anger.

"Where? The former Court of Accounts, which was burned down during the Commune. But, as you can see, it is still a Court. And of course, what we are going to do is settle some accounts."

"Is this some kind of trial?"

"It is more than that, I am afraid. It is an execution." He made a slight move of his plump hand, and two Wolf-men stepped up onto the flat stone, and pulled the black drape off the large structure.

The guillotine appeared, vertiginous, its oblique blade gleaming in the torchlight. Its posts were laced with vines or ivy and topped with bunches of mistletoe. Two metallic horns darted from the upper mantle, fastened to curved tubes of steel that were themselves inserted into mechanical contraptions on either side of the legs. The heavy "mutton" that held and weighed the blade was not suspended by a rope but fixed to a pair of telescopic pistons, which were in turn connected to some sort of engine. It was, in short, *a steam guillotine.*

All of the Wolf-men had dropped to their knees, heads down, as soon as the death machine had appeared, and now they slowly got back on their feet.

Blankbate knew this was the end. He stood fascinated, for a while unable to summon the strength to fight.

"Meet our Queen, the Widow, the Mother of Men and Eternal Maiden, She who turns Life into Death and Death into Life. She demands blood to bring spring back to our accursed land," the man in the wheelchair declaimed, encompassing the snowy ruins with a wide swipe of his arm. "It is our great honour to offer a sacrifice to her, and a great privilege for you to have been chosen as her consort."

"Why me?" Blankbate howled. He felt the anger building up in him, streams of strength flowing to his aching muscles. But there was nothing he could do.

The man in the wheelchair gave a smile that the torchlight twisted into a grimace.

"It is well known that a stranger brings either trouble or abundance. In both cases, sacrifice is required. And, as a benefit, we get rid of strangers—all these Jews and Dagoes, all the vermin that invade France these days. It used to be a land of Plenty, but it has been abused and defiled, and it is our mission to purify it from its waste, so that it can grow again, back to the full splendour of its past abundance."

Reasoning with these men, Blankbate realized in a drench of cold sweat, was as useless as fighting them. The word "waste," though, struck him. This man was not only an enemy but also a colleague, a garbage collector. That was why he had the Blackamoor. But he had committed the most basic mistake and, in Blankbate's eyes, the ultimate sin: that of thinking that the mess should or could be cleaned, that it was not part of some mysterious balance. And of course, that mistake had made him crazy.

But it was too late for understanding. Another wave of the man's hand sent one of the Wolf-men over to the Widow. With careful, solemn gestures, the screw that blocked the spring of the lunette was undone. A fat piece of rope from a figure-eight-shaped ring was unfastened and hooked to the blade. Pulling the rope, the Wolf-man lifted the mutton up to the crossbar mantle, then coiled the cord around a hook on the left post.

Another Wolf-man had joined him, feeding charcoal to the firebox of the steam engine. The glow was reflected on his feral head, and embers flickered in his black, opaque eyes.

"*I made two journeys: one through the forest, one through the fire,*" the bearded man in the wheelchair suddenly declaimed. The engine started to puff and purr in the silent night. From time to time, the Wolf-men spoke among themselves in a language that sounded like twisted, inverted French, but Blankbate could not understand them. He tried to focus, dispel his fears, find a way out, but his mind, too, seemed bound in tight chains.

He watched hopelessly as the dressing of the Bride continued. A large wicker trunk, padded with vine leaves, was brought alongside the platform. A zinc pail was hung over the lunette, and another Wolf-man, perhaps the tall one who had framed him, stood near the Widow, a crude curvaceous metal vase in his hand.

Blankbate knew what it was before the man in the wheelchair had time to tell him.

"The *Blackamoor*. Your blood will be the wine of our harvest. We'll feed the earth with it."

"Let an impure blood water our furrows!" the Wolf-men chanted, as, with a hiss of pressure, wraithlike smoke from the engine rose around the guillotine.

Blankbate closed his eyes. He suddenly understood that his mistake at the Red Castle had only been the outcome of another, earlier, bigger blunder. His dream of the Blackamoor had been a dream of his own death. He had come to Paris not to prevail, but to meet his fate. Some part of him, he realized, had known it all along. This was why he had walked into the Hall of the Dead. The grail was to be filled with his blood.

He took a deep breath, summoning courage. Hands seized him and pushed him towards the stone. He elbowed them back and straightened his spine.

"I'll walk," he spat out at them.

The man in the wheelchair nodded.

"Actually, the ritual demands a fight," he decreed.

And the Wolf-men grasped Blankbate again and he fought back in despair, twisted, kicked their shins, but they were strong and they were many and they dragged him up to the stone. The time came for them to tear off his collar, and he faced the guillotine rising darkly against the night sky, and he looked for the Great Bear to say his prayers. But before he could find it, he was toppled, face down, over the teeter. Someone tried to pull his hair to pass it through the lunette, but it was too short-cropped, and the hands had to take purchase below the neck, strangling Blankbate as they pulled him forward. He had lived most of his life as a pariah; couldn't he die with dignity? His head was forced into the lunette and its upper half-moon was lowered to hold him in place, and locked. He felt he was going crazy as multiple hands held him down on the teeter and a large, masked man advanced towards him, holding a spiked hammer.

"You'll be pleased to know that we are not barbarians," the man in the wheelchair said. "Unlike the unclean Jews and Musselmans, we are merciful enough to kill the offering before we cut its throat. Proceed, please."

The hammer was lifted, passing against the face of the moon.

"Long live the Widow, Mother of the Universe!" the Wolf-men shouted.

Blankbate held his last breath, and watched the hammer as it fell.

To be continued . . .

EPISODE IX

THE SECRET CHIEF

I

A Morning at the Morgue

W hen Gabriel woke up, his brain like a sponge full of cold gravy, the first thing he did was to check the hasty squiggle on his bedside table.

Boy meets girls, it read.

With a sigh, he noticed that another piece of paper had been slid under his door. Shivering, he got out of bed and picked it up. It was from Brentford: "Meet me at Notre-Dame at eleven o'clock."

Outside, it was sunny, but awfully cold, with a near-gale-force wind blowing from the north that went through his bones like an X-ray. Brentford was waiting for him on the Pont-au-Double with a paper bag in his hand, and greeted him as if he hadn't seen him in months.

"Holy Cod!" he exclaimed. "Your eyes are in the middle of your cheeks. Too much static or something?"

Gabriel almost confessed his nightmare, but fought the impulse. "I have an intense inner life, I suppose."

"Well, I've never doubted that."

"What have you got there?" Gabriel asked, pointing to the paper bag, hoping to change the topic.

"Why, don't tell me you've never heard of the famous *Lunchpack of Notre-Dame*."

Gabriel stifled his laughter and frowned instead. "You've got to get this interpherence fixed, Brentford," he said. "It's becoming a bit like *The Strange Case of Dr. Jekyll and Mr. Hyde*."

"All right, sorry."

"That was funny, actually. Your best so far. But I doubt you made me come here just for these fireworks of wit."

"Just a little laughter before a hard day's work. Next, we're supposed to meet Tripotte. I got another *téléphonage* this morning, but he was very elusive about why he wanted to meet. Ah, *quand on parle du loup* . . . Here's Tripotte."

The commissaire was approaching from the nearby prefecture, his bulk made more portentous by the fur-lined greatcoat he wore. He licked his lips before saluting Brentford, and he, too, pointed his pudgy finger at the paper bag.

"You'd better eat now, Mr. Orsini," he intoned, "because I'm taking you to the morgue."

The morgue was located in the shadow of Notre-Dame, at the stern of the Île de la Cité, in an austere, single-story building. Its large, central gate was closed, but a long queue twisted out of a small gate on one side, while a few people trickled out of another gate on the other. Along the fence surrounding the building, muffled street peddlers proposed coffee, roasted chestnuts, apples, gingerbread, and whatever "morgue paté" was. Showing his police card, Tripotte hurried the apprehensive Brentford and Gabriel past the queue and inside. It was as busy as a theatre lobby just before the play. Inside, people of all ages and walks of life pressed themselves against two notice boards, one with photographs of corpses, the other with lists of distinguishing marks. The anguish building in Brentford's gut started to crystallize into something angular and piercing.

Tripotte, however, did not give them much time to think. He hurried them through the wooden barrier that separated the lobby from the display hall. Once in the hall, they faced a tall window split in three by two black columns, dividing the view of a dozen sluice tables with bodies on them, each naked except for a small loincloth. People passed in front of the glass for a few moments of half-shocked, half-voyeuristic staring, exchanging comments in voices that might have been lower while the guard urged them to move along. It took a while for Brentford to understand that this ghastly take on the Grévin had actually been devised as a means of identifying anonymous bodies. He lowered his eyes for fear of recognizing one of them himself, even though he felt quite sure now that it would indeed come to that, and he tried to block the names that sprang into his mind.

After exchanging a few words with a clerk from the registry, Tripotte turned towards Brentford and Gabriel and said, "Now, step up and tell me if you identify this *bit-player* here. Actually, he's quite the leading man today."

Brentford took a long, reluctant walk to the window, then, finally, looked up. There, where Tripotte pointed his stubby index like a typographic hand, lay a muscular body, its neatly decapitated head resting near its shoulder, the forehead bashed to a pulp. Even though it was the first time Brentford had ever seen his face, he had not a doubt that it was Blankbate.

He shook and felt the tears well up in his eyes.

"So?" Tripotte asked.

Brentford mastered his nerves and managed to say, "What makes you think I know him?"

"I had some doubt . . . but I no longer do. All I know is that this man lived in the same hotel as you do."

"Alan Blankbate is his name," Brentford admitted. He felt his sadness charging with anger. "What happened?"

"Some rare domestic accident, I would say," Tripotte replied. "He was found in a wicker trunk in the middle of the Seine, his head in his hands, with tinted glasses on."

"Was he . . . beaten?"

Tripotte shrugged his shoulders. "I doubt he did all that to himself," he said. "Come with me for a minute."

He led them to a smaller room where some coroners and policemen were writing and filing reports.

"Docteur Demain?" Tripotte called out.

The doctor, a young but already balding man with a head like a lightbulb, got up and shook their hands.

"These gentlemen here are very curious about our latest finding," Tripotte told him.

Demain glanced at the paper he had in his hand. "I've just finished the report," he said, and read aloud, "The victim was about thirty-eight, tall and vigorous and in overall good condition, with a tattoo on his back showing a skull over crossed hooks that look like those used by ragpickers, and a motto in English: 'Dust to Dust.' Another tattoo on the right forearm simply says—in neat cursive letters— *Legio Patria Nostra*."

"That's the motto of the French Foreign Legion," Tripotte observed. "A man with a past."

"I never knew he was in the Foreign Legion," Brentford whispered to Gabriel.

"Rigor mortis is observable," Demain went on, "but difficult to distinguish from the effects of freezing. In any case, death was fairly recent, less than twelve hours ago, I would say. The wrists show rope marks. Longitudinal traces on both temporal zones may mean that the subject was tightly blindfolded. Both arms reveal pressure bruises— probably from a tight grasp while the subject was resisiting—and so does the back. There are traces of four blows to the scalp and the temples, coming from blunt objects—bull's pizzles probably. The malar region and the upper lip show some traces of glue, and there are skin blotches—as if a false beard had been ripped off."

"Did you know he had a false beard?" Tripotte asked point-blank to Brentford.

Brentford sensed the danger behind Tripotte's question, and changed his shiver of disgust to a shrug. "If he had one, no one was meant to know, I suppose."

The doctor, who observed them beyond the rim of his glasses, hemmed and resumed his gruesome reading.

"Now, on the frontal bone we have a deep, intrusive wound two inches in diameter roughly in the shape of an O, but with the edges quite dented where the skull has caved in. The blow evidently comes from a heavy, pointed object."

"A pickaxe?" suggested Tripotte, staring straight at Demain.

The coroner hesitated but finally nodded. "Well, almost surely, yes."

"With all the icepicks around, nowadays, it's not going to be easy to find this one," Tripotte sighed, as if to himself.

"The angle of the blow suggests that the victim was somehow looking up. Which leads to the *other* cause of death: decapitation. The cut is very neat, like that of a guillotine, although slightly oblique at the nape, as if the victim had raised his head at the last moment."

"Guillotine?" Brentford muttered, stunned.

"*Like* a guillotine is what I said," the doctor insisted under Tripotte's severe stare. "It is the same kind of wound—it's just that the pressure exerted on the blade was much, much more powerful than a normal guillotine. The cervical area of the body is crushed to splinters. I've never seen a guillotine powerful enough do that. However, there's no other explanation."

"A guillotine's a guillotine," Tripotte said impatiently. "What did he die from—the blow or the blade?"

"Judging by the two haemorrhages, I would say that they happened almost simultaneously, and it's difficult to say which came first—except of course that it does not seem very logical to stun a beheaded man."

"Would it be more logical to behead a man whose skull you have just broken?" Brentford inquired.

"It would not be more logical to me, but I have observed that criminals tend to have a logic of their own," Demain answered perfunctorily. "There's nothing more I can tell without an autopsy."

Tripotte sighed. "Well, that means asking for permission from the Canadian Commission. I'll get in touch with you about it, Doctor. Meanwhile, you should start charging entry. This is a very popular corpse that you've got on your hands."

"We certainly should, yes. That might help us pay for a better laboratory."

Tripotte ignored him. "Now, Mr. Orsini, would you care to join me with your friend at the Pointy Tower for a few questions?"

"The Pointy Tower?"

"That's what we call the Police Prefecture," he explained, leading them out without waiting for a reply.

The questions had been basic enough. How long had they known Blankbate, and where did they know him from? What was his occupation? What had they talked about these past few days? A few ameliorations of the truth later—since they met on the ferry from Jersey a few days ago, he introduced himself as a collector, but he wasn't talkative and seldom appeared in the hotel—they were free to go, as long as they remained in Paris. But it was clear to them that Tripotte was less interested in solving Blankbate's murder than he was in cornering Brentford and Co.

Once outside, Brentford leaned disconsolately on the parapet that overlooked the frozen Seine.

"Listen," Gabriel said. "If you're busy finding reasons to blame yourself, I'm not going to help." Gabriel was having one of his brief spells of behaving like the older, wiser brother. He was a few months older, actually.

"All right," Brentford conceded. "It's not my fault. Except I brought him here and I wanted to take him back."

"Peterswarden—and, I suspect, a bit of ill-luck—are responsible for us being here, not you. And Blankbate was big enough to take care of himself anyway. Holy Cod, Brentford, he didn't even tell you what he was looking for."

"He may have been close to finding it, though. A little too close, perhaps."

"Do you think this Dr. Demain might have an idea of what really happened?"

"Why are you asking?"

"I don't know. I watched him closely and felt him hesitate—taking his cue from Tripotte, but, you know, slightly embarrassed to be doing so."

"Perhaps. But what is he going to tell us? That it was the Wolves of the Wood of Justice? We already suspect as much. And he if is in league with Tripotte, questioning him would bring us more trouble than answers."

"As you wish. It would be foolish to get into trouble when everything else is just dandy."

Brentford looked at Gabriel. "Maybe what Blankbate was looking for has nothing to do with our situation."

"It's not so much what Blankbate was looking for as *who was looking for him*. Who knows which one of us is next? If we're to go back to the morgue, I'd rather walk there than be rolled in."

Brentford gave it some thought. "Well, Gabriel," he finally said. "I'll walk with you, then, and we'll speak to Dr. Demain. But let's call Jean-Klein first and explain the situation to him. He'll know what questions to ask."

✳

They had to queue for a good half hour before being admitted again, which gave Lavis time to come down and meet them during his lunch break. For reasons he couldn't explain to himself, he felt a tremendous sympathy for this group of Canadian expatriates, and, learning of their loss, he had quickly agreed to consult with them. As he happened to know Demain from his student years, he felt calling at the morgue might make things easier for everyone.

"I'm afraid I can't stay very long," Lavis explained. He was elegantly dressed as a sportsman, Brentford noted as he watched him bang a pair of skis to get rid of the sticky snow. Skis were very rare in Paris, Brentford had noticed, but he had also noticed that Lavis was one step ahead when it came to fashions. "Tourette has really tormented me for leaving yesterday afternoon," he told them.

"Sorry to hear that." Gabriel said.

"It is nothing. I was glad to see d'Arsonval."

By chance the registry clerk remembered them and fetched Dr. Demain for them, before being entrusted, much to his dismay, with a pair of skis. One could not say that the coroner was overjoyed at seeing them again, but neither did he seem much surprised. That Lavis accompanied them somehow reassured him. He warmly saluted his colleague and took them all not into the tiny cabinet but into the dismal autopsy room itself, mercifully empty for the moment and more suitable for a quiet discussion.

Brentford had regained his drive. "Sorry to disturb you again, but there's something that we forgot to ask you."

"Please," the doctor said. "I'll be glad to help if I can."

"Would it be possible to have a look at the retina of the victim?" Jean-Klein intervened.

The doctor made a face. "You mean you want to make an optogram?"

"Yes. Mr. Orsini told me on the telephone that the victim was *looking up*. That may leave us a chance. I have all the necessary equipment at the Salpêtrière."

"It may be too late. And you know that our master Brouardel is really sceptical about the process."

"But he mentions it," Jean-Klein answered. "As far as we know, only two optograms were ever made. A rabbit and a German convict. Both of them decapitated."

"But the conditions were very special. The rabbit was kept in the darkness for a long while before it was beheaded."

"You told us that Mr. Blankbate was blindfolded," Brentford interjected, despite being rather uncertain as to what the argument was about. "He may have had only a few minutes of exposure to light."

"But the death happened hours ago. I doubt the victim's retinas will be in good shape."

"The rhodopsin can last as long as forty-eight hours, and the effects of the frost may help us too," Jean-Klein countered.

"Not to mention that afterwards he was in the trunk with his tinted glasses on his eyes, if our information is correct," Gabriel added.

"You see," Jean-Klein insisted. "We lose nothing by trying."

Demain shook his head. "On a strictly professional level, I would be the first to try. It's not that I'm afraid it won't work, you understand. It's more what will happen if it *does* that worries me."

"You have my word of honour that it will stay strictly between us," Brentford reassured him. "And if I have yours that you won't speak of it to anyone, I'll be perfectly satisfied."

"Not even to the police?" the doctor wondered.

"And would the police be helpful in this matter?" Gabriel asked him in return.

"Perhaps not," Demain sighed. "For the love of science, then. And for the love of justice, if there is such a thing. Let me turn on the sodium light and bring the body here. Jean-Klein, if you would prepare a six-thousandths solution of saltwater. It will take us a few minutes, and then you'd better run back to your lab."

II

The Demigod of Les Halles

L ilian was surprised when, coming straight from Morgane's enchanted bed, she knocked on Brentford's door and found herself facing Pirouette.

"Lilian!" the child exclaimed, hugging her. "I missed you so much."

Lilian knew little French beside what she had picked up in New Venice and a few recent acquisitions from Morgane's pillow, but she knew enough to be moved.

"Okay," she finally murmured. "Let me go now. Is Brentford here?"

"No. He left this morning."

Lilian entered the room and noticed the notes and drawings Brentford had left behind on his desk—maps of New Venice that were full of blank zones, sketches of buildings whose perspectives vanished in the fog of the white page, names of places crossed out or followed by question marks . . . She smiled at them sadly and not without tenderness. Was her love for Morgane softening her?

"It's a pity you don't like him," Pirouette was saying. She was sitting on the bed swinging her legs and watching them as if they were a puppet show.

"What?"

"Mr. Orsini. I find him very nice, and very handsome."

Lilian let out a small puff of laughter. "Yes. He is all that, I guess." She caught a glance of herself in the mirror and saw that, behind her back, Pirouette was watching her intently.

"I know only"—she pretended to count on her fingers—"one man who is more handsome. And then, he is not as nice."

"Who would that be?" Lilian asked politely, still gazing into the mirror and smoothing the skin around her eyes. She could do with a beauty sleep, she thought. Morgane had revealed herself to be an enthusiastic somnambulist, and Lilian had spent half the night trying to coo and coax her into going back to bed. And the other half had been even less restful, she thought, with a blush she hoped Pirouette wouldn't notice.

But no. The child kept on prattling.

"You don't know him. He's called Swell-in-the-Sack. And you know what? He has a tattoo, down there, you know, that says *Au Bonheur des Dames*. And when I say down there, I should say "up there.""

Pirouette rolled back on the bed, laughing at this fine morsel of French wit.

Lilian turned back, her hands on her hips. "Pirouette! Who tells you things like that?"

"My mother," the child answered honestly.

"She takes your education to heart, doesn't she?"

Pirouette was not laughing anymore, and she sat at the edge of the bed, staring in front of her. "I wish you were my mother," she finally said with a pout.

"I am glad I'm not." The corners of Pirouette's mouth turned down as if she were going to cry. Lilian sighed and went to her, hugging her. "Okay, I'm sorry. I'd like to be your mother. I truly would."

Then she realized that the tears were not real. Pirouette gave a yelp of mirth and bounced on the bed. Lively child, thought Lilian.

"And then Mr. Orsini could be my father? If I were your age, I would marry him," Pirouette declared, nodding to herself with great conviction.

"If I were your age, I would mind my own own business," Lilian told her curtly, although she was more amused than angry. Still, it occurred to her that, perhaps without realizing it himself, Brentford had brought the child here to foster exactly that suggestion. She felt faintly flattered, but the shortest jokes were the best, and this one was well past its prime.

"But I know that you like girls better," the little girl went on, devilishly, primly pointing her chin, as if to defy her.

Once again, Lilian was taken aback. "How do you know that?"

"It's easy. Your clothes smell of a perfume that is not yours. And this is a cloakroom ticket from Le Rat Mort. Everyone knows what kind of women go there. Don't look so shocked. I play games with my friends, too, but . . ."

"Pirouette. Please. That's enough. You're a nice little girl, but I'm sure your mother must be very worried about you. Shouldn't we go and reassure her? You don't want her to call the police and get Bren—I mean Mr. Orsini—in trouble, do you?"

Pirouette looked gloomily at the tips of her new shoes. She had known this would happen sooner or later.

"She'll beat me."

Lilian paused, then leaned over to gently pat her head. She felt sorry for Pirouette, but she couldn't let her—nor Brentford, for that matter—pretend they really were a family.

"There, there . . . I'll go with you, okay? I'll give her some money and make it all right, okay?"

Pirouette nodded sadly and looked off. It was her lot in life, after all, not to have much of a choice. These people had been nice to her, but she had always supposed it wouldn't last forever. She got down from the bed, trying not to cry.

✳

As they passed his doorway a few minutes later, the Colonel's voice called from inside his room.

Lilian sighed and went in.

"Ah, Miss Lake—err, Tuluk, can you leave us alone?"

"Of course," Tuluk said amenably, and headed towards the door, leaving on the bedside table the oil-bulb syringe that he used for the maintenance of the Colonel's gears.

"And please close my lid. There are ladies in the room."

Once Tuluk had gone, the Colonel harrumphed.

"Miss Lake. I owe you an apology for my conduct a few nights ago. I want you to know that it won't happen again," he recited in his grumpy phonographic voice.

"That it won't happen again, I can guarantee you," Lilian said. "Unless you wish me to unscrew your head and use it to play skittles."

The Colonel's eyes rolled in their orbits and for a moment Lilian had the feeling that his tremulous moustache was going to jump at her throat like a rabid ferret. He blushed a deep burgundy and finally exhaled a whining sigh, the way a pierced balloon would.

"I stand corrected," he growled. "Well, maybe not *stand . . .*"

"Very well. Now, let's forget all about it," Lilian said. She walked up to the Colonel and, delicately, put a kiss on his blushing forehead. She then lifted Pirouette in order for her to perform a more slobbery version of the same, which delighted him.

"Are you taking her away?" he inquired worriedly, as they left the room hand in hand.

"Just to see her mother. I'll be back."

"Be careful, you two," the Colonel muttered, wondering if heartache could ever be said to apply in his case.

❄

In spite of the bad weather, Les Halles was thriving that morning, with rows and rows of women lining the pavements to sell dismal vegetables and fruits to the crowds thronging the streets surrounding the glass pavilions. The women's cries rang through the cold air as if it were an aviary, and when carts full of wicker baskets tried to pass through it got so crowded that Lilian was afraid she might lose Pirouette in the press. She herself got lost for a moment in angry contemplation of a man beating a duck with a stick as if the creature were a pillow.

"A *bombeur*," Pirouette explained. "It makes the ducks look fatter."

Lilian could feel Pirouette's little fist gripping her hand; the closer they got to the rue Pirouette, the stronger the grip.

"Listen," Lilian said, kneeling beside her as they drew near her mother's place. "I'll go with you to her door and give her some money. She will be pleased to see you, I am sure. If anything bad happens, you know where to find us." The sulky Pirouette withdrew her cheek from Lilian's tentative lips, a dejected pout on her face. "Promise you'll come back, if it goes wrong, all right?" Lilian said in a softer voice.

"How touching," said a voice above them that sounded very male and, from Lilian's perspective, had every reason to do so. She quickly got up.

"Your mother will be delighted to see you, Pirouette," the man went on. "She's been polishing the silverware in your honour. Especially that ladle."

Lilian knew this must be Swell-in-the-Sack. He was handsome indeed, with his black curly hair and deep black eyes, but he looked disheveled, as if he had been up all night. He was probably on his way to bed now, and Lilian had no desire to detain him.

"Excuse us," she said, as she tried to move past him to the door.

He put his arm across their way, his long hand on the doorjamb.

"Saturnin Loupart," he said. He spoke softly, but Lilian had smelled better breath. "Swell-in-the-Sack to the ladies. And you would be?"

"A different kind of lady," Lilian said curtly.

"Looking for a job in the Quarter? It's rather lively, and pretty girls haven't the time to get bored."

"I'm bored already. Goodbye, Mr. Smelly Sacks, or whatever your name is."

She ducked and passed quickly under his arm. Still, Pirouette had time to smile suavely towards Saturnin, who winked his velvety eye in return.

✳

Two minutes later, he was in the upstairs room of the Ange Gabriel, facing a man whose disguise as an English tourist (checked jacket, deerstalker hat, red muttonchops, beer belly, glasses hung on a chain resting on his portly chest) was a little too obvious.

"Come on, Tripotte," Swell-in-the-Sack joked, "it's not the Quat'z'arts masked ball yet." He'd known the policeman since the days when he'd been a simple commissaire's dog supervising public executions, and so felt he had some leeway with him.

"*Shhh!* Don't say my name here. It's not exactly one of your cute nicknames."

"Leave my nickname alone. It's not as if it's something anyone could call you."

"Listen, my dear little Saturnin," said Tripotte with a frown. "It's lucky for you that I find that your abilities are better employed in the streets than behind bars—which, you will readily admit, is where you belong. Or perhaps on the teeter of the guillotine?"

Swell-in-the-Sack sniggered. "I've been close enough to the guillotine as it is, thank you. As recently as last night, in fact."

"If you don't want to get closer, you'd best show me a little more gratitude—a word I don't suppose you know, but it means, roughly, that you shouldn't bite the hand that feeds you."

"I'm not sure who's feeding whom, though."

"Nature, when well ordered, is a perfectly balanced cycle. You feed me, and then I'll feed you. Let's keep it as God in his infinite wisdom wanted it. Now"—he silenced the retort he saw coming from Swell-in-the-Sack with a wave of the hand—"did the little girl come back from the hotel?"

"As it happens, just now. But it wasn't your Canadian spy who returned her—it was a woman. Thirty-something, well groomed. She thinks herself brave, it seems."

"French?"

"No, though she speaks it a little, with an English accent. Or would it be Canadian?"

"That would be the one who has papers under the name of Lilian Lake. Don't congratulate me; she's the only woman of the lot. I wonder what Orsini needed this Pirouette for."

"I can think of plenty of things he would have needed her for. She's quite a little devil, you know."

Another gesture from Tripotte signalled his disappointment.

"He's not the type. The people at the hotel would have told me. I told them to watch him closely, but nothing unseemly happened. No, there's something to this that I don't understand . . ."

Swell-in-the-Sack smirked. "It's called kindness—a word I don't suppose you know, but roughly it means that these people should be easy to deal with."

III

The Talk of the Hashisheens

oming back from Notre-Dame along the Boulevard St. Michel, Gabriel decided to call at Paul Vassily's flat. It was barely two o'clock in the afternoon, but as a disheveled, red-eyed, grey-faced Vassily opened the door, Gabriel realized that his friend lived in a different time zone, one where the rosy fingers of Dawn pointed towards the bed, and the bird of Minerva took its flight around breakfast time.

He excused himself profusely as Vassily introduced him into a red-draped living-room that remained totally impervious to the light of day. Here, thought Gabriel, was a man who re-created for himself the long perpetual winter of the Arctic wilderness. Thulé-des-Brumes, indeed. Vassily himself looked pretty rough, not unlike something at the tip of a ragpicker's crook.

"Just a cigarette and I'll be ready," he drawled.

But as it turned out, it was a cigarette that involved long and meticulous preparation and, when he finally managed to ignite it, had the rich smell of the mysterious Orient.

"Be my guest," he said, offering the cigarette to Gabriel. "You are used to it, I suppose."

"I'd even say it is used to me," Gabriel answered, snuggling back in the armchair. He took a puff, and quite instantaneously, freshness sparkled round his head and a luminous draught softly whistled through his bones. It also loosened his tongue.

"Sorry to disturb you, Paul. I wondered if, among all your strange books, you would have a book . . . a book about . . . succubi."

Vassily nodded silently for a moment, then extended his hand with somnambulistic grace. Gabriel gave him back the cigarette. "Sorry, no," Vassily finally answered through a wisp of sweet-scented smoke. "I wouldn't have much use for one." He looked at Gabriel. "Have you had a visit?"

Gabriel hesitated. "Something very faint . . . forcing itself out of the darkness."

"Female?"

"Thank God, yes."

More nods, and then: "Anything carnal?"

"Perhaps. But I did not find it arousing, to say the least."

A long time elapsed in silence, and then Vassily said suddenly, "Gourmont." He was pointing rather dramatically towards Gabriel, but then Gabriel realized he just wanted the cigarette back. He obliged him.

"Gourmont. Rémy de Gourmont?" Gabriel asked.

"You know him? I am supposed to go and see one of his new dramas tonight. 'Silent Theatre' he calls it. You will find it, I presume, more soothing than Mallarmé. And the location is wonderful."

"The location?"

"The Théâtre-Salon, in Pigalle. It is said to be the smallest theatre in Paris. It's a former chapel and a former painter's studio. The theatre they run there now is for . . . the happy few. And you can be a part of it."

"I'd be delighted. And what is Gourmont's relationship with succubi?"

A pause expanded, stretched, and slithered slowly around the room.

"With what?"

"The succubi."

"The succubi?" Vassily exhaled a plume of smoke behind which he disappeared. "Ah! Gourmont is writing a book on them, I've heard. Not under his own name. But I'm sure it will be magnificently researched. His erudition is delicious, delicious . . ."

"Delicious, that's a word to snuggle in."

"To smuggle in. In the word—the word *itself*."

"It's exactly that." Gabriel nodded. "You feel how it slurps. How it drips."

"Dripple. Dripple. Dripple-icious. Drool precious."

"You can blunder with a blunderbuss but you can't omni with an omnibus," Gabriel noted.

"*Omni soit qui mal y bus.*"

"I just said that."

"No, *you* did . . ."

Several hours passed in this manner. It was night by the time they tottered off to St. Sulpice to catch the brown omnibus to Pigalle.

IV
The Golden Dawn at Dusk

Brentford would have done anything to shake off the weight of Blankbate's death. Of course, Gabriel had been right when he tried to reassure him by observing that there should be another Blankbate still living in New Venice, but still . . . The *tattvas* were, he found, a diversion as good as any other while he waited for Lavis's laboratory results, and, perhaps, he hoped, they were not a totally useless distraction at that. In spite of his efforts to jot down everything he could remember, his recall of New Venice hadn't improved a whit since their arrival and had even, he suspected, deteriorated—the city had grown nebulous and patchy in his mind, as if he couldn't convince himself of its existence or, more exactly, as if *it* couldn't convince *him* of its existence.

So, with de Couard's recommendation neatly tucked in his breast pocket, Brentford took a ride to the western suburb of Auteuil, where the Ahathoor temple had recently been relocated. What he had gathered from the painter's hesitant and confusing explanations the day before was that it had been founded a few years earlier by a certain McGregor Mathers as the Parisian branch of the Hermetic Order of the Golden Dawn. The move to Paris, de Couard supposed, had been a way for Mathers to get closer to the Secret Chiefs who had given him original—and extremely important, as well as extremely valuable—Rosicrucian documents. There was also something fashionable to it, probably, Paris currently being not just the Capital of the Arts but the Capital of the Occult. Moreover, Mathers's artist wife, Moina, was French—the sister of a young rising star of French philosophy, Henri Bergson, who, could perhaps, contribute some funds.

In any event the neighbourhood looked rather affluent to Brentford. It was residential and uncannily calm, and the snow made it still more lifeless. He never ceased to wonder why people would live in such dead-quiet residential areas—it felt like walking through a necropolis. The address, 43 rue Ribeira, supposedly the entrance to the temple, had behind its green door a curious tunnel-like passage guarded by griffins. This, at least, had some allure. He noticed a small calling card on the doorstep and bent down to pick it up. It was entirely white on both sides. Not sure what to do with it, he put it in his pocket. Then, using a secret code that de Couard had given him, he banged on the door.

It was opened by a slightly square-jawed woman with burning eyes under a shock of jet-black hair: Mrs. Mathers herself, a figure straight off a Tarot card, and not without a wild kind of beauty. There was no servant, Brentford realized: clearly, the Rosicrucian documents passed on by the Secret Chiefs had not included the philosopher's stone and the recipe for gold.

At first, the high priestess of Isis looked rather uncertain about the visitor: Brentford supposed that the occultists—always imagining themselves at the centre of a network of rival lodges and dark forces—tended to develop wariness as a second nature. On the other hand, the glint in her eyes made Brentford feel that she welcomed the visit . . . any visit, perhaps . . .

Mr. Mathers, she informed him—or the Hierophant Ramses, as he apparently liked to be called—was indeed at home and would soon join them. A tall, taut man with a military moustache, he had a certain charisma, but also a definite nervousness, and a heavy whiff of whiskey on his breath. Brentford quickly got the sense that this was a man who had launched himself into an adventure that he now doubted increasingly that he could control. Not that he pitied him—Brentford didn't understand people like Papus or this fellow, nor did he understand exactly what they were after.

In any event, de Couard's recommendation was well received, and the colourful couple promptly gave Brentford a guided tour of the Temple, during which he noticed with surprise that they referred to each other as Monsieur le Comte and Madame la Comtesse. He had to give them credit for living their personal myth to the full. As a New Venetian, this was something he respected.

As it turned out, however, it was a short tour. As Brentford understood it, the entrance hall of the villa was the temple itself. This was a purely domestic operation, with the sort of grandiloquent cheapness he had observed at Papus's lodge. The white-marble staircase at one end, probably used as tiers during ceremonies, was surrounded by homemade painted panels of Egyptian deities, among whom Brentford recognized only Osiris. On an altar that still smelled of heavy incense, beside a nosegay of lotus flowers, a little white flame sprang from a Tibetan lamp made of green stone.

"It comes from Lhasa, the sacred city," Mathers explained with great reverence. "Observe how its three sides are slightly uneven," he added, nodding in appreciation, as if Brentford was supposed to understand the mystical meaning of the observation. There was more than a hint of the confidence man about the "Count," but there was also a strange intensity of conviction, and it was hard to draw a line between the two—even, perhaps, Brentford surmised, for the man himself.

"And this is a sistrum," he went on, lifting another curious object off the altar: a metal loop on a handle, crossed by four bars hooked on both sides and fitted with rings. "It's traditionally used for the worship of Ahathoor. The handle is the alpha and the other end is the omega. Each metal rod signifies an element, and the five jangling rings represent the action of the forces of nature as moved by the Divine spirit."

"Of course," Brentford replied, as he watched with a benevolent irony this grown man waving his rattle. Brentford doubted that this was what the gods asked of men . . . but who knew, maybe the gods liked a good laugh.

"So," Mathers asked, after leading Brentford to a small, quiet drawing room. "What is it you are seeking?" De Couard's recommendation, it seemed, had indeed helped him pass muster.

"Enlightenment through inner vision," Brentford said, honestly enough. "I was especially impressed by the *tattvas* I saw at Monsieur de Couard's."

"That is indeed part of our early initiation. But first you have to be given the grade of neophyte, which requires a course of studies.

Although . . . are you by any chance an advanced student of the tradition?"

"Not really, but I have had experiences of astral flight with an entity whom I have good reason to believe was the Helen of Simon Magus."

Which, roughly, was the truth. Still, Brentford was surprised that he'd managed to keep a straight face while telling it, although it always felt good to talk about Helen.

And his candour seemed to have worked wonders, for Mathers looked deeply impressed.

"Good reason?" he asked.

"She said so herself."

Mathers pondered this and found it convincing.

"If that's the case, I'm not worried about your ability to master the mysteries of the grade. I'll just give you a list of readings. You read hieroglyphs, don't you?"

"Oh. Only the big print," Brentford said modestly, thinking it was a good line until he realized he had stolen it from someone. That goddamn Sson of a wizard. What could he be doing "now"?

Mathers gave a short snort, which Brentford preferred to think was a laugh.

"The Egyptian Book of the Dead, that's the key for a start," he said, handing the list to Brentford.

Suddenly Brentford had a memory of riding towards the pyramid of Giza and almost falling from his horse, Gabriel laughing somewhere behind him. He had never been there, but he could feel it all, the muffled galloping, the sand in the eyes, being wrapped in a woolen heat. He kicked the vision shut and resurfaced. Not a second had lapsed.

"Of course, if I can contribute in any way to the order . . ." he said, as he imagined the situation demanded.

Mathers's swarthy face brightened.

"Come back to me when you're ready, Mr. Orsini. We'll have time to discuss these things later. Let not the material world get in the way of our real aims."

"Oh, by the way," Brentford said abruptly, retrieving the blank calling card from his coat pocket. "This was on your doorstep."

The swarthy face paled this time, and the subdued agitation Brentford had earlier remarked in the man now came to the fore. Count McGregor trembled. He snatched the blank card and ran to the hall, where he passed it over the flame of the Tibetan lamp. He changed colour, trembled more violently, and in two strides, took up his greatcoat and flew out of the room, as if expelled by a charm.

Moina and Brentford found themselves alone. They stared at each other for an embarrassing while. She looked troubled, but he could also see that she had no intention of mentioning what had just happened. She closed over the secret like an oyster over a pearl, but in that silence, he could hear, somewhere at the back of the house, a door banging shut.

"I'll be on my way, madame," Brentford said with a bow. "It was a pleasure and an honour to meet you and your husband."

Moina looked at him absent-mindedly, then quickly refocussed.

"If you want to come back for beginner-level *tattva* lessons, I suppose it's not important that you are not a 0=0 brother."

"That's very generous of you," Brentford said noncommittally, because he had no idea what a 0=0 brother was. He was close to the altar, where, he noticed, Mathers had left the card. He picked it up before Moina could move. Quickly, he made out, typed in fading blue ink:

fr. lux e septentrione.

Light from the North. "FR" must be *Frater*, "brother."

He turned towards Moina, and could see her struggling to appear calm, so that Brentford might suppose that the card was nothing out of the ordinary.

"But there is nothing on this card," he said, to let her off the hook, and indeed the inscription had now evaporated. "I apologize for my curiosity. I was worried for Monsieur le Comte."

"Thank you for your concern," Moina said unconvincingly. "The Count will be perfectly fine."

But as soon as Brentford was out the door, instead of going back to the avenue Mozart, he turned right, towards the rue de la Source, where he estimated the sound of the banging door had come from. And sure enough, there was, as he had deduced, another entrance to the villa. Mathers had disappeared but not, as the phrase goes, "without a trace."

"There's something to be said for snow," Brentford thought as he started the chase.

The tracks led through more sleepy, deserted streets, until they turned south along the sturdy arcades of the Circular Railway. Then, at the Auteuil station, they turned again, this time westward, into the Bois de Boulogne. The footprints were becoming less distinct, and Brentford almost missed them as they veered north again, along what looked like an abandoned racetrack. There was but one path to follow, and once or twice Brentford thought he caught a glimpse of the Highland hierophant in front of him. He forced himself to be more prudent.

The path reached the Upper Lake, where its water usually fell below to the Lower Lake via a picturesque cascade. But the cascade was frozen now, and the Upper and Lower Lakes were each an expanse of mirror-like ice that shone in the moonlight like spilled mercury. The ice must have been thick, too, for a tall man with a top hat stood in the middle of the Upper Lake wrapped in a greatcoat, a cane in his hand and a packet under his arm. Mathers was on his knees before him.

Brentford crouched at the edge of the treeline, but he was too far away to hear what they were saying. However, he saw, or thought he saw, Mathers fold and twist as if suffering great pain. The conversation did not last very long, in any case: the tall man forced Mathers to his feet to take the packet from him, and Mathers turned away, moving in a cautious, uncomfortable-looking walk across the ice, reaching the shore just a few steps away from where Brentford was hiding. By the time he got to solid ground he was running more than walking, the packet held tightly to his chest, and as he passed, Brentford thought he saw his nose bleeding purple in the moonlight, although Brentford hadn't seen him being hit.

And so Mathers faded into the night, while the other man hadn't budged an inch. He held still for a very long time before walking calmly back to the shore, the ice squeaking under his feet.

He came to a stop immediately opposite where Brentford hid in the trees, and casually took out a cigarette from a case.

"Excuse me, sir," his voice boomed out, "would you happen to have a light?"

Brentford felt pinned where he was like a chloroformed butterfly. The man approached slowly, less out of caution, Brentford thought, than to make an impression. It worked rather well.

Brentford rose from his crouch and reluctantly stepped out from cover. "Sorry, no," he said, faintly hoping these were not his last words.

Reaching into his greatcoat, the man brought out a silver lighter. "It is fortunate that I always carry a light," he said with a curious laugh. In the lighter's yellow flare, his inclined, malevolent face finally appeared and remained suspended in the flame.

Lucifer, Brentford thought with a shiver.

"Nothing of the sort. Lyonel Owain Savnock, at your service," Lord Lodestone said calmly.

"Brentford Orsini," Brentford heard himself answering. "How . . ."

"How do I know what you were thinking? Because it was written on your face. And because I put it there myself. I gave you a single, fleeting image, and for a while it triggered in you something you could not quite master."

Brentford had regained his breath. He still had trouble reconciling the man in front of him with one of the Seven Sleepers. He felt torn in half: ready to fight the man for his life, but wanting to ask for his autograph first.

"This little magic show," he said, "is what you do to Mathers, I suppose?"

Lord Lodestone didn't seem to take offence. He was clearly a man confident enough not to feel threatened by mere words.

"For one thing, it's not magic," he replied. "Magic is just an excuse for failure. As for Mathers, he does it to himself. He always has exaggerated physiological reactions during our little audiences. But given the choice, you can rest assured that he would not want it any other way. It makes him feel important, and that is exactly why he chooses to believe in me. If you always wondered what sort of idiot would sell his soul to the devil, you just met the ideal type."

It took a while for Brentford to realize that perhaps Lord Lodestone was actually merely interested in having a chat. But whether that was true or not, the obvious course to avoid was to take him for a dimwit. Sincerity and openness, he gathered, would be appreciated, and perhaps even rewarded with clues about his plans.

"He thinks you're one of the . . . Secret Chiefs?"

For a second, Brentford thought he had committed a *faux pas.* "You are of an inquisitive nature, Mr. Orsini," Lodestone answered quietly.

But, again much to Brentford's surprise, Lodestone seemed more interested in chatting.

"Such an inquisitive nature is, to my mind, a precious quality among human beings," he went on. "It is, truly, what makes us what we are. Since we ate of that damned fruit in Eden, it has been our curse to gather knowledge—it is even, perhaps, our *mission.* I cannot but congratulate you on your curiosity, and you will not find me a man to shy away from the truth—within, of course, certain practical limits. So to answer your question: he *does* think I'm one of the Secret Chiefs, or Unknown Superiors. I rather like him, nevertheless. His business is a hard one. There is more magic in money than there is money in magic. A simple piece of paper is worth more than the philosopher's stone, these days."

Brentford let this piece of wisdom sink in.

"There are no Secret Chiefs, then?"

"Well, as a matter of fact, now that you ask, I *do* happen to be a kind of Secret Chief—but that has nothing to do with this conversation . . . unless, perhaps, you are the man who dined yesterday at Thélème with Alexandre Vialatte."

Brentford expected his confirmation to be followed by a thundering: "*What were you trying to get out of him?*" perhaps accompanied by a few lightning bolts. But Lodestone simply replied, "Clever fellow. And efficient. Do you find him agreeable?"

"Why yes, very much so . . ."

"That is fortunate."

At a simple gesture from Lodestone, they had started to walk towards the north end of the park. Brentford had the feeling that, if he didn't say anything, silence would not be a problem. He had begun to imagine Lodestone as a solitary man, in search of understanding, yet he also sensed that this was probably just another disguise—perhaps even a trap.

"I am surprised that you recognized me," he ventured, as their steps crunched simultaneously in the snow. On their left, the frozen cascade hung out of time.

"An honest face in Paris? It would be harder to forget it," Lodestone answered. "So where all does this honesty lead you? I would say not very far, but I wish I were wrong."

"No, you're right, Milord. It hasn't led me as far as I wish to go, currently."

"Is this why you are interested in the Golden Dawn?"

"Indirectly, yes. I have, shall I say, developed an interest in inner vision."

"Only an idiot would not be interested in the workings of his mind. But do you think these people of the Golden Dawn, for all their comedic virtues, will really be of any help to you?"

"I admit I doubt it. I was raised a mathematician, and grew up an engineer. I usually have little patience for this sort of abracadabra. Recently, however, things have happened to me for which I haven't found my grounding very helpful. Though I doubt that, were such things happening to them, those mystics would find their *grimoires* very useful either. Knowledge comes from experience, not the other way round."

"It is perhaps more complicated than that, but you state it very clearly," Lodestone commented appreciatively.

Brentford felt encouraged to go further. "But still, they seem to be of some use to you?" he asked. But, once again, his bravery, such as it was, went unnoticed. Lodestone, no doubt, expected it.

"Oh, these occultists have many great qualities. For one thing, they save from oblivion and ignorance a tradition that is truly rather precious, even if they seem to have an innate inability to tell the wheat

from the chaff. Then too, they have a sound sense of ritual and symbolism, an art that is unfortunately being lost, and a very powerful
one at that. And last, but not least, few as they are, their networks
are intricate and far-reaching. They cover the whole globe and have
nerve endings in the highest places. I have found that you can achieve
surprising results if you know how to use them."

"You mean that they have a real power?"

"They try to make it appear that they do, certainly. They have
plans for the world. For Mankind. There is a lot of politicking done in
the astral, these days. A lone occultist is little more than a fool. But the
quack who gets the ear of a king or an emperor is a very dangerous
animal. These kinds of networks are blueprints for the politics of the
century to come. Sooner or later, their schemes will come to fruition,
and I can tell you, *we* shall be glad to live far away from them, somewhere that they can't reach *us*."

Brentford appreciated the "us," though he supposed that it
referred to the Sleepers.

"And how do you use this network?"

"I have a hand in it. The left one, that is." He lifted it, and for the
first time Brentford saw the lion at the knob of his cane, though it
wasn't exactly a lion: more like one of those slightly clownish Tibetan
snow lions, with a wavy mane and big square teeth.

"I give them objects or information," he went on, "in exchange
for the same, or for contacts. For I, too, you see, have plans for the
world and mankind. I admire tradition, I appreciate the use of symbols and rituals. The difference is that I am a businessman and a poli-
tician. I know how to get money, and I actually do like to get things
done. I'm sure that, as an engineer, you can understand that."

Brentford could, even if the type that Lodestone incarnated, part
magus, part robber baron, was more of a prototype. But he was, without doubt, the kind of man it took to get a thing like New Venice
done.

They were now close to the Porte de Passy. Brentford felt it was
time to say goodbye. Lodestone shook his hand quite cordially at first,
but then Brentford felt the pressure of the grasp increasing, until it
was more a threat than any sort of Masonic sign.

"Mr. Orsini," Lodestone said, "before we part, I would like you to take both a very deep breath of this fresh air and a look at the multitude of stars above your head. Aren't they beautiful tonight? Isn't this air wonderfully bracing? Isn't it, in a word, extremely pleasant to be alive?"

"It is, indeed," Brentford said, after he had fulfilled each of his curious directives.

"It will be, I hope, all the more pleasant for you if you were to know that if I hadn't seen you with Monsieur Vialatte at the Thélème Abbey, you would now be dead under the ice of the Upper Lake. I suppose it is unnecessary to add that if I ever see you in my path a third time, it would be much better if it were for a very good reason."

"Thank you for adding that, Milord. I wish you a very good night," said Brentford, with a slight quaver in his voice, before hurrying off to the Passy-Hôtel de Ville Omnibus to queue in front of the station. It was only as he arrived that a restrospective fear shook him and drenched him in cold sweat.

It was a stern warning that he had just received, but at least Lodestone had not ruled out the possibility that there might be a good reason for their meeting again. Brentford was inclined to think that his own reasons were excellent. Whether they could be explained as such to Lord Lodestone was an altogether different problem.

The English tourist walked out of his hiding place, a tree that would have had to grow another dozen years before it could entirely conceal his *embonpoint*. But the tourist had no intention of waiting for so long. He felt exhausted, his feet ice-cold from the walk in the snowy woods. He watched the tramway clang by and, farther off, a man with a cane walking back towards the obscure treeline of the woods. "So," he said to himself, "That must be the man."

IV

The Silent Theatre of Snow

I t had been a long, maddeningly slow trip, but the Théâtre-Salon was well worth it on its own picturesque merits. With its two large angels hovering above the orchestra, and its tiny boxes lined with iron railings above dark gothic paneling, the place looked more like a chapel than a theatre. Its gloomy solemnity proved a fitting jewel case for *Snow*, the play that had already started when Gabriel and Vassily arrived—if *started* was the right word, which Gabriel doubted.

The backdrop was a projection of plates from a Reynaud's praxinoscope. It depicted, in a naïve, vapourous, wholly artificial, but—to Gabriel's still hasheeshed eyes—singularly luminous way, a wintry mountain landscape and a wood of skeletal tree stumps sprinkled with holly. At first the scene was touched by the faintest glow of sun. But by and by, through a rather amteurish optical illusion, the edge of the mountains became a reclining nude woman, an immense idol lazily floating in the blue. Then, all claws out, a golden-maned lion attacked her, drawing long streaks of blood that trailed like clouds in the sky. Next, an old woodsman and his wife, doing their best to look poor and burdened by unbearable tasks, trudged by, when suddenly the man got a stone in his clog. Act II ended on this cliffhanger.

In Act III, the family trudged back miserably in the other direction, but this time with a child in tow, then ate bread and chopped wood in insufferable pantomine. Gabriel was starting to wonder if he could borrow the axe to massacre everyone, but then *something actually happened* in the next tableau: the clouds opened and the Woman raised herself and stood on the ground. Two flamelike lights, one red and one purple (*Like Od!* Gabriel thought), scintillated off her fingertips, and in these lights, figures were starting to move: in the red lights, there were plump, nude women, a Boucher avalanche of pink flesh; in the purple, devilish, priapic men. So this was to be a spectacle for adults, after all. The two lights spilled over each other, and the figures blended in unspeakable antics, so violently that blood dripped down towards the earth. But then, hermaphroditic angels (and Gabriel of course had a spasm of homesickness, thinking of the gorgeous Elphinstone twins) glided from the tree trunks and harvested the blood in ruby cups, from which they drank in ecstasy. Then the figures paled, the angels glided back into the trees, and so ended the fourth act.

Compared to the play's beginning, Act V was positively hectic. On the stage there were now two young lovers, draped in black capes, frolicking and kissing, with a kind of stupid amorous joviality that made the lonesome Gabriel wish that one of them would step on the teeth of a rake. Act VI, however, dampened their enthusiasm. A thick snow started to fall (and the cotton balls, as they drifted down, instilled in Gabriel a sense of childish wonder and wonderful well-being), until by and by it buried the lovers and the family, and all that remained of the scene was the tops of the trees.

The epilogue was equally cruel: the moon shone down on the desolate scene for a while and then was extinguished as the Woman burst into laughter in the darkness. So the Universe is just a cold, dark night lit by chaotic flares of cruel desires. Thanks for the news, thought Gabriel, as a volley of applause erupted, as thunderous as twenty half-asleep people could make it.

As the curtain fell one last time, Gabriel felt as if he had been released from a cage. That said, he felt privileged, too, as if he had just witnessed the birth of an art: one that would have no future anywhere, except in the phantascopic, phantasmagoric phantasies staged in the Circus of Carnal Knowledge, in New Venice, Northwasteland. He was almost surprised not to see d'Ussonville here, scouting for new ideas.

"You know the man we saw yesterday at Mallarmé's, the one that Fénéon brought? D'Ussonville?" Gabriel whispered to Vassily. "I should invite him here. I am sure he would be interested."

"Why not?" Vassily said. "We'll ask Gourmont. He'll be interested in someone interested."

The author was in the small courtyard in front of the theatre, saluting the spectators, most of them friends or relations. A nervous, stocky little man, with glistening cheekbones and a thick dark moustache, harangued the air nearby.

"He should do this with puppets," the man said with a curious metallic twang. However much Gabriel liked absinthe, another man's breath was not his favourite mode of enjoying it.

"I'll do it with puppets," the short dypsomaniac automaton went on. "Actors make it too personal. Only puppets, whose masters we are, can translate our exact thoughts. It's like in politics . . . Honourable monsieur, where are you from?"

Gabriel pointed an incredulous finger at himself. Once again he had failed to hide his interest, or perhaps he had an unfortunate gift for attracting the attention of demented writers.

"Polar lands," said Gabriel with candour, to cut a long story short. "Nowhere, so to speak."

"Ah! Excellent!" The man approved loudly. "Poland! Nowhere, so to speak. Excellent."

Before Gabriel could clear up the misunderstanding, Vassily pulled him over to Gourmont. Not naturally keen to meet people's eyes, Gabriel could not bring himself to look at Gourmont's lupus, which devoured half his face and curled his upper lip into a grin of disdain. Sometimes lowering his own eyes, sometimes raising them up to the stars, he let himself be introduced by Vassily.

The aging writer put his hand on Gabriel's shoulder and took him a few yards away, in the shadows of the courtyard.

"What is it I can do for you?"

"Paul told me you were an expert on succubi."

Gourmont rolled his bulbous eye towards Gabriel.

"You were . . . visited?"

"I'm afraid so."

"Interesting, interesting," the writer whispered. "Have you been around occultist circles, lately?"

"More than I would have cared to be."

Gourmont nodded, his lips pursed.

"You were visited against your will? Is that it?"

"Certainly."

"Since you do not seem to me to be a madman or a hysteric, and since I suppose you would not admit to it if you were, I will then assume, *cher monsieur*, that a spell has been cast on you. Someone who uses fluidic coagulations of the astral plane to obsess your astral body."

"I know of no one who . . ."

Gourmont's wife called in the background. He raised his hand.

"Just two minutes, Berthe, I'm finishing with this gentleman. You know, this is what I was trying to show with that little farce of mine," he said, with triumphant false modesty. "The astral life is *violent*, the living fluids that circulate through the immensity are charged with genital instincts. At times, it feels as if the whole universe is about to surrender to a vague, voluptuous dream . . . or a monstrous kiss." He paused, as his lupus shone in the moonlight. "We are all sensitive to this mysterious atmosphere. But it is dangerous. Very dangerous. Each one of our thoughts and our fantasies, our memories, imprints itself on the stuff the astral plane is made of, and resounds there like a wake-up call for the love-thirsty larvae. It leads them to your astral body as surely as a blood trail will lead a dog to its prey. The question is, do they come of their own accord—or, excuse me for saying so—attracted by your desires? Or is it that someone masters them and sends them to you? Or is it that someone projects themselves into the astral to connect with you in that fearsome, repulsive manner? If you don't—yes Berthe, I'm coming!—if you don't have the time or courage to ponder those grave questions, you could always go and meet Père Tonnerre, the exorcist of Notre-Dame. He had Satan tattooed on the soles of his feet to better trample him, and he swats succubi like flies. Now, if you will excuse me, we all have our chain . . . be it in this world or others."

V

The Visual Purple

When, after his exhausting odyssey, Brentford eventually reached the Hôtel des Écoles, it was with the firm intention of immediately resting his head on a pillow. But when he saw Jean-Klein's skis in front of the Colonel's door, he knew it meant the results were back from the tests on Blankbate's retinas. He clenched his jaw and strode in. He had, among other things on his overbooked itinerary, a murder to solve.

It was moving to see Jean-Klein reunited with members of the Most Serene Seven. Thomas was there, a slightly smug smile on his face, his eyes glinting with fresh morphine, and so was Lilian, nervously chain-smoking near an ashtray that looked like a mass grave for cigarette butts. The Colonel of course had remained hidden but had deputized Tuluk to attend on his behalf. Gabriel, however, wasn't there, and neither was Pirouette. Perhaps, speculated Brentford, she had simply gone to bed.

The cliché was on the desk, waiting in an envelope addressed to him.

"Sorry to have kept you waiting, Jean-Klein," Brentford warmly apologized. "I was detained." The fact that he'd been detained by Lord Lodestone himself somehow did not seem that important anymore.

"Don't worry," Jean-Klein said. "I haven't been here long, and I've had a pleasant time with your friends. It's like we've known each other for years."

"Well, I'm glad," Brentford said. "You could have opened it, though."

But he realized that to the Seven, he was still the Regent-Doge. No one, probably, had imagined opening an envelope with his name on it.

He tore the envelope open and looked at the photograph, not without emotion. It was a confused mass of particles that, frozen, nonetheless seemed to be agitated by a Brownian motion. Fuzzy blocks of light and darkness drew an abstract pattern that seemed indecipherable.

"So?" he asked Jean-Klein. "What do we have here?"

"It's a cliché, or *optogram*, of what we call Visual Purple, a biological pigment found in the retina—also known as rhodopsin—which is responsible for the perception of light and which immediately bleaches once it's been exposed to light. Professor Kühne, from Heidelberg, compared it not to a photographic plate, but to a plate that can renew itself, erasing old images in favour of new. But there's always a certain latency, and it takes some time for the trace of the old image to vanish entirely. That's one the reasons certain murderers recently have taken to destroying their victims' eyes after the deed, fearing that tell-tale images might be printed on their retinas."

"So what we have here are the last images seen by Blankbate?"

"We should consider ourselves lucky to have gotten anything. I think that violent death, especially by guillotine, somehow helps to fix the image—as if the falling blade acted as a kind of shutter. But optograms always look messy, and we lack any information about the surroundings to help us know what we're seeing."

Brentford focussed on the image. A kind of luminous sphere appeared in the top corner, barred by a blurry, oblique object. Could it be the guillotine's lunette? If it was, it was curiously located in relation to Blankbate's eyes.

"I don't get it," Brentford admitted. He passed the picture around. Lilian frowned at it, too.

"This ball of light. It looks rather like the moon, doesn't it?" she observed at last.

They all looked at one another.

"Well. Good guess, I'd say," Jean-Klein agreed. "Usually guillotine executions take place outside, in the last hours of the night. So, there's a definite possibility that it is indeed the moon."

Lilian passed on the picture to Thomas, who was sitting on Brentford's bed with his boots on, but he hardly looked at it before passing it back to Jean-Klein.

Brentford sighed. "Well, thanks very much, Dr. Lavis," he said. The expected revelation had failed, it seemed. A hard day's work had resulted in more lost time and frustration.

"Wait a minute," Thomas suddenly said, flushed by inspiration. "Can I see it again?"

"As much as you'd like," Brentford said. Jean-Klein passed the optogram back to Thomas.

The ensign examined it closely and closed his eyes, as if trying to pin down some image forming behind his lids.

"I've seen this object before. I don't really know where . . ." he said quietly, as if speaking to himself.

There was a moment of silent expectation, and then Thomas burst out laughing: it was all so evident and easy. Implicitly, woven in a web of crossing looks, a common view was forming among the Most Serene Seven that something should be done before Thomas's little morphine problem got out of hand.

"The slaughterhouse at La Villette," Thomas announced proudly. "This object is the spiked hammer the butchers use to stun the animal before they cut its throat."

"A *merlin*?" Jean-Klein blurted.

"What were you doing there?" Lilian asked.

Thomas laughed again. He was happy to be the centre of attention for once, and quite pleased with his discovery.

"I was with a nice girl, for a change. She was waiting for a drink of fresh blood, something of a custom here, apparently. I was struck by the way a tall fellow wielded this thing. Look at the little curve here at the back of this mass—it's the hook."

Brentford wavered between the importance of the news and the horror of the scene he couldn't help picturing in his mind.

"Why would anyone want to do that to Blankbate?" he asked.

Thomas suddenly took on the look of an inspired poet. "I remember now," he said. "I saw Blankbate that morning, waiting for someone in front of the abattoir. He was with a curious old man, rather uncouth, and he didn't seem to want to talk much. It could be linked, couldn't it? His murder may have something to do with the butchers of la Villette."

"You may well be right . . ." Brentford muttered, thinking out loud. "He was in Paris for a mission of his own that he never revealed to me nor, I imagine, to any of you. I suppose it was a Scavenger thing. He must have been after something the Butchers had, or they were in his way. Thomas, Lilian—I'd be grateful if you would go to La Villette tomorrow and observe what happens there. See if you can find that old man again."

Lilian and Thomas looked each other. The idea of going to the other end of Paris in the icy morning did not quite agree with their personal projects. But it was a case of patriotic duty, and if there was a chance of avenging Blankbate . . . Lilian, at least, sighed her approval. Thomas did not.

"I liked Blankbate. Quite an able man," he began. "But should we let this distract us from the more urgent matters at hand? We're closing in on the Sleepers—shouldn't we concentrate on that and let the police work on the rest?"

"Would you, as an officer, leave the life of one of your men unavenged?" the Colonel shot back.

"And I doubt that the police will be very helpful," Brentford added. "As we've learned, some of them have more than a paw in this Wolves of the Woods business."

Thomas conceded the point gallantly. "We'll go, then."

Suddenly an enormous din was heard coming from the hallway.

The Most Serene Seven hurried out, only to find that Tuluk had snuck out to try out Jean-Klein's skis on the staircase. He had made an edging mistake between the second and third floors and lay on the *entresol*, a confused tumble of clothes and limbs, one of the skis stuck in the elevator grille and an embarrassed smile on his flushed face.

"Are you all right?" Jean-Klein asked, as hotel clients trickled out of their rooms and gathered in dressing gowns all around the staircase.

Tuluk seemed to find the whole affair rather funny . . . or at least his laughter was an attempt to convince the others that it was.

❋

Brentford shook his head in despair and went back to his room. He noticed that Lilian was following him.

"Brentford," she began, joining him as he unlocked the door.

"Yes?" he asked, taking a step aside so she could enter.

She walked in and Brentford closed the door behind them. As happened now when he found himself alone with her, he could feel a certain anguish whirling in his stomach, like a goldfish choking in a muddled bowl.

Lilian spoke quickly. "I have to tell you that I took Pirouette back to her mother's place."

Brentford was unhappy with the news, but not quite surprised. "And why is that? She won't be safe there."

"I couldn't take care of her, day in, day out."

Brentford nodded. "I suppose I understand," he said, though understanding did not mean that he approved.

Lilian had turned, and she grasped the railings at the foot of the bed so strongly that her knuckles turned white. Brentford braced himself for a confession that he did not want to hear.

"You see . . ." she began. She hesitated for a while. "I've met someone." She hesitated again. "I'm in love, Brent."

Brentford felt something inside sink. "Thomas?" he asked, paling, and trying to hide his anger.

Lilian sniggered. "I can do a little better than that, I hope. Even if he has been amazing tonight."

"Am I supposed to know who it is?"

"Do you really care?"

"For you, yes."

Lilian bent her head down and gave a slight, twisted smile. "Well, I'll tell you who it is, but only because I think she can help us."

"*She*?" he asked, wide-eyed, although it was hardly a surprise. "Sorry. Carry on." He felt his fury cascading down into a pool of sadness and getting lost there.

"She's called Morgane Roth. She's the girl we met at the hospital the day we arrived, when our Jean-Klein died."

"The one whose séance you went to?"

"Exactly. It was the séance that gave me the idea. She had a rather odd take on spirits herself, but the fact is that the one that manifested itself that night knew about New Venice and that it was going to be built. Lord Lodestone seemed to be embarrassed by the mention of it, and last night I found him completely unwilling to discuss it."

"You dined with Lodestone yesterday?" Brentford blurted out.

"Oh, did I forget to mention that? I learned nothing, really, beyond the fact that he is thinking hard about a religious system for what we suppose is New Venice. As I say, he was especially cagey."

Brentford thought of the open-mindedness with which the Sleeper had talked to him a few hours ago. For a man who feared nothing but the discovery of his secrets, his reaction at the séance might point to something important indeed.

"I met him by chance this evening. I found him rather . . . *pleasant* would not be the right word . . . communicative, let us say. But I did not get a chance to talk about New Venice, nor was I encouraged to. However, I must say he is a rather impressive character."

"You have to like the type. But, yes, I suppose so," Lilian approved.

"So, what do you suggest?"

"We should try a séance at Morgane's place, just the Seven, and see what comes out of it. Whether there's a way out of here or a chance to communicate. Perhaps we'll learn more about Lodestone."

"Would tomorrow night be possible?"

"I'm sure."

"All right, then," Brentford said, albeit with some difficulty. Meeting his love's lover was not exactly his idea of a good night out. But he would do it. For New Venice. And for Lilian.

"Are you angry at me?" Lilian asked. "For Pirouette—or Morgane?"

"No, Lilian," he said, then thought about it. "I'm angry at the people who treated Blankbate like beef."

As she left, her back a pearlescent blur, he was about to thank her for her idea, but decided there was a limit to his self-abasement.

❋

Lilian had not been gone a minute when someone knocked at Brentford's door. Technically, it could have been anyone but the Colonel; however, it was Thomas who he found standing in front of him, his opiated smile a tad too persistent.

"Yes?"

"There is something I remembered that I forgot to tell you. Or something I forgot to remember to tell you."

"What is it, Thomas?" Brentford sighed.

"It may seem strange to you, and at the time I didn't pay any attention to it. But when we went to that séance with Lilian at Morgane's . . . D'you know Morgane, by the way? A very beautiful woman, not my type, but very much Lilian's, I gather . . ."

"It's been another long day, Thomas," Brentford said with more impatience than he meant. "If you could get straight to the point . . ."

"Right. So when we went to that séance, there was this little harbour before the Bastille. And in that harbour, I thought I saw a yacht that was flying the New Venetian flag. That's all."

Brentford was impressed again. "That's a lot, Thomas. Thank you very much."

Thomas clicked his heels and walked out, absorbed by the dark corridor. "Take care of yourself, mate," Brentford was about to say, but it was already too late.

VI

The Mysteries of Montmartre

After Gabriel had spoken with Gourmont and he and Vassily were leaving the Théâtre-Salon, Vassily had met a "friend" whom Gabriel found quite charming, although her name, Hermine de Candore, sounded too good to be true. Vassily offered to see her home—*his* home, Gabriel surmised—and they vanished in the busy night. Not that Gabriel felt abandoned: he was still disappointed with himself for not having recognized, until it was too late, Alfred Jarry standing in front of the theatre, and he could feel himself beginning the slow slide that marked the start of his sulking spells. A little loneliness, he decided, was exactly what he needed.

But he did not feel like going home right then, if his hotel room could be called a home. As he was already halfway up to Montmartre, he decided to continue rambling. He took the rue Blanche and merged into the chaotic glitter of the boulevard, buying a cornet-bag of hot chestnuts to munch on a leisurely stroll among the street hawkers, the song-sellers and the paper flower–girls, among faceless but hurried silhouettes whose heads were enveloped in clouds of breath charged with the static of desire. He walked without a destination, ignoring the raucous love-calls of feathered females, following whims, perspectives, clusters of blurry lights. He angled off to climb the rue Lepic, where busy ragpickers reminded him of poor Blankbate, and then swerved towards the Abbesses, watching people in the cafés trying to dispel the cold and wetness from their minds, their yellow faces waving like weak flames behind the misty windows.

On the rue Ravignan, he came across the Zut!, a drab little tavern off the tourist circuit whose name (which meant "Damn!") sounded familiar. Wasn't this where, what were their names, Raymond and Lucie, the anarchist couple he and Brentford had met at the cemetery, had said they could sometimes be found in the evening? He pushed open the door to find himself in a fuliginous dump, bare of all ornaments, except the word "Zut!" scratched on the wall and trembling in the uncertain light of wick lamps. The bar was a row of wooden casks, and it served unhealthy drinks to a clientele that was on a par with the decoration: the lower dregs of bohemia, black-nailed and thinly clothed, bellowing dubious anarchist rants through the thick fog of cheap pipe tobacco, while tousled-haired muses applauded them, vibrant with alcohol-fueled love. Charming place, thought Gabriel, as he made his way towards the bar.

Having ordered a Putois demi-fine absinthe, he slithered towards the back room, whose ceiling looked as if seawrack had been glued to it and now dangled in enamelled stalactites. Lucie and Raymond were indeed there, drinking wine with a heavyset, long-haired man, whose soft voice and unctuous courtesy did not quite hide a tough, almost brutal, streak. They introduced him to Gabriel as Olivier Deligny, the publisher of a respected anarchist newspaper, *Le Niveleur*—"the Leveller." He had a book in front of him that immediately triggered a warmth on Gabriel's tattooed arm.

"May I have a look?"

"Be my guest. I have just bought it second-hand," Deligny said. "It has become rare."

It had been published in 1872 and written by Auguste Blanqui, the famous—for some, infamous—French conspirator. The title alone—*L'Eternité par les astres*, "Eternity Through the Stars"—made Gabriel salivate. He flipped through it rapidly but cautiously, sensing that Deligny was a rather fastidious fellow when it came to books.

"It was written in jail, at the Fort of the Bull, as it is called. It's the work of a desperate man," Deligny elaborated.

To Gabriel, it looked like some kind of Gallic version of Poe's *Eureka*. From what Deligny explained, this cosmic speculation was founded on a rather simple line of reasoning: if the elements of matter are in finite numbers, and if the universe is truly infinite, then all combinations of material bodies have necessarily to be repeated endlessly along with all their possible permutations. For the convict that Blanqui was, this made the universe itself a gigantic jailhouse, full of eternal routines, but it also allowed the possibility of what he called "happy variants": brother-stars where lost loves were found again and failed revolutions were successful for once. It suddenly dawned on Gabriel that perhaps this was for the Most Serene Seven a better theory than that of time travel; it could at least explain why this Paris was different—its climate, for example—from Jean-Klein's Paris of 1895. But how they might have found themselves on a brother planet was another matter altogether.

Seeing that Deligny was getting slightly impatient for the return of his treasured book, Gabriel closed it softly and started to tell his own story.

"I was at the morgue this morning," he said grimly. "One of our friends has been beheaded."

The French anarchists looked at each other and expressed their deepest sympathy, simply but seriously. They regarded these murders as acts of war and the victims as fallen comrades.

"Yes, I've read this in the papers, where it was labelled as an unfortunate accident," Raymond said with a sigh. In the next room, a certain Frédé had started playing a lullaby on his guitar, by tone-deaf public demand. "As usual, the journalists would rather write about the so-called anarchist menace, and not one of them dares touch what's behind the beheadings. There are deep ramifications, you know, up to the highest levels."

"The president?" Gabriel asked, between two bitter sips of his rather louche absinthe.

"Perhaps." Lucie began to explain, "Or at least, Faure is a staunch supporter of the Franco-Russian alliance that was signed in 'Ninety-three. The price of the alliance has always been that France gets rid of its troublesome foreigners, including, of course, Russian refugees."

"Ah!" Gabriel said. "The Russians again. Someone at the Canadian Commission said that Tripotte was on the Okhrana payroll."

The three exchanged looks. "It is quite likely," Deligny replied, in his soft, edgy voice. "Since Rachkovsky took over at the Okhrana, he has always employed people from the Sûreté—some retired and some not. He has a whole brigade of them. I hear that the Sûreté is divided about the cooperation, but, nevertheless, the Okhrana provocateurs are always very well informed, and it is more than probable that files from Notebook B are copied and transmitted to Rachkovsky."

"But," Gabriel surmised, "it's not Rachkovsky or provocateurs, or the Okhrana, who commit these beheadings, is it?"

"Not directly, of course," Deligny went on patiently. "But, with the unfortunate Dreyfus affair on top of this, the hatred of Jews and foreigners has taken on monstrous proportions in this country. Some 'true patriots,' as these imbeciles call themselves, have decided to 'clean up the mess,' to use their rhetoric, and recruit Butcher-Boys from La Villette. They're a bunch of brutes full of thicker-than-mud 'old' French blood, who still live in the days of guilds and paternalism, and have only hatred for trade unions and the Republic. Edouard Drumont hires them as stewards for all his anti-Semitic rallies, and we even gave them a serious drubbing in the Vauxhall back in 'Ninety-three. Their leader was a sight to see—Antoine Manca de Vallombrosa, Marquis of Morès, isn't that a name out of a dime novel? He has now retired to the Sahara, I hear, where he wages a guerrilla war against the British. But his successors are so stupid they can't share a thought among themselves. And of course all these people are staunch supporters of the Czarist regime. Since the interests of these patriots merge, at least temporarily, with those of Rachkovsky and his clique, I suppose that favours are done, and information exchanged, if not manpower."

"But who runs them now, these Wolves?" Gabriel asked.

"Since the departure of Morès, it seems that his stand-ins have rooted for a certain Hébert," Raymond answered. "The King of Garbage, as he calls himself."

"That's some title," Gabriel said with a frown. "Garbage, you say? My dead friend was in this line, too. Perhaps his death has something to do with Monsieur Hébert's business."

"Perhaps," Raymond answered with a shrug. "It is a business, certainly, and a lucrative one at that, and I doubt that Hébert would regard favourably any attempts at interfering with it. He has become filthy rich, literally. He has thousands of ragpickers slaving for him, and he sells Paris's own refuse back to it at a very dear price. This is where his fortune comes from."

"Money has no smell," Lucie observed wryly.

"Now," Deligny went on, "Hébert has his political ideas, but dumb as they are, he is shrewd enough to know he won't go anywhere with an army of dustmen. So he turned to the bigger fellows."

Well, there is a lot that can be achieved with an army of dustmen, Gabriel could testify from experience, and the memory of Blankbate filled him with bitterness and resentment. But then, what was possible in New Venice . . .

"Hey, look who's here," Lucie whispered, pointing her chin towards a corner of the back room.

Gabriel turned around to see a tall man rising from a dark corner, wearing a high-collared navy-blue coat of military cut. In the dim light, he recognized his profile and started with surprise.

"D'Ussonville," he whispered to himself, hiding his face behind his hand.

The Sleeper nodded discreetly towards another tall man with white cropped hair who sat near the door, then went over to talk a little with him, apparently without having noticed Gabriel's presence.

"Who's that?" Gabriel asked his friends in a low voice.

"Captain Boulogne," Lucie answered.

"*Shh!*" Raymond murmured, a finger on his lips.

"Or so they say," Deligny added all the same.

The "captain" left the tavern, and the other man followed him a few seconds later—after scanning the room, Gabriel observed, as if for potential foes.

"So who's Captain Boulogne?" Gabriel inquired after they'd gone, with what he hoped would pass for a light touch.

Raymond sighed as Lucie explained, "Some sort of anarchist legend, actually. He's rumoured to be preparing a terrible coup. The ultimate propaganda by deed . . ."

"For a legend, he looks rather real," Gabriel commented, wondering if d'Ussonville really had started as a Captain Boulogne, or was just playing his part for some end Gabriel couldn't discern . . . yet . . .

"Oh, he's real," Deligny said. "It's the coup that's hypothetical. A lot of us think it's a trap. Even these naifs who advocate direct action have been conned so many times by provocateurs that he may have trouble recruiting anyone who isn't a policeman. I'm anxiously waiting the time when there are only secret agents in terrorist groups."

"Well, he's recruited someone, at least," Raymond commented.

"Well, excuse me," Gabriel said abruptly, as he rose. "This is rather important to me. I must go."

"Are you going to apply?" Deligny asked, and something nasty in his tone of voice implied that, for a brief second, he'd suspected Gabriel of being an undercover policeman.

"I'm just interested in legends," Gabriel said as he saluted them. "Goodbye and good luck."

Deligny nodded solemnly. "Good luck to you," he replied.

✷

For a while Gabriel thought he had lost track of D'Ussonville and his companion, until a shadow cast on a streetcorner wall gave him some hope of catching up. He hurried along the slushy pavement, walking cautiously, almost on tiptoe, so close to the wall that he could feel its humidity on his back, until eventually the two silhouettes came into his line of sight. He followed them up narrow stairs, along snowy vineyards, past derelict windmills, through winding streets with the distinct feel of a small village—a complicated route, which Gabriel understood was meant to avoid the crowd that trickled from the Place du Tertre, even at this time of night.

But their destination was suddenly hard to miss: the half-finished church of Sacré-Cœur abruptly loomed over them, bluish in the moonlight. The works were still going, and scaffolding bristled around the gigantic dummy teat that was supposed to appease God's anger at France's socialist tendencies. Gabriel had to admit that the whole thing had something faintly New Venetian about it—its sheer unashamed improbability, its vague dreamlike quality, the sensation that it was less a real building than some trompe-l'œil set up for a drama not yet played, or maybe a cutout glued on a trick postcard photograph.

Obviously, "Captain Boulogne" had not come here as a tourist. His accomplice in tow, he disappeared through an opening in the palisade and remained invisible for several minutes. Gabriel didn't dare to follow them; he would have to wait until they came out. But then he saw, emerging from the shadows, a third man who had evidently been waiting surreptitiously near the Sacré-Cœur. It was sheer luck that he had not spotted Gabriel. From where Gabriel stood, this man looked like a typical Parisian thug with his casquette and his neckerchief. He came close to the rent in the fence and tried to peep through it, but he didn't enter and soon retreated back into the shadows. Moments later, the pseudo-Boulogne and the tall man accompanying him stepped out. The two men separated immediately and went their own ways off into the labyrinth of Montmartre. The spy chose to follow d'Ussonville. Gabriel saw him undoing his neckerchief and stretching it between his fists as he came up behind d'Ussonville.

"Look out, Captain!" Gabriel cried, as the man closed in on d'Ussonville, ready to jump on his back and strangle him from behind—the famous *Father Francis's* trick.

D'Ussonville turned quickly and sent a perfect *fouetté chausson* kick towards his opponent, catching him in the ribs with a crack that Gabriel could hear across the street. The man swayed, and before he could recover his balance, d'Ussonville, a sportsman for his age, had followed up with a swift pass of his cane (Gabriel, a canist himself, recognized it as a perfect *latéral croisé*) that slapped the man across his ears and cheeks so violently that it cut a gash as if he had been lashed with a whip. The thug doubled up in pain, offering d'Ussonville the opportunity to kick him in the face, which he did without the slightest hesitation and with a certain prancing elegance. The mugger collapsed into the gutter with a self-pitying moan.

"Thank you, sir, and good night," d'Ussonville called to the invisible Gabriel while straightening his clothes. Then, lightly touching his hat with the tip of his cane, he blended into the night.

To be continued . . .

EPISODE X

RECOGNITIONS

I

The Cult of the Wolf

Things had gotten so intense that it wasn't difficult for Gabriel to think of six impossible things that had to be done before breakfast. This particular morning was worse than usual, and he had in fact lost count after ten or twelve, his muddy mind refusing to go further. He hadn't slept for days, not even the proverbial wink, and while insomnia had its merits—it kept the succubus at bay—in the long run, it had become clear to him that it simply would not do.

Brentford found him in the hotel restaurant, slumped in his chair, lucky to have a table to prop him up.

"I know," Gabriel muttered as Brentford sat down. "I've aged ten years since we got here. I'm probably the only person who's ever managed to get older when travelling back in time."

"You could do with injections of testicular liquid. I seem to understand from the papers that it's quite the tonic, and very fashionable now."

"I already have more testicular liquid than I can shake a stick at, if you get my meaning."

"It is my misfortune that I always get it, yes."

Gabriel felt it was time to steer the conversation towards less personal matters.

"I met Thomas and Lilian on their way out. Did I miss something last night?"

Brentford told him succinctly about his meeting with Lodestone, and filled him in on Lilian's plans for a séance with Morgane Roth.

"You'll have to go without me, Brentford. I'm not quite in the mood for spirits," Gabriel warned him. "Any news on Blankbate's murder?"

"We've made inroads." He took the optogram out of his wallet and passed it to Gabriel, who struggled to keep his eyes open and focussed on the luminous chaos of the image.

"According to Thomas, this thing in front of the moon is a merlin," Brentford explained, "a butcher's spiked hammer. It was used before the decapitation."

Gabriel looked more closely, until suddenly the mysterious dots made sense. Brentford saw his eyes light up, like a pale Arctic sun behind a veil of clouds.

"It's a ritual murder, Brentford," Gabriel said. "A sacrifice. I saw Raymond and Lucy last night, and they seem to think that the Wolves are indeed Butcher-Boys from La Villette, who are longtime darlings of radical right-wing nuts. I suppose they incarnate the good old France of yore, and the sacrifices that are needed to wash away its current sins, preferably with blood."

"Butcher-Boys . . . He was killed like an animal, yes. But I thought animal offerings were meant to replace human victims. Wasn't that the metaphor?"

"Some people have an innate inability to grasp metaphors. Occultists in particular. Nationalists, of course. Some people here seem to have reverted to a mode of *very* primitive thinking. For one thing, look at the moon under the arch. It's aligned perfectly with the blade of the guillotine, like an eyeball inside its socket. And this little curved mass on the left, look at its beak—it looks like a vase or something, probably to collect the blood as it spurts from the wound. And isn't that an ivy leaf, on the top corner? As if the guillotine were wreathed in it. I don't know for sure, but it certainly looks like the work of a twisted fertility cult, a sacrifice designed to ensure the renewal of the natural cycle of growth."

"But I thought that the Wolves of the Wood of Justice were more of a political or even a racial operation?"

"What's the difference, really? Politics and magic . . . basically, it's all about ensuring that there's enough food, and finding someone to blame if there's not. It's mostly what New Venice is about, too, isn't it?"

Brentford, thinking of his stint at the Greenhouse, couldn't really disagree.

"As to taking it out on the foreigners," Gabriel went on, "that's the ABC of magical thinking. It used be a time-tested feature of human sacrifices: the passing stranger whose ritual murder will bring luck to the crop. It's not as passé as it seems. It even has a bright future, I guess. You know the Marseillaise, don't you?"

"The fish soup?"

"That's *bouillabaisse*. I mean the French national anthem. *Let an impure blood water our furrows*. It's a sentence that *sticks*, is it not?"

"But the guillotine—it's hardly primitive equipment," Gabriel persisted.

"It depends on how you look at it, I suppose. But it's turned into a myth of its own. It's certainly a potent totem for a tribe. Don't forget it's usually made of oak, one of the trees most commonly held sacred, and one that was worshipped at druid sacrifices for its fertilizing power. From what I've heard, the butchers like to dress as druids at least once a year, when they parade an ox through the streets."

"And the wolves?"

"Hmmm . . . something to do with the Luperci, perhaps—the Brothers of the Wolves," Gabriel speculated. "They were Roman priests who would sacrifice a goat in honour of the she-wolf who had fed Romulus and Remus. Also, in old French peasant traditions the wolf is often a corn-spirit. I also seem to remember that 'wolf' is the name for the nonadept in the radical Wood Masonry of the *carbonari*—the charcoal-burners. It could be a kind of private joke. But really, anything goes in these rituals. It only starts to make sense when you're lying trussed up on the altar."

"Well, all that might make some sort of sense regarding the current situation in France. But I still don't see what Blankbate had to do with these butchers."

"From what I gather, the wolves are run by a local trash tycoon named Hébert. Blankbate may have been scavenging in forbidden territory and found himself the perfect offering for their cult."

"And where can we find this Hébert? I suppose turning to the police will do more harm than good."

"I have a hunch he is more the kind of person who finds *you*."

Brentford sighed, his eyes closed in deep thought.

"Perhaps the Colonel is right; we should forget about this story for the moment and simply watch our backs. There are so many things going on that I was beginning to forget about de Lanternois and the magnetic crown. I feel he is the key to our next step . . . the next step towards home."

"Oh, by the way," Gabriel said, as he got up. "I forgot something, too. A trifle, really. I met d'Ussonville again, prowling in the streets of Montmartre under the name Captain Boulogne, and apparently he's hatching a plan to blow the Sacré-Cœur to bits."

Brentford stared at his cup of coffee as if it were the slough of despond. He eventually nodded and muttered, "Oh, great."

II

Ladies' Delight

It was so foggy at the abbatoir in La Villette that morning that you couldn't see the clock in the esplanade from the nearby entrance gate, and the pavilions of the slaughterhouse loomed uncertainly as the queue of Blood Drinkers advanced towards them. In civilian clothes for once, Thomas checked the muffled silhouettes around him to make sure that Blanche wasn't among them. Knowing her as he did (which was, he admitted, too little), he guessed that she didn't actually visit as often as she claimed and that perhaps she had only been putting on a show when she had brought him here earlier. Thank Cod, in any event, that she wasn't there now; he didn't want her to see him with Lilian, who was walking beside him in moody silence. Even if they didn't mention it, the two of them shared something: blurry visions of their lovers softly sleeping between warm sheets.

The queue snaked towards its destination, its fits of chesty coughing diffusing steam into the mist, breaking Lilian's reverie with the way it reminded her of a herd about to be sacrificed. She noticed with revulsion the painting above the door of the scalding-house, which showed a man in a blue butcher blouse slitting another man's throat. MORT AUX JUIFS, the legend above it read. No one else seemed to even notice it.

She nudged Thomas.

"See that fresco over there?"

"Oh. I didn't even see that when I was here the other day. What does it say?"

"'Death to the Jews.'"

Thomas raised his eyebrows.

"Why would they want to kill the Jews?"

"They probably don't know themselves," Lilian said, in a quiet but contemptuous tone.

A faint smell of blood and manure, rising from the greasy ground, pervaded the place and made her feel queasy. The Butcher-Boys waited in aprons, with defiant looks, charged breath, and knives on their belts. As the cow was brought to the gate, people shuffled and fanned out as if to get a better view. Lilian was among them, taking special note of the man whom the others called Le Bzou, who wielded the merlin, his muscles bulging under his shirt as if they had been cast in bronze. As Le Bzou lifted the hammer, Lilian recognized the curious hook at the back: it was the same object that she had seen on the optogram. She closed her eyes and the merlin came down with a squishy thud that brought her heart to her lips. She tried not to think about Blankbate.

"Over there," Thomas suddenly whispered, nodding towards the entrance arch of the pavilion. Lilian took a quick glance. Two men were at the end of the queue, spectral shapes just emerging from the fog. One was an old man in rags, the other a tall officer with a red uniform under his cape and a pith helmet above his long sad face. Something black and shiny appeared at the end of his right arm, as if he were carrying a weapon, but it wasn't clear from that distance.

"The old man," Thomas whispered, "He was the one with Blankbate. And I met the other one, too. He's not the kind of figure you forget. He knows Blanche."

"Blanche?"

"The girl we saw at the séance, remember? She was the one who first brought me here."

In Lilian's mind, the jigsaw puzzle that had been Thomas's whereabouts during the past few days was suddenly completed. But now there was a new conundrum to exercise her mind.

"What do these two have to do with this . . . Blanche?"

"She seemed to be very troubled by the sight of the old man. As to the Major," he added with disgust, "he claims to be a very good friend of hers. I'll go and talk to him."

Thomas walked briskly across the few yards that separated him from the two men. As he approached, he could see the old man hunch up like a hedgehog, but Yronwoode kept his uncanny composure—half man, half tin soldier.

"We meet again, Major," Thomas said, full of morphine poise, as he saluted the British officer, then turned to the other. "As to you, sir, didn't I see you here two days ago? You were with a tall fellow, with a beard and tinted glasses, you remember?"

The old man looked at the Major as if in panic, then said something in French that Thomas didn't need translated to understand—the old man simply wanted to get away.

"Do you know the man I'm talking about, Major?"

"Listen, Mr. Paynes-Grey," the Major said. "I have already taken the occasion to warn you about getting involved in all this. None of it is your business—and you should believe me when I say that that's rather good news for you."

"*Partons . . .* " the old man begged.

"I am sorry to insist, Major," Thomas said firmly. "But that man was a friend of mine, and the last time I saw him alive was with this person."

Lilian was too far away to hear anything, but she could feel the tension just by watching Thomas's back. It quivered like a wild horse's. She felt a twinge of remorse about the morphine solution Morgane and she had so lightly offered him. It was then that she saw Swell-in-the-Sack.

He was walking up along the queue, a few steps away. She lowered her head, congratulating herself on the veil she wore, but he was not paying attention to the Blood Drinkers: his eyes were fixed on Thomas and the two men. He put his fist in his pocket, clenching something. Lilian immediately sensed the danger.

She lifted her head, and then her veil.

"Well, if it isn't Mr. Swell-in-the-Sack," she said softly as he walked by.

The handsome ruffian's eyes lit up as he recognized her. Lilian had been right in assessing him. He might pride himself on his manhood, but women were his weakness. She noticed—it was hard to miss—the purplish gash that flashed along his right cheek. She also noticed that he was one of those men who seem embellished by their wounds. Up to a certain point, at least.

"Why! It's Pirouette's chaperone! Come here for a little thrill, did you?"

His malevolent mien had abruptly given way to an easy charm that Lilian could well imagine effective, despite her distaste for him. He was a steamroller of relentless seduction. Many women must have surrendered while knowing all the time that the charm was only a show, but it was not a bad show. Somehow, and unlike the spiel of most men, you felt it had *content*.

"Not the thrill I expected," she answered.

"There may be other kinds," Swell-in-the-Sack said. Lilian wished she had a gramophone to record the crapulous and honeyed tone of his voice.

"I'll show you the sights, if you wish," he went on softly, his eyes indicating an open door on the side of the abattoir.

It would soon be Lilian's turn to drink from the frothy blood that was bubbling on the ground. She knew her stomach could not take it. Not that it could take this fellow, either. But perhaps, besides keeping him away from Thomas a little longer, she would learn what the devil he was doing here, among the Butcher-Boys, and why he had been so wound up to see the Major and the old man talking to Thomas.

Swiftly stepping out of the crowd now elbowing its way to the fountain of blood, she followed Swell-in-the-Sack through the door and into the abbatoir. There, hanging from hooks, rows and rows of mutilated carcasses extended into the distance, it seemed indefinitely, waiting to be sold in the Carré de Vente. Lilian thought of Blankbate again and a shiver ran through her as she looked at the red scarf around Saturnin's neck.

He stopped and turned towards her, his half-mittened hand caressing one of the carcasses. He had broken, unclean nails, but his slender fingers were beautiful, and he obviously knew it.

"I didn't know you worked here," Lilian said, trying to sound more troubled than she was and surprised it came to her so easily.

"Oh, I used to, some years ago, and I still have a lot of friends here. But I decided that I much prefer to deal with meat that's alive and smiling."

Lilian felt her blood rushing to her face, and knew from the passing smugness of his smile that he took her flush of anger for a blush of sudden arousal. That he could even think this, however, only stoked her fury.

It was already too late for the conversation she'd been hoping for, and the situation now struck her as terribly unseemly. Already Swell-in-the-Sack had taken a step towards her, lightly placing a large hand on her arm. Lilian looked at him a little from below, her head slightly inclined, her eyes flashing "Don't you dare," and then again she saw that he understood this as "Please, no," which, in his huge pocket dictionary, evidently translated as "Please." It maddened her that every one of her reactions seemed to him like an invitation. He moved his head an inch closer, and beamed a sparkling smile. His teeth were so white they reminded her of the rib bones that she saw all about, and for a moment she was dizzy, raw meat whirling all around her.

"I'm glad you've thought things over since yesterday," he said. "I've been thinking about you myself." He announced this as if it were an especially flattering compliment. Lilian shook herself from her paralysis.

"That's when you hit that lamp post, I suppose," she quipped, nodding towards the gash on his cheek.

His smile froze and his grasp tightened on Lilian's arm. Before she could react, Saturnin's face loomed close before her, a blur in which his smile seemed a red wound, as if he were smiling with his whole wound.

"I'll show you how this happened," he whispered hoarsely.

Lilian tried to push him away, but he was too strong. She turned her face from him, her gloves fumbling for a purchase on his clothes. He slapped her hands away and moved against her. She now could feel his breath and the way he pushed his pelvis against the front of her dress. Lilian quavered as she felt his powerful fists wrinkle her dress and slowly raise it above her ankles and her calves, crumpling her petticoat as they went. Suddenly, he dived for her mouth. Lilian closed her eyes, and as the lips brushed hers, took a deep bite. She felt the blood spurt in her mouth, strangely insipid. Saturnin cried out, losing his grip a little.

"You bitch!" he spat out.

He still had hold of Lilian's dress, but he'd staggered back a step. It was her chance—her legs freed from their cotton cocoon, she kicked him in exactly the right place to fold him at a right angle. Swell-in-the Sack knelt down with a squeal, and then moaned in agony. She thought about what Pirouette had told her: *Au bonheur des Dames*— Ladies' Delight.

Drawing a long hatpin out of her chapeau she pointed it at him like a stiletto.

"Well, *that*'s Ladies' Delight to me!" she hissed. "If you ever try that again, I'll burst your eye like a rotten grape. See if the women still like you with an eye patch beside that hideous wound."

Swell-in-the-Sack looked up at her, his anger, disbelief, and pain fighting for control of his face. Anger won, and he was about to leap for her throat when a voice barked behind them, "Lilian, what are you doing here?"

It was Thomas. "Who is this goon?" he asked. "Hey, I know him. He was here the other day. He spoke to Blanche."

Swell-in-the-Sack, still on the ground and throbbing with pain, seemed less inclined to avenge himself. Someone called from outside in a language neither Lilian nor Thomas understood, though Thomas thought he had heard it before. They watched Swell-in-the-Sack hesitate: he could answer the call and get reinforcements, perhaps even Le Bzou, the colossus with the hammer. But Lilian could read on his face that he felt no desire to be found on his knees with another dishonourable wound, and one received from a woman at that. Proud little bastard, she thought. He looked up at them with wounded hatred. Thomas grabbed Lilian's hand and dragged her back into the fog and away from the slaughterhouse.

"I couldn't get any information about Blankbate," he explained later as they waited for an omnibus on rue d'Allemagne. "The old beggar was clearly troubled to see me again, but you should have seen his face when he saw your little friend talking to you in the queue. He utterly panicked. That's why, when I saw you following him inside, I thought something bad was happening, so I followed you."

"Very chivalrous of you, but by then I had done the hard part," she said, patting him on the back. Then, as if distracted, she said, "I wouldn't be at all surprised if Swell-in-the-Sack had something to do with Blankbate's death."

Thomas took this in and frowned. "I really have to speak to Blanche about this straightaway."

III

Father Tonnerre

*C*ity Isle lay like an ice-bound ship in the middle of the Seine, the funnels of Notre-Dame standing out against the empty skies. On the quay, a sleepy Gabriel bought a one-sou coffee in a large, white, cracked-china bowl from an old woman who promised him it was "hot as hell, black as night, and sweet as sin." Hot and black it certainly was, and having gulped it (straight from the crack, of course), he headed with a springier gait towards the archbishopric nestled at the side of the cathedral.

Introducing himself to a mummified concierge, he asked to see Father Tonnerre, mentioning M. de Gourmont's recommendation. For half an hour he waited in a drab corridor, meditating on a crucifix that shone pale in a slant of sickly light and finding it one of the most depressing objects he'd ever laid eyes on. He had been brought up a Catholic, in a family that had counted so many priests in its number it was a miracle that there was still a family. He had been tutored into stupor—*perinde ac papaver*—by a murder of Jesuits. In spite of all this, or more probably because of it, he had never felt the faintest spark of faith kindling his selfish little heart.

Living in New Venice had more than once put his sceptical mind to the test, and certainly the nights he had had telepathic contact with the Polar Kangaroo, brushed the hair of a part-time Eskimo goddess, and started an affair with hermaphrodite albino Siamese twins born from a dead woman in a crystal castle on a mythical island, had mightily extended his sense of possibility. Not to mention his book-demon tattoo, which, though he'd gotten it as a joke when he was a student, now actually helped him find books. So it was no wonder that even he now had his moments of metaphysical musing.

Recent events had worsened that tendency in him, but even so he was surprised to find himself looking for even vague comfort in the religion of his childhood. What did he really expect from one those priests whom he had always regarded as little more than solemn clowns with a smattering of second-rate Latin? Nothing miraculous, surely. The content in itself was not that important. After all, magic, like poetry, is the art of conjuring real effects from imperfect metaphors. Hocus-pocus, robes and masks, sparks and smoke—anything was welcome as long as it kicked open the doors of the cellars and attics of your mind. He supposed that the abracadabra of his own family tradition was, whether he liked or not, always going to be the thing that had the strongest influence on him, something that would resonate within his deepest memories. Still, all he really expected of it was to be disappointed.

What did not disappoint him, however, was Father Tonnerre's appearance.

He was bulky more than tall, hiding his coarse face behind a grizzled beard that reached down to his chest, beneath which a charred, twisted crucifix was stabbed into the belt of his frock. He wore no socks with his sandals, as if the wool would be inconveniently soft when it came to trampling Satan's face. His eyes were sparkling with a light that could hardly be described as heavenly. He looked, in short, like a man who ate demons for breakfast and washed them down with a full bottle of communion wine.

"Yes?" he inquired, with a passable stab at geniality.

"Gabriel d'Allier. I've come to you on the advice of Monsieur de Gourmont."

Father Tonnerre's furrowed brow informed Gabriel that there were better credentials, but still the priest invited him into his office, a place that was painstakingly designed to reassure the visitor of its occupant's total contempt for the luxuries of this world. That didn't help to elevate him in Gabriel's esteem.

"I have to pray first. It is the normal procedure," he said as he knelt on a prie-dieu and made something of a show of it for a moment.

But then he got up and sat behind his desk, and spoke with a refreshing straightforwardness.

"As it was Monsieur de Gourmont who sent you, I don't expect anything edifying."

"I cannot speak for him," Gabriel said, "but my interest in these matters is, unfortunately, not merely bookish, and I am grateful for his help in finding someone who can help me. I have been . . . visited."

Tonnerre heaved an audible sigh, but his eyes winked rapidly. "What sort of visitor? We get many visitors in this country today. I doubt he left his card."

"I haven't seen him, but I have felt him very distinctly. Or perhaps I should say *her*."

Tonnerre leaned across the table and, in a furious whisper, asked Gabriel, "Are you, sir, an onanist?"

This wasn't a topic that Gabriel especially wished to discuss with a stranger, especially one on whom his own enlightened thoughts would so obviously be wasted. In his opinion, people usually—ridiculously—mistook onanism for a sexual practice and completely failed to understand that in its nature it was essentially mystical, a spiritual exercise—the melancholy shamanism of afternoon reveries. Beyond that, for a species dumb enough to have traded the penile bone for the opposable thumb, it had possibly been the key factor in the rise of imagination, not to mention the cornerstone of that most noble art known as Literature.

Gabriel forced himself to look mildly shocked. *Not since Jesuit school*, he was about to say, but what came out was, "Not lately. Certainly not in this case."

"So you did not evoke it, so to speak. That's the most common cause, you know. And how do you know it was a woman?"

"There are certain signs in nature . . ."

"I am aware of that, thank you. What sort of consistency had she?"

"Our acquaintance did not proceed that far. But I felt her touch very distinctly. Cold. Slightly gelatinous, perhaps."

He nodded his head. "So, no marks on your body, I suppose. Have you suffered nervous trouble lately? Or mental, perhaps?"

"No. Nor do I want them to start. Hence my visit."

The answer apparently satisfied Tonnerre. Momentarily. His eyes narrowed again.

"Any episodes of glossolalia? Premonitory visions?"

These, Gabriel guessed, must be symptoms of a real possession. If he didn't want his visit to be for nothing, he thought he should make an effort to play along. "Just a few attempts at French, as you can hear," he offered. "And sometimes I see sudden images that I think belong to the future." He was actually referring to memories—of New Venice—but they would have to do.

"What sorts of images?"

"Distant cities, mostly."

Tonnerre flinched almost imperceptibly, but went on with his questions. "Any bad . . . readings connected to these visions?"

"All my reading is good."

"I do hope so. Most possessions are self-induced through reading. Nothing is more pernicious that the contagious effect of occultist literature, or of any literature, on weak minds—and this is a time of weak minds. Cursed are the poor of spirit, for theirs is the kingdom of hell."

It was quite unorthodox, but Gabriel let it pass, and saw one second too late that it had been a sort of trap.

"Are you a Christian, Monsieur d'Allier?"

"Technically, yes."

"Technically? I do not know of such a way of being a Christian. Have you Faith in God?"

"The usual, yes."

"The usual is the most useless. 'So then, because you are lukewarm, and neither cold nor hot, I will vomit you out of My mouth.' "

Talk about defective metaphors, Gabriel thought, wondering what business God had putting people in His mouth in the first place.

"If you have not brought this on yourself, then it is very possible that a spell has been cast on you," Tonnerre continued. "Have you had any commerce with occultists recently?"

"Indeed, I have, yes. A certain Monsieur Papus."

The exorcist frowned, and his voice rang with reproach as he spoke. "Based upon what I know of him, although I don't share his view of things, Monsieur Papus is a good Christian and a dedicated enemy of Satan. Perhaps it is towards other sources that we should look. Have you ever heard of the Palladians?"

"A little," Gabriel answered, trying to hide the sudden flare of interest that the question ignited in him.

"These Freemasons are the true followers of Lucifer. They steal hosts from churches and use them in black masses. Now that Diana Vaughan has returned to the bosom of the true faith, and exposed their power and relics, we have to expect a violent counterattack. Magical duels, perhaps, as happened not so long ago in this very city. Paris lies in the hands of Satan. We are in the middle of a spiritual war, a merciless combat of wills."

"But why me?" Gabriel asked. "Why would someone cast a spell on me?" The word *relics* had caught his attention, but he was at a loss as to how to gather more information on that particular point.

"Maybe it is not altogether personal. Succubi are demons, but with them it is often the *place* that has to be exorcised. Most often, when men come to see me, the problem is within the house itself. It is, it appears, somewhat different with females," he added, with a knowing look that Gabriel found rather unpleasant. "Where do you live?"

"The Grand Hôtel des Écoles, rue Delambre, in Montparnasse."

Tonnerre nodded. "Not an especially notorious place—it used to be ragpickers' slums, if memory serves. But it is close to a cemetery and right above the catacombs. In any event, it will have to be purified, and quickly: three or four such visits of a succubus can deplete your strength and even cause death. I'll be at the hotel tonight, at around eight p.m. I must warn you that you are about to undergo an intensive and difficult process. It is not to be taken lightly."

He seized the charred crucifix from his belt and waved it under Gabriel's nose. "Demons are strong!" he exclaimed. "One of them once knocked the cross out of my hand and hurled it against the wall. If you're not serious about this, you are in great danger. You must be thoroughly prepared. Prayer and faith, that's all there is. I'll hear your confession and lay my hands on you now, before you leave."

Nothing was more unwelcome to Gabriel than the mere idea of confession. Not that there was any risk he would run out of inspiration, but even beyond his mortal hatred of any kind of thought police, it was one of his ideas that talking about things made them worse, and, curiously, more real.

With Tonnerre's slightly acrid breath one inch from his face, Gabriel mumbled a résumé of rather tame sins and was given as penance twenty aves and as many paters. Perhaps that was the good side of Catholicism: there was nothing that could not be fixed, making all your sins come to seem rather common, boring, and insignificant. Or maybe this was exactly what Gabriel did not like.

He bowed his head, and shivered with repulsion as the priest put his warm hands on his head and murmured a prayer.

"I can feel your fear," Tonnerre said sonorously. "But with the help of the Lord, I'll clean up this mess."

IV

The Hypnotized Explorer

I f Brentford wanted to examine newspapers from the last few months, his best bet, the hotel manager explained, was to go to the Arsenal Library, where copies of all the Parisian newspapers were conserved. As for foreign newspapers, the reading cabinet at the passage Jouffroy, on the boulevards, would be the place. The name "Arsenal" banged a tiny golden gong in Brentford's mind.

"Is it near the Arsenal harbour?"

"A few yards away."

He knew where to go first.

"Sir . . . ?" the hotel manager asked as Brentford took his leave.

"Yes, what is it?"

"We certainly appreciate your business in these dire times, and I'm sorry to have to tell you this, but . . ."

"Please, tell me."

The man fiddled with his moustache as if he were tuning an antenna to the correct wavelength of inspiration. "If you'll allow me to say so, the little girl is gone, and that's one less problem. But now we have this other situation, you see . . ."

Brentford's smile stilled and remained fixed. It was meant to encourage the manager, but seemed to have the opposite effect. The man blushed and began to perspire.

"Yesterday, one of our maids complained about seeing a . . . talking head, in your room. She was very frightened."

"A talking head? You mean that little mechanical device? It's just a trick. I'm an amateur magician."

"That's what the head told us," the manager said doubtfully.

"I'll be more careful not to scare your employees," Brentford tried to reassure him. "So . . . it's all right, then?

"Well . . ." The manager hesitated. "Then it seems you had this . . . sav—native . . . person . . . skiing down the stairs . . ."

"A most unfortunate accident, and not likely to happen again. Our Eskimo friends are full of curiosity, but they learn quickly from their mistakes."

"We also suspect . . . in fact . . . and I regret to have to say this . . . that we found morphine in one room."

"You Frenchmen really like to clean thoroughly, don't you? Morphine is not forbidden, I hope?"

"Not really, but . . ."

"We were, you remember, part of the Montparnasse train wreck, which was a mere six days ago. The drug was prescribed by a physician to my friend to alleviate his pain." Then, a bit impatient with the general drift of the conversation, Brentford decided to change gears. "I suppose this explanation will satisfy Commissaire Tripotte, who seems to take a keen interest indeed in your hotel."

The manager paled. "You don't think . . . ?"

Brentford had scored his point and now made an appeasing gesture. "Collaboration with the police is to be expected from a law-abiding citizen." It was an elegant way to call the manager a snitch.

The manager looked embarrassed.

"As I said, we appreciate your business. But, strictly between us, I would appreciate it more if Monsieur Tripotte were not so involved." Then he whispered, "You see, in France, nobody likes the police."

Brentford smiled at the paradox, for, on the whole, the French seemed to him a rather suspicious lot, and especially gifted at finding faults in others. But apparently even the police didn't like the police, since people like Tripotte seemed to prefer hanging out with assassins. It reminded Brentford that there was no time to lose, but perhaps some to buy.

"By the way, since you appreciate our business so much, may I pay you the next week in advance?"

"Of course!" The manager replied, visibly delighted. "I'd like to see this magic trick of yours one day," he said as Brentford left the hotel.

Brentford paused only long enough to mutter, "Now that you know how it works, it wouldn't be amusing."

✳

The fog had evaporated to reveal a skyless day, misty and wet, the horizon hanging white and damp like a sheet on a clothesline, and diffusing a dull, migrainy light. It was so cold that for the first time since they arrived, Brentford had to take "boilers"—glycerine pills—to see himself through the trip.

The Arsenal was a long, narrow, and austere building, not far from the Bastille and almost on the bank of the Seine. Brentford didn't really know how to start his research, but the bespectacled librarian had heard of de Lanternois. The death of the explorer had first been reported in March, he noted, so any newspaper issued around that time might contain useful information.

Brentford was made to fill in cards, then led to one of the long tables in the reading room, where he waited tedious minutes for the newspapers to be delivered. However, there were about sixty dailies in Paris, and so when the bulky stack was finally delivered he received it with mixed feelings. He decided to concentrate on the most popular sheets, based on what he had seen people reading in the cafes: *Le Journal*, *Le Matin*, *Le Petit Journal*, *Le Petit Parisien*, many of which were further thickened by spectacular illustrated supplements. Even if his French were up to the task, it would take the whole day.

He'd been searching for hours without finding anything useful, the rustle of the overlarge pages nearly deafening in the otherwise silent reading room, when, from just over his shoulder, a voice whispered, "Excuse me. Louis d'Ussonville. Interesting case, isn't it?"

He turned to find himself looking up at a tall, thin, stooped man with a quixotic expression, and his heart jumped as he recognized the Sleeper come to life. He had known that d'Ussonville was in Paris, but still, this was like dreaming about New Venice . . . and then seeing it for real.

"Brentford Orsini," he stammered as he returned the handshake that was offered him, hoping that Lord Lodestone hadn't already mentioned his name to d'Ussonville. But the Sleeper showed no sign of knowing it. "Indeed," Brentford pressed on, "this case is quite hard to crack."

"May I . . . ?" D'Ussonville sat beside Brentford and stared at him with something like amusement. He finally whispered, "De Lanternois is an interest that I happen to share. We are not that many, I must say. It is rare to meet someone concerned with this unfortunate hero. Or with what lies behind his story."

"What lies behind it?" Brentford asked, as it came to him that the librarian had probably warned d'Ussonville that someone had shown an interest in the explorer's fate.

D'Ussonville folded his wrinkles into a patient smile; he didn't believe Brentford was as naïve as he was trying to appear. "It is my experience that de Lanternois mostly interests people who want to make what happened to him fit into, shall we say, a larger scheme of things. But perhaps you are different in that respect."

Brentford understood immediately that he would learn more about de Lanternois from d'Ussonville than he would from scraps of yellowing paper. He decided to follow the same course that had saved his life when talking with Lord Lodestone—that is, to be as honest as he could. Trying to fool the Sleepers did not seem a good idea, and moreover, Brentford felt more than a little loyalty towards them. Wasn't he, after all, a native New Venetian, a Doges College alumnus, and a highly placed member of the Arctic Administration, not to mention a former Regent-Doge? Loyalty to the Sleepers and their work was his job, quite simply.

"I am not. I happen to have in my possession an object that belonged to de Lanternois—and to a larger scheme of things, I suspect."

D'Ussonville was not a dramatically expressive man, but his nod spoke volumes about his appreciation for Brentford's goodwill.

"Aha," he said, raising a finger. "You've just earned yourself a lunch."

✳

The lunch was at a small place on the Île St. Louis that was called Les Mariniers but which was actually less filled with bargees than with petits-bourgeois and half-convincing bohemian types. As they took their table, there was no way for Brentford to reconcile the serious but affable man sitting opposite him with the character of a dangerous bomb-thrower. Though a millionaire, d'Ussonville looked at ease in his surroundings, like a man who knows how to behave properly in every level of society, and who takes a keen interest in every walk of life. Brentford quickly perceived that this was less an acquired behaviour in him than it was in Lord Lodestone . . . But he was soon overcome by the strangeness of meeting the two Sleepers and seeing them as human beings, instead of as wax figures that time had rendered more and more difficult to distinguish from one another, until all Seven had eventually been fused into a single mythical protoplasmic entity. How had they met? How had they gotten along? These were, curiously, questions that Brentford had never wondered about before. Stranger still was the fact that knowing about d'Ussonville's future did not quite seem to put Brentford at an advantage—probably because, he realized, the future of New Venice was much more in d'Ussonville's hands than it was in his.

D'Ussonville got straight to the point.

"There is a good reason," he said, "why this case is hard to crack, as you mentioned earlier. It was never meant to be one of those heavily publicized expeditions that's in all the newspapers. It was more of a classified operation."

"Classified by whom?"

"The French authorities. As you know, the British Crown gave over the District of Franklin to Canada last year, which then, de facto, gave Canada rights to the Northwest Passage and the territory ranging up to the pole. Nonetheless, the question of whom the pole belongs to is a sensitive one. It is not properly mapped yet—there may be more islands to discover, and then there are rumours of an open sea, vegetation, an entrance to the centre of the earth, and every possible natural resource . . . Meanwhile, Denmark, Norway, Russia, the United States, and others of course claim freedom of navigation over the pole and the Northwest Passage—in the name, of course, of international scientific cooperation, while trying to extend their own borders at any opportunity. The Americans have been the most interested in, shall we say, leading the pack: they've funded numerous expeditions and even attempted a permanent settlement, much to their woe."

"The Greeley expedition?" asked Brentford, suddenly remembering meeting the Phantom Patrol during his own polar expedition, and their stitched, mutilated, half-gnawed bodies.

"Among other attempts, yes."

Shaking it off, Brentford said, "I didn't think France was concerned in this scramble."

"It's not—directly," replied d'Ussonville. "But, for one thing, France is always happy to put a little pressure on the British, and more specifically, now that the French shore of Newfoundland is threatened and St. Pierre close to its demise, it's trying to make up for the loss elsewhere. What's more, as you know, France is very keen to please the Russians, who are themselves very interested in the polar regions. It's even likely that France will support Russia's claims as far as possible . . . in the hope of getting some crumbs from its table."

"So, de Lanternois was as much a secret agent as an explorer?"

"More of a secret agent, judging by his fate. The idea was to supersede Markham's Farthest North and see what the terrain looked like for future enterprises. Apparently, de Lanternois made it as far as Ellesmere Island and disappeared there."

"Wasn't his body found?" Brentford asked, a bit disingenuously.

"Maybe it will be someday, like Franklin's crew . . ." said d'Ussonville. ". . . if anyone is crazy enough to go and look for him. But I doubt very much that the discovery would give France anything to put on a stamp."

"But I saw de Lanternois' wax figure at the Musée Grévin!"

"A young journalist named Gaston Leroux let the cat out of the bag. The state does its best, but it has insufficient control of the press, and accordingly they had to dance to the newspaper's tune and make de Lanternois the hero of the week. But then, with these atrocious winters, the notion of a Frenchman dying of cold has come to seem rather unremarkable, and the newspapers dropped the topic. Right now, they'd rather attack the government about its handling of the current weather situation than about why de Lanternois' ill-fated excursion was kept a state secret."

Brentford wanted to ask why the wax effigy had a snow-globe eye, but thought this a bit premature, so he tried another angle. "I had a feeling that there was something a little more than just politics to it," he ventured. "As I told you, while I was above the Arctic Circle on personal business, I happened to come into possession of a rather curious object, which was presented to me as having belonged to a dead French explorer. This object is a magnetic crown."

D'Ussonville tried to hide his interest, but a glint in his eyes betrayed him.

"You must have an interesting personal business," he commented, with a slight but distinct chill in his voice.

"Oh!" Brentford said, his mind racing to find an alibi that would pass muster. "Not really. I'm in insurance. Shipwrecks. Lost cargo. That sort of thing. I have to survey a lot of flotsam. We got the crown from some Baffin Bay Eskimos."

For a man who wasn't a liar it was a big blubbery fib. He feared that d'Ussonville would inquire about the cost of coverage for a 46,000-ton line ship sailing through the Arctic, but instead the Sleeper asked, "And what is a magnetic crown?"

Brentford suspected that this disingenuity was a part of his repertoire, unless he simply wanted to flatter Brentford that he had things to learn from him. "From what I've been told," he said, "it's a device that allows one to store—and, it would seem, pass on—hypnotic suggestions."

D'Ussonville knitted his eyebrows. "And what makes you sure it belonged to de Lanternois?"

Brentford improvised. "It shows Paris when you put it on your head." He doubted that d'Ussonville bought this story, but the Sleeper chose to remain noncommittal for the moment. "That certainly beats panoramic pens," he said.

Brentford took a deep breath. "In fact, the crown is what brought me to Paris. I'm hoping to assess its actual value. Though the magnetic crown has also been used in medical research, it seems that it was first devised by occultists—Papus, not to put too fine a point on it. What I can't figure out is why they would have given one to de Lanternois."

D'Ussonville gave the impression of already knowing the answer. "I don't believe there's anything 'more than just politics' to it," he said. "These really are the politics of our day, and it's not for me to say whether that's good or bad. Last year Papus published a book entitled *Anarchy, Indolence and Synarchy*, in which he advocated, through rather childish physiological analogies, a strongly autocratic political system devised by his mentor, a certain St. Yves d'Alveydre. His praise of the Czar is quite strong, and not limited, I'm afraid, to his writing in this book: two years ago, for example, he became involved in a Franco-Russian cabal whose aim was to cause an uprising in the Punjab that would drive the English out. He had—or at least this is what I have been told—a certain occult interest in the operation, relating to sacred cities in the region. And the presence of one of his devices on de Lanternois' head might make a little more sense in that context—the Arctic being something of a sacred place for certain traditions."

"I still don't see the point of the device," Brentford persisted. "Were they trying to record his thoughts?"

"The important point you miss is that, according to your own explanation, a magnetic crown works by *suggestion*—de Lanternois may have been hypnotized into risking that insane adventure, and the crown was there to reinforce the suggestion during a difficult expedition. Or perhaps it was meant as a kind of telepathic device, either to receive thought transmissions or to send them to some clairvoyant—at the Czar's residence in Tsarskoye-Selo, for instance, where clairvoyants are said to abound. Telepathy is all the rage in occult circles these days."

Horrified, Brentford imagined the mesmerized de Lanternois fighting the blizzard like a clockwork toy, straight ahead, straight ahead . . . He shook off the image. "I met Papus a few days ago, by the way," he said. "He seemed to be very concerned with Palladian activity in the Arctic."

D'Ussonville smiled, an inch wider than before. "He would be, yes."

Brentford understood that the Sleeper was done discussing the matter. But, as he was to discover over coffee, that didn't mean that d'Ussonville had finished with him.

"I'm afraid I will soon have to take my leave. I have a rather busy day ahead of me," he began, placing his napkin on the table. "Shouldn't we get on to business and discuss our little deal, Mr. Orsini?"

"I wasn't aware we had business," Brentford said cautiously.

"Well, I'm buying you lunch, am I not? What else could that mean in this city but business? To put it simply, how much do you want for the crown?"

Holy Cod! thought Brentford. He hadn't foreseen this. The crown wasn't really his to sell nor to give away, for one thing. On the other hand, the Sleepers knew what to do with it better than he did. Yet he also felt certain that the Most Serene Seven, or what was left of them, would need the crown in order to get back to New Venice—a point it would be difficult to explain to d'Ussonville.

He cleared his throat. "If it were for me to decide, I would call a lunch a fair price. But I'm afraid the crown does not belong to me. There might be a legitimate owner—the family, for example . . ."

D'Ussonville's gaze was unblinking. "I suspected you are not one to be bought. I congratulate you on this virtue, which is becoming ever more rare. I only hope that it doesn't put you in—shall we say—an uncomfortable position."

Brentford wondered if this was meant as a threat, but nothing in d'Ussonville's demeanour supported that hypothesis. Words that would have rung ominously in Lodestone's mouth sounded more like polite concern in d'Ussonville's . . .

And suddenly it all made sense: the men behind de Lanternois' mission simply wanted the crown back. Of course. Brentford was relieved that he had used a false name when introduced to Papus, as he now realized that they were no doubt looking for him. The Sleepers, he reckoned, would be better placed to protect the crown from Papus and his goons, and Brentford sensed that they needed it as badly as the Most Serene Seven did. After all, the French conspiracy to reach the Farthest North had directly threatened the Sleepers' interests in the region. New Venice might be at stake.

And so Brentford found himself facing a hard choice: to give the crown to the Sleepers and run the risk of never going home . . . or to keep it to himself and run the risk that there would be no home to go to.

D'Ussonville seemed to realize his unease and spoke mildly as he rose from his seat. "In case you change your mind, you can reach me at my sister's place—the Baroness de Bramentombes," he said. "I may even take the liberty of inviting you to one of her salons tomorrow night. Perhaps then you will be more inclined to discuss the possibility of a deal. I trust you to make the right choice, Mr. Orsini."

He held out his hand, and Brentford, rising before the legendary Sleeper, couldn't help a slight tremor as he took it . . .

As soon as they had parted and d'Ussonville had turned the corner of the boulevard Henri IV, Brentford set about following him from what he deemed a safe distance. He did not have to stalk the Sleeper for long: d'Ussonville swerved towards the Arsenal harbour—just as Brentford had hoped he would—and, after crossing a brand-new iron footbridge, descended onto the quay via a narrow flight of stairs. Passing snowy sand heaps that looked like the Alps in miniature, then moving along a row of low wooden huts, d'Ussonville finally turned up the gangway of a yacht that stood among the long black *mont-luçon* barges like a swan trooping among aquatic crows that flew a familiar flag.

So Thomas had been right. The New Venetian flag flew in Aresenal Harbour—a name that must have reminded the Sleepers of the *Arsenale* shipyards in Venice.

Feeling exposed as he watched from the parapet overlooking the docks, Brentford circled back to approach the quay from the Place de la Bastille. With its dozen useless boats listing in the early ice, the Arsenal from that approach looked more like a scrapyard than a harbour, which didn't bode well for a city that depended so much on the river for its supplies. No wonder there hadn't been any boaters at the restaurant—the quays were deserted. Brentford drew up in the shadows to look out at the unguarded yacht. The steam-powered vessel was impressive, not so much because of its size—he estimated it at barely longer than one hundred feet—as because of its obvious robustness. Brentford knew enough about boats to know that this one would have no problem with the Parisian ice; it was clearly fit for much more northerly climes. And, indeed, as Thomas had told him, it flew the flag of the Winged Sea Lion of New Venice—*Or* on a field of sable and silver. Metal on metal—a bold heraldic statement. Only Jerusalem and the Vatican had such a distinguished coat of arms. Brentford almost felt the tears welling up. He couldn't make out the name blurred under a fine layer of frost on the ship's prow, but after briskly crossing the open space to huddle out of sight beneath it, he couldn't resist the impulse to reach up and give the frost a swift swipe. He was only half surprised when the word *Dukedominion* appeared.

But there was no time to waste. Using the anchor chain, he pulled himself up to where he could grasp the top-rail and managed, on the third try, to hoist himself up, winded, onto the deck. From there, he tiptoed to the deckhouse, thanking the snow for muffling his footsteps, and keeping to the starboard side, where he would not be so easily spotted by passers-by.

The portholes of the deckhouse were curtained but, thankfully, the curtains were open. Hugging the side of the deckhouse, Brentford took a quick peep through the first porthole, but all he could see through the thin film of frost were blurry lights and insubstantial shapes, among which he was uncertain whether he recognized d'Ussonville. Afraid that his ear would freeze to the glass, he couldn't make out more than muffled conversation, either. He quickly felt he was risking too much for too little, and was about to retrace his steps when he heard voices that sounded as if they were coming from the dock. He hurried aft to catch a glimpse and saw two men—one thickset and black-bearded, the other fairer and moustachioed—walking towards the yacht, accompanied by a nun, talking quietly. All that Brentford could make out was a certain note of haste and concern. They boarded and were admitted to the deckhouse, where they stayed for approximately half an hour—Brentford shivering all the while as he hid in the shadows—after which they walked out, hurried across the quay to climb the stairs, and stepped into a waiting hackney cab.

After Brentford could no longer hear the cab horse's hooves and had decided that he could safely make his exit, the deckhouse door opened again and d'Ussonville, now in a navy-blue coat of military cut, crossed the gangplank and headed across the quay towards the stairs in turn. Crouching below the portholes, Brentford watched him until he saw the Sleeper's top hat bobbing along the parapet overlooking the harbour. For a second it crossed his mind that he should try to slip into the deckhouse, but a stern voice in his head told him that in its humble opinion this was the lousiest idea he'd had in quite a while. At times Brentford found the voice of his conscience something of a bore, but he had learned to trust its advice. He turned away and was scanning the deck for the anchor chain when a slight crunch on the ice below made him dart his eyes fast enough to spot a checked jacket and a pair of fuzzy sideburns, and a hand carrying a rifle vanishing behind an abandoned barge. Brentford dashed to the foredeck, twined himself around the anchor chain, and—why complicate things?—fell down to the dock, then ran for the stairs, hoping to get lost in the busy thoroughfares around the Bastille.

But the spy who had caught Brentford spying did not take up the chase. He was heading towards the prefecture to develop the contents of his new photographic rifle.

V

Three Drops of Blood

When Thomas had first arranged with Blanche for a rendezvous, he'd had something more enjoyable in mind than a walk in a cemetery, even if a little shot of morphine in a Vespasian toilet (to calm himself down after he had just pushed away a stout, jowly, blond, ether-smelling man who had called him "handsome sailor") had added some brightness to the prospect.

The Cimetière du Père-Lachaise, he had to admit, was impressive, if you enjoyed that sort of atmosphere. It looked like a half-scale model of a city, with its streets, and various crypts and mausoleums like so many houses, mansions, palaces, and monuments. And half-smothered in snow as it was, it gleamed blindingly, at least to an opiated eye.

A dim memory of New Venice's Boreal Grounds passed through his mind. Père-Lachaise was much smaller, of course, but equally magnificent, and, like its New Venetian equivalent, a step closer to a real city. The mausoleums had windows through which you could see statues of the deceased eternally playing out some moment of their domestic lives, and doors through which you could pay them a courtesy call, a bouquet of flowers in your hand. Other statues had invaded the paved paths and could be seen strolling around in stilled steps of weathered bronze, or sitting on the stone benches reading never-changing headlines from unruffled newspapers, or engaged in suspended conversations. Near rows of little graves, effigies of dead children played hopscotch or hoops with brazen abandon. Living people, however, had made themselves scarce. The place, some explained, was a tad too uncanny for comfortable meditation . . .

Maybe, Thomas thought, the Boreal Grounds had only ever existed in his mind, in one of those mysterious cities of which you sometimes dream. As the days passed, everything about his home had receded further into uncertain morphine mists, and he found it harder and harder to believe in it.

Trying to shake off his dream, he turned to Blanche and said, "This is a strange place for a meeting." Over her shoulder he noticed a half-faded white rose laid on the nearby tomb of some poet, and he reached out to pluck it and offer it to her.

"Why is everyone always giving me flowers?" she asked with a wince. "I've told you before—it's like a little funeral every day."

"You seem to be very interested in death," he said—a little hesitantly, for he wasn't very fond of serious conversations. However, ever since the time—during one of their more feverish trysts—that she'd told him she would like to make love to him while he was strapped supine into a guillotine, he had decided that there were things he needed to know about her.

Blanche, seemingly by way of answering, dropped her lace handkerchief on the snow, and when he bent to pick it up he was shocked to see bloodstains blooming in its folds. He stared at the crumpled lace in his hand, which was bloodied like an old bandage.

"Tuberculosis," she said simply. "I hope you don't mind the blood." She extended her hand for the handkerchief. "Said the young girl to the sailor."

"No, I don't," he said as he gave it back. "It's more that I refuse to believe it."

"I did, too, when I first learned I had it. Then the man I was to be married to died . . . and after that it occurred to me that I should make myself familiar with death . . . and if possible have a little fun with it."

"I'm sorry for your loss," Thomas said, embarrassed. "Who was he?"

"A naval officer and a promising explorer who didn't live up to his promise. He disappeared in the North, not far from where you're from, and was never found again. All I have to remember him by is a wax figure in the Grévin Museum."

Thomas must have made a face, for she went on somewhat apologetically. "I realize that this isn't a very becoming conversation to have with a young girl who isn't even twenty years old, but you started it. Nevertheless, if it reassures you, let me tell you that I have discovered that if in the midst of life we are in death, the reverse is equally true. I met you here to show you something that I hope will amuse you." She took his arm, and wheezing softly at his side—he noticed now—she led him up the stairs leading to the top of the slope.

"By the way," he told her, "I went to la Villette this morning, hoping to see you."

"Oh, sorry . . . I felt lazy," she said in the kittenish tone at which French girls, he had noticed, were so bloody excellent.

"Never mind. I just wondered . . . I saw that fellow—you know, the tall fellow you spoke with the other day . . ."

She turned towards him showing signs of a nascent smile. "The very handsome one?"

"To you, perhaps."

"He seemed to have caught your eye as well."

Thomas hesitated. "I just wondered where you knew him from."

"From La Villette. That seems obvious."

"And you struck up a friendship *there*?"

"Exactly. And, believe me, long and enduring it is." This time a note of mirth was unmistakable. At least I entertain her, thought Thomas, piqued.

"You make friends easily, it seems."

"And you're a fine one to complain about it, Mr. Paynes-Grey." She looked at him in all seriousness this time. "Love is easy, free, and for all. If there's wisdom in dying, that's the piece of it I got. Now look over here—" A bit out of breath, she pointed to a strange monument that resembled a megalithic temple, all covered with flowers. "Allan Kardec's grave. 'The father of French spiritualism.' "

"Is that what you wanted to show me? Is this what you meant by 'Life in Death'?"

"Spiritualism? I wouldn't call that life."

"Perhaps your mother would, judging by the question she asked at the séance."

Blanche hesitated and then said, "My father was reported dead before I was born. His body was never found. My mother has long tried to find it. That's where her spiritualism comes from. But I don't like to talk about all that. I promised you something amusing."

They swerved to the left and stopped at a low tombstone where a man of dark greenish bronze lay collapsed flat on his back, exposing the soles of his boots, an upturned top hat beside his hand as if he had just dropped it. He looked as if he had been felled just minutes before.

"Victor Noir," Blanche explained.

"You should marry him," suggested Thomas. "Then you would be Mrs. Blanche Noir."

"That's what's known as black humour, I suppose," Blanche said. "This man was a young journalist, who, twenty-five years ago, was shot point-blank by a cousin of the Emperor himself. The cousin didn't like something the reporter's boss had written, and when Monsieur Noir came on his boss's behalf to arrange for a duel, the Emperor's cousin simply shot him dead. He became a symbol for the Republic and was relocated here five years ago. But take a closer look."

"I see nothing special."

"This bulge in his trousers. Doesn't it inspire respect?"

Thomas gave her what he hoped was an arch look. "I've seen better," he said.

"Look more closely, idiot. See how the bulge is a slightly different colour, almost coppery?"

"Why is that?"

"Life in death."

Tugging his arm, she dragged him behind a nearby monument.

"Wait here. You'll see," she whispered.

Twenty cold minutes must have passed before a woman, her face almost entirely hidden by a fox stole, cautiously approached the effigy of Victor Noir. Looking around to make sure nobody was watching, she pulled aside her coattails, lifted up her heavy dress, sat astride the statue, and began feverishly rubbing herself against what Blanche had referred to as a bulge. The woman continued for a few minutes, her breath increasingly short under her veil, then she stopped abruptly, deposited a nosegay of chrysanthemums in the upturned hat, and left in a hurry.

Thomas was dumbfounded. His first impulse was to impart his personal opinion of the mental health of French women, then he realized that was hardly the reaction Blanche expected, and, confused, kept his real conclusions to himself.

"What's going on here?" he blurted out at last, turning towards Blanche and noticing, finally, that tears glittered in her eyes, like smithereens of diamond.

"It's a ritual for some women in Paris. They believe it's a way to cast love spells, or a fertility rite to help them beget children. I find it very moving—it makes me sad to think I will never have children."

Thomas racked his brains for a sensitive comment but, finding none, settled for leaning towards Blanche and saying, "I want you."

Blanche turned and quickly flung herself at him, in a hurried rustle of silk. For a few moments, their clinch looked more like a fight than an embrace . . . Then, just as a trembling Thomas finally found his purchase, a voice interrupted them.

"Blanche?"

It was Yronwoode and the old beggar Thomas had seen at La Villette, standing like ghosts among the graves. Slowly the lovers rose from the stone on which they'd tumbled.

It wasn't in Blanche's power to turn any paler than she already was, but she stood rigid and trembling, and Thomas could see how upset she was. He moved in front her.

"What do you want? You didn't seem so talkative this morning."

"You're not the one we were looking for," Yronwoode said calmly. "Now we have found her, but it seems that you are always in the way. Bad luck for you."

Blanche stepped forward.

"Who is this old man?" she asked Yronwoode, trying to sound collected, "Why is he following me everywhere?"

The old man was stooped, his head down, not daring, it seemed, to look up at Blanche.

Yronwoode maintained his calm tone of voice. "His name is Amédée de Bramentombes. He is your father."

Blanche shivered, looked closer at him, and then pulled back and clenched her jaw. "My father died a long time ago," she spat out.

"As you can see, he did not," Yronwoode persisted. "Tell her yourself, Monsieur."

"And why would she believe him?" Thomas asked. "He's surely some goddamn impostor."

The old man looked up and whispered in a hoarse voice, "It's true, Blanche. I am your father . . . I'm sorry."

Blanche put her gloved hand to her veil as if to smother a scream. At first Thomas thought she was about to faint and moved to support her, but she pushed his arm away. The old man stood, not daring to draw any closer to her, and sobbing now into his filthy moustache.

"You are in danger, Blanche," Yronwoode said. "Your father's death was a scam, to get rid of him. There's money at stake, you see."

Blanche was fumbling for words. Thomas stepped in. "Money?" he asked. But Yronwoode wasn't talking to him.

"Your father was very ill when you were a child. Your mother's friends decided to stage his death, so that they could get their hands on the money. Your inheritance . . ."

Blanche stood motionless as the statues surrounding them.

"At first it wasn't all that much money. Things changed, though, when your uncle came back from Australia a millionaire. You are *his* only heiress, as well. The people around your mother wanted to ensure that this fortune wouldn't go to waste. That's why, for instance, your fiancé Amadis de Lanternois was sent to his death, thinking he went of his own free will. He was beginning to suspect things, you see, and had developed a habit of standing in the way."

Thomas saw that Blanche had straightened her spine at this. "Where did you learn all this?" she asked.

"I was commissioned by the British Embassy to investigate de Lanternois' death."

She took this in, never taking her eyes off him. "This is why we met, I suppose?"

"Well, yes. But it is not why we kept seeing each other, is it?" Blanche blushed but he continued. "To get on with the story: you will soon be of an age to receive your father's money, and perhaps your uncle's, too—his life may well be in danger. But should something happen to you, the money would go to your mother—or rather, to the people who hold her under their sway."

Blanche's voice had gone wan. "I'm going to die anyway."

"So are we all, Blanche," the Major said softly. "But it seems someone is in a hurry on your behalf. Recent mysterious events involving your uncle have put his enemies on alert, and they realize that they are going to need his money a little sooner than expected. Which will put not only your uncle in danger, but also *you*—and soon. That's why, after I tracked him down and explained the situation to him, your father agreed to come out of hiding. If he makes himself known, then you will not be his heiress so soon—a much safer position for you, especially as long as we keep your uncle alive, too."

"Why are you doing all this, Major?" Thomas asked.

Yronwoode looked him up and down before saying, "It may sound a bit old-fashioned to you, but I make it my duty to protect the ones I love."

"I appreciate that, Ivanhoe," Blanche said in a low voice. "But who is it exactly that you're saying is a danger to me?"

"Just about everyone from your mother's salon—especially Papus and Tonnerre, who are after the money for different reasons."

"I've never liked them," Blanche muttered to her father, who was watching her as if in wonder.

"But most of all," Yronwoode insisted, "you have to fear the man who found your father when he was sick and gave him a job as a ragpicker—a man named Hébert. He's been successful in the waste business and has big plans for expansion—plans that will require rather a lot of funds. Hébert is a dangerous fellow, and your father bitterly regrets any service he has done him in the past. He wants nothing more now than to rehabilitate himself in your eyes."

Blanche sighed deeply, then walked up to her trembling father. She hugged him closely, even though he stank as if he had been freshly dug up from a nearby grave. He shook like a leaf.

"You smell so bad it makes my eyes sting," she said softly to him when she finally pulled away.

"I've missed you so much," Amédée stammered.

Thomas averted his eyes, as did Yronwoode, who scratched a match against a gravestone to light a cigarette he was holding in his claw-hand.

"You smoke, Ensign?" he asked Thomas, with only the slightest hint of benevolence.

"No, thanks. I suppose I ought to thank you for all this, Major," Thomas said.

"At the risk of repeating myself, I still say you'd better stay out of it."

"And away from her, I suppose?"

Yronwoode took a long drag on his cigarette. "It's probably too late for that," he exhaled. Then he turned to Amédée. "We should go now, my dear Baron. It isn't safe for you two to be seen together. I think we've made our point to Mademoiselle de Bramentombes. When you're in trouble, Blanche, I'll bring your father back from the dead and expose the whole scheme. You are not alone."

His tongs on the reluctant Amédée's back, the Major pushed him up the slope towards the columbarium. Blanche sat on a gravestone and watched them go, one hunched, the other limping, finally disappearing among the snow-covered crosses. Thomas sat beside her. He thought she was sobbing, and perhaps she was at first, but suddenly she lifted her veil and shook with a fit of coughing that sounded like silky thunder. Before she could seize her handkerchief, three little drops of blood fell in the snow.

For a long while, Thomas stared at them, transfixed, unable to take his eyes off them.

VI

A Sweet Succubus

The roar of a petrol engine grew and then ebbed to silence in front of the Hôtel des Écoles. From the half-frosted window Gabriel could see Père Tonnerre stepping down from his motorbike, a Millet model with a rotary engine that looked like a starfish inside the back wheel. Evidently this was the easiest way to chase demons around a snow-smothered Paris. Seeing the priest's sturdy silhouette enter the building, carrying a suitcase full of what he supposed was holy paraphernalia, Gabriel suddenly felt bat-sized butterflies fluttering in his stomach. He wasn't so sure he really wanted to go through with this ritual anymore.

A thunderous knocking on the door subsequently made him start, and he had to calm himself before he could open it. Father Tonnerre stood framed by the light in the doorway, his legs apart, the blackened crucifix once again like a dagger in his belt.

"Good evening. Have we been a good Christian today, Mr. d'Allier?" the priest asked as he stepped past Gabriel and entered the room.

"God only knows," Gabriel muttered.

"Let us pray together, then," Tonnerre said, a hand on Gabriel's shoulder pressuring him to kneel on the floorboards. Gabriel, feeling humiliated, mumbled something that had less to do with the salvation of his soul than with the damnation of Tonnerre's. From the corner of his eye he could see, sticking out of the priest's sandals, two calloused, tattooed heels showing Satan crushed and vanquished. It disgusted him.

"Now stay there on your knees," Tonnerre ordered as he unlocked the suitcase and placed pictures of the Virgin Mary and the crucified Christ on the bed. His own crucifix he placed on the pillow.

"We act directly in their names," Tonnerre said, indicating the pictures, as he donned a violet stole over his surplice. "It is they whom the demons must obey, not a simple man like me. But first for the place . . ."

He took a phial of holy water and poured it into a small cup, adding a pinch of salt with a cross-shaped flourish. Grasping an aspergillum, which he wielded like a bull's pizzle, he began sprinkling the saltwater around in large, determined movements, reciting in Latin as he did so: "*Blessed Saint Michael, Archangel of the Lord; I call on you to drive from this home the spirit that dwells here in unrest. As you drove out the Devil from the Abode of Heaven so too drive out this devilish presence. Oh purest of the Heavenly Host, Oh Commander of the Lord's Host, cleanse this house! In the name of the Father, the Son, and the Holy Ghost, Amen.*"

This seemed to Gabriel to be taking forever, but then Tonnerre turned to him.

"Now, you," he ordered, sprinkling Gabriel liberally with the holy water. Curiously, it felt fresh and pleasant to Gabriel. The exorcist knelt down again in front of him, making the boards squeak, and, his eyes closed, started spooling off the never-ending litany of the saints, cuing Gabriel's regular response of either "Lord have mercy," or "Pray for us." The list seemed to go on forever, and Gabriel quickly tired of the drab hum of it. So that's the Catholic method, he thought: boring demons until they can't stand it anymore. It was an old technique, that of inducing a trance through repetition, and Gabriel had to admit that after the fiftieth name he did feel somewhat less lonely in his fight against the demons . . .

When the list was complete, Tonnerre launched immediately into psalm 54—"Save me, O God, by thy name"—and went on to adjure Him: "*Holy Lord, almighty Father, everlasting God and Father of our Lord Jesus Christ, who once and for all consigned that fallen and apostate tyrant to the flames of hell, who sent your only begotten Son*

*into the world to crush that roaring lion; hasten to our call for help
and snatch from ruination and from the clutches of the noonday devil
this man made in your image and likeness. Strike terror, Lord, into the
beast now laying waste your vineyard . . ."*

"Amen," Gabriel said, as prompted, when this was finally done.
He had to admit this was powerful rhetoric, and he'd always believed
there was no end to what good metaphors could actually accomplish.

He thought the exorcism proper was about to begin, but instead
there was still a reading from the Gospels to endure. He almost wished
he were at Gourmont's play again.

But Gabriel was distracted from the tedium when he began to
notice that something was happening to Tonnerre—the priest's face
reddened more and more as he spoke, to the point of threatening apo-
plexy at any moment. But that wasn't all: spasms twisted Tonnerre's
features, he emitted something like a barely contained giggle, and his
eyes sparkled with a kind of panicked glee.

Whatever was happening to him, Tonnerre made a mighty effort
to pull himself together and shake it off, and he headed stubbornly
into the first exorcism. His hands slightly trembling, he draped his
long violet stole around Gabriel's neck, as if to build a protective circuit around them both. Then, putting his large, clammy palm atop
Gabriel's head, he took a deep breath and began speaking again: *"I
cast you out, unclean spirit, along with every satanic power of the
enemy, every spectre from hell, and all your fell companions, in the
name of our Lord Jesus Christ."*

He made a rapid sign of the cross and, again, with his every utter-
ance, seemed about to crack apart at the seams. Tears welled up in his
eyes as he stammered his way through the formula. He stopped, closed
his eyes, tried to catch his breath, and pressed on, saying, *"Begone and
stay far from . . . this creature of God. For it is He, Hi . . . hi who com-
mands you, He who flung you headlong from the heights of heaven
into the depths of he . . . he . . . hell—"*

And then Tonnerre could hold it in no longer. He burst into
laughter, flinging himself backwards, his belly heaving like a plunging
whale, his tattooed feet kicking in the air, taking Satan into a wild,
midair dance just in front of Gabriel's eyes. Gabriel felt the laughter

creep over him, too, but there was something so frightening in the priest's eyes that it kept Gabriel's laughter at bay. Tonnerre was absolutely roaring while simultaneously looking at him with an air of utter distress and disbelief—and fear.

Gabriel was utterly baffled, and without a clue as to how to react until, calling upon a willpower that Gabriel judged tremendous, Tonnerre forced his face to mould its features into a more serene expression, and he finally stopped laughing. The brief silence that followed was torn apart by the sudden deep rumbling of a motor that immediately brought the priest to his feet.

"My motorcycle!" he exclaimed, still breathless from his fit of laughter. He ran to the window, followed by Gabriel, who joined him in time to see Tuluk astride the Millet and skidding dangerously at the slippery corner of boulevard Edgar Quinet.

"*Blasting Hell,*" growled Tonnerre, with another sign of the cross.

He gave Gabriel a withering dark look, then ignored him as he stuffed his paraphernalia back into the suitcase as quickly as he could, before rushing out of the room without bothering to say goodbye. Gabriel heard him tumble down the steps and then saw him pop out of the building like a cannonball onto the sidewalk, running towards the corner where Tuluk had disappeared.

Still watching from the window, Gabriel finally let loose his own laughter.

✳

The whole show had so exhausted and baffled Gabriel that he soon went to bed, lying there on his back for a while, smoking cigarettes from a packet of Liberty Caps, musing about the Phrygian hat depicted on the packet and about the days when those who wore it proudly called themselves *libertines*. He let the smoke coat his lungs with warm tar and his brain with pleasant feathery thoughts, and it wasn't until he had turned off the bedside lamp and tucked himself between the sheets with a nervous giggle of pleasure that he felt her, just beside him on the bed. He bit his lip and, trying to be brave, turned quickly to face her.

Her presence was not exactly real, more like a grainy, trembling image, with a faint halo that may have come from the moonlight pervading the room. She was sitting on the bed, or suspended just above it, nude but posed modestly, with her blond curly hair falling softly on her plump shoulders and her chubby white arms hugging her round kneecaps. He could see, pressed against her thighs, the soft folds of her ample breasts and her velvety belly rolls. Two frail dragonfly wings that seemed made of the finest stained glass bristled on her back, sometimes beating with little buzzes and clicks. She was the Fat Fairy, and he knew her from a forgotten dream.

"Flap?" he whispered.

"Of course. Who did you expect, the Green Fairy?"

"I'll be damned . . ."

"Nobody ever is. What an unpleasant old man that was that you had in here," she said, with a voice that was not really a voice, but more like the soundless words one hears in dreams. "And how ticklish he was," she added, giggling to herself.

"You did that?" Gabriel asked. "He was laughing because of you?" Well, he told himself, that takes care of one religious mystery. "You mean you weren't afraid of him?"

She turned her face towards him, her small sapphire eyes sparkling in the moonlight. She looked more like an angel than a demon. "Afraid of him? He was so boring I barely caught a word he said!"

Gabriel thought for a while. "What are you doing here?" he asked.

"Here, you mean?" she answered with the cutest frown, pointing at Gabriel's head.

"Wherever . . ."

"A friend told me you were calling, looking for a girlfriend. I am your girlfriend, am I not?"

"I suppose so, yes . . ." Gabriel answered hesitantly. He felt a tug in his guts, but fear had always been close to desire for him, and the two reactions shared quite a few symptoms. In this situation it was hard to guess which it was.

"A friend, you said . . ."

Flap gave a smile that spread her dimpled cheeks like a theatre curtain, and she pointed a stubby finger at the umbrella stand near the door. Then Gabriel understood: the moonlight that bathed her shone at a different angle from the moonlight coming through the curtains. It was as if there was a second moonlight, pouring forth from another source. And this source was the little Polar Kangaroo amulet that he had mounted on the knob of his walking stick. Like a phantascope, it projected Flap's uncertain, white-gold image onto the bed—straight, no doubt, from New Venice, or at least from the dream bubble that at times seemed to surround that lost city.

He looked at her and smiled.

"What are you, exactly?" he asked. "What sort of being?"

She made a funny face. "It's difficult to explain. I'm more like a *maybeing*—a dream extra . . . a fantasy."

"But I wasn't dreaming."

"You're always dreaming, Gabriel. And always desiring in your dreams. That's how we found you."

"Like that? Far away and out of time as I am right now?"

"I don't have much time for time and place."

Hope fluttered in Gabriel's ribcage. "Then . . . can you take us back home?" he asked.

"You'd better ask your friend," she said, a tad impatiently, pointing to the figure of Kiggertarpoq gleaming at the tip of the cane. "He'll know. But you didn't call me just to talk, did you?" She moved lightly and knelt down in front of him, her arms pushing her breasts forward, her small nipples as pale pink and soft as the muzzle of a white mouse. Softly, she bent over him and blew lightly on his hurt temple, and it felt fresh and whole again. "There," she said.

So beautiful, Gabriel thought, with an overwhelming sense of relief as he reached out to embrace her.

"Hey!" she complained. "Careful with the wings!"

VII

Lilian Unveiled!

It was already late that night when Brentford and Thomas finally found the place where they were to meet Lilian. Le Furet, a small nondescript bar on the boulevard du Temple, did indeed display, crudely painted on the glass pane of its entrance door, a ferret goring and sucking the blood of a rabbit. Charming, thought Brentford. He opened the door with a sigh, wondering why Lilian had chosen such a dump for their rendezvous.

But he quickly understood when he took in the clientele: except for a senile waiter carrying a tray of quaking, clinking beer *bocks*, there were only women there. They were huddled around the tables, playing lotto, poker, and dominos, smoking and talking, shouting and laughing. "Lively place," Brentford muttered to Thomas. It was always striking to see women in the absence of men, their relief, their happy, loud abandon. And a clear message from Lilian, if he ever needed it.

The women suddenly stopped talking as they noticed the newcomers, then quickly resumed their games as if in a purposeful hum of busy indifference. Brentford and Thomas saw that Lilian was already there, and she got up and came over to them, followed by a lithe, dark-robed woman whom a jealous Brentford tried very hard not to look straight in the eyes.

"This is Morgane, the woman I told you about," Lilian said.

Brentford stiffened his backbone and, taking a deep breath, bravely faced the woman who now stood before him. Ah, well, he quickly decided—you couldn't blame Lilian for falling in love with her. It stung, nevertheless, to kiss her hand, and a bitter shame coursed through his veins.

"I'm glad to make your acquaintance, Mr. Orsini," Morgane said huskily. "Lilian has told me a lot about you."

"I have heard about your gifts myself, Miss Roth," read the subtitle under Brentford's awkward mumble. "But I suppose the séance will not be taking place here."

"No, we're here for Thomas, actually," Lilian said. "You'll agree he deserves a reward for the brilliant deductions he came up with the other night, I'm sure. Follow me, sailor. And wait for us here, Brent—we won't be long."

Leaving Brentford to his dark thoughts, Thomas let Lilian and Morgane steer him towards the back of the room. On the way he noticed, as they passed by the door of the loo, a horrid trompe-l'œil painting of a man squatting with his trousers round his ankles, his features distorted and his veins bulging horribly from his frustrated efforts. Then they reached and climbed a narrow staircase that spiralled so steeply that Thomas had to pull himself up with his hands as if it were a ladder. It led to a small, narrow bedroom or boudoir entirely hung in turkey-red, and which in the spare light of the gas lamp seemed to throb as if it were alive. The space was stifling, and encumbered more than decorated with porcelain dolls. Unfurled fans tacked up all over the walls like pinned butterflies worsened Thomas's growing feeling of unease. A fat blond woman was slumped on a sofa, near a table where Thomas recognized the accoutrements of morphine cookery.

"Ah, hello, bloaties," she said. "This is the man you've told me about?"

"Yes, Angèle . . ." Morgane answered.

With a visible effort, the blond woman opened the bedside table, took out a bottle full of crystal cubes, and handed it to Morgane.

"Here. It was poor Didine's reserve," Angèle said, her face twisted like that of a child about to sob.

Morgane patted her back while Thomas and Lilian exchanged embarrassed looks. "We're not going to detain you any longer, Angèle," Morgane said softly. "Thanks for everything."

Angèle nodded, and sniffled. "Don't pay attention, darlings. You girls have fun. That's all there is to it, right?"

"Didine?" asked Thomas, as he once again extracted himself with difficulty from the narrow staircase and faced the monstrous rest-room door painting again.

"Angèle's sweetheart," Morgane explained. "She recently died from an overdose. She had become so bloated that she couldn't go down the stairs, and had to stay in her room in agony for weeks."

Thomas looked at his bottle and frowned.

"The first symptom is usually constipation," Morgane went on, pointing at the door of the loo.

"The reminder's rather hard to forget," Thomas said, trying to look unconcerned.

They found Brentford looking miserable at a table near the door. Lilian almost regretted having tricked him into coming here. "Okay, we can go now," she said.

"Hey, Lili, you promised us a song," a woman shouted.

"Yes, show us what kind of singer you were!"

Lilian turned towards Brentford and took off her coat again. "Sorry. They're right, I did promise."

She jumped up on one of the tables, the little crowd cheering and clapping around her in a heady maelstrom of perfume and smoke. With a quick gesture of the hand, Lilian commanded silence, and started *a cappella*, before the crowd joined in with jaunty albeit ill-timed clapping:

> They pass away these nights and days
> Like zebras in a ha-a-aze
> Turned to moonrays turned to sunrays
> They gleam upon the gla-a-aze
> But in the same places
> we still breathe the same way
> And your face is
> As white as . . .

It didn't take long for Brentford to recognize one of his favourite songs by the Sandmovers, Lilian's band back when she still called herself Sandy Lake—a reminder of a time long gone, in more ways than one.

Turned to moonrays turned to sunrays
They gleam upon the gla-a-aze
Another day feels like always
The same old frozen bla-a-a-aze
But with the same faces
We still play the same way
And your face is . . .
As white as . . . ice is.

The reason why she was singing it slowly dawned on him: it was
a conniving, bittersweet recognition of their common life in New
Venice, and a definitive valediction to it. The parting gift pierced his
heart, and noticing the fun Lilian seemed to be having now, waving
and rolling her narrow hips as she danced on the table, basking in
the audience's enthusiastic attention, he wondered if the song made
the pain worse or actually soothed it . . . and he decided that it was
soothing. He had lost her already, anyway, a long time ago in the
future.

�֍

It was a relief to Brentford when they finally arrived at Morgane's.
He expected little from the séance, except, perhaps, that it would distract him from his brooding and put him back on track. *New Venice,
remember?* he asked himself. *You may have lost a piece of it, but that
means you need the rest all the more.*

Their hostess motioned Lilian, Brentford, and Thomas towards
the round table where the Writing Ball awaited, distorted candlelight
mirrored in its sheen. They sat down around it, and Brentford started
when Lilian put her hand on his.

"So," Morgane said, tucking her long jet-black hair behind her
small ears. "Did Lilian explain what our plans were?"

"I'm not sure I understood them," Brentford answered, his mind
once again revolting against his submission to the situation.

"What I told them," Lilian explained to Morgane, "is that the
spirit that contacted you the other day seemed to know all about a
certain city in the Arctic that we asked him about. I suggested that

perhaps, if you could get in touch with that same spirit again, he could tell us more about that city, and maybe even put us in contact with someone of our . . . you know . . . *milieu.*" She turned to Brentford and Thomas, and said, "Morgane told me earlier that she thought this was indeed possible."

"From what I must call the very vague explanations I was given," Morgane hastened to add, "I am not sure I understand the situation, except that some things are either none of my business or better left unspoken. But, indeed, as I explained to Lilian, spirits pay no attention to distance or time . . . but that doesn't mean that they're always keen to run errands for you."

"But is it *technically* possible for a spirit to contact a living person?" Brentford persisted. "Someone living in the future, for instance?"

"It's not exactly simple," she replied. "We can always try to ask the spirit. Provided, of course, the person you have in mind is sensitive to that kind of encounter."

Brentford looked at the other New Venetians in the room. "Let's try Woland Brokker Sson," he suggested.

Morgane turned off the light and, asking the others to close their eyes, started the Skylark-Mirror. Soon, with a little backwards jerk of her head, she lapsed into a trance. Brentford opened his eyes and watched her eyelids fluttering like trapped Dusky Brocade moths. A thrill ran down his spine; he wasn't sure that he liked this sort of thing at all.

"Spirit," Lilian asked, fumbling for her words, "We were here five nights ago. We asked you questions about a city in the Arctic. A city called New Venice. Can you tell us any more about it?"

A heavy silence weighed on the darkened room as Morgane slowly extended her arms towards the keyboard, then began to type fitfully, a supple bronze automaton banging on a clockwork beetle, finally stopping abruptly.

Lilian slowly took the sheet from the machine. It read:

No! But perhaps *you* could tell us more, you little dark horse.

Thomas and Brentford turned towards Lilian. "What does this mean, Lil?" Brentford asked.

"How would I know?" she snapped.

"Perhaps it's just his way of saying he knows we know about the city. Just like he did last time," Thomas proposed. Brentford noticed that although he looked collected, Thomas's hand clutched in his own was trembling.

Brentford sighed and leaned towards Morgane.

"Do you know a man there, in New Venice, called Woland Brokker Sson?"

A swarm of iron letters clacked over the white sheet like locusts. Brentford pulled out the page. This was serious ghostwriting, he thought.

That senile old quack! And his tin-toy Colonel!
Useless old fogeys, both of them!

Brentford frowned, following the lines with his finger as if they were Braille. Not only did the spirit seem to know a thing or two, but there was something faintly familiar about it, something he couldn't quite put his finger on. He nodded to signify he was going to speak again, even if what he had to say sounded damned stupid to his own ears.

"Could you talk to him? Ask him to get in touch with us?"

A little time elapsed before Morgane moved her hands to the machine, then hesitated slightly before pounding the keys like a volley of shots.

Brentford extended a hand cautiously, as if afraid of a last stray bullet, then retrieved retrieved the page, and read it aloud:

I wish I could, Brenty Boy. I surely wish I could.

They all looked at each other, the truth dawning on them with the same strange reluctance as that of the sun after months of polar night.

"Lilian? Is that you?" Thomas asked. "Was it you all the time?"

"I don't . . ." she began.

Morgane slowly came back to herself, looking around the table, winking like an owl. "What happened?" she eventually asked, as she noticed the disappointed faces surrounding her.

Lilian pushed forward the typed pages for her to read.

"I should have guessed it!" Morgane said. "This one was too close to be very far. It was just at my side, actually. These things happen sometimes." She seemed to find the confusion funny. Turning to Lilian, she added, with a sort of gruff tenderness, "Well, Lili, I've been channelling you since the first minute, haven't I?"

Lilian looked pale and thoughtful, even as she smiled back. "I'm really sorry. I thought . . ."

"It's okay," Brentford said, with more nastiness than he had intended. "It was just your true self speaking."

"But if it was you all the time," Thomas asked, "how did you know that the woman who was with us last time was lying about her husband?"

"Even you could have guessed it, if you had looked at her instead of at her daughter," Lilian answered, a little moodily. "What does it matter, anyway?"

"Because I know for a fact that you were right. I met the father, and he is alive and well. And Blanche is d'Ussonville's niece."

VIII

Night Hunt

Driving a motorcycle was not as easy as Tuluk had expected. The Millet's tyres were narrow, for one thing, making the icy cobblestone streets a nightmare to navigate. The first curve had proven almost fatal when he had skidded extremely close to the little chalet in the middle of the boulevard Edgar Quinet. A U-turn later, he crossed Montparnasse Square.

Totally oblivious to the surrounding traffic, which was, luckily, rather light at the moment, he drove on furiously down the boulevard, the motor throbbing inside his chilled bones as if it were a part of him, revving up to a wobbly, noisy speed that filled his heart with elation. It was like being the wind itself, and he laughed at the looks he was getting from passers-by—their expressions suddenly desperate, as if in dismayed realization of the fact that the weather had finally turned so bad that Eskimos were now invading Paris.

The gawking strollers became rarer, though, as Tuluk left the flickering avenue for a darker, more austere neighbourhood of forbidding façades. He couldn't help wondering why it was the most deserted quarters that got the widest avenues. Passing near the square of Missions-Étrangères, where an owl was hooting, he approached a gigantic gilded dome that recalled New Venice's Blazing Building in its otherworldly poise. But it was the moon playing hide-and-seek behind the dome that interested him, distracting him from his sense of elation at velocity alone. Never taking his eyes off it, he throttled down and cruised along the immense structure until he reached a vast expanse of snow that led directly to the bluish strip of ice that used to be the Seine. Stopping when he reached the parapet, he got off the Millet and left it where it fell and, in full Inuk dress, walked down a wooden staircase towards a disused omnibus boathouse resting on uneven pontoons just off the riverbank.

Tuluk felt good as soon as he stepped out on the ice: his lungs opened up, his sight became clearer and his muscles more responsive to the slightest command. The city looked miles away from out on the ice, just a sullen hum sprinkled with the dying embers of street-lights . . . although he was momentarily mesmerized by the Eiffel Tower, which shone in the distance like a ladder to the stars. *When it came to creating useless things,* he thought, *the qallunaat were the best, no doubt about that, and yet*—it was hard for Tuluk to explain, but this thing was not totally useless: it fed your soul with a curi-ous blend of wonder and pride and gave you a little more courage than you had before. A pleasant draught chilled the inside of his head, cleaning from it the fumes and noises of city life. He felt like running across the icy Seine like a loose sled dog, but the moon eventually reminded him of what he had come to do . . .

From what Brentford had told the group, the trunk containing Blankbate's body had been found near the Pont des Invalides but had been dragged there from another place. Given the position of the moon yesterday, this place—the place of Blankbate's death, Tuluk told himself grimly—must have been slightly upstream. Turning towards the west, he walked cautiously to the middle of the cracking, frozen river. He took his time, step after step, stopping occasionally to look around, trying to imagine where the moon might appear as it had in the optogram. It was so easy, really, that he almost laughed when he finally found the location.

The tall, charred ruins of what looked like it had been a pal-ace stood a few hundred yards above the Invalides. Two-story-tall archways—bathed by the moonlight whenever the clouds allowed—had the shape of eyebrows and were overgrown with dead branches and brambles. It had happened here, Tuluk had no doubt. He trudged with regret towards the riverbank and up the ramp that led onto the quay. Hiding behind a dead tree, on the opposite sidewalk, he could see that the overgrown ruins would not be so easy to enter. And the ragged glow of a fire somewhere inside told him that the place wasn't deserted, either.

With a final look to make sure no one else was around, he crossed the street swiftly and lifted himself onto the balustrade, getting entangled in ivy and scratched by thorns as he did, but tumbling over nonetheless to crouch beneath an arch. Peering into the inner courtyard, he saw two men watching over the fire—as well as the guillotine standing nearby, curtained in black.

As silently as he could, he crept around the surrounding arcade to get a better view of the guards. He finally spotted them: two men in thick fur coats and wolf masks sitting next to a brazier near a small makeshift tent, cleaning their guns and from time to time exchanging words that sounded more like grunts.

Tuluk slowly drew the knife from under his anorak, ate a little snow so that his breath would not betray him, and with his other hand fumbled in the snowy rubble for stones or debris. If they wanted to play animals, they would be dealt with as such.

Once he felt ready—and even, perhaps, a little excited—he threw a stone under the arcades, not very far from his hiding spot. It rolled and echoed, but the wolves simply pricked up their ears for a moment before going back to their task. Two throws later, however, and after a whispered but heated debate, one of the wolves stood up and, clean gun in hand, walked towards the arcade.

From Tuluk's perspective, he appeared in the moonlight with his pointy ears pricking but his eyes askance just as Tuluk wanted them: turned to the emptiness where the columns cast their shadows in oblique stripes on the snow.

By the time he turned back it was too late: Tuluk had already plunged his knife into his neck where coat and mask met. The blade went in quite easily, and Tuluk could feel the exact moment when life resisted—a big jolt of reluctant meat—and quickly gave up in a gush of warm blood that trickled down his wrists.

Tuluk caught the man up in his arms as he sagged and dragged him to a spot where he'd be visible to his companion. The sound of the dead man's falling gun had rung through the arches and the other Wolf-man ran towards it. Tuluk had hidden behind a column, careful to leave no shadow showing. The second wolf, he knew, would have to choose, in a split second, between checking his mate's pulse and watching his surroundings. This would be the time to attack.

The second man grew cautious and called his friend's name: "Pierre? Pierre?" Then he spotted him and made the last mistake of his life when he knelt down to undo the dead man's mask. In two steps, Tuluk had pushed the knife between the man's shoulders until he heard the bone cracking. Blood spurted into his face. He pulled out the knife and stood, his hands trembling slightly, thankful for the masks that hid their faces and made it all seem more like a hunt than murder.

It was the first time that Tuluk had taken human life, and he felt for it what he felt for animals: a sense of shame, less for himself than for a world where death was the price of life. It was the only way that the wolves could be dealt with—or perhaps only the simplest, but where Tuluk came from, the simplest way was always the best. Surely, these men had families, children, friends . . . But they were also the ones who had killed Blankbate without a second thought. One can only take care of one's own kin. They had not done this, but Tuluk had.

And with that, he refocussed: now, he would destroy the thing that had actually killed Blankbate. Tuluk looked up at the dark silhouette that seemed to grow with each approaching step. If he ever needed a reminder of what was wrong with the *qallunaat*, this disgusting object would be it. So much cleverness lost on bad ideas, so much work wasted on death instead of life. He headed towards the brazier, grabbing up some sticks and twigs on the way and then trying to set them on fire. But they proved too wet from the snow.

It took him a short while to decide to fetch the Millet. When he got to it, two *flâneurs* were examining it, but the sight of an Eskimo covered in blood running at full speed towards them quickly dissuaded them from loitering any longer. Tuluk grabbed the bike and pushed it through the deserted streets back to the ruins.

He lifted the motorcycle over the railings, then, struggling through the snowy rubble, carried it to the dais where the draped guillotine stood. He opened the gas tank of the Millet and poured the petrol on the thick felt covers cloaking the machine. A lit match later, it flared up, first hesitantly, almost timidly . . . and then with a hot *whoosh* that lit the courtyard like a lightning flash. Tuluk's face broke out into a big smile as the air around him became blurry and pungent and golden. He took a few steps back and, warming his hands at the growing inferno, watched the dark instrument of death rising amidst the flames, its lunette like an empty moon eclipsed by drifting fumes.

To be continued . . .

EPISODE XI

THE EMPIRE OF DEATH

I

The Telepathophone

"Come in," said Brentford, as he realized that the knocking he had just heard in his dream had drifted into reality. He felt slightly disappointed, though, when the dark shape in the doorway turned out to be Tuluk and not Lilian. "Lili" hadn't come back to the hotel the night before, leaving Brentford to ponder on his own the thousand-piece jigsaw puzzle that was his heart. But she had been in his dream, he remembered now. He was lying in a coffin, paralyzed and mute, and she was knocking in the first nail with a miniature spiked hammer.

Without a word, Tuluk walked over to the bed Brentford had just vacated and carefully placed something large on the bedspread.

"For Mr. Blankbate," Tuluk said.

"What?" Brentford wondered, still half-asleep and trying to get his bearings in the gloomy room. "Open the curtains, will you?"

Tuluk did so, thus revealing a day that seemed to have had a bad night: two wolves' heads were lying on the bed, their fur caked with blood. It took Brentford a moment to realize they were actually masks, and a moment more to understand what they were doing there. Disgust and a grim satisfaction struggled to find a way to share his soul. He opened his mouth to explain that although he appreciated the intention, he had his reservations about the result. But all that came out of his mouth was, "Thank you, Tuluk."

Tuluk nodded and walked out of the room, his steps springing with pride.

"Well," Brentford said aloud to the heads after a few long moments staring at them. "Maybe it would be better if the maid didn't find you here."

❄

Tuluk went back to his room to join the Colonel, who had been relocated there to make it easier for his batman to take care of him. The Colonel's maintenance didn't take very long, but it had to be done with care: filling the syringes with nutrients, oiling the gears, tightening a few nuts and bolts and, in the Colonel's words, "trimming the old tash."

The sessions had also become a time of increasingly open and friendly conversation between them. The Colonel appreciated Tuluk's single-minded commitment to whatever he was doing, as well as his efficiency and ingenuity in all things technical. And he was glad to speak with someone about the Inuit, a people he had fought against and come to respect deeply. As he was fond of saying, "There's nothing like going to war against someone to appreciate what they're really worth."

He began this session by asking Tuluk, "Did I tell you what happened that time I got lost in the blizzard, eh?"

"No, sir," said Tuluk, fascinated as ever by the workings of the rubber bellows that heaved as the Colonel spoke.

"It was in the Thirties A.B., I'd say, and one of my last missions. We were doing a routine patrol near Strathcona Fjord when we found ourselves in the middle of the worst bloody blizzard I've ever been in. I quickly lost contact with my men, and Victoria, my camel, broke a leg in a crevasse, and I had to shoot her, poor thing. So there I was, lost in the middle of nowhere. I said to myself, 'Branwell, old sweat, it was a privilege to know you, but I guess this is where we part.' Since walking would have done nothing but tire me to death, I huddled in my fur blanket like a goddamn croaker, and waited to see who would pass away first, the blizzard or me. I must have fainted, for when I woke up I was lying in an igloo with a bunch of your compatriots watching over me as if I were a baby in a crib. I was covered in blubber and wrapped in blankets and I realized that they had saved my life—those people I had regarded as a bunch of half-wit huskies. I had lost only a few toes—ah, those were the good old days!—and I was feeling rather punk, but they took care of me for weeks on end, and as I spoke a bit of the lingo, it all went on rather well. After that, I retired from service, and I sometimes rode to Strathcona on my own, bringing nails and hammers, you know, the kind of stuff you people are so fond of, and we all had a wonderful time."

"Nails and hammers?" Tuluk asked, with a frown.

"Yes, sir. I befriended the shaman, a nice chap named Siqiniq."

"Siqiniq?"

"Yes, did I mispronounce it? He taught me a trick or two, and let me tell you, Tuluk, he had a sister . . . Sweet little snowflake, I called her."

"*Qaniq*?" Tuluk said, lifting his head slowly from the gears, his face gone pale.

The Colonel looked at him, eyes wide in surprise, but before he could react, Tuluk had punched him in the face.

"Blimey!" the Colonel said, jerking back into place and feeling his left eye bloom with pain. "Are you insane?"

Tuluk was crying. "You left us! You left us!" he shouted.

The Colonel understood instantly—*Tuluk*. That was what the Inuit called Englishmen. A fine name for a métis child, born from a *qallunaaq* stranger.

"I never knew . . ." he stammered. "I was already an old man, and I never thought that . . . Then I had that little accident, and mmmmmph . . ."

Tuluk had now smothered the Colonel in an embrace, saying "*Ataata, Ataata*"—Father, Father . . .

"There, there," the Colonel said, wishing he had arms to hug him back . . . and that Tuluk had already changed the saltwater from his tear ducts, for right at that moment, it stung like hell.

✳

Brentford, washed and dressed and carrying the wolf-masks Tuluk had presented to him bundled up in a sheet, walked quickly through the hotel lobby, hoping to find a dustbin out in the street where he could get rid of them. But before he could reach the door the hotel manager stopped him.

"Ah, Mr. Orsini," he said, so embarrassed that he immediately put Brentford ill at ease. "Sorry to disturb you, but it seems there was another problem yesterday. Someone complained that your Eskimo friend, er . . . shall we say . . . *borrowed* a petrol bike, right in front of the hotel."

Brentford pressed his eyes closed with his fingers and released a sigh that could have moved curtains. "If he borrowed it, then I'm sure he'll give it back soon," he answered, making a mental note to strangle Tuluk at the first opportunity, possibly with the manager's intestines.

"Exactly, sir, exactly. This is why the police haven't been called yet. But if you could make sure that he actually gives it back, it would reassure everyone. By the way, may I help you with those dirty sheets? I'll have them brought to the laundry."

"Well, um, no," Brentford said, hugging the bundle to his chest as if it were his long-lost baby blanket. "I'd like to keep them with me, if you don't mind . . . they just need a little fresh air."

The manager looked at him, puzzled, and then caught sight of something that made him turn pale.

"Is that blood?" he inquired, pointing at the bundled sheets with a trembling finger.

Before Brentford could find a plausible answer, a rumble made them turn their eyes. It was Gabriel, scrambling down the stairs, brandishing his cane.

"Ah, Brentford," he said. "I've been searching this dump through and through. I was afraid I'd missed you."

Taking hold of Brentford's arm to lead him off, and without paying any attention to the manager, he announced: "Kiggertarpoq sent me a sign last night. I've made telepathic contact with the Polar Kangaroo!"

"What?" Brentford exclaimed, mindlessly putting the bundle into the gaping manager's hands.

"Come on," Gabriel said, dragging Brentford back to the stairs. "I'll explain it all."

A thud made them turn their eyes. The manager had passed out, dropping the bundle of sheets, out of which the two wolf heads had rolled onto the carpet beside him.

"What is this mess?" Gabriel asked with disgust.

"Just that," Brentford said, hastily pushing the wolf heads under a sofa before the manager could come to. "A mess. So, a sign, you said? What sign?"

Gabriel stopped on the mezzanine. "Never mind the sign. It was somewhat personal. The point is, communication is *possible.*"

Brentford frowned, but then hope flooded his expression. "Can it work both ways?"

"There's the rub. I tried and I tried with no luck." He stared off pensively for a moment. "But there *must* be a way . . ."

❄

Tuluk, his vision still blurred by tears, went to Gabriel's room, and having knocked to no avail, decided to enter anyway. (There were advantages, after all, to being a "savage.") He found the Wimshurst influence engine and brought it back to his own room, where he installed it as well as he could beside the Colonel.

"What are you doing, son?" the Colonel asked, trying to crane his neck, then wondering why he had bothered.

"I'll take care of you," Tuluk answered. "Hold this," he added, handing one of the rods to the Colonel.

"And how the dickens am I supposed to hold it, you big oaf?" barked the Colonel. "And they say that intelligence is inherited."

But Tuluk was a resourceful fellow, and picking up a spool of butcher's twine out of the mess that was his room—for a man worthy of the name always has twine at hand—strapped the rod to the Colonel's head, ignoring his protests.

"It cures everything. It will be good for your eye."

"You'll blow us to kingdom come, you bloody ice wog!"

Tuluk paid no attention, and having grounded the machine to the pipes as Brentford had explained, waved the other rod while cranking the influence machine.

"It won't hurt you, *Ataata.*"

"It'd better not, let me tell you," the Colonel mumbled, while a few violet sparks began to fill the air. "I may not be able to kick your arse, but I can still bite off your nose."

Tuluk brought the rods closer together and kept cranking.

"Is this doing any good?" he asked, as the Colonel grimaced.

"As much good as ether on a wooden leg," he replied. "Where did you get your M.D., son? Off the corpse of Octave Pavy?"

Tuluk cranked more frantically, his brow sweating with exertion.

Just at that moment, Brentford swept into the room with Gabriel in tow, after only a perfunctory knock. (There were advantages, after all, to having been the Regent-Doge.) "Can we have a word—" he began. "What the pole is going on here?"

"Nothing, nothing," Tuluk panted as he continued to crank. "Just taking care of my father!"

"Father?" Brentford and Gabriel looked at each other.

"That's what he said!" the Colonel shouted over the whirring.

Brentford and Gabriel decided they had no time to figure this one out. They'd come to make a much more important announcement.

"We've made contact with New Venice!" Gabriel said, taking a few steps forward, his cane extended towards the Colonel triumphantly.

But as soon as the cane came close to the Colonel's rod, a burst of sparks lit the room, and the Colonel's face abruptly froze and remained fixed, his mouth half-open as if about to say something.

"What have you done?" Tuluk shouted, his face red with worry and anger.

Then the Colonel spoke—but in a booming voice that wasn't his.

"HELLO? HELLO? MR. ORSINI? IS THAT YOU?"

Deafeningly loud as it was, Brentford could instantly recognize the unmistakeable voice of W. B. Sson.

"MR. ORSINI! MR. ORSINI! WHERE ARE YOU?"

Brentford looked at Gabriel, who looked at Tuluk, who looked at Gabriel, who looked at Brentford, who was now shouting: "It seems we made it!"

"What?" asked Gabriel.

"That voice belongs to Woland Brokker Sson! He's talking to us!"

"I'VE BEEN LOOKING FOR YOU! WHERE THE HELL ARE YOU? IS THERE ANYONE THERE?" Sson shouted, making the windows rattle.

"Speak to him!!" Gabriel advised. "Quickly!"

Addressing the open-mouthed head of the Colonel, Brentford said, "Mr. Sson? Mr. Sson? Hello? Can you hear us?"

"Is that you, Mr. Orsini?"

"Yes, it's me! Mr. Sson, I'm mightily pleased to hear you."

"So am I, Orsini! So am I! Are you safe?"

"Mostly, yes!"

"Speak up!"

It was not in Brentford's nature to shout, but it was now or never. "We're safe, yes! But we have a problem!"

"I know that! I am in the Psychomotive. I just found your bodies."

"What? We're not dead!"

"I can hear that! I'm in the *other* Psychomotive. The one that did not fork out."

Brentford looked at the others and they looked back, just as confused. "Sorry, Mr. Sson. I don't understand."

The Polar Kangaroo was now alight and the cane vibrated in Gabriel's hand. A few furious knocks, coming from the floor below, were now distinctly audible. "Is there a way to turn this down a little?" Gabriel asked timidly.

"You forked out in time while crossing a Black Aurora. Like bilocation but in time. Bichronism, if you like. The Psychomotive and your bodies were duplicated in the process. Except Time stopped for you in the first Psychomotive and went on in the second one."

"How is that possible?" Brentford wondered aloud.

"Don't ask me. I didn't create the universe! It would work much better if I had, believe me. Where and when are you, exactly?"

"Paris! 1895!"

"Paris? Ah! At least we got that part right!" Sson bellowed with some satisfaction.

There was a hubbub in the corridor—a chorus of scandalized comments, the kind of complaints people make while hastily tying their dressing gowns and shoving their feet into the wrong slippers.

"What happened, for God's sake?" Brentford inquired. Typical of his friend, Gabriel thought. The need to understand before doing anything.

"I'm not sure. It may be the magnetic crown you took aboard. Things that belong to the same age are charged with the same, shall we call it . . . chronomagnetic force! They are powerfully attracted to one another. Usually matter is resistant to chronomagnetism, but when there's a tear in the fabric, like a Black Aurora, they just gravitate towards one another."

This was something Brentford could understand, as could anyone who had ever walked through a museum or among ruins . . . the strange air that you breathe there, that vibration, as if the objects were waiting to be made whole again, longing for their missing parts, attracting them by a low, relentless hum of desire. The sense of the past, almost palpable as it is, was nothing but this, then—a "chronomagnetic field." And it was the most satisfying explanation of ghost sightings that he could think of.

Brentford was about to speak, but the hotel manager, a handkerchief pressed to his pale, sweaty forehead, now stood in the doorframe, staring at the scene. He pointed a shaky, indignant finger towards the Colonel.

"What . . ."

"If you don't mind sodding off," Gabriel invited him, as he strained to keep the Polar Kangaroo next to the rod strapped to the Colonel. "And don't stop cranking, Tuluk!"

"That's enough! I'm calling the police," the manager huffed, with a little sulky nod.

The New Venetians exchanged a worried look, but no sooner did the manager storm out of the room than he flew back into it to collapse in a heap on the floor. Thomas appeared at the door, casually rubbing his fist. Though just out of bed, he had grasped the situation in a luminous flash and done the manly thing. Rapidly the hotel guests shuffled back to their rooms, muttering oaths under their morning breath.

"Are you still there?" Sson was howling.

Brentford contemplated the shambles around them and realized that their situation was spiralling out of control. Obviously, they had outstayed a welcome in Paris that hadn't exactly been warm to start with. Brentford felt nervous as he asked the next question.

"Mr. Sson. Could you get us back to New Venice?"

"I'm not sure yet. Can we speak later?"

"I hope so," Brentford said, more to himself than to Sson.

"What? Just do what you did this time and I'll be here. In any case, I'm glad this little device works. I knew the tele-pathophone would come in handy."

"It works very well, Mr. Sson. Very well indeed." Brentford thought he'd broach the volume problem on a later occasion.

The transmission stopped and, with a flutter of the eyelids, the Colonel slowly came back to life.

"By Jove! What was that?" he asked, wishing he had elbows to push away Tuluk, who was so happy at his return that he'd started hugging him again. "And for God's sake, Tuluk, untie that bloody wand!"

"It was Sson, Colonel," Brentford explained, as Tuluk obeyed his father. "He was using you as a telephonic device."

The Colonel waxed furious.

"What? Do you think he might have told me? Oh no, not him! After all, I'm just his plaything, eh?"

"We should look on the bright side, Colonel," Brentford said dubiously, as he watched Thomas and Gabriel sit the unconscious manager on a nearby armchair. "He's going to get us out of here."

"I'm surprised that the device worked through time, though," the Colonel mused.

"This is what worked through time," Gabriel said, showing the knob of his cane. The Polar Kangaroo had reverted to its normal narwhal-ivory hue.

"It's probably powerfully charged with chronomagnetism," Brentford reflected aloud. "Like a time compass pointing to New Venice. Whatever it is, we'll have to find a way to use it more discreetly."

"Oh, I think I know a place," Thomas said casually, as he stepped back and admired how well he had fixed the still-unconscious manager's tie.

✳

"That's certainly a lot," the manager admitted, now restored to his senses and swabbing at his cut lip with his bloodstained handkerchief. His eyes were clouded with that most prurient of French passions: other people's money.

"And in gold," Brentford insisted. "Give us two days to find another place and it's yours. But remember: if you say anything to the police, you won't need more than an ashtray to hold what will be left of your hotel."

Brentford had no intention of carrying out this threat, but he felt it was the right kind of rhetoric to use on a man with a yellow liver and a price tag stamped on his forehead.

The manager mulled over this groundbreaking form of blackmail—which actually gave him money—and eventually nodded his assent. "Agreed, then," he said.

Brentford nodded, then crossed to the door and held it open for him. The manager rose, crossed the room, and turned on the doorsill to offer his hand. Brentford looked at it as it if were a piece of old meat. "Oh, I don't need that," he said, before slamming the door in his face.

"*Whew*." He sighed, turning back to the Most Serene Seven, as he still insisted on calling them, despite Jean-Klein's accident and Blankbate's horrendous death. It was one way, he supposed, of keeping those lost comrades alive. But nor was Lilian there, which was another kind of punch to the stomach. Cupido's arrow—what a silly image! Everyone knew Cupido was no cherub, but a seven-foot-tall, grunting, drooling thug wielding a club.

But the sight of Tuluk helping the Colonel with his pipe revived him somewhat from his melancholy. As an emblem of the kind of collaboration between Inuk and qallunaaq that *A Blast on the Barren Land* had advocated, he liked it better than the repulsive Tiblit eloping with his ex-wife Sybil.

"So, Thomas," he said, trying to revive the others, too. "What was your idea?"

Thomas shone like a transfigured saint, so happy with himself that Brentford wondered if he should try a shot of morphine himself.

"Blanche, the girl I told you about—"

"D'Ussonville's niece, yes."

"She invited me to one of her mother's salons tonight and said I could bring some friends with me."

"This must be the same function that d'Ussonville invited me to," observed Brentford. "It would certainly liven up the party if we brought the Colonel."

Thomas laughed. "No, no. My idea's about her house—she told me it has a passage to the catacombs! We couldn't be accused of bothering anyone there! And we'd be on hand to protect her if anything happens."

Brentford was genuinely excited. "Excellent, Thomas, excellent!" he exclaimed. "We'll do just that. We'll be safe from Tripotte there, and it will be the perfect place to continue our discussion with Mr. Sson on how to get out of here! I hope you can bear some more time with the Wimshurst machine, Colonel. We need to get back to Sson as soon as possible." Then he remembered something. "Anyone want to send a *pneu* to Morgane's place? I would like very much for Lilian to be there."

The remaining four looked at each other.

"Fine, I'll do it myself," Brentford said, shrugging his shoulders. He shook off the last of his sadness, carved a smile into his face, and—with the pride of a ship's captain marrying two passengers— announced, "Now, Colonel, let's celebrate your reunion with your son. Champagne!"

II

The Subterranean City

The bronze Lion of Belfort was barely visible through the evening mist when the so-called Seven stepped out of the carriage that had taken them sluggishly to the deserted end of the avenue Denfert. The Colonel was sealed in his aerated Gladstone bag, and the Wimshurst was hidden in a trunk now being painstakingly unloaded from the roof of the cab along with the rest of their bags. The whole operation was unfolding not quite so discreetly as Brentford would have liked, but there had been no sign of Tripotte, so perhaps the manager was being true to his word. Meanwhile, he told himself he had learned to be content with what the circumstances allowed. Or at least, he thought he had: Lilian was nowhere to be seen, and he realized with a pang that there were still some things he hadn't learned to be content with after all.

The carriage door to number 87 was open. Exactly as Thomas had described, an archway, flanked on each side by apartment buildings, opened onto a paved courtyard where, tucked out of sight behind its evergreen hedge, stood the house of Mme. de Bramentombes. Blanche, who had cajoled the concierge into remaining silent once he had opened the gate for them, was waiting under the archway, as arranged. At first she looked to Brentford like a lively, smallish girl dressed for a country excursion, but as he drew closer he saw the determination, and the fatigue, on her face. He couldn't stop staring at her as Thomas, extraordinarily happy to see her, swept her up in his arms. Despite the fact that Brentford was still glowing from the Sunday-supplement reunion of Tuluk and the Colonel, he couldn't help wondering whether the reunion of Blanche and Thomas would lead to a similarly happy ending. It was his mission, after all, to make that impossible, by taking Thomas back to New Venice. Unless—what if Thomas wanted to stay? Another dilemma that he could do without. But would it really be that much of a dilemma? For he had no right, of course, to stop Thomas from remaining in Paris, if that was what he wanted.

Brentford bowed to Blanche and thanked her for her help, while Gabriel's eyes searched her face for a likeness to the Elphinstone twins, to whom, unless he was mistaken (family ties not being his strong suit), she was supposed to be some sort of distant great-aunt. He did not find anything in her features, however, except his own worry for the Twins.

"Nice to meet all of you," she said, "whoever you are."

"We're ready," Thomas announced.

"All right, then," she said. "I'll take all of you to the catacombs, except for you two—" She nodded at Brentford and Gabriel. "You two go to the party first. Then Thomas and I will slip back into the house, get changed, and fetch you there for whatever it is you have to do."

The plan was for Gabriel and Brentford to put in an appearance at the salon to see if they could learn anything further about the Sleepers' plans, or their foes', before joining the others.

"This is where we separate, then," Brentford told her. "Our deepest gratitude for your help." Turning towards Thomas and the Branwells, he added, "And good luck to you three."

Brentford and Gabriel headed across the courtyard to Mme. de Bramentombes's, while Tuluk, carrying the Colonel in his satchel, and Thomas, carrying the trunk, followed Blanche. She crossed off to another door that led them down a rickety staircase to the interconnected cellars beneath the houses. At the foot of the stairs, doors to the individual basements stretched off in a line along a dirt-floored corridor, and in the light of a petrol lamp Blanche had taken from the wall at the top of the stairs, the rough-hewn wooden doors reminded

Thomas of a prison row. What they were doing, he reflected, was not exactly legal, but he liked to think, as Brentford did, that their current status of *diplomatic extra-temporality* gave them a little leeway in regard to the law.

As if reading his mind, Blanche unbolted one of the doors with the easy swiftness of habit.

"I spent my childhood playing here," she explained.

The cellar was dry and surprisingly warm, and full of spectral furniture hidden under dusty sheets, although some of it, half undraped, revealed in the moving lamplight Empire-style gilded mythological figures. A black ebony Empire cabinet, decorated with a faded laurel wreath, stood against the wall opposite them. When Blanche opened it with a small golden key, a gust of acrid darkness blew into the cellar.

"Here," she said, stepping back to show them the black hole. Thomas put down the bag to lean through the door frame and found that the cabinet was bottomless. All he could make out behind it was a steep, narrow staircase made of stone that faded down into the depths. Dizzy, he stepped back and wondered whether their trunk would make it through the narrow opening, but Tuluk, as if reading his thoughts, had already opened it and taken out the Wimshurst machine. Wrapping it in a blanket with all the fastidious care that an Inuk can deploy, then fastening it on his back with straps torn from the blanket, he handed Thomas the Gladstone bag containing the Colonel and nodded to them that everything was all right. Thomas did not especially like the approving look that Blanche gave to Tuluk, however. He felt the urge to reassert himself.

"You'd better let me go first," he said, extending his hand to take the lamp.

Blanche gave him the lamp and shrugged her shoulders, but took the lead all the same.

The slippery limestone stairs seemed to go on forever, but at least it was relatively warm down there, Thomas observed. Three hundred steps later, they reached a crunching layer of gravel, and a tunnel, barely six feet high and three feet wide, that led straight into more darkness.

"It's not very far," Blanche reassured them, "before we come to the part that's open to tourists."

"Should we worry about coming across guards?" Thomas whispered.

"Not at this time of night," she replied, before moving off again silently.

So far, the place simply looked like the quarry that it had been for ages. In the echoing hush, Blanche, wavering like a flame under the lamp she held, swerved into a narrower passage, which led to a small door made of crude planks.

"The part that's open to the public is just a few yards away," she explained before releasing a cough that ripped the silence apart and made Thomas wince with unease. She took a pin from her hat and put it in the padlock.

"Here," she said as it swung open.

They entered a place with more corridors, roomier spaces with arrows and stars painted on their walls. Then the tunnel widened further still, and the gates of the catacombs opened in front of them, two white rhombs on black pillars.

"Stop! Here is the Empire of Death," Blanche said, and it took two seconds for Thomas to understand that she was translating from an angular inscription above their heads. She smiled weakly. "I'll go first," she said.

Not funny, thought Thomas as he followed her.

The place was a maze of walls constructed entirely of bones and skulls, as far as the trembling light could show. Tuluk found it repulsive at first. Coming as he did from a lonely race numbering only a few hundred people, the sheer number of these remains filled him with a disturbed awe, as if all the dead from all times and places had been crammed down into these walls. But, ever quick to adapt, he soon reconciled himself to an awe at the fastidiousness of the work, at the very idea of building a city of bones—all the remains, carefully arranged as they were, came to seem like decorative patterns, making them less fearsome. Besides, the sheer number of them overwhelmed his sense that they had once belonged to a definite people. It was Death as a faceless force that was pictured here—Death as it blows like an ill wind through generations of men. In a sense, perhaps because the air was so warm, it felt curiously cosy, even pleasant, like a family reunion.

From time to time Blanche translated one of the numerous tablets that were affixed to pillars or mounted on the walls and inscribed with clichés that recalled how fleeting life was and how soon we would all be like these skeletons. Tuluk remained quiet, but Thomas felt that the messages were all the more depressing because they were so true—and ultimately so useless. It was the last thing he wanted to read about. "So you played in here when you were a little girl?" he whispered to Blanche.

"I did," she replied dreamily. "Isn't it a magic kingdom? If we had time, I'd show you where lies the embalmed heart of a particular officer—"

"I'd rather not see it, thank you very much."

Thye trudged on, until after what seemed like miles of skulls—all Princess Blanche's subjects, admiring her as her cortege passed by—she warned them that they were nearing their destination. "Port-Mahon," she announced.

It was a most curious thing, and Tuluk joined Thomas in his awe: an engineer had sculpted a model of a fortress city in the limestone, a fortress in which, Blanche explained, he had been imprisoned during a war, although she wasn't sure which one. It made for an imposing wall, bristling with turrets, and in front of it, a half-circular plateau that Thomas immediately thought was a perfect spot for the telepathophone.

"It's astonishing," he said. He was an enthusiast of forts and fortresses, and there were few things that he liked as much as patrolling the wards and parapets of Belknap Base. It had always made him feel heroic.

"I don't know if it's finished or not," Blanche said. "The sculptor fell down a well and died not too far from here."

Thomas's face darkened. After a moment, he said, "Let's get to work." Though it was his mission not to let anyone see the contents of the Gladstone bag, in such surroundings it didn't seem to matter whether Blanche saw the Colonel or not. He opened the bag and lifted out the head of the Colonel.

"Phew. About time," the Colonel said. He took in his surroundings and his eyes fell on the gaping Blanche.

"Good evening, Miss. A pleasure to meet you," the Colonel said in his suavest voice, which was not so suave as he thought.

"Good evening . . ." Blanche said waveringly, looking wide-eyed to Thomas for an explanation.

"And you thought you could impress me with Major Yronwoode," Thomas bragged good-naturedly. "*This* is a colonel."

The Colonel went on as if unawares. "Truly charming place, by the way," he said. "So you're going to fry my brain again, Tuluk? Is that any way to treat your own father?"

Blanche looked at Thomas with an expression both quizzical and stunned, but he merely shrugged. "All right," he said to Tuluk and the Colonel. "We'll leave you fellows to yourselves. We'll be back in a jiffy with Brentford and Gabriel. Keep your eyes open, Tuluk."

Blanche led Thomas off along another route, through more corridors of skulls and bones, towards a location she said was directly beneath her mother's house.

"Is that thing truly his father?" she finally asked.

"So it seems."

It was a few moments before she observed, "They're strange things, families, aren't they? Even your own doesn't always seem familiar."

After a few more twists and turns, they passed by a small fountain. "They called it Lethe," Blanche said.

"I've heard that name somewhere before," Thomas commented.

"The river of forgetfulness," Blanche reminded him. "The dead who drink from it forget their past lives."

"Oh, really?" He kept to himself that he had, in effect, crossed it once before, and all that remained of his past life was an uncertain, shimmering city, as fleeting as a dream at dawn. He knew that he wasn't ready to forget Blanche the way he'd forgotten New Venice. He was about to tell her so when she suddenly raised her hand.

"*Shh!* I hear footsteps," she hissed.

They hid behind a pillar and, a few seconds later, saw Louis d'Ussonville pass before them in his evening jacket, an electric light shining from the tip of his cane and sending twisting shadows up the walls. He held a crumpled note in his hand.

"What's he doing here?" Thomas whispered, once he judged that her uncle was out of earshot.

Blanche looked embarrassed, but shrugged her slight shoulders.

"Some business of his own, I suppose. Let's hope he doesn't come across your friends. It's too late to warn them now."

After following yet more corridors, they reached a narrow staircase. They were almost at the top when suddenly they heard the sound of echoing mayhem coming down the halls they'd left only moments before—shouts at first, and then the distinct and unmistakeable sound of a gunshot.

They froze on the spot.

"My uncle!" Blanche exclaimed, growing even paler.

"I'll go and see what's going on," said Thomas, squeezing her hand. "You go ahead and fetch Brentford. Hurry!"

Blanche nodded and did her best to rush ahead, huffing so he could smell her breath through her veil as she passed him. It pained him to be separated from her, to watch her leave and to remain on his own in the Empire of Death, an inverted Orpheus, trapped in the Hades from which he wanted to set her free.

III

Ebony Whistles

From the courtyard, Mme. de Bramentombes's house looked like a shop window at Christmas, full of expensive clockwork toys. There were about sixty people inside, ladies in blooming dresses and men in severe dark tailcoats—"ebony whistles," as they were called. White hair wavered everywhere like an opium field rippling in the breeze. It was not a particularly young crowd—old people, rich people, important people . . . even the former Regent-Doge of New Venice felt a twinge of backwater shyness as he was about to be introduced. He stored it next to the twinge that came from Lilian's absence.

"Whom may I announce?" a servant asked, with the air of someone about to sneeze.

Gabriel d'Allier and Brentford Orsini introduced themselves, and it was d'Ussonville himself who came to greet them. "Oh! You two know each other?" the Sleeper asked genially, not bothering to hide his surprise. "Freight insurance and poetry walking hand in hand, so to speak. What a pleasant allegory," he went on.

"Just like Plutus and the Boy Charioteer," Gabriel said, pleasantly enough, although Brentford understood that it was also meant to put the Sleeper off balance a little. Apparently Gabriel succeeded, for d'Ussonville gave only a short laugh in response, then said, "Consider this house yours. Maybe we can talk later, when it's a little calmer around here. Now, if you'll excuse me, I have business to attend to."

As he left the room, the two New Venetians summoned faded memories of their future-past life as bright young things, and bravely entered the crowd. Like dutiful bees in a field of flowers, they went from cluster to cluster, hoping to make a little honey from the pollen of gossip. Whatever they could learn about the Loups des Bois de Justice or the de Lanternois affair might well prove crucially important. And Thomas had intimated that there might well be a lot to learn here.

But no such luck.

"D'Allier, d'Allier . . . Interesting name," said a bald man with a moustache that would have been at home on a walrus, as he focussed his look on Gabriel through his eyeglass like a man studying a germ through a microscope. "I take it that you are of French descent?"

"I would not dare claim so grand a privilege without being sure," Gabriel said impatiently—he'd never been able to tell his French stock from his Irish, nor had he ever found a compelling reason to do so— "but only the autopsy will tell, I'm afraid."

The man, who had begun to bow in appreciation of the patriotic compliment, straightened up suddenly, a flash of worry crossing his face. Had he detected a lapse in taste? A whiff of insolence?

"The autopsy? What do you mean?"

"I mean that being French . . ." Gabriel kept on, feeling he was skidding a bit but already too far gone to help it, ". . . is in your marrow, I suppose, or written all over your internal organs. Does not ontogeny recapitulate nationality? Or does it? Could it be, God forbid, that nationality is only a superficial, insignificant layer of the onion that is your being? What would you think of the man who would say of himself 'I am an overcoat' just because he happened to be wearing one?"

Flabbergasted, the man muttered, "I suppose I'd never thought of it that way."

"How very French," Gabriel said with a smirk, raising his glass of Bourgueil. The man nodded, but then went suddenly empty-eyed, and, pretending to spot an acquaintance across the room, briskly walked off.

Brentford was no luckier in his own first encounter, which was with a short young fellow who said his name was Marcel and who had a ridiculous moustache and rings around his eyes that would have made Gabriel green with envy. He was mostly boasting about a novel he had just started to write—*Jean* something—but from time to time through his tangled sentences glinted innuendos of a rather improper nature about the male servants of the house. Once or twice, it even seemed to Brentford that the little fellow was giving *him* the eye.

He tried to steer the young man back to safer topics. "So what were you saying just now, about writing? That was interesting . . ."

"Oh, nothing!" the young man blushed. "All these intellectual theories, they're so useless in the end, don't you think? It is all about memory, the memories of our past loves"—here he fluttered his eyelids—"and how they came to pass. Memories are what define our true selves, don't you agree?"

"Memories?" Brentford reflected. The little fellow didn't realize how right he was, he thought. These past few days, the rare moments when Brentford had felt like himself were those when New Venice had appeared to him in dreams and sketchy visions; the moments when—thanks to a gesture, an arrangement of buildings and light, a fleeting emotion that recalled another—he had breathed again the air of his city. And he thought about how a sudden recollection of a scene with Lilian could pierce his heart as neatly as the first time . . . and perhaps even more deeply.

"Involuntary memories, mostly, yes," Brentford sighed. "They represent what we truly are. We have to be as true to them as to our own country."

The little writer gaped at Brentford, as if some fundamental truth had been revealed to him, and Brentford took advantage of his stupefaction to take leave with a bow.

Meanwhile, no sooner had Gabriel extricated himself from the French patriot than he'd fallen prey to that most dreaded species of conversationalist: the heraldry fiend. He'd met plenty of them in New Venice, especially in the heyday of the arcticocracy craze, when, in homage to the Two Hundred and Ten builders of the city, the Rossinis had magically become Orsinis and the Daleys changed to d'Alliers, all allowed to drape themselves in imaginary peerages. His own father, in fact, had worked for the House of Honours and Heraldry, and so Gabriel had been raised among the glamorous grammar of coats-of-arms and the obscure boasts of mottos, and he saw both the fascination with them and the inherent futility of it all. And what gave them such allure? Did it come from some ingrained need to scrawl an instant history on the blank-page whiteness of the brand-new city? Or, on the contrary, did it have more to do with a desperate attempt by the founders to train the inhabitants of New Venice with this stuttering tendency to quote from the past? Or was it simply an aspect of the classic, fatal mitosis of Mankind: Us against Them?

Whatever the reasons, Gabriel recognized in titles and nobiliary particles a childish dream of grandeur, the safety of a self-assertion grounded entirely on mimicry, the white-gloved but still slightly simian rituals of reciprocal back-scratching. As such, it was a lesson in the way mere words could redefine reality. But it still amazed him that grown-ups could take these magical *noms de scène* as seriously as they did.

The heraldist, rubbing his long-nailed hands like a fastidious dung fly, swayed softly as he spoke, diffusing as he did so greasy whiffs from his long, unkempt, greyish hair.

"I seem to remember there was a Gabriel d'Allier in the fifteenth century," he insisted, as if to reassure his interlocutor that if his nobility were to be tested, it would not be found wanting. All the same, a sly, dreamy, condescending smile on his face suggested that the name was not exactly first-class.

"You don't say," Gabriel replied. "Probably some puffed-up, illiterate peasant, as they all were to begin with. Or someone servile or brutal or self-serving enough to have earned a particle in the first place."

As the heraldist stopped oscillating to stare at him in bafflement, Gabriel excused himself and got lost in the crowd. They tired him out, these people who had no idea of their own lives beyond what could be classified and tagged, as if they were potted plants in a botanical garden.

On the other side of the room, the conversation wafting towards Brentford stopped him in his tracks and he looked up to see, encircled by onlookers, a stocky man with an Alpine Hunter officer's uniform and a Napoleon III moustache who held a telephone receiver in one hand while applying his other palm upon the ear of a fellow guest. The listener smiled in astonishment, not so much at the sound of music coming from the theatrophone network that linked the city opera house to private homes, than at the fact that he could hear the performance streaming right through a clammy hand.

"It's incredible!" the man with the hand clamped to his head declared.

"Has it anything to do with effluvia?" one of the ladies looking on asked.

"No, no," the stocky man with the moustache explained. "It is our muscular fibres that carry the signal as well as any wire. Effluvia are a different thing."

"I've never understood them, anyway," someone was saying, as Brentford approached.

"There are two kinds of effluvia," the Alpine Hunter explained with evident pleasure. "*Static*, which is like a fluff of little sparks that surrounds you, and *dynamic*, which is when the nervous fluid is projected outwards and is more like flames."

This man must be Colonel de Rochas, Brentford thought—the very man I planned to see and then never had the time.

"So it's the vibration rate of the projection that changes the colour?" some young polytechnician in uniform was asking.

"No, no," de Rochas responded. "The colour depends on the polarization. The right side of the body is usually blue, or violet, while the left side is red."

Odic force, effluvia—they were one and the same, then, or close enough, thought Brentford. It reassured him to know that the machine that had brought him here would be considered vaguely possible by these crazy Parisians. Somehow, he felt that this raised the odds of his getting home.

"Ha! Colonel! I was looking for you . . ." a man just behind Brentford called out to de Rochas. The voice was familiar, and it was Brentford's good luck to recognize it before he turned his face towards its owner: Dr. Gérard "Papus" Encausse.

Brentford ducked his head and in a few strides was back at the side of the young writer with the circles around his eyes. Brentford took him by the arm. "I'm sorry—what was your name again?—Marcel?—you were telling me about your memories . . . ?"

While the unflappable young fellow spooled off his silky sentences as if they'd never been interrupted, Brentford observed Papus and de Rochas from the corner of his eye. They had drifted over beside the curtained windows and, half-hidden there from the shimmering, clinking crowd, they spoke with animation.

Suddenly, at the other end of the salon, the maître d'hôtel announced: "Monsieur Pierre Hébert."

There was a ripple of silence, and Hébert's wheelchair rolled in, creaking on the parquet floor, pushed by a colossal servant who looked more like a bodyguard. Brentford had no doubt that this was the white-bearded druid he had seen in the torchlight procession some nights ago (how many? he had lost count). But he saw him now as someone else: Blankbate's murderer.

Papus and de Rochas went to shake his hand, and the ripple of silence turned to a hum of whispers.

"The kind of man who does no good to a salon's reputation," the young writer murmured to Brentford. "It is strange to see what the world is coming to these days."

"Did you see what I saw?" a voice whispered at Brentford's shoulder. Gabriel had glided closer—unnoticed by Papus, thank God.

"It's what I'm seeing now that worries me," Brentford answered through his teeth.

Mme. de Bramentombes, who had been waddling through the salon like a turkey in peacock's feathers, had a brief word with Hébert. Then the *maîtresse de maison*, turning a chalky shade of pale, took her guest and Papus towards another room—a library, Brentford guessed, judging by a golden flash of book spines. She closed the door behind them, instantly fanning the whispering, which spread and crackled through the crowd. D'Ussonville, Brentford noticed, was nowhere to be seen. Perhaps he was in the library as well.

"Not him!" Gabriel hissed, signalling with his head towards the door of the salon, where he'd just noticed a new entrant.

"Who's that?"

"The priest. Father Tonnerre."

Brentford watched the bulky robed figure slithering towards the door of the library. "You know him? Is that the priest Tuluk stole a petrol bike from?"

"The same, yes. Though maybe a bit humbler now."

"And what do you think he's doing here?"

"I have no idea."

"What in heaven's name could they all have to say to one another?" Brentford asked, as if talking to himself. "Occultists and Catholic priests. Aristocrats and garbage collectors . . ." Meanwhile, it was obvious that many of the other guests were asking themselves the same question—albeit in cautious, almost timorous terms.

"Shouldn't we find out?" Gabriel pressed. "If we want to learn anything, we should act while they're all talking together. There must be a way to listen in."

"We need to find Blanche and Thomas," said Brentford. "They know the house." His growing sense of urgency was only interrupted by a sudden worry. "Shouldn't they be here already?"

Gabriel thought for a moment. "There's something I could try. I've never done it before, but theoretically it's possible."

"What is it? Wait—there's Blanche!"

She was at the other end of the room, pale as death and giving Brentford a look that implored him to come closer.

"Try whatever it is that you have in mind," he told Gabriel as he moved towards her. "It's vital that we know what's going on."

"All right. Find me in the bathroom in twenty minutes," Gabriel said, as he bumped into the young writer, who had continued to hover near Brentford.

"Sorry?" said Marcel.

"I was talking to my friend," Gabriel replied hastily.

The young writer sighed, a little spitefully, as he watched Brentford making his way through the crowd towards Blanche de Bramentombes.

✳

Gabriel lost no time after locking himself in the white marble bathroom. Searching the pocket of his paisley waistcoat, he drew out a sandpacket, then perched on the toilet to unfold it on his knees. He had only done Supreme Selenium Standard once before, and it was not a pleasant memory, but *Needs must when the devil drives*. And after all, the effect lasted only ten minutes or so, he told himself, and there was very little chance he wouldn't find his way back.

So, summoning his courage, he bent close to the packet, rigid in his fear of exhaling, inserted an index finger into it and—lifting one eyelid after the other—gently daubed the shimmering crystals into the corner of each eye, mumbling, "Okay. See you later . . . or not . . ." as the crystals stung and blurred his view.

He'd barely had time to press his eyes shut before the buzz started.

Like every potent drug, the first lesson Supreme Selenium Standard imparted was submission, though Gabriel doubted that the so-called *spirits* of such drugs were the wise teachers that some users claimed they were. If there are spirits, they are probably as panicked as we are to encounter a foreign, unknown mind, and would blow the same gasket as we would. But before Gabriel could develop this theory, he found himself wearing an ice helmet, with a dagger of freshness stuck in his spinal cord, his bones like translucent lemon candy and his veins full of lime juice.

"Whaa . . ." he whispered, his forehead suddenly drenched in cold sweat.

But the buzz quickly resorbed, and now Gabriel felt as if his body were sinking down inside itself—as if his bones, as heavy as stones, had slowly fallen down and piled up into a heap in the darkest, muddiest silt, forever severed from his will. It was like fainting and still remaining conscious, for his mind, although foggy, still struggled in this quicksand. And yet quite easily, with nothing more painful than a tug, he felt himself abruptly float up to the surface, pass through the top of his own head with an electric thrill, and when he opened his eyes, he found himself hovering a few inches over his own slumped body. Not a pretty sight, he had to admit.

His soul had expanded as if freed from a crate. It was both scary as hell—that fear of not coming back—and almost pleasant at the same time, with Gabriel having the curiously physical feeling of being able to move his soul with muscles made of air. It was not much more difficult—nor much easier—than swimming at night after two glasses of absinthe, he observed. And so, still keenly conscious of having only limited time, his Self paddled off like a dog, and the wall he went through was more an afterthought than a physical obstacle.

Reduced to a floating, gliding eye, he crossed the salon, a few inches above the heads of the guests, exhilarated by the view even if they flickered eerily and threatened to revert to the haphazard dots of his luminous chaos. Had he not *really* left his body, then? What a useless word *really* was, really. He swerved towards the library door and as he crossed it felt a wave of fear: would Papus or de Rochas notice him? But there was nothing to fear; the Plick and Plock of the arcane would not know a stray soul if it came and kicked their astral butts. The angel Gabriel, however, had no trouble spotting Tripotte among the damned.

Their voices weren't very clear, and Gabriel, waving his imaginary limbs, decided that a phonograph horn in a shadowy corner of the room would be a better spot to hear them from. He dabbled towards it, lowered himself to curl snugly into the horn, and crouched there, staring out. It felt warm and comfortable, and he could hear perfectly, provided he didn't lose his focus.

". . . and you'll never guess . . ." Hébert was saying, ". . . but we found Father Tonnerre's Millet bike in the remains of the Widow."

"That savage stole it from me," Tonnerre muttered.

"What savage?" Tripotte asked.

"What do you call them—Eskimos?"

"Not that many Eskimos in Paris, eh?" Hébert said to Tripotte, barely controlling his rage. "One of your crazy Canadians again? They go around asking for the Blackamoor, they haunt La Villette, and now they kill my men and burn the Widow! It's a crime against our national genius!"

"Who liveth by the sword, shall perish by the sword," Tonnerre intoned.

"Come now, Father," Hébert answered. "I don't think Christianity has ever shunned violence against its enemies."

"Perhaps not," the priest admitted. "But at least it avoided such abominations as your little pagan ritual."

"We need something to instill a fearful respect in the people, Father, and Catholicism has become unable to achieve that in our day and age."

"Oh no? Sacré-Cœur is being made for precisely that purpose—to instill respect and a God-fearing awe in the heart of our countrymen."

"The Sacred Heart is for sissies," Hébert protested. "It's for women and little girls. It won't clean the country the way I'm cleaning it, because, you see, I'm not afraid to dip my hands into a little blood."

Tonnerre stood up, red with anger.

"If it weren't for the present threat to the Sacré-Cœur, I'd leave this room and be done with you immediately."

"And renounce the money that Madame de Bramentombes has promised you on her daughter's death?" Hébert said.

"Promised to *God*," Mme. de Bramentombes corrected him, pursing her lips. "Poor little girl," she added, as if to herself . . .

Hébert sniggered at her and, ignoring Tonnerre completely, turned to Tripotte.

"The Sacré-Cœur, then—do we even know what threatens it?"

"Swell-in-the-Sack couldn't tell. But the man d'Ussonville was with, Guillaume Froment, is a chemist. A disciple—" Tripotte added with a grin, "—of Berthelot."

"Ah, Berthelot. A brother alchemist," Papus said. "But his politics are abominable."

"Froment is rumoured to be working on especially powerful explosives," Tripotte went on. "We searched the whole damned church—pardon, Father—but found nothing at all. Imagine the scene if the Sacré-Cœur was blown up . . . You may not believe it, Hébert, but the effect would be disastrous."

"It would certainly put us in a very bad way with the Czar," Papus interjected. "He might even decide not to visit Paris next year—especially, if, as rumour has it, we'll soon have a new Socialist government that's not so favourable to the alliance with Russia in the first place. All of which would cost us the benefits of our success in the de Lanternois case."

"Which reminds me," Tripotte said. "The Eskimo you suspect of having murdered your Wolves was caught fiddling with Lanternois' wax figure in the Musée Grévin, trying to steal something from it. I wanted to be sure before I alarmed you, but it seems that those damned Canadians are on de Lanternois' tracks, too."

"And this Eskimo!" Papus exclaimed. "Where do you think he comes from? Where de Lanternois disappeared from, of course! These Canadians are on his tracks, and—" suddenly he stood gaping and whispered, as if to himself, "*They have the crown!*"

"What?" de Rochas exclaimed.

"Two Canadians came to see me the other day," Papus recalled. "They had allegedly inherited a magnetic crown. How could I not understand! They have found de Lanternois' crown, and they are after us."

"They may not have read it," de Rochas tried to reassure Papus.

"Either way, it's evidence against us. It should be in no hands but ours."

They were all silent for a moment, weighing the implications, before Tripotte said, "I'll send someone to get it from their hotel."

At this, the disincarnate Gabriel made a mental note. But he was becoming tired and distracted and felt as if he were being sucked into the horn, slowly sliding like treacle down its sides. It seemed as though his body was tugging him back, like a dog on a leash. Clenching his teeth, he listened with renewed energy. As he refocussed on the scene, trying to coax every word into his uncertain memory, he heard a crackle somewhere below him. It took him a while to understand that it was the wax roll of the phonograph, which had started to spin and record the conversation. It was as if his mind had decided to use the machine as an extension of itself, replacing his absent body, saving the memories that he was bound to forget. For a while Gabriel feared that the conspirators would hear the whirring mechanism, but no, they were talking too loudly.

"This is getting out of hand," Hébert declared. "Why don't we just clean the whole mess up the simple way? These Canadians to start with, and d'Ussonville and his English Lord of a friend. I'll bet they're all in it together anyway."

Mme. de Bramentombes yelped, "My brother is not to be 'cleaned up the simple way'!"

"Why not?" Hébert snarled back at her. "Your daughter is still alive and his only heir. And your brother is becoming dangerous with his anarchist whims and Arctic projects—we should act quickly to make sure that his fortune isn't pocketed by some other cause. Not to mention that you know a little too much to change your mind now."

There was a distinct note of menace in Hébert's words. Mme. de Bramentombes had to take a seat as it finally dawned on her how deep she was in the mire.

But Father Tonnerre was not so easily intimidated. "I cannot condone such murder," he said calmly.

"Oh, really?" snapped Hébert. "What's the problem? I'll confess it to you and you'll absolve me, while keeping the secret of the confession."

"You take these things too lightly, Hébert."

"Oh, do I? Believe me, I've thought of the consequences. If we get d'Ussonville out of the way we save the Sacré-Cœur, and we stop his plans to colonize the North Pole, for which our Russian friends will be very grateful. It's war, my dear Venus, and your brother is a traitor to his country and its faithful Russian ally. Where is he, by the way? Shouldn't he be here somewhere?"

"He got a note twenty minutes ago and had to leave," Mme. de Bramentombes sniffed, her handkerchief in her hand, not noticing the knowing look that Hébert and Tripotte exchanged. Father Tonnerre had put a hand on her shoulder to comfort her.

"Let's start by finding Froment," Hébert said to Tripotte, "and *persuading* him to write a note, asking d'Ussonville to meet him at the Sacré-Cœur tomorrow night. There he'll have to face some wolves, and we'll see if he's the hunter that he claims to be."

"And d'Ussonville's accomplice, the English lord?" Papus asked.

"Yes, he's also dangerous," Tripotte commented. "I watched him closely, cleverly disguised as one of his fellow citizens. And guess who I saw boarding this yacht of his—none other that Monsieur Taxil and Diana Vaughan."

"What?" de Rochas exclaimed.

"It's worse than you think, Albert," Papus said. "I've heard rumours that Diana is about to surrender to Lord Savnock a sacred relic that she's stolen from the Palladians, as a retaliation for their persecution of her. With this relic, he'll soon have as much power as the Palladians themselves."

"A *relic* from the Palladians?" Tonnerre interrupted. "No instrument of the Devil can be called a relic!"

Papus ignored him. "He must never obtain it. He already holds the Golden Dawn under his sway—with this, he'd be too powerful, and too feared among the initiates for us to act against him. It's now or never, gentlemen."

"I'll take care of it personally," Tripotte said. "I'll just need a few wolf skins."

Suddenly a coded knock rang out on the door. "Come in," Hébert ordered immediately, as if he were at home.

It was Swell-in-the-Sack. He stood in his fur coat, his face pale as death, his curls stuck to his sweaty forehead. "Something has happened in the catacombs!" he cried, in a voice somewhere between a shout and a plea.

Gabriel started at the news and, with a violent pull, felt himself expelled from the horn and flung backwards, hurtling over the heads of the guests in the salon to be sucked back into his body, like a fish reeled in at enormous speed. It was all so violent that, soul returned or not, his body refused to react at first and remained paralyzed on the toilet seat. His mind was hardly more useful: groggy from the shock, his brain was suddenly overcome by an immense exhaustion and an overwhelming need to sleep.

"Warn . . . Brentford . . ." someone slow-witted whispered inside his head, where all the lights were going out one after the other, "warn . . . Brentford . . ."

IV

The Battle of the Catacombs

"I'm proud to have a son like you," the Colonel said to Tuluk, who had just finished rigging up the Wimshurst machine. "But, believe me, boy, I could do without this damned rod protruding from my head. Makes me feel like a bloody unicorn."

"*Shhh. . .*" Tuluk interrupted him. He'd heard voices, not very far away. How close, it was hard to tell, with all the whirling echoes of the Catacombs.

"Wait for me here," Tuluk whispered to the Colonel.

"Surely, boy," the Colonel whispered back. "I can hardly run away."

Tuluk checked the seal-shaped hunting knife in his boot and darted off towards the voices.

He didn't mind the darkness that quickly engulfed him, and, following the walls with his hand, he concentrated on the sounds, which were becoming clearer and clearer. It didn't take him long to find their source, in a gleam of the faintest light.

Crouching warily against the skulls until his eyes had adjusted enough to make things out, he saw three men standing over a lamp in a sort of recess. One of them had a cane that was somehow also a light, and for a moment Tuluk marvelled at the device. It was the man he had seen at the skating rink a few days before, the one who had asked him so many questions about where he was from. He was speaking to a man who appeared to be some kind of military officer, and who was equipped with one of those mechanical limbs that *qallunaat* were so good at constructing. The third man, meanwhile, hung back from the conversation and appeared to be, simply, a tired, old man, dressed in what looked like rags.

What little speech Tuluk could hear was in French, so he couldn't understand it anyway, and it left him at a loss as to what to do. But at least these men didn't seem to pose any danger to the Colonel . . . although he had a sense that Brentford might not be happy to see them when he arrived.

However, Brentford's appearance might be momentary, judging by the sudden pounding of footsteps he heard approaching rapidly. Then he noticed that the three men had gone stock still, their eyes full of worry. An instant later, he saw why.

Wolves.

There were six of them, carrying torches and bull's pizzles, and they burst out of the darkness to charge the three men. The half-iron man pulled out a gun and without pause fired point-blank at the clustered pack of furs and masks. One slammed backwards, hitting the floor with a grunt, but the others were too close now for another shot and, after stunning one with his metal arm, the military man tried to unsheathe his sword. The tall man from the ice rink, with a swift sweep of his luminous cane, sent one opponent to his knees, then kicked him in the face.

Meanwhile, the ragged old man had been seized by a Wolf and dragged away, screaming for mercy.

To attack an old man! It made Tuluk crazy. Before he knew what he was doing, he had grasped the handle of his knife and was running towards the Wolf, who now had the old man pinned to the ground. Tuluk tackled him from his blind side, and as the Wolf writhed to get away, pushed his blade through the throbbing fur until he felt it skid against a rib. The man was still kicking and thrashing, and Tuluk, pulling the blade out with an effort, reached back for the final plunge. Instantly, however, he knew something wasn't right—a shadow engulfed him and a furry arm wrapped around his throat, and, holding him tightly, pulled his head back as if to tear it off. Tuluk tried to strike behind him but found nothing. Then there was a flash of bitter cold in his throat, before he saw the blade come away. He felt his life bubbling out of him. In a sphere of exploding pain, images sparkled: ice fields, fires, faces, friends, and light.

Now, it would be all auroras.

❋

Thomas had lost his way. His pocket flashlight—an anachronism here that he realized he'd best hide from Blanche—had shown him nothing but mind-boggling knots of tunnels and skulls. He would lose track of the voices, then find them again; but now, as he drew close, he recognized more than voices. He'd been in enough brawls to know what was happening.

He hurried onto the scene only to discern an indistinct dark mass of people so violently tangled that he couldn't tell the sides apart at first. Then in the light of a fallen torch he recognized Tuluk as he lifted himself off the body of a writhing werewolf. But it seemed barely a second had elapsed before the same Tuluk slid forward, his throat a gaping, toothless smile. Thomas threw his flashlight away, pulled out his gun, and shot the Wolf that emerged behind Tuluk with a dripping knife in his hand, sending him crashing into the wall of bones behind him. Another wolf turned his head at the detonation, and that second was enough for Yronwoode to plunge his blade into his chest. The last remaining wolf, who had been fighting d'Ussonville with no success, saw himself outnumbered, and, leaping over a wolf-headed corpse, headed for the nearest dark tunnel. Thomas started after him, but d'Ussonville stopped him.

"It's no use. He could ambush you anywhere."

Thomas realized it was true and, gaining control of his adrenaline, rushed over to Tuluk, wondering whether he should turn him face-up and not finding himself able to do it.

"Friend of yours?" Yronwoode asked. Thomas nodded. "Sorry, young fellow. Truly sorry."

"What were you doing here?" Thomas asked. "What led to this?" He felt sadness numbing his senses, but knew he could not blame the incident on something other than Tuluk's recklessness.

It was d'Ussonville who spoke: "Major Yronwoode judged that it was time for me to get acquainted with certain aspects of the current situation. Your friend, I'm afraid, got mixed up in it of his own accord. He just appeared, and fought valiantly. I, too, am truly sorry."

"The wolves were after Monsieur de Bramentombes," Yronwoode explained, indicating the old man still huddled against the wall. "As you know, there is a price on his life. I think he has become too fond of seeing his daughter these past few days, and that put them on our track. But it's even more unfortunate that these wolves have now discovered that Monsieur de Bramentombes and his stepbrother are both, shall we say, *in the know*. They will have to act quickly now . . ."

"Can we help you with your late friend?" d'Ussonville asked, putting a hand on Thomas's shoulder.

"Uncle? Daddy?"

They all turned to see Blanche, in her evening dress, stepping into the light with Brentford at her side.

She advanced slowly, stunned. "What happened here?"

"Wolves, my dear," d'Ussonville explained. "They have been following Amédée and the Major. So our idea for an appointment wasn't as safe as we would have liked think."

"We?" Thomas asked.

"Yes," Blanche explained, still staring at the pile of bodies in horror. "The major asked me to arrange a meeting with my uncle. I thought it would be safe here. And then you called and I couldn't say no. I'm sorry it all got mixed up together like this."

Brentford held back in shock, trying to make sense of a scene that featured skulls everywhere, an assortment of men lying on the floor in fur clothing, a half-mechanical British officer, an old tramp, and a founder of New Venice.

"Why would the Wolves try to kill you?" he finally muttered, still examining the carnage.

"They wanted to kill us both, I think. They were first of all after Monsieur de Bramentombes," d'Ussonville explained patiently, pointing to the cowering old man. "Since he obviously isn't as dead as they thought, the fortune he has bequeathed to his daughter could return to him. But if they killed him for good, they could then count on Blanche's poor health to get the money back—through my subservient sister, who would inherit it on her daughter's death. Likewise, Blanche is also my heiress. And of course, if they shorten my life, it would also solve some of their other problems—but of those I'm not at liberty to say more."

But Brentford wasn't listening anymore, for his eyes had come to rest on something he did not want to believe. His voice barely a whisper, he uttered, "Tuluk?"

"Yes," Thomas nodded sadly. "They slit his throat. I shot the bastard that did it."

Brentford's first thought was for the Colonel. His second thought was that he would have to tell him. He looked around him, at all the insane heaps of human bones, and an anger swelled in him: an anger at the universe for finding nothing better than death to make life lovable. It was then that Brentford made his decision.

"Blanche, please," he said, "would you go home and send Gabriel down to join us with the Colonel? He should be in the bathroom, and please make sure he doesn't forget his cane. Thomas and I will carry Tuluk to the Colonel. Monsieur d'Ussonville, yesterday we talked about a certain object that is in my possession. I did not realize the danger you were in and will bring you this object tomorrow, to use as you please."

D'Ussonville gave him a long look, then bowed his head: "I would be immensely grateful. It will be put to good use, believe me."

Brentford nodded, biting his lip.

It had better be, he said to himself.

✳

Brentford thought that he had been through hard times before—Helen's death came to mind—but carrying the heavy, bloody corpse of his friend through these narrow, harrowing catacombs struck him as the hardest so far. And there was worse to come: he didn't even want to think about facing the Colonel.

But they trudged on until, from the centre of a curious miniature city, rose the back of Branwell's head, the Wimshurst at its side—an image of utter serenity that Brentford would have to shatter.

"Tuluk, is that you?" he asked. "You bloody son of a sled bitch! Leaving your old dad like that!"

Setting down Tuluk's body just out of sight, Brentford stepped before the Colonel and spoke as softly as possible. "Tuluk has been killed, Colonel. Fighting very bravely."

From his perch in front of the stone city the Colonel fell silent. He gave Brentford a puzzled look, then looked away. Eventually, however, he returned his gaze to Brentford, with steady but reddened eyes. "Can I see him?" he asked quietly.

"Of course." Brentford and Thomas brought Tuluk's body into the circle and placed him in front of his father.

"The bastard who did this is dead, I presume?" the Colonel asked.

Brentford admired the Colonel's effort to bite the bullet. But he also found it absurd.

"I shot him myself," Thomas said, realizing as he did not only that he had killed his first man, but also that it pleased him immensely.

When Thomas's words had finished echoing down the tunnels, the Colonel simply said, "Let's call that ass of a wizard and be done with all this."

"Now?" Brentford asked.

"Right now!"

Brentford paused before explaining, "We have to wait for Gabriel. He has the Polar Kangaroo. Meanwhile, we should have some sort of ceremony for Tuluk."

"A ceremony? He's better off where he is, believe me," replied the Colonel. "Just bury him here, where he died."

"You mean . . ."

"Aye! Right here! On the battlefield. Among these bones. There is no better place."

Brentford looked at Thomas and nodded his assent. Together they walked up to the nearest wall of bones, and began pulling it cautiously apart. Once they had overcome their initial reluctance, and their fear, there was something almost soothing in moving the bones about. They were light as husks, as if to suggest that they were not so serious, not so essential, after all, but just a waste product of something more luminous and worthwhile.

Once Brentford and Thomas had cleared a deep, roughly human shape in the top layers of bones, they took Tuluk's body and laid it down among his fellows, "white" as they were. After all, among skel-etons, race looked like a rather uncertain and daft notion.

But when it came time for a prayer, Brentford had no idea, although the Colonel did.

"A prayer?" he said. "To Eskimos, Christian prayers are just magic formulas. They'd rather use their own—like that Inuk poem."

And, after clearing some oil from his throat, and in a voice no less steady than a phonograph's, he recited:

You earth
Our great earth
See, oh see,
All those heaps of bleached bones.

But only one thing
Is great,
Only one.
It is
In the hut by the path
To see the day
Coming out of its mother
And the light filling the world.

Without a word, Thomas and Brentford put the bones back over Tuluk's body, one by one, watching him disappear under them, until once again there were nothing but bones where a man's face had been.

Brentford sighed and turned towards the Colonel.

"Colonel," he announced solemnly, "I promise that if we get back to New Venice, you'll see Tuluk again."

❋

These comings and goings had exhausted Blanche, not to mention the emotions she had felt. Her heart beat like a caged animal, and a chesty, acid cough tore holes in her lungs as if they were paper lan-terns. She could feel her palate fill with blood and phlegm, and for a while she doubted she could make it to the top of the stairs that led into her mother's house. She thought she might do what lost children did in fairy tales: leave some traces of her passage, for Mr. d'Allier to follow when he came down. She carried no pebbles or breadcrumbs that could be thrown behind her, but it did not take her long to find a solution. Putting down her lamp, she lifted up her evening dress and started tearing at the hem of her petticoat, which, thank God, came off easily. Every few steps she put a strip of white cloth behind her, until her petticoat was almost entirely shredded. The time came when she had to start tugging at her drawers as well, and the feeling of the subterranean air on her thighs woke her up a little. Finally, trailing a hem that was drenched and dirty from her roamings in the tunnels, and not caring a whit, Blanche made her entrance at her mother's soirée. Impervious to the stares that followed her muddy tracks, she parted the crowd and headed to the bathroom in search of Gabriel.

"Mr. d'Allier?" she called, knocking on the door. It was hardly a decorous way for a young woman to behave, but if she had ever cared about decorum, she certainly didn't now.

A faint grunt answered, but the door did not open. She knocked again, and all she heard this time were strange, unidentifiable sounds.

Finally the door opened—on nothing. Or so she thought until she saw Gabriel d'Allier slumped on the floor, as if he had used up all his strength crawling to the door. She helped him up as well as she could. He was pale and sweaty, his bloodshot eyes peering from beneath swollen lids. Behind her, people were starting to gather to see what was happening. Only now was Blanche embarrassed.

"The wax roll," Gabriel was slurring into her ear. "Get the wax roll from the phonograph. Give it to your uncle."

"I will," Blanche answered, although not sure at all what she'd understood. "Can we have a little fresh air here, please?" she asked the onlookers who had surrounded her.

"Do you need a doctor?" someone asked.

Blanche almost giggled at this. She had seen enough doctors in her life not to think much of them.

"Leave us alone, please," she pleaded, as she made her way through the crowd, her lungs on fire. "This man needs some rest."

Her arm around Gabriel's shoulders, she slowly helped him out of the room, closing the door behind her. Once away from everyone's sight, she swerved towards the broom cupboard, where the passage to the catacombs started. It seemed to take forever, but finally she propped him against the doorjamb and put in his unsteady hand the lamp she had taken from the floor. She whispered to a maid, who brought Gabriel's hat, cloak, and cane.

"There. You go ahead while I get the wax roll. Down the stairs and just follow the white—the white things."

"White . . . things," Gabriel answered, nodding his heavy head.

"And I'll get the wax roll," she repeated, as if talking to a child.

"Wax roll," Gabriel said.

She steered him to the top of the stairs and closed the door behind him. She almost expected to hear him tumbling down, but no.

Taking a deep breath that burned her chest, she made her way back to the library, pursued by whispers that sounded not a little like those you hear at funerals. She entered the library without even bothering to knock. Swell-in-the-Sack, still standing in the middle of the room, interrupted his explanations, and everyone from the whole cabal—the greasy policeman, the unpleasant cripple, the ridiculous magus, the lunatic officer, the scruffy priest, the pale widow—exchanged puzzled looks as she passed between them like a ghost.

"Blanche! What . . . ?" her mother gasped.

But Blanche said nothing, walked up to the phonograph, and unfastened the roll. Without a word, she turned on her heel and walked back to the door through a thick curtain of flabbergasted silence.

"Where are you going, Blanche?" her mother finally asked in a hushed voice.

But Blanche was gone.

✳

Following women's lingerie unto the empire of death—that's the story of my life, Gabriel thought as he recognized the "white things" upon entering the catacombs, his lamp flickering on the bright silky rags strewn on the floor. Strangely, he was not bothered by the human remains that surrounded him. In the state he was in, reality remained optional, like the attention you either lend to or withhold from an obnoxious, sputtering stranger. In fact, these remains—the bones upon bones—were the only kind of crowd he could have tolerated at that moment. Inoffensive, trustworthy, and all equal, they had achieved something humankind had always dreamed about. Death wasn't an empire, it was a republic.

But then he stumbled upon a heap of corpses, a Valhalla of wolf-like berserkers that, unlike the bones that lined the walls, made him shiver through and through. Dripping blood, they were fresh, and he hurried past as quickly as he could, which was not very quickly, and stumbled on until he heard voices, and something like an Eskimo chant. *Home*, he thought.

"Well, you took your time," Brentford said when he stepped into the light. It was clear to Gabriel that, beyond the pile of bodies he'd just seen, there was something dreadfully wrong, but he wasn't yet lucid enough to guess what it was, or even to bother to ask.

So Brentford explained it to him. "Tuluk died while trying to save someone," he said simply.

Gabriel shrugged his shoulders. By the look of this place, many people had died, and, in his fuzzy mind, one more did not seem so important. Then the memory that Tuluk had once saved his life struggled to the surface of his mind, and he felt vaguely sorry for the debt that had to remain unpaid.

Brentford, meanwhile, had moved on: "We don't have a second to lose. Just put your cane near the Colonel's rod. Thomas, if you would, crank that thing."

The three New Venetians encircled the Colonel in his sculpted city, and soon enough, violet sparks flew once again between the rod and the cane. As had happened in the hotel, the Colonel's face froze and his mouth opened wide. A deafening voice echoed throughout the catacombs.

"AT LAST! I WAS GETTING WORRIED!" Sson bellowed.

Praying that there were no lurking Wolves or policemen, and suspecting grimly that they amounted to the same thing, Brentford tried to gather his wits. "We've had a few setbacks. It's extremely urgent that we leave as soon as possible."

It was eerie, Brentford thought, and he shivered at the thought of his voice travelling to another time.

"I've been working on it!" Sson answered, his voice filling the sculpted cave. "Not as easy as it seems, hey? I am sending a Black Aurora for you to pass through."

"You can do that?" Brentford said, wondering aloud more than really asking.

"I'm a wizard, am I not? But there's something else you might not like."

"Which would be?" Brentford asked apprehensively. His greatest fear was being asked to choose, from among his fellow New Venetians, those who would be allowed to go back.

"As I told you, your bodies have been duplicated, but the bad news is, the bodies you are in now cannot travel back in the same way. What we need to do is send your souls back to their original place, back into the bodies that are still in the first Psychomotive. One soul, one body, see?"

"But how do we do that?"

"Well, that's the hard part. You have to get rid of the extra weight . . . and the best way to do that is to die."

"What?" Brentford looked at Gabriel and Thomas, who looked back in disbelief.

"Only physically, of course," Sson continued. "While the Black Aurora is open. Preferably by falling from a high building or tower, and well apart from one another, so that I can get a clear soul signal without getting you mixed up."

"You mean you want us to kill ourselves?" the stupefied Brentford asked, his eyes still on his friends.

"Kill yourself or get yourself killed, whichever suits you best. The most important thing is that at the very moment of your death, you have to have a very clear image of New Venice in your mind. It's your desire to see it that will bring you back."

"But we've almost forgotten it. It's anything but clear."

"That's what I feared. But there's nothing I can do. Just try to concentrate together and do your best. This part is entirely in your hands."

"As is the dying . . ." Brentford muttered.

"Sorry, it's hard to hear you . . . is everything clear? Tomorrow at about midnight, you'll see a Black Aurora over Paris. I think I can hold it for a few hours, but no more. If you all die during that time, with a little luck, we'll meet again in the Psychomotive on the very day where you forked out in time."

"A little luck?"

"Magic is nothing but luck, Mr. Orsini."

Brentford hung his head and thought. The promise he had made to the Colonel while standing over Tuluk's corpse came back to him forcefully.

"Listen, Dr. Sson. I have a request."

"Yes . . . ?"

Brentford took a breath.

"Could you bring us back to before the time we, as you say, *forked out*? To two or three days before Peterswarden's Wedding with the Sea?"

There was a long silence at the other end of the connection before Sson's voice crepitated back.

"I suppose it could be done. But it would create complications. I could bring you back to your bodies in the Psychomotive a little earlier than proposed, but once you resume your lives in the city, you will meet your selves as they were in the days before you left. It is somewhat . . . hazardous."

"We'll take care of that," Brentford answered with determination.

Sson was silent long enough for Brentford to find it unbearable. Then he said, "If that's what you want, so be it. I'll be waiting for you tomorrow night, ten days ago. Best of luck."

The Colonel crackled, then his face went slack and he was silent, before fluttering his eyelids and seeming to regain consciousness—which he clearly, instantly regretted: the thought of Tuluk had almost stopped his clockwork heart.

Brentford was speechless with compassion for a moment, before the Colonel finally seemed to cock his chin in redetermination and blurted out, "So, what happened?"

The other three looked at each other with the eyes of men who know themselves to be condemned.

"I promised you you'd see Tuluk again, Colonel. And you will. But you'll have to sacrifice yourself first." It was a promise that cost nothing, because if it didn't work they would all be dead.

The Colonel didn't seem to need further explanation. "That's hardly a problem," he answered immediately. "I'm a soldier. Sacrifice is what we do . . ." Then he looked at them expectantly and said, "When do we start, gentlemen?" and Brentford leaned forward to put him in his leather bag.

To be continued . . .

EPISODE XII

THE BLACK AURORA

I

The "Ḣotel Rat"

I t was well past midnight when the four New Venetians stepped out of the empire cabinet and headed for the deserted avenue. They quickly discovered, however, that it was too late to get a coach and that they would have to walk in the pinching cold all the way back to the hotel. As they set off, Brentford did his best to feel alive, letting the sharp air fill his lungs, but did not derive much pleasure from what might possibly be his last night on earth. He thought of Tuluk, mostly, and the loneliness of the Colonel in his satchel. Gabriel lagged a few yards behind, sometimes stopping to lean against a lamppost or a wall. Thomas mulled over Blanche, furious with himself for not finding an opportunity to talk to her once more, perhaps for the last time. Together, they looked like a cortege behind a hearse, except that it was their own funeral.

Brentford walked back to Gabriel, propped against a lamppost.

"Are you all right?"

Gabriel took a while to absorb the question, thinking it over as if it were especially tricky to answer.

"Thinking of high places," he finally answered.

"The *I fell* tower came to mind," Brentford answered sombrely. "And you?"

Gabriel simply shrugged, and Brentford knew him well enough to realize that this signified that he had an idea but would not share it. He was like a cat who would go off and hide itself to die in peace.

When they finally reached the hotel, the desk clerk looked at them as if they were lepers. Brentford quickly convinced everyone to simply go to bed—Gabriel to an oblivious sleep, Thomas (Brentford suspected) to a rendezvous with a needle, and the Colonel to—what? Brentford wasn't sure whether the Colonel ever slept. In fact, given events, he could now well imagine the old man—once the door was closed—with his eyes wide open, staring at the empty darkness.

Staggering, finally, into his own bedroom, Brentford was surprised to find Lilian waiting for him, sitting on his bed. He was still more amazed to stumble over a body lying on the carpet—a woman wearing a domino mask and the skin-tight black bodysuit typical of the hotel thieves that the French called *rats d'hôtel*. She was tightly trussed up with tasseled curtain cords, apparently unconscious, and gagged with a lace handkerchief bearing Lilian's initials. For a split second, Brentford felt so exhausted that dying the next day seemed almost like good news.

"What in hell happened here?" he finally asked Lilian.

"Sorry I missed the party," she said. "I found your *pneu* after I came back from a *café chantant*. As I wasn't sure if I'd still find you there, I thought I'd better come here. I've been waiting for hours now."

"I can see you kept yourself busy." He knelt down next to the Hotel Rat and lifted the domino off her face. It took him some time to remember where he had seen her before: the girl who'd been with that big fellow—Swell-in-the-Sack—at the Ange Gabriel. Marie-Honnête, he had called her. This puppet had her strings attached, now.

"She came in through the window," Lilian explained calmly. "I was waiting in the dark, so she didn't see me until . . . well, she didn't see me at all, actually, although she did *feel* my presence when I hit her on the head with the candelabra."

Brentford checked that the hotel rat was indeed alive, then asked, "What was she looking for? Could you tell?"

"This," Lilian said, suddenly brandishing the magnetic crown.

"Ah . . ." He wasn't ready to tell her more yet.

Meanwhile he wondered who had sent the woman, and decided it must be some accomplice of the Wolf gang. After all, he had seen with his own eyes that Papus, who coveted the crown, was in league with Hébert. In any event, he had promised the crown to

d'Ussonville, and he would see to it that it was delivered tomorrow.
As a parting gift.

"Well, thank you, Lilian." He was about to stand up, but it felt
right, somehow, to be at Lilian's feet.

But Lilian waved his thanks away with a nonchalant gesture, as if
she knocked out hotel rats as a pastime.

"So did you hear from Sson?" she asked.

"More than I would have wished."

"Meaning?"

"Well . . . it seems that the price for the return ticket is somewhat
high."

"That doesn't surprise me. What is it?"

"Death," Brentford admitted as soberly as he could. "We have to
die tomorrow night for our souls to travel back to the fork in time. A
little beyond that, even—I want us to go back to a time just before we
left, to make sure that we're all alive again."

Lilian nodded. "You mean we have to kill ourselves?"

Brentford shrugged his shoulders resignedly. "Or be killed. The
trick is that we have to think about New Venice at the precise moment
that it happens."

"Don't we do that all the time? Most of the time, at least."

"A clear picture is needed, apparently. I don't get them that often,
and can't conjure them at will. That part worries me almost as much
as the—well, you know."

Lilian was quiet for a long time before saying. "How do you think
you'll manage?"

"Well, I was thinking about paying a visit to this crazy painter—
Wait, what do you mean 'you'?"

Lilian looked so intently at Brentford that for a second he thought
she was going to cry. "I'm not going, Brent," she finally said.

"What do you mean?"

Lilian struggled to find the right words, then language tumbled
out of her as if she'd finally decided there were no right words. "I told
you, Brent. I'm in love. I've decided to stay with Morgane. I—I've
been performing again. We've thought of an act—I'll call myself Liane
de Thyane, and sing in cabarets."

Brentford panicked.

"But you can't stay," he said, remembering even as the words came out of his mouth that he was ready to leave Thomas with Blanche. "Not that I can forbid you."

"Of course you can't. Especially as all you have to offer is death."

His answer was swift. "It's New Venice that I offer you."

Lilian thought about it for a while as Brentford waited anxiously, surprised to find another death penalty within the death he had already accepted. Then she said, "You'll return to a time just before we left?" and Brentford saw his mistake immediately. "If it works, then, you'll find me there already, won't you, whether I come or not? You'll go back to that Lilian, and perhaps try to reconcile with her. You may think that Lilian is a bitch, but she likes you, Brenty boy. Perhaps you should try your luck."

There was little he could answer to this. He wondered momentarily whether they should go back to New Venice without her, but in the next moment he regretted his selfishness. The Colonel would find Tuluk again, and Gabriel would find, well, whatever it was that he missed in New Venice. It was the right thing to do, if there was such a thing as a right thing in this failed universe. He said, "I've been trying my luck a little too much lately. Will you make me one promise?"

"If I can keep it, yes."

"Come with us to de Couard's studio. We need your memories of New Venice as much as we need our own."

"Of course, Brent. I don't see why I couldn't do that."

"And another thing. I need someone to take care of the Colonel."

"Take care? You mean kill him?"

"No. Just help him to pass away. I don't think he'll cause any trouble. He just lost his son, and—"

"What? What son?"

"Tuluk." Brentford explained wearily, then told her of his death. There was a moment of silence, so full of Tuluk that Brentford could almost hear him breathe. "All I mean is, the Colonel is ready," he concluded.

Lilian heaved a sigh that chased the ghost away. "This one I'll do because you asked me," she told him. "Go back to New Venice and say hello for me, Brenty boy. For now, though, I'm going to my room, and I'm leaving you with this girl. She's just the way you like them: pretty and quiet." She stood up, and, much to his surprise, bent down and kissed him on the forehead. The warmth melted his brain.

"There should be more men like you, Your Most Serene Highness. Good night."

Brentford watched her go, still on his knees, wondering whether a Highness had ever felt so low.

✻

Brentford had brooded as much as his exhausted brain allowed. The French, he remembered, called this "grinding some black," and indeed he had ground enough black now to set up shop as an alchemist. Eventually he fell into a deep, dirty sleep, haunted by Arctic dreams wherein he found himself on an ice field, fighting a blizzard and repeating to himself, "To the north, to the north," although he knew deep in his heart that he couldn't go much farther. He crawled up a hillock and suddenly saw the lights of a distant city, and extended his hands as if to pick up the golden fruits that lay in front of him. But as he did so he understood with crystal clarity that it was but a mirage, and that he would die there on the hillock. He lay on the snow and all he could hear was his heart, beating, beating, beating . . .

Then Brentford realized that what he was hearing was a steady and brutal knocking on his door, and he roused himself to find Tripotte standing on the landing wearing a smug look. Murder was the first thought Brentford entertained, if only for a split second. But Tripotte hadn't come alone. Surrounded by agents whose panoply apparently came with a filthy moustache, the bent copper waved a search warrant under Brentford's nose, proving that from time to time official methods were not to be shunned, especially when they caused more hassle than the devious ones. Realizing that the stakes were high, Brentford quickly regained his self control.

"Yes?" he inquired, as if Tripotte were just another door-to-door salesman.

"We are here for a certain object that doesn't belong to you," he said brusquely.

"If it doesn't belong to me, there's little chance that I have it," Brentford answered, more curtly than he intended.

His tone wasn't lost on Tripotte. "This isn't the time for bravado, Mr. Orsini," he said.

Brentford couldn't help himself. "No, it isn't," he said. "Perhaps you could come back later?"

"Enough!" barked Tripotte. "Let us in."

Brentford stood fast in the doorway, ready to play his trump card.

"By the way," he said, "since you're here, I want to report an incident."

Tripotte was immediately *en garde*. "An incident?" he asked warily.

Brentford stepped aside to reveal the hotel rat, who hadn't budged an inch during the short night. "I've been attacked by a burglar."

The look on Tripotte's face, embarrassed but not the least bit surprised, said it all. Indeed, he'd come to see what had happened to his confederate and, possibly, to retrieve the crown for himself and his other associates.

"We'll take care of her," he said grudgingly. "Is anything missing?"

"My patience, perhaps."

Tripotte's teeth were clenched so tightly he could barely reply. "We'll see if we can find you some while we search your place," he finally got out.

Despite his calm demeanour, Brentford was in a near-panic as he tried to remember whether Lilian had taken the crown with her or not. With a triple fisherman's knot in his stomach, he watched the navy-blue-clad gendarmes rummage through his things, displaying, thank Cod, more enthusiasm than efficiency. They took so much pleasure in making a mess that it began to seem like the real point of the operation was to render his room a shambles.

Half an hour later, among strewn shirts and burst suitcases, they had found nothing suspicious.

The pacing Tripotte was furious, which made Brentford rather happy for the first time in days. "Well . . ." the policeman muttered as he prepared to beat his retreat. "There are other rooms to visit."

"That's not what I read on your warrant, Commissaire," Brentford said. "I wouldn't want to press more charges were you to unnecessarily harass my colleagues."

The angry realization of his mistake led to another black stare. "Don't worry," he finally uttered. "You can trust that we'll get other warrants. Now, if you'd like to come and report your incident."

"Oh, it can wait. I'll drop by the prefecture this afternoon."

Tripotte extended a pudgy finger that Brentford would gladly have bitten off.

"It's not going to end here, Monsieur Orsini," he growled, "and it's not going to end well." Behind him, the policemen charged with removing the hotel rat were doing more handling than was strictly necessary.

"Tell me something I don't know," Brentford answered, thinking that in a few hours he would either be dead, or back home, or both. He closed the door on Tripotte's glaring visage.

Brentford fell back on his bed, hoping sleep might return to him for a few last moments. But there was something a little different about his pillow—something hard. He slid his hand into the pillowcase and pulled out the magnetic crown. The one thing Tripotte's men hadn't inspected, he realized. It was then that he remembered his dream about the lights of a distant city.

II

The Commonwealth of Vision

Brentford had no intention of paying a visit to the prefecture, not in this life or the next. By one o'clock he was banging the knocker on de Couard's door, surrounded by the remnants of his diplomatic delegation.

The painter was his usual shifty self—with perhaps a touch of embarrassment added. For one thing, he must have felt crowded by this sudden invasion of strangers, which included a woman, no less.

But Brentford quickly sensed that something else was troubling him, even as he said, "I took the liberty of bringing some friends, in connection with a very urgent matter. A matter of life and death." Realizing this was perhaps not the best way of putting his host at ease, he quickly added, "Not that it concerns you personally. It has to do with the work I commissioned."

"Ah . . ." de Couard stammered. "There has been a slight p-problem."

"I'll take slight problems over serious ones, these days," Brentford answered in a conciliatory tone. "What happened?"

"It's . . . the notes and sketches you gave me. They've been t-t-taken away."

The little mercury ball in Brentford's stomach fell below zero. Cautiously, he asked, "Would it be indiscreet to ask by whom?"

"I am not allowed to tell you . . . But there's a little n-note for you." The painter reached over to a pedestal side table and picked up a card that was white—pure white—and handed it to Brentford.

"Gabriel, can I have your lighter, please?" Brentford asked.

Gabriel, still looking exhausted from his out-of-body adventure, took the monogrammed silver Foley & Ruse lighter from his waistcoat pocket and handed it to Brentford, who coaxed a short flame from its sulphur pellet. Words slowly appeared on the card in French . . .

> Dear Mr. Orsini,
> We would be delighted and honoured to discuss your most fascinating documents. Please meet us at ten o'clock tonight on Lord Savnock's yacht in the Arsenal Harbour.
> And please don't forget the crown.
>
> S∴H∴H∴

Whatever "S∴H∴H∴" meant, the note was clearly from d'Ussonville. And if the tone was not threatening, it was not especially benevolent either. It was, after all, more an order than an invitation. On the bright side of things, if they condemned him to death for disclosing information about the foundation of the secret city that would become New Venice, he wouldn't have to worry about the way he would die, and he would certainly be thinking of New Venice at the fatal instant. But dying at the hands of the Sleeper—that was a cruel destiny, *poletics* at its most freezing cold.

Brentford tried to pull himself together.

"So," he said with a sigh, "Monsieur d'Ussonville has paid you a visit?"

At the name of d'Ussonville, de Couard seemed to nearly have a seizure. It amazed Brentford that a man with such a tremor in his hand could make a living in pointillism. But more than that, it amazed him to see the power the Sleepers held over people. Himself included, he supposed.

"Yes," de Couard began slowly, ". . . last night. He came to take his painting, the one I s-showed you—*Villes*. But he saw your sketches . . . and took them, too."

Seeing Brentford's face turn a waxy shade of pale, the painter quickly added, "I worked all night to make another one—from memory."

Brentford was surprised that de Couard had taken such a risk, which amounted to an act of disobedience. Even if it had been done less for Brentford's sake than for his own artistic pride, it was still commendable.

"I'm very grateful to you," he told de Couard.

The painter rejected his gratitude with a slight shrug of his stooped shoulders. "I had to do it," he simply said. "This city is . . ." But rather than find the end of his sentence, he invited the strangers to his studio. There, hanging from the picture rails, was a curious installation. Pencil drawings of the city, cut out in the middle to form smaller and smaller frames, were aligned in a perspective, so as to give depth and relief to the scene. It looked sketchy at first, and blurry in places, but drawing closer, Brentford could see that de Couard had seen the city right down to the most minute details, and in many respects, it was more precise than Brentford's half-amnesiac scrawls. There were, he was sure, buildings he had not even remembered before seeing them in de Couard's work. For a while he wondered if a vision of his own future as a New Venetian had played a part in the artist's inspiration.

Lilian had noticed, too. "You have a good memory of my friend's memory, sir," she said in her tentative French,

"Oh, it's n-nothing, really, madame," he said, blushing like a glowworm.

Gabriel suspected immediately that the man was still a virgin. If that was the case, his art was an advertisement for sublimation. The city, on these frail pillars of graphite, seemed to tremble like a mirage, and looked as if it might fade at any second. But it was there.

"Monsieur de Couard, we need to use this painting for an experiment," Brentford announced.

"I don't understand—"

"We need a *vision*. As if we were seeing this city for real, as if we were there." This, he knew, would interest the painter. "My colleagues and I need to concentrate together on the picture."

Brentford's reasoning was this: if the Most Serene Seven had forgotten things about New Venice, they had not forgotten the *same* things. It was like a jigsaw puzzle of partial memories whose pieces could be made to fit together.

And, as Brentford had expected, the idea triggered something in de Couard—more tics, of course, but also a certain curiosity.

"We want to make the picture *real*," Brentford insisted.

And de Couard's tics flickered about his face . . . until they finally took the shape of a smile on his thin lips.

The smile disappeared as soon as Thomas extracted the Colonel from his bag. For a man like de Couard, who was wary of even the slightest shock, a talking head was close to a lethal blow.

"Please calm yourself, sir," the Colonel said. "If it doesn't bother me, it certainly shouldn't bother you, eh?"

"I sup-suppose so . . ." de Couard stammered, shaking with unease.

A few busy minutes later, the five remaining New Venetians—Gabriel, Brentford, the Colonel, Lilian, and Thomas—were sitting in a half-circle in front of the painting. The lights had been turned down, except for a lamp set behind the drawings, which made their outlines clearer. Gabriel's cane stood upright in front of the New Venetians, with the figure of Kiggertarpoq facing them, like a gunsight on which all eyes focussed.

"And what is the use of this thing, sir?" de Couard asked Gabriel.

"It is my own experience that this object can establish a telepathic bond between us and this place," he explained, indicating the sketchy city to his future fellow-citizen, not even sure that what he said made sense to himself.

"Oh, I see." De Couard nodded. "Quite fascinating."

He stood behind them, waiting to pull the rope that made the blue *tattva* go down just in front of the drawings.

"Remember," he said. "First, you should prepare yourself for the vision by concentrating on this figure. When you see the negative image of the circle, just wave and I'll lift up the *tattva*. Focus on the drawing and the vision should begin."

Brentford stared ahead intently, hoping he'd know a negative image when he saw one.

"A little help wouldn't hurt," Gabriel said. "This is what I'd taken when Kiggertarpoq contacted me." He unfolded a packet of Diamond Diviner's Dust and handed it around.

"What does it do, exactly?" Brentford inquired.

"Mostly, it channels for the imagination the other sensations that you can feel in dreams but can't imagine otherwise. For me, it made my wish come true—in fact a little bit truer than true, even if only in my imagination. Desire is the key—isn't that what Sson said?"

Lilian didn't hesitate to help herself, and neither did Thomas, but Brentford was reluctant to be playing tricks on his brain while he still had use for it—until he remembered his motto, *Do All, Be All*, and decided that if he was going to die tonight, he had little to lose by experimenting.

Meanwhile, Lilian took care of the Colonel.

"What a charming sandman you make, Miss Lake," the Colonel told her.

"Sandwoman, if you don't mind."

"Now," Gabriel said, "when I was a kid at St. Anthony's, and it was too cold to go out, my grandfather would take me by the hand, ask me to close my eyes, and we would walk around the living room, pretending it was the town, and he would describe the monuments to me so that I could picture them in my head . . . Let's do something similar: let us imagine that we're taking a walk together, and oh, let's make it a winter day. There's nothing like snow to help in forming good mental images."

The New Venetians nodded and joined hands—except for the Colonel, of course, who had to endure Brentford and Lilian pinching his cheeks.

"Now," Brentford said. De Couard turned off the lights, except for the oil lamp that shone behind the drawings.

Their eyes stinging and pulsing from the sand, the New Venetians locked their gazes onto the *tattva*, until it seemed less a surface than a deep blue hole leading to the other side of the sky. Its edges throbbed as if something inside was trying to break out of it. They closed their eyes to a red flash, at last, and, on de Couard's command opened them again while the curtain rose on the miraginous city. In front of it, the Kiggertarpoq effigy, as if heated by the looks that crossed it, had now assumed a gentle glow that made the space around it tremble slightly. Sweating and shivering from the diamond dust and trying to ignore their aching muscles and stomach cramps (the Colonel being by far the most successful), the time exiles focussed on the drawings and projected their memories with all their will onto the spots they recognized, street after street, bridge after bridge, canal after canal. By and by, as they tried to imagine themselves passing amongst the buildings, they sensed the city growing around them, almost organically, taking on more weight, assuming more precise, more angular shapes, though some parts always remained blurry and indefinite. And when they found themselves stuck in some featureless place, they would see a white furry shape hopping in the distance, and, following it, would always find their bearings again.

The crunch of their steps (or in the Colonel's case, the grating of his sled) on the ground-diamond snow, the thrill of the Arctic air, the weight of the winter clothes—it all came back to them. Even in a snow-socked Paris they'd almost forgotten the extremity of it all. From time to time, as they raised their minds' eyes, each could see that some location that his or her own brain had left unfinished would be gaining in substance and detail because—this much they understood—someone else strolling not far away was remembering it better. And indeed, when this happened, the Polar Kangaroo would appear and steer them so that they could see one another, walking in the distance or just turning a corner, linking and weaving their memories together. Brentford almost bumped into Lilian coming out of the Xanadu Arcades, and felt his heart leap into his throat, but at the moment it happened, it was if the drawing were suddenly filled with colour and sound and became so tangible that Brentford could lean on one of the Arcade's columns to regain his breath, and feel the pressure of it on his back as clearly as in the reality of a dream.

For hours they walked around, each one's memory growing more precise as it fed from the others' and connected with them, until they couldn't tell any longer whose recollections were whose, and their walk was like a promenade in other people's dreams. But it was more than that. Each crossing and knotting of their paths was making the city more solid and sharp in the pale polar sun. Now they could feel that what they passed remained behind them, so that they could turn around and see it still there, rising and spreading and gleaming, the whole of it, sparkling as if it were made of salt. That it was really made out of memories and dreams only made it more real—for, after all, that was what New Venice had always been: *a commonwealth of visions*. Their five dark silhouettes converged on Bears' Bridge and found de Couard waiting for them in the middle of it, unusually radiant. He, too, it seemed, had at last found a home.

"I can see it. Around your heads. Like a model made of thin air," he announced. "Occultists call these *clichés*. It's all so beautiful."

As they painfully, slowly, and regretfully came back to their senses, all they could see through their stinging eyes was the pencil drawing and the narwhal-tusk carving of the miniature kangaroo.

But the city, they knew, was inside them, and would remain there till they died.

III

New Venice Must Be Built

When they finally left de Couard's house the night had already seeped in and bathed Paris in a fine mist that made the lights plushy like dandelion clocks. They said not a word to one another about what had just happened, but with the vision of their home still lingering behind their bloodshot eyes, they felt like New Venetians more than ever before as they walked into the Place de la République—the last place they would ever see each other in Paris . . . or perhaps anywhere.

"So, this is where we say goodbye," Brentford said in a husky voice. Thinking it unsafe to go back to the hotel, they had agreed earlier that everyone would go their own separate ways from here.

"Good luck with your new career," he said to Lilian, trying not to sound bitter and, judging from Lilian's crooked smile, not quite managing it.

"Say hello to me when you see her," she said. "Or to her when you see me."

"Be sure I'll do that. Thomas, give my regards to Blanche. What about a little fencing tomorrow at the Academy?"

"With pleasure," Thomas nodded, with a click of the heels that the snow almost smothered. "I'm sure my arm will feel better," he added with a smile.

"And, Colonel, I wish you a safe journey home," Brentford whispered to the bag, hoping no one was looking.

"As long as I have a good head on my shoulders," came his muffled voice from the dark interior, "I'm sure I'll do damn fine."

Brentford sighed and turned, finally, towards Gabriel.

"I know what you're thinking," Gabriel said with a smirk. "Don't think you'll get rid of me that easily. Remember," he added, lifting his cane to show Kiggertarpoq: "The thirteenth returns and it still is the first."

"Says who?"

"Gérard de Nerval."

"Gérard the Narwhal, you mean."

They both smiled, but weakly.

❊

By the time Brentford reached the Arsenal, there were so many sparkling stars overhead that the night sky looked like a suspended, motionless snowstorm. The portholes of the *Dukedominion* were lit, so, knowing he was expected, he crossed the footbridge over the harbour and headed for the gangway. The yacht was not guarded, and he made his way to the door of the cabin with no trouble other than a knot of fear in his stomach. The knot spasmed when a man dressed in black and wearing a raven mask opened the door and motioned him inside, without so much as a croak, before he had time to introduce himself.

Savnock was sitting in the luxurious stateroom, poring over a long ebony box on his lap. On a table beside him, a model of New Venice spread its canals and avenues. A huge tower with a light on top stood in the middle, and Brentford struggled for a moment to remember it, before deciding he was sure it did not belong to New Venice. Not as he remembered it.

Savnock looked up. "Ah, Mr. Orsini. I am mightily pleased to see you again. And for a rather good reason, this time. Monsieur d'Ussonville apologizes, by the way—he had some other business to attend to. Please take a seat. And please," Savnock said to the Raven, "bring us two flutes of champagne."

Brentford sat cautiously, wondering whether he should fear for his life, but then he knew very well that this was not a concern anymore. He bent to open his satchel—causing a hurried movement from the Raven behind him that Savnock stopped with a quick gesture—and extracted the magnetic crown.

"Mr. d'Ussonville asked me to bring him this," he said as he handed it to Savnock.

"Thank you. I'm sure he'll be delighted." Savnock said, barely looking at it as he took it and—much to Brentford's annoyance—set it aside before going on. "I'm celebrating a very important event, today. Not so much important for me as for my enemies."

Without bothering to ask what they were celebrating, Brentford said instead, "I wonder whether you count me in that number."

"We'll have plenty of time to discuss that," Savnock told him. "For the time being, I'd be happy if you'd join me in celebrating my new acquisition."

He turned the box towards Brentford, and opening its gilded locks revealed what looked like a cane resting on purple velvet.

"The Tail of Saint Mark's Lion," he announced with a grin. "Monsieur Achille Laviarde, King of Patagonia and Auracania, accompanied by Monsieur Taxil, brought it to me this afternoon, as a present from Diana Vaughan. She stole it, allegedly, from the Eleven Seven, who run the whole Palladian organization. Did you know that this tail is actually possessed by the demon Asmodea?"

Brentford frowned. "The Tail of St. Mark's Lion? But the lion is just a metaphor."

"A metaphor come true," Lodestone answered with a sly smile. "Isn't that truly miraculous?"

"I thought the whole affair about the Palladians was a hoax," Brentford muttered, trying to remember Gabriel's confused explanations.

"I should know all about that," the Sleeper declared. "I funded Taxil's entire scheme."

"I don't understand."

Savnock smiled suavely. "Thanks to this Palladian hoax, the occultist underworld now considers me invested with supernatural powers that make me a rather dangerous fellow to contradict," he said, clearly enjoying himself. "Not to mention that I am also, as you have yourself witnessed, a secret chief of the Golden Dawn, and, accordingly, one of the supreme hierophants that command Mankind's destiny!" This seemed to greatly amuse him. "If that doesn't keep the Czar's minion magi in line, and disincline them to meddle in my personal affairs, I wonder what would?" He lifted his champagne glass and said, "To your health, Mr. Orsini," clinking his glass firmly against Brentford's with a crystalline ring.

Brentford wondered whether there was anything ironical in the toast, but there were two things he was sure of: he didn't find it funny, and he didn't like the champagne very much.

His chilly reaction did not go unnoticed. "Let us return to more important matters," Savnock said abruptly. Brentford noticed that the Raven still stood behind him in the shadows, and he braced himself for what was next—discovering that his fear was not for his life, as he had first thought, but of making an ass of himself in front of a Sleeper.

"What do you think of my little model, Mr. Orsini?" he asked, his tone now a notch icier.

"Well, it's very—" Brentford was about to say "familiar," but thought it wiser to settle for "—interesting. And the tower is impressive."

"Ah yes, the Tower of the Sun. The Eiffel Tower beat it to a slot at the 1889 World's Fair. The light at the top was supposed to shine all night, and it was so high that they had planned to build a sanatorium at the summit. We're still hesitating about it. Personally I'm inclined to give darkness a chance."

"We? Monsieur d'Ussonville and you?" Brentford asked, surprised at his own boldness.

Savnock did not seem to mind.

"We—the *Seven Hierophants of Henochia*, as we like to call ourselves."

"Is it . . . a Masonic lodge?" Brentford asked cautiously.

"Do you ask because of the ridiculous name?" Savnock said with a smile, as well as a gesture that cut off Brentford's protestations. "We are masons, certainly—but masons in a way undreamed of by the useless wig clubs known as Freemasonry. We are neither ancient nor much accepted, but we are real masons and we're about as operative as they get: We build *cities,* not cardboard temples."

Brentford had neither the time nor the inclination to play dumb. If these were to be the last moments of his life, then he would spend them in the way he had imagined the first moments after his death in some imagined heaven: having a good, eye-to-eye conversation with one of the Seven Sleepers, wherein he could ask what the pole they thought they were doing.

"Is this what you plan to build on Ellesmere Island?" he asked. "What Monsieur Vialatte described to me was a much smaller operation."

"It *is* small. No bigger than Venice, really. But Venice never needed to be big to be a great and powerful city. The greatness is in the vision, not in the actual size. '*One hundred men invent a solitude and they call it Venice.*' "

It was the opportunity Brentford had never imagined he would have, to ask the question that had always wanted to ask. "Why Venice?" he asked, as calmly as he could.

"Why Venice?" mused Savnock. "Well, we thought of many names. New Henochia, New Hermopolis, New Golgonooza, New Hurqalya . . . But Venice has an advantage over other legendary cities: *It is an imaginary city that is real.* Or more exactly, it's a real city that through the centuries has managed to remain imaginary. Three or four years ago, when I was in London to meet the commander Markham about his Farthest North, I took him to a show at the Olympia, staged by a certain Imre Kiralfy. This Kiralfy had managed to reconstruct a decent portion of Venice right there in the theatre, and it was such a wonder that it left on us, shall I say, an indelible *mark*. When, later on, Markham and I discussed Marco Polo Bay, the idea flashed through me, and I *saw* it, of an imposing, spotlessly white city of palaces, domes, and towers, intersected by many bridged canals—all as close to the North Pole as man could possibly go."

"It did not come as a surprise to me then that the Chicago Columbian Exhibitions, two years ago, had exactly the same design. From that it became evident that Venice was still, for the men of today, the ultimate utopia, *a World's Fair in Eden.* This is quite simply what we aimed to achieve: not as an ephemeral entertainment or a three-dimensional daydream, but as a real human settlement, where men of good and strong will would have no excuse, no *choice* but to live to the best of their abilities the life they all dreamed of. So at this very moment, some of the buildings from the Chicago World's Fair, as well as some others from the San Francisco and Atlanta fairs, are being dismantled and will be carried towards Marco Polo Bay as soon as the weather allows. Our brother hierophants are seeing to it, as they are seeing to it that we get supplies for the workers that we've sent."

Brentford was still cautious, taking it in—this was his own history in the making, after all. "You're building it based on models from the World's Fairs?" he asked.

"Indeed, we are," said Savnock, still declaiming as if for posterity. "We, the Seven Hierophants, are now in a position to influence, by various means, every World's Fair that is about to take place. Watch what will happen in Berlin, Nashville, Stockholm, Turin, or Omaha, and you will see New Venice rising right from the Dreams of Men. Monsieur d'Ussonville is working right now on the Paris 1900 World's Fair—you will find little there that we haven't designed or approved. New Venice is man's last chance to put things right, to bring light where there is darkness, and to support life where death rules. We are taking no chances with this chance."

"You sound like . . . a philanthropist," Brentford essayed.

Savnock shook his head.

"God forbid!" he answered. "Being human is enough. I do not like men for what they are—I have no inclination towards sainthood or idiocy—but for what they could and should be. By building a city we build ourselves. We are deeply persuaded, Mr. Orsini, that Architecture can raise people to a higher degree of knowledge, of sensation, of individual and collective self-consciousness—to the heights of a living myth, to . . . illumination. Building is the only way we have to live up to the power of Nature in us."

He looked Brenford straight in the eyes.

"*Let us look each other in the face. We are Hyperboreans—we know well enough how remote our place is. Beyond the North, beyond the ice, beyond death—our life, our happiness.*"

Brentford smiled in recognition of that phrase known to all New Venetians—before catching himself and hoping the reflex would pass as connivance. "It hardly seems possible," he said, as if to himself.

"Possible? Let me tell you something, Mr. Orsini. Two nights ago I had the opportunity to dine with two Jewish gentlemen, Messrs. Herzl and Nordau from the Vienna press. Very interesting fellows, very intelligent. And do you know what they consider possible? Nothing less than a state for the Jews in Palestine, despite the fact that their people are being persecuted just about everywhere. And as they talked, they almost convinced me that, unlikely as it seems, it could well happen. I was almost jealous, Mr. Orsini, to hear of a project you might call more ambitious than ours. In any event, if our project is not possible and we fail, let the world judge us by our ruins and see how they compare with those of our democracies."

"And pole—politically?" Brentford said. Savnock observed him quizzically. "I mean . . . is it a political utopia, as well?"

"Oh," said Savnock. "I take it you mean some sort of democracy? It is certainly a noble philosophical notion, but like many others it tends to look best on paper. Perhaps you have been in France long enough to see how unsatisfying theory can be, to the eye and to the mind. Listen to everyone's selfish little opinions and interests and all you get is a world of compromises and half-baked ideas, a world for clerks and shopkeepers, which is by and by drained of its beauty, because beauty demands strength of will and single-mindedness, as any artist will tell you. There are Seven of us, from many countries and many walks of life. Altogether we know all there is to know about our endeavour, and when a discussion arises about the best way to carry it out, we certainly work as equals to the best of our abilities. But a democracy it certainly is not—*not as long as we live*."

For a long, weird moment, Brentford had the eerie feeling that Savnock recognized him as the man who would bring democracy to New Venice and, still more eerily, that he was deviously giving him some sort of permission to do so. I'm going crazy, he thought.

Brentford was oscillating between his respect for Savnock and the instinctive distate he felt for autocrats as he asked, "And you think people will just . . . obey you?"

Savnock fetched a little book from a nearby pedestal table.

"For some reason, people usually obey me," he said, "but I doubt such an argument would satisfy an intelligent man like you. Here's an interesting little work by a certain M. Tarde that Monsieur d'Ussonville lent me, kindly overestimating my French. But at least I understood this: '*Society is imitation and imitation is a kind of somnambulism.*'

We are good examples and good magnetizers, and we have the most powerful magnets of them all: symbols and *money*."

Brentford was stunned by the baldness of it all. Was it for these ideas that he was about to kill himself, for these ideas that he had lost Lavis and Blankbate and Tuluk? He was disgusted but tried to hide it, and in spite of it all he couldn't help gazing at the model before him with all the fascination of a child. "Yes . . ." he said dreamily, "it must be expensive."

"Beyond reason," Savnock agreed. "But *New Venice must be built*, and we are rich beyond reason as well. It has always struck me that all past beauty of some significance is always a monument to the wealth that built it. Beauty needed money to exist as much as money needed beauty to make itself legitimate. But now we have arrived at a turning point, where for the first time in the history of mankind, a rich man can say to himself, 'I don't care if it's ugly as a long as it makes or saves me some money.' I'm not afraid to say that, currently, it's capital that makes the world an uglier place. And yet we think that money should not be divorced from beauty. It is the responsibility and honour of rich men to leave behind them more splendour than they destroy. And believe me, that's a lot of splendour to start with."

"But money isn't everything. I mean, technically—"

"As I told you, we're taking no chances. Everywhere, we recruit the best, and there is not a single invention that we do not study thoroughly, even if it has failed elsewhere. That said, I would be lying if I claimed that the climate had not remained something of a concern."

"Oh," Brentford said, before he could stop himself, "One could always use the methane clathrates in the ground, you know, to—er . . ."

"Clathrates? Really?" Savnock said with an arched brow. He jotted down the word in a notebook and said, "I'll have to talk to d'Ussonville about this. He is our engineering expert. But how is it that you are yourself a specialist in these questions? I was told you worked in insurance."

"Well . . . I talked about this with a man called Felice Rossini . . ."

This, too, went down in the notebook. And then Brentford knew that his ordeal was about to begin.

"If memory serves me," said Savnock, "you mentioned Rossini to Monsieur Vialatte. We tend to be extremely picky about our collaborators, but I take your recommendations quite seriously. You see, Mr. Orsini, I haven't known you for a long time, but you seem to me a very knowledgeable person. And by perusing your little notebooks and sketches—which Monsieur d'Ussonville could not help borrowing—I find the nature of your preoccupations uncannily similar to ours. Sometimes down to the most minute details."

Saying that he came from the future just didn't seem like a reasonable option to Brentford. He finally settled on an untruth that accommodated a good amount of truth.

"I have visions . . . I told you that in the Bois de Boulogne."

"Ah yes, the Visionary Insurance Salesman . . ." said Savnock. "Interesting character. Listen, Mr. Orsini, I am not a torturer unless it is strictly necessary, and I know men well enough to know that, if you are lying to us, you do not do it out of enmity. Whatever your reasons for hiding the truth, I have to suppose they must be good. But you will understand that I cannot take chances. As I said, New Venice must be built. What I'll do is leave you a choice. You either join us or face your execution. You have one minute to decide, while I help myself to another glass of champagne."

As the champagne foam crackled in the flute, Brentford imagined himself accepting Savnock's offer. After all, even if the others died tonight and found themselves back in New Venice, it was written nowhere that Brentford himself had to be among them. The Colonel would find Tuluk all the same, Gabriel would see the twins again, the New Venetian Lilian had proved rather well that she could live without Brentford, and so did it really matter if he stayed in Paris? Not only that, but moreover, if Sson really brought them back to a week before they had left, there would be another Brentford living in New Venice, totally ignorant of a Paris where an older or younger Brentford was working with the Polaris Guild not too far from Liane de Thyane, or perhaps even with the first Two Hundred and Ten, alongside his grandfather. It was like vertigo, imagining oneself living these two lives.

But he knew that he could not leave the others. It was his mission to see them home. Perhaps they could do without him, but he wasn't sure he could do without them. And it seemed cowardice to try to evade the death that he had accepted yesterday in the catacombs.

"The minute is over, Mr. Orsini. What do you choose?"

He was almost in tears as he answered, "I cannot accept your offer."

Savnock nodded, and for a moment, in the shadow of the lamp, it seemed to Brentford that anger and sadness fought in the Sleeper's face. But perhaps it was a trick of the light, and before it could really register, the Sleeper appeared to Brentford to be perfectly collected.

"Very well." Savnock turned to the Raven, "Will you please go out and put a gun to Mr. Orsini's head. I take it he's well insured."

Brentford felt a claw grasp his arm.

He looked at the model of the city and felt nothing but love and longing.

"See you in a minute," he whispered to it in his head.

IV

The First Death of Brentford Orsini

The Raven took Brentford by the arm and led him out of the stateroom, down the gangplank and off the yacht, and off towards one of the shacks that were lined along the quay. Brentford's hands were free, and escape seemed an option, but now that he had sealed his fate himself, the only thing that mattered was thinking of New Venice with all his might in the seconds before his death.

"Kneel down, please," the Raven asked, once they were inside the shack and he'd lit an oil lamp.

Brentford stared at this bizarre figure, wavering out of focus in the shifting light of the lamp. "I'd rather stand, if you don't mind," he said.

"I suppose that counts as a last request," the Raven said. "Turn towards the wall, then."

Brentford did as he was told. Closing his eyes tightly, he summoned the vision he'd had at de Couard's and started walking around New Venice in his mind, crossing Bears' Bridge on his way to the Greenhouse . . . taking one step at a time . . . trying to imagine the crunch of the snow and the effect of the cold . . . But he felt himself trembling, and however hard he tried, the images wavered, uncertain and feeble.

Drenched in a cold sweat, he held his breath and tightened his sphincter.

The Raven pulled the trigger.

The whole world ended with a click. And yet when, trembling, Brentford opened his eyes, it was still there. He had never been so happy to see timber, and in the light of the oil lamp the plank walls of the shack looked like heaven to him. He did not even really care that he wasn't in New Venice.

"Well. It seems I misfired," he heard the Raven say, in a voice that echoed as if he were speaking in a cathedral—but with an accent that had a familiar ring to it.

It was a while before Brentford's heartbeat returned to an acceptable rate, at which point he turned and saw Alexandre Vialatte sitting on a crate. The Raven mask was at his feet, a gun dangling from his hands, and an impish smile on his face.

"But—he ordered you to shoot me—" Brentford began.

"That's not what I heard him say," Vialatte cut in firmly. "Little as I know him, one thing I do know is that he's a stickler for the small details, and he has a fastidious way with words. If he had wanted me to shoot you, he would have used the word *shoot*."

"He did not want me to die, then?" Brentford said, looking down at himself as if still trying to convince himself that he was alive.

"That's my interpretation of his order," Vialatte replied. "For whatever it's worth."

"It's certainly worth a lot to me," Brentford said in a gush of sincerity. "It makes me feel ashamed to have lied to you."

Vialatte smiled. "No offence taken. I lied to you as well. You were only keeping a secret. It's a quality we have come to appreciate. We've found it's becoming very rare indeed."

"And you're sure you haven't disobeyed him?"

"Would I stick my neck out for you, Mr. Orsini?"

Brentford shrugged. "From what I know of you, you might."

Vialatte's smile turned from impish to friendly. Brentford had now regained his foothold on reality—a reality that meant he would have to find another way to die. He sighed just as someone banged on the door.

Vialatte, gun in hand, opened it swiftly, and Brentford was shocked to see Lilian storm into the shack.

"Brentford!" she shouted. "Thank Cod you're alive!"

"You'd better thank this gentleman, Lilian," he informed her.

But Lilian had no time for Vialatte. "The Wolves! They're going to attack! Pirouette came to tell me Swell-in-the-Sack was up to something and—"

"And you came for me," Brentford said, a glow in his plexus.

Lilian pulled herself together. "I saw you from the walkway," she said curtly. "Look, they're very close. You need to warn Lodestone."

Brentford walked up to Vialatte and held out his hand, palm up.

"Would you allow me?" he asked.

Vialatte seemed about to protest when a cascade of brittle echoes sounded nearby, like fireworks in the frozen air. He looked into Brentford's eyes, nodded, and gave him the gun.

"Too late," Lilian said, as Brentford walked to the door, vaguely wondering whether he was holding the weapon correctly. His cadet years suddenly seemed very long ago.

"You know, time doesn't mean much to me anymore," he answered as he threw open the door, feeling every inch the hero. "See you later, Lilian."

He burst onto the quay, trying to acclimate his vision to the darkness of the harbour area as he ran. He could see faint silhouettes and wolf-headed shadows skittering about on the ice between the wrecked barges, amidst sparks that exploded in the dark with champagne-cork pops. He ran towards the yacht, hoping to get there before they did, his head hunched into his shoulders in the midst of the pinging of bullets until he finally barrelled up the gangway to the deck. He found Savnock outside, his back to the cabin wall, a revolver in his hand, calmly shooting with aplomb at fleeting shadows.

Suddenly, Brentford saw a chubby shape he knew well—Tripotte—coming out from behind a reversed keel to take aim at the Sleeper. Brentford reacted quickly and shot, but the pistol merely clicked—it was empty, of course. He threw himself on Savnock, and as they toppled he felt a hot burning in his shoulders and an explosion in his chest. Tingling as if being eaten by ants, he sank to his knees, and found himself breathing fire in a world suddenly moving in slow motion. He could still see the Wolves advancing, shooting at every step, becoming more and more numerous, unless . . . unless . . . Weren't they falling, one after the other? Coming from behind the Wolves, as if spawned by the slanted barges, a dozen Ravens appeared, firing mercilessly at their opponents' backs. The Wolves slumped on the ice in strange contorted shapes, like puppets suddenly unstrung. Some tried to fire back, but it was too late.

Ravens were now stepping forth from all around them, and one by one, the army of Wolves fell into a furry heap.

But Brentford no longer cared. I'm dying, he thought as blood gushed from his chest, soaking his clothes with warmth. He tried to envision New Venice, but found he couldn't think past the pain crushing his chest.

He could feel Vialatte and Lilian coming to his rescue, but they were already distant, as if seen through a windowpane being rapidly devoured by frost. "Brent! Brent!" Lilian was saying, sounding just like an old, half-forgotten song. He shook himself from the reverie, and tried to turn his eyes to face her.

Above her head, like a halo, the Black Aurora was unfolding, a gentle sway of the darkest nothingness . . .

"Take me to a high place . . ." he managed to say, while the sickly taste of blood invaded his mouth.

The strain was too much. A bottle of ink slowly spilled onto his brain, and then everything went black, softly, softly, until his mind was all blackness.

It was the cold air that woke him. He was propped against a wall or a column, the Black Aurora almost within his reach, if only he could have moved his hand. Lilian was kneeling beside him, and leaning on the curlicued balustrade, draped in his bloodstreaked cape, stood Lord Savnock, holding his own wounded shoulder.

"Where . . . ?" Brentford groaned.

"The Bastille column," Lilian said softly. "High enough for you?"

Brentford rolled up his eyes and saw the golden Génie de la Liberté gleaming above his head, the broken chains in its hands.

"Perfect," he said.

"Good choice," Savnock was saying. "Did you know Egyptian mummies were buried here by mistake with the dead revolutionaries?"

Lilian threw him a dark look, which did not seem to trouble him.

Vialatte's voice resounded near Brentford.

"Here he is, sir."

Turning his head with difficulty, Brentford could see Tripotte standing, scared and silent, between two Ravens holding him fast. But

Brentford felt less hatred for the policeman now than a detached curiosity, or a growing indifference. Savnock walked up to Tripotte and knocked his bowler hat off with a backhanded slap. The hat flew over the railing, gliding and dwindling down into the night river.

"Now, Commissaire," he said in his most commanding voice, "Would you be so kind as to follow my fingers?" He made a fork with his index and middle fingers and slowly waved it in front of Tripotte as if preparing to burst his eyes. The policeman looked too shocked to react. Savnock spoke now very slowly, in a way that almost rocked Brentford to sleep. He struggled to stay awake.

"You are exhausted," the Sleeper told the policeman. "You cannot stand, or move your limbs, Monsieur Tripotte. You wish to sleep, as you have never wished for anything before. All you have to do is let yourself go, yes . . . like that . . . When I count to three, you'll be soundly asleep, with all your troubles over . . . you understand, Monsieur Tripotte . . . One . . . Two . . . Three . . ."

On a sign from Savnock, the Ravens each took a step to the side. Tripotte stood on his own, staring at nothing, his sparse hair ruffled by the wind.

"Now, Alexandre," Savnock said to Vialatte, who handed him the magnetic crown. Savnock took it and put it on Tripotte's head. "Now," he whispered, "this crown, Monsieur Tripotte, what does it tell you?"

Tripotte blinked.

"To the North," he whispered. "To the North . . ."

"To the North, Tripotte, that's where you're going. *The North of the World.*"

Tripotte nodded and slowly turned on his heel, heading towards the staircase that spiralled inside the column.

"The north, the north of the world station . . ." he muttered under his breath before disappearing.

Savnock turned to Brentford and smiled. "Good riddance," he said. "D'Ussonville will be angry with me, but I couldn't resist the temptation to put that crown to good use."

He came closer to Brentford, and knelt at his side. "Mr. Orsini, you saved my life and my city. Here," he said, taking a medal from his pocket, with a wince of pain he did his best to hide. With his bloodstained glove, he pinned it to Brentford's lapel. "It's all I have to offer you. It was given to me by the King of Patagonia, and is totally valueless—until someone like you wears it, that is."

From below a cloud of dull, relentless pain, something like happiness made its way into Brentford's head. Had he not saved Savnock, there would have been no city for any of them to return to. Now he could die, his duty done.

Savnock got up and stood surrounded by his Ravens. "Mr. Orsini. This charming lady told me you that wish to be left alone. I've detained you too long and besides, it's high time I changed shirts. Perhaps we'll meet again. That would be my honour and pleasure. Goodbye, Miss . . . ? I'm afraid I've forgotten your last name again."

"Lake," Lilian said.

"Lake. I'll try to remember it." He put a finger to the rim of his hat, and with a sweep of his cape went down the staircase.

"Do you want me to stay?" Vialatte asked.

Brentford shook his head: No, he wished to be left alone with Lilian. Vialatte put a hand on Brentford's shoulder, nodded a slow farewell, and then followed the other Ravens down the stairs.

Brentford and Lilian were alone. Brentford shivered, and occasionally went rigid from a burst of pain. Lilian passed a hand over his forehead. It seemed odd to them both but there was, unmistakably, something vaguely pleasant behind the tragedy of it all—something like adolescent fantasies, Lilian decided, when you dream you're suffering agonies on a hospital bed but you don't care because your hand is in the hand of Someone Who Loves You.

"The Colonel—" Brentford suddenly said, his mouth sweet with blood.

"The Colonel is in good hands. He's with Morgane and Pirouette. They'll take care of everything."

"And the . . . others?"

"Thomas is with Blanche. They're going to the Sacré-Cœur. Something to do with a wax roll. I'm not sure I understood."

"Gabriel?"

"I don't know, really."

"Do you see it?"

"What?"

"The Black . . . Aurora . . ."

Lilian lifted her eyes to the sky. "Let's say it helps to know there is one," she said eventually.

A thorny pain shot out through Brentford's body, as though his veins were choked full of crystals.

"I'm slipping away, Lil," he said. With a nervous gesture, he clutched something in his watch pocket, keeping his fist clenched. Lilian sat near him and, holding his hand, started to speak softly.

"You remember that day, a few weeks after the coup, just before we got together? It was the last night of the season, the day before the sun came out for good. It was barely night, more like a dawn or a dusk, but still very cold, so that we shivered constantly, a bit like tonight. We'd been drinking and talking all night. We were walking up to Great Pan Place, and we stopped to look at the vista, the sleeping city, all in shades of blue, the sun coming over the horizon—do you remember?"

She didn't know whether she heard a sigh or a yes, but she chose to think it was a yes. "You were behind me, just a few inches, and any other man would have put his hands on my shoulders right at that moment . . . but you just stood there, silent except for your chattering teeth. In my head, I called you an idiot, but at the same time I was there, listening to your clacking teeth, so happy that you didn't move, that by your restraint, you made that moment last forever, and . . . Brent? Brent?"

The hand holding hers had gone limp, and his other hand had unclenched to reveal a small glass eye, full of whirling snow. She leaned over him and saw his wide-open eyes reflecting the Black Aurora.

"Idiot," she said, biting her lip. Very softly she closed his eyes, before her sobs took her over.

V

The First Death of Colonel Branwell

I t was while she was locked up in a closet in her mother's flat that Pirouette overheard Loupart. He had come in the morning, looking for Marie-Honnête, who sometimes brought Pirouette's mother some trinkets from her burglaries. After one or two glasses, Loupart had confided that something big was planned for the evening, near the Arsenal, and that the Canadian swell who had kidnapped Pirouette would also be dealt with. He himself, he added, was going to the Sacré-Cœur with Hébert. Something was happening there, too, but he wouldn't say what.

As soon as Pirouette's punishment was over—her mother needed her on the street that night—she ran to the rue Delambre, hoping to talk to Lilian, only to find the Grand Hôtel des Écoles surrounded by policemen. Before she could leave she saw Tripotte and a dozen of his men, furious and empty-handed, hurrying towards a paddy wagon. As they opened the door, she caught a glimpse of wolf disguises hanging from the pegs inside.

By chance she had in her blouse pocket a very precious treasure: a business card that she had stolen from Lilian's own coat while she was staying at the hotel. *Morgane Roth, Médium Mécanique, 42 rue Montgallet*. That was awfully far from Montparnasse, but she had no choice but to try. Jumping from cart to omnibus, taking purchase on everything her small cold hands could grasp and crouching at the rear to hide herself from the drivers and controllers, she finally made it as night fell.

Morgane's apartment was warm and cosy, a heaven on earth after her afternoon of being out in the cold. She found the Colonel and a dark-haired lady playing checkers near the fire while Lilian nervously paced up and down, casting dark looks at the mantelpiece clock.

After an enormous hug from Lilian and in front of a warm chocolate that was unlike anything she'd ever had before, and that greatly revived her, Pirouette explained what she knew of the plot being hatched by the Wolves—who, by the way, consisted of not only Butcher-Boys, but policemen as well. In short, she said, something was going to happen in the Arsenal, and something at the Sacré-Cœur, but she didn't know what. Weapons, however, were being gathered.

It didn't take long for Lilian to decide what to do: she had to go to the Arsenal to warn Brentford. She put on her Monte Carlo coat immediately.

"If I don't come back," she said, "would you be so kind as to help the Colonel? All he needs is a quiet, high place."

Morgane and Pirouette looked at each other.

"I know one," said Pirouette.

❉

The Astrological Column raised its slender, enigmatic silhouette above Les Halles, just beside the Bourse du Travail, in a circular street of its own that had no beginning or end. Built by a foreign queen for her astrologers, it had remained impervious to the centuries, charged with so much superstition that it had in effect protected itself.

Thanks to lessons in the general sciences she'd been given by Marie-Honnête and Swell-in-the-Sack, the ancient lock on the heavily emblazoned door proved no match for Pirouette. It was what came next that turned out to be difficult: carrying the Colonel in his big Gladstone bag up the 150 steps of one of the narrowest, darkest spiral staircase ever built. The Colonel's muffled protests about being mis-handled did not make things more pleasant.

The platform at the top was encased by a curious, curlicued, spherical, metal structure, open to the October winds and topped by a needle that would have pleased Thomas Paynes-Grey. But as Mor-gane—a heavy smoker trying to catch her breath—looked around at it, the structure began to make sense: it cut the night sky into neat quadrants. For a moment she regretted not having taken up astrology instead of spiritualism—for when the spirit fad faded, the night sky would still be there, magnificent and dependably mute. Looking long enough over the balustrade that faced north, she thought she could make out curtain-like folds of pure darkness: the Black Aurora Lilian had told her about? Farther off, in the east, she thought she could glimpse in the dim moonlight a silhouette moving upon the Saint Jacques tower, but when she looked again, it seemed to have disappeared. Despite the wind she tried to light a cigarette with her Magicienne-brand lighter, but every attempt failed miserably.

Giving up, she helped Pirouette carefully take the Colonel out of his bag and put him on the edge of the balustrade, his face to the north.

"Miss Roth?" the Colonel said. Morgane started at his creaky voice. Medium or not, it was taking her a while to get accustomed to this . . . creature. She would like to have seen Lilian's face when she first encountered it. But there was no denying that the Colonel was as human as human could be, and she did not especially care to be a witness to his demise.

"Yes, Colonel."

"Would you be so kind as to leave me alone with Pirouette?"

"Certainly, Colonel. I was about to go down for a quick puff."

"*Tssk*," the Colonel said after she left and he was alone with Pirouette. "Women who smoke . . ."

"Is it true you're going to die?" Pirouette asked abruptly.

"Not for real, Pirouette," the Colonel answered. As always when speaking with the little girl, he felt his French was barely intelligible . . . but she seemed to understand him clearly enough this time.

"You promise?"

"I promise you, yes," he said. "As it was promised to me."

Pirouette looked at him dubiously. "And why do I have to do this to you?"

"Because we're good friends, aren't we? I don't want a stranger fiddling about with my gears—all I need is a friend with very small fingers. And, this Miss Roth—she scares me."

Pirouette gave a short laugh.

"You're jealous because of Lilian," she teased him.

"Not at all. It's you I prefer." He could see Pirouette's face blush, red from the cold as it already was.

"All right then," she said quickly. "If you want me to, I'll do it."

The Colonel straightened his head. "Fine, Pirouette. Open the gear box."

Pirouette, on tiptoe, unlocked the door that revealed the Colonel's workings. She looked at it all for for a moment, fascinated by the whirring of the cogs.

The Colonel interrupted her reverie. "You see those coils near the rotating ring?"

"What?"

The Colonel heaved a sigh. "There's a thing that is going in circles, right?"

"I can just about see it," Pirouette said, straining her ankles, her tongue lolling out of her mouth.

"You can *just about see it*?" the Colonel asked. "Good Lord. Now, by any chance, can you *just about see* some rolls of copper wire next to it?"

"Hmm . . . yes . . ." Pirouette said, though the Colonel suspected she was just saying so to please him.

He pressed on. "Now, just beside this wire, you have a little commutator, haven't you?"

"A what?"

"A toggle, a thingummy."

"This?" she said, reaching her arm all the way inside.

"Stop! Not now!" the Colonel yelped. He shook his head and regathered his senses. "Wait until I tell you, okay?"

"At your command, my Colonel," she said, clowning a little.

The Colonel gave a short snort that meant that he was laughing, though it was more a snort of relief that she hadn't killed him before he was ready. "All right," he began again. "I'm going to close my eyes. You will count up to ten and then switch that damn thing off, understand?"

Pirouette suddenly looked terrified, and about to cry, realizing the full import of what was about to happen . . . but she managed to nod sombrely.

The Colonel closed his eyes.

"One . . ." Pirouette started.

The Colonel's eyes popped open. "No! Silently, please," he barked. Then, after another sigh. "Let's start again."

"All right," Pirouette replied. She sounded a little vexed, and when she resumed the Colonel could still hear her whispering the numbers under her breath.

He tried to concentrate, to conjure up the memories of a vision he'd had at de Couard's—of himself on one of the observation decks at Sson's cast-iron Uraniborg. He didn't know whether the scene was supposed to be based on actual memory, so he imagined Tuluk at his side . . . He imagined, in fact, that he was teaching his son to look through a telescope . . .

"What is it, Ataata?" Tuluk was asking.

"This, my son, is a Black Aurora."

At this, he opened his eyes—just as Pirouette switched the toggle.

For a while, afterwards, she stood watching him, her head tilted, not really knowing what to do. Close his eyes? One of her friends had told her that when her little brother had died, her mother had closed his eyes. But wasn't the Colonel supposed to be looking at the Aurora?

Finally, bracing her elbows on the ledge of the pedestal, she hoisted herself up to place a small kiss on the Colonel's lips. His moustache was bristly and as she lowered herself to the ground, she could still feel the tingle on her upper lip, and a little sting on her cheek.

"You took forever," Morgane said—through a cloud of smoke—when Pirouette rejoined her downstairs.

"Do we leave him up there?" Pirouette asked anxiously.

Morgane thought of the head facing the stars, and the image pleased her.

"Why not? Nobody ever goes up there."

Pirouette was uncertain. "Are we going to go find Lilian now? She might know better what to do."

"She'll join us later, don't worry. Give me your hand."

Distractedly, Pirouette did as she was told. Poor thing, Morgane thought. They walked away, looking back at the tower every now and then.

But Pirouette was on the verge of panic. Now that she'd taken care of the Colonel, perhaps there was no use for her. "You won't take me home tomorrow, will you?" she suddenly burst out to Morgane. "My mother will kill me."

Morgane stopped where she was and looked down at the little girl. "Who needs a mother when you have good friends?" she said. "You'll come and stay with Lili and me instead. By the way, do you like long white dresses?"

Startled, Pirouette admitted, "I *adore* them."

"Sparkling makeup?"

"I've never worn makeup. But I'd like to try."

"Do you like to play the fool?"

Pirouette, suddenly feeling hopeful, replied with a cross-eyed face that made Morgane giggle.

"Well, I may have something for you to do, then," Morgane enthused. "You see, there are ladies who've lost their little daughters and come to see me, and sometimes it makes them very happy to see their little girls again, you know—like little luminous white ghosts."

"Oh, yes!" Pirouette clapped her hands. "I'll be the *Môme fantôme*."

Morgane smiled. "The *Môme fantôme*. I like that. You'll go far . . ."

Hand in hand, they vanished into the night.

VI

The First Death of Thomas Paynes-Grey

Just before leaving for Edgar de Couard's studio in the early afternoon, Thomas had received a phone call from Blanche, asking him to meet her later that evening at the foot of the Butte Montmartre.

When he saw her waiting at the cosy Bon Bock, he immediately regretted that it was his duty to go back to New Venice, although her coughing, which seemed to rip through his own chest, reminded him of why he'd rather go back: he did not want to be here on the day she died. His heroism, his loyalty, his sense of duty and sacrifice were all mere cowardice in light of that decision. So be it. However hard he tried, he could not imagine himself surviving her—not in Paris, at least. And, a coward to the end, he could not bring himself to tell her that tonight would be the last time they would see each other. Unconsciously, he patted the pocket where he had put his syringe, already loaded with a lethal dose of morphine.

Daydreaming about being reincarnated as the dead stoat around her neck, he found it hard to concentrate on what she was saying about the wax roll in her hand.

"I don't know how your friend Gabriel did it, but, I listened to it, and it contains all the evidence of a plot against my uncle, and more. I must take it to him before it is too late."

"A plot?" Thomas asked, quickly coming into focus. "Here in Montmartre?"

"At the Sacré-Cœur," she told him. "I couldn't locate my uncle today, but there was a note on his desk from a certain "Monsieur

Froment," making a midnight appointment in the dome of the basilica. The conspirators on the wax roll say it's a trap."

Thomas looked at his watch. "Perhaps we should go now, to warn him."

"You're right," Blanche said, as she dissolved a spoon of granulated hemoglobin in a glass of water. "But it's a steep way up." And she looked so spent at the very thought of it that for a moment Thomas thought she wouldn't make it.

But she did, and an endless flight of stairs led them closer to the basilica itself. Its silhouette grew at each step, rising in the middle of a wasteland of snowy rubble, becoming so enormous that it seemed about to burst from the scaffolding encasing the dome. At the top of the stairs, it took five minutes for Blanche to catch her wheezing breath, while Thomas at first pretended not to notice, then looked on with sorry concern, not knowing what else to do.

Once Blanche had regained her strength, they learned that of course at such a late hour the entrance was closed. But finding a loose plank in the wooden palisade surrounding the construction site was easy enough. Blanche, who had been dragged by her mother to the Blessing of the still-unfinished church a few years before, knew her way around the place, and without hesitation she led Thomas inside the building via an office that, she explained, sold tickets to tourists and pilgrims. They stopped short when they saw the office door hanging open. Thomas assured Blanche that d'Ussonville had most likely gotten there before them . . . but he was on the alert as they moved on. Climbing a flight of stairs that crossed what Blanche called a *saut-de-loup* ("A what?" Thomas asked. "A wolf's leap?"), they found themselves inside the church proper. It was dark except for a few lit tapers, and Thomas could feel its immensity more than he could see it. What little he could perceive was bare, without any paintings, and the nave seemed to be half-blocked by an enormous framework. It was sinister and drafty, and Thomas wondered what sort of god would use this as a house. The kind of god that did not mind snuffing out a bright candle like Blanche, he decided.

But he was distracted from such gloomy reverie when he noticed that Blanche had stopped short again and was staring at the nearby door to the stairway that led up to the dome—it, too, was slightly ajar.

Thomas's suspicions were heightened, but nevertheless they pressed on, the staircase proving less steep than he had expected, and open to the moonlight. It landed them above the chapel, where still another staircase awaited them, its wooden steps creaking so loudly that they had to advance on tiptoe. The effort seemed to make it all the harder for Blanche. Every few yards, she had to stop and lean against the wall, trying to breathe in deeply, her eyes glinting and a smile on her face that scared Thomas more than it reassured him. They were not yet halfway to the dome.

After reaching another platform at the top of the chapel, they had to move along a stretch of slightly sloping flagstones that circled the apse at a vertiginous height. Through the windows and the scaffolding outside they could see the north of Paris, and Thomas searched the sky for the Black Aurora, but he saw no sign of it.

They moved on to what Thomas prayed for Blanche's sake would be the last staircase. Spiralling and narrower, it took them outside the construction area into the night air again until, amidst cranes and hoists, they picked their way across stone steps that imitated tiles and past scaffolding that gently squeaked in the cold air, and finally reached the archways that surrounded the dome.

But it was too late.

Peering out from behind a half-finished statue, they saw d'Ussonville standing on the scaffolding, surrounded by six or seven Wolves, who most likely had waited in the dark for him to show up. The leader of the pack was Swell-in-the-Sack, whose bearing no disguise could conceal. But by the weak light of the Sleeper's Leclanché, fallen at his feet, they could see that it was a standoff: d'Ussonville, held at gunpoint by Swell-in-the-Sack, had opened his coat to reveal that his chest was wrapped in dynamite—the Wolf-man would die too if he shot d'Ussonville, and God only knew what would happen to the Dome. Time seemed to stand still.

"Look down," Blanche whispered.

On the outer layer of scaffolding below them, living shadows were swarming, shadows that looked human but with what seemed to be polished beaks glinting in the dim moonlight. The figures were incredibly swift, and silent. *But what were they—friend or foe?* Thomas wondered desperately.

He turned back to Blanche, but she was gone—hopping from scaffold to scaffold, heading for the platform to join her besieged uncle.

"No!" Thomas started to cry out—but d'Ussonville shouted it first.

As did someone else—from the shadows charged Yronwoode, his pistol in his hand and his sword in his claw, with Amédée de Bramentombes just behind him, a ragpicker's crook in his hand. Thomas leapt after Blanche, but she'd already landed on the platform, brandishing the wax cylinder like a weapon.

"Leave him alone!" she shouted between short breaths. "I have the proof of your conspiracy!"

Swell-in-the-Sack turned towards her and shot her point-blank in the chest, flooring her on the spot. Bramentombes, who had outflanked Swell-in-the-Sack a second too late, tackled him with a vicious scream of despair that froze Thomas's blood as much as the sight of Blanche falling. The Wolf and Blanche's father rolled over the edge of the platform and plummeted down, crashing through the scaffolding below and off stone ledges and statues, their screams resounding off the walls of the basilica as they fell.

With his single working hand, Thomas turned and gripped the throat of the nearest Wolf, choking him with all his might, while out of the corner of his eye he saw Yronwoode toss his gun to d'Ussonville and then turn to brandish his sword. But during the distraction, Thomas's opponent kneed him in the ribs and he tumbled backwards to the platform. The Wolf quickly leapt on top of him with his knife raised for the kill—only to have half his mask ripped off by a bullet. It was the Wolf-man's turn to fall back on the platform, his legs writhing, then, merely, twitching on the boards. Thomas scrambled back to his feet, turned to d'Ussonville to thank or help him, and saw the Sleeper taking aim at another Wolf rushing at Yronwoode from the rear. D'Ussonville shot him, and the Wolf tumbled over the edge of the scaffold into the blackness.

Thomas could reach Blanche now, and he leaned over her, trying to use his hand to stop her spurting wound. But her eyes had rolled up and her mouth was gasping for air like never before, dribbling foamy and bloody saliva.

"It . . . hurts . . ." she groaned.

Thomas, his eyes brimming, abruptly drew out the morphine syringe. His mind had fastened onto one idea: he would give her the full dosage, so that she wouldn't suffer and could die in peace. And as he searched for a vein in her arms, raven-masked men were suddenly climbing the scaffolding all around him, like a dream or a nightmare. He heard gunfire, screams, bodies crashing to the floor, but it seemed to Thomas that it was all happening far, far away. He was focussed on finding the vein in Blanche's arm . . . but when he finally did, he realized that she was already dead. And with one quick movement and no further thought, he stabbed the needle into his own chest, pressing the plunger all the way down.

Within seconds he had melted onto his back, his eyes fixed on the night sky, which now seemed to be bursting with blackness. The Aurora, he suddenly remembered. But then the morphine hit his brain, the night sky became dazzling, and the open top of the dome was gradually covered with gold. He became more and more numb, his limbs one after the other freezing and turning to bronze . . . then his chest, then his head . . . New Venice, he whispered, vaguely remembering what his final thoughts must be . . . But the last thing he saw was not his city: it was Blanche looming above him, a skeleton enveloped in a black cape over a transparent muslin robe, her face intact and mischievous under her black beret. Inside her naked ribs, he could see her little heart glowing red.

At the foot of the Sacré-Cœur, a temporary chapel had been built to house Françoise Marguerite, also known as the Savoyarde: a three-yard high, two-ton jewel of a bell with a lace of inscriptions. It had been carried up Montmartre to the cathedral in a torchlight procession a fortnight before.

Hébert, trussed to his wheelchair, sat before it, surrounded by the Ravens—and faced by d'Ussonville, who wore an expression of fearsome determination. Hébert had been caught when, his men fallen or fled, he had tried to wheel himself away in the snowy mud. His last defender, a colossus with a merlin, was now lying a few yards away, both of his eyes put out: the mark of the Ravens.

"You're going to pay dearly for this!" d'Ussonville told him through gritted teeth, waving an arm at the three bodies laid out nearby: the broken, absurdly dislocated remains of Amédée; the white shape of his daughter, so small in her winter clothes; the corpse of a gallant foreigner with his arm in a sling.

"I just wanted to save the Sacré-Cœur—to save France!" the crippled druid insisted.

D'Ussonville would have none of it. "As if you cared about France," he spit out. "You wanted to kill me. And you did kill people who were very dear to me! I never intended to blow up the Sacré-Cœur—I only wanted to steal this goddamn bell." A wry smile curled his lips. "At least now I've found a better use for it."

With a nod, he ordered the Ravens to seize Hébert's wheelchair and roll it under the bell.

"What—what are you doing?" Hébert shouted. "I wasn't the only one—"

"Don't worry about your friends," the Sleeper replied, brandishing the wax cylinder at Hébert as the Ravens gagged him. "I have here something that should keep Papus and his associates out of my way for a while. You should worry about yourself—I'm giving you a chance to cleanse your soul of your sins. In three weeks' time, this bell will be blessed and installed in its chapel. Perhaps a bit of this blessing will reach you."

At another nod of d'Ussonville's head, the Ravens laid hands on the pulleys and began to lower the bell until Hébert's wheelchair and his muffled shouts were swallowed in its enormous bronze maw.

"Three weeks to think about your mistakes, Hébert! Just three little weeks . . ."

But Hébert was not to be heard from again.

D'Ussonville took his handkerchief and wiped his eyes, although nobody had seen him shed a single tear. He straightened himself and turned towards Yronwoode, whose half-human expression was always hard to read.

"How did you come to be here, sir?"

"We followed your niece as soon as she left home. I was afraid that you'd got into trouble, and I thought that perhaps she could lead me to you. Her father . . . insisted on coming with me."

"It is most unfortunate,"d'Ussonville said. There was nothing accusatory in his tone, and his sigh spoke of weary acceptance. "I had promised the bell to Lord Savnock. He'll be angry," he said, as if to himself, while the Ravens began to silently drift off, one by one.

"Who are these men?" Yronwoode asked, as he watched the bird-headed fighters slipping off.

"Oh—the Ravens. They're Lord Savnock's private guard. He was kind enough to lend them to me. He sometimes calls them his Little Scavengers. I hardly know more than that." He stared off, lost in thought. But then something occurred to him and he turned to Yronwoode once more. "By the way, Major," he said, ". . . are you looking for a job?"

VII

The First Death of Gabriel d'Allier

Gabriel had always thought that every man died alone, and that he would, too, if only to prove himself a man.

He thought his choice of a high place was also telling: a church steeple without a church, and bristling with flamboyant Gothic ornaments, St. Jacques-de-la-Boucherie towered over its own square, lonely, brooding, vaguely malevolent. If Gabriel had been asked to choose a spot that would be quintessentially Parisian, he would have chosen this tower. It was not the most ancient, nor the most famous, nor the highest monument, but, stubborn—it had somehow survived when its church had been burned down during the Revolution, after all—and self-contained, it remained charged with history and vibrant with some sort of louche magic. It was not even especially authentic—like the city itself, it was a crazy motley of ruined parts and fancy restorations. That it had also been founded by a guild of butchers was only a small touch of irony in the present circumstances.

There was another reason the location struck him as apropos—it was only a few demented, desperate steps from where Gérard de Nerval had hanged himself. Brentford's asinine pun on the Place de la République had suddenly brought it to mind. *Don't wait for me tonight, the night is black and white*, the poet had written a few hours before his death; Gabriel thought that it prettily summed up his situation. When in doubt, do what they do in books, was one of Gabriel's secret mottos and—that rarest of things—a principle that he actually lived by.

Stoically, he decided to ignore the fact that the lining of his overcoat had been torn by the railings he had just climbed: God is in the details, he told himself, although he hoped he wasn't about to meet God. Crossing the square that—he recalled—doubled as a mass grave of Communards, he hurried up the few steps that led to the tower's first platform, where he found a statue of the mystic mathematical wizard Blaise Pascal, mistakenly placed here to commemorate his experiments on the void. Gabriel muttered, "I'll show you an experiment on the void, you hysterical old stoup-frog," as he passed, and then found himself facing a wooden door—nothing that his evertrusty helping spirit couldn't open. He simply tapped on the lock with the small Polar Kangaroo on the knob of his cane. The effigy shone like the candle stuck in these shriveled, pickled "hands of glory" that superstitious burglars cut from the corpses of hanged men and carry around in the belief that will they break any lock. The door squeaked open on a narrow staircase that spiralled up into the dark.

Many steps and another lock or two later, Gabriel reached the top platform, which he found occupied by a puny wooden weather station sitting on a web of beams and chicken wire covering the platform. He chuckled at this derisory effort to complicate his plans. But the laughter caught in his throat when he thought he saw, just to the north, a starless zone floating in the night sky that could only have been . . . the Black Aurora.

"Ah, your vehicle awaits," he muttered to himself.

Opening his coat, he unspooled a long, tasseled curtain cord he'd stolen from the hotel and wrapped around his chest, and set about knotting it into a noose. Noose-making was an art he'd mastered as a suicidal adolescent, or even before that, for one of his first memories was of trying to strangle himself with shoelaces when he was no older than three or four. When he thought about it now, those attempts seemed less about dying than about locating the emergency exits. Now, however, it was the real deal, and he was even more flustered that it was proving tricky with half-frozen fingers, and for a nervous while Gabriel thought he wouldn't finish before the Black Aurora closed.

By the time he finished he was feeling even more pressed for time, and he struggled, lugging the cord towards the ledge, almost stumbling at every step, like a clumsy tightrope walker. And that was nothing: finally managing to reach the statues at the ledge, he realized that he had left his cane near the weather station. This suicide business was starting to get a little too bothersome.

So back he went, sighing and swearing as he moved over the beams with a care that even he found curious in a man about to die. But thank God, or thank Sson, the aurora was still visible when he was, finally, back at the ledge and ready.

The statue that he chose to anchor the cord around was, of course, the Winged Lion of Saint Mark.

"See, he's got wings," Gabriel said, speaking to Kiggertarpoq, a habit he had developed lately. "They should have made you with wings. You're in sore need of some, if you want my opinion. Of course, there isn't an animal in the world that wouldn't look better with wings. I certainly would." But all he got from the kangaroo was a subdued glow.

With a sigh he passed the tasseled noose around his neck and sat cautiously on the narrow ledge, the city lavished at his feet. Someone had not yet written, but would soon, that "Paris looked like a brain or the sex of a woman." Gabriel suspected that this sentence said more about French writers than about Paris, but he still felt happy to remember it.

After carefully placing the cane at his side, he couldn't resist taking a Liberty Cap out of his coat pocket. He lit it and sat there for a while, idly watching the wisps of smoke dissipating and the embers flying off into the cold midnight air. Puff after puff, the cigarette gave a hazy sheen to the lights of the city below, filling every lamplight with bright fire . . . It sharpened the angles of the buildings and deepened the avenues into velvet ravines . . . It made the city so real that it looked unreal. Even the distant Sacré-Cœur, half-built as it was, shone like the silk shade of an electric light . . .

For a while, Gabriel didn't want to leave—either the ledge or Paris. But he had to, didn't he? He thought of Brentford, of the Colonel, of Thomas; he tried to dispel images of their deaths and wondered instead whether they were already home.

He crushed out what was left of the cigarette on the stone ledge.

"Now," he said, rising to stand on unsteady legs and clutching his Kiggertarpoq cane. He looked for something to say, but found his mind a blank.

He leaned over the void, and the vertigo he felt quickly turned to something else: his body refused to die. It clung to life like a miserable leech.

"Come on," Gabriel encouraged it. "Don't be such an ass."

It wasn't death, he tried to convince himself, just switching bodies, a little out-of-body experience, as he now seemed to have on a daily basis. Nothing to be afraid of, really—though all he had to prove it was the word of a wizard. His body didn't accept it as easily as his New Venetian mind, leaving him disappointed in himself: he had always thought that the will to live wasn't his strong point, judging by his appetite for sleep, lethargy, and losses of consciousness. But now every cell in the streets of his veins protested and threatened to riot, and he sat, a coward king, in the ivory tower of his skull.

"I'm not even listening," he said to himself. Holding his breath and closing his eyes, he bullied his spirit to let the tip of his shoe glide off the ledge.

Then he looked again and almost fainted.

But as he struggled with his willpower the city suddenly changed. It lost its muted, hazy glow and instead throbbed and hummed like a loud motor. It smelled of petrol and filth, and his throat felt as if he had smoked ten cigarettes at once. People were moving along the side-walks in ugly clothes, talking loudly, waving outrageously, as if they had forgotten how to move normally. Gabriel wondered what sort of hell he had found himself in—this seemed even more barbaric than the Paris he had known during his stay as part of the Press Gang. He closed his eyes, and when he opened them found himself, with relief, back in 1895. So this was what staying meant? He'd rather be in New Venice.

He took a deep breath, and let the other shoe glide closer to the edge, feeling a knot in his stomach like he was a kid on a diving board.

His heart was beating fast, pumping blood into his brain, which was full of fleeting, half-lit and whirling images—his life spun out in meaningless and vapourous flashes, just as he had lived it. But one thing remained meaningful for him, and that was New Venice. You could take the boy out of the pole, but not the pole out of the boy. Whether he'd been aware of it or not, he had inhaled it with every breath, known it with every step, sung it with every word, built it in every dream. He was but a cutout from its backdrop and he had no doubt now that his soul would fly directly back to where it belonged.

Kiggertarpoq was now fully aglow, as if pulling on a leash.

Gabriel patted the Lion's head.

"Good boy," he said. "Daddy's going home."

He faced the Aurora and got ready to plunge, turning to take one last, solemn look at the city.

At which point, the fear crushed his chest, and he couldn't do it. Stepping back abruptly, he tripped over his own feet, got tangled in a coil of rope, and, in a panic, tried to regain his foothold. He teetered, waving his arms over the void.

"Holy Cod!" he thought, trying to grab hold of the Winged Lion at his side and simultaneously dropping the cane which, suddenly blazing, twirled down towards the snowy ground. Trying to catch it, he lost his footing and flew like black sperm into the night, the rope tail undulating in his wake with Kiggertarpoq whirling on just out of his grasp.

In the early morning the crowds of unemployed workers who streamed from Belleville and Ménilmontant to the foot of the tower, and gathered there in hope of employement, found a body dangling from the statue of the Winged Lion. Just below it, through a crack of the pavement, a little mandrake was growing.

Go see for yourself if you don't believe me.

To be continued . . .

EPISODE XIII

THE DOPPELGANGER GANG MURDERS

I

One Week Ago in the Future . . .

There was a time without time and a space without space.
And it was wonderful.

❉

"What are you, some sort of mad scientist? Using me, your friend—
Ha!—as a blasted telephone!"

Brentford opened his eyes and found he was in the half-lit Psychomotive, with the Colonel arguing with Woland Brokker Sson nearby.
For a moment he wasn't sure if it was a dream or reality, but it was so
luminous and loud that eventually he became convinced that it was
the latter. His headache seemed very real, too.

"Am I alive?" he croaked.

"*Ah!*. . . Well, you never really died," Sson reassured him, obviously glad at Brentford's revival, and grateful for the diversion.
"Your soul just changed places and times. But I admit it's a troubling
experience."

"It seemed like death to me."

"Only physical. The old reluctance to leave one's body! Not that
I can criticize that. If it hadn't been for your spare body waiting for
you, you would have died for good and never known it. Souls need
bodies, you know, as much as bodies need air."

The wizard looked like an old man tonight, his cheeks sallow and
his eyes puffy, even though, Brentford remembered, he was seven days
younger than he had been when Brentford had seen him last. Perhaps
the effort of creating a Black Aurora had exhausted him. He knew

from Helen's experience (as little as you can know from someone else's experience, especially when that someone is a goddess of sorts) that whatever miracles you perform must be purchased from nature, and some of them carry an exacting price.

"How are the others?" he asked, suddenly worried.

Sson looked embarrassed. "There's good news and, then, there's bad news," he said.

"Let's hear the bad first," Brentford told him, with a sigh.

"Ensign Paynes-Grey never made it. There was a little jolt but then—nothing. And neither did Miss Lake, nor Mr. Blankbate nor Mr. Tuluk nor Dr. Lavis. Their bodies have shown no signs of reanimation."

"Lavis, Blankbate, and Tuluk died before tonight," Brentford pronounced curtly. "And Ms. Lake chose not to come back. I should have told you. But Ensign Paynes-Grey—he should have . . ." Brentford caught himself. Perhaps Thomas, too, had chosen to remain where his heart was? Brentford decided that he'd rather see it that way than think of Thomas suffering some dreadful accident.

"I took the liberty of getting rid of their bodies while you were recovering," Sson said quietly. "I thought it might be uncomfortable for you to do it yourself."

"I thank you for that," Brentford said. "But . . . they're all still alive, aren't they . . . somewhere in New Venice?"

"Very much so, and quite their younger selves," Sson reassured him. "All of them, but here's the rub: you are as well—but more on that later. So that was the bad news. But I must say, three out of eight is rather a good ratio for a wizard, and three out of four is simply excellent." Sson's smile was nonetheless weary.

"The good news, then?" Brentford asked.

"The Colonel, as you see, is in good health but somewhat troubled, and . . ."

"Who are you calling *troubled*, you senile old quack?"

". . . and your friend Mr. d'Allier mumbled a lot of nonsense."

Brentford chuckled. "That sounds like his normal state."

"And to think I called you a friend," Gabriel said from behind him.

Elated, Brentford whirled around. "How was it for you?" he asked.

"I haven't had that much fun since Acteon's stag party," Gabriel replied.

Whatever that meant.

"And you, Colonel?" Brentford asked, taking him in with relief, too.

"I'd rather not think about any of it ever again."

Brentford nodded. He understood. "We are very grateful, Mr. Sson," he said.

"I think you can be, yes. The Aurora was a lot of work, but believe me, the hardest part was getting that Psychomotive one week back in time—speaking of which, there's something I'd like you to see."

✻

"It ain't a fit night out for man or beast . . ." Gabriel said with a wink as he stepped from the Psychomotive and was almost blown over by a gust of cold wind. Their complaints about the cold in Paris seemed rather petty now.

Fur-clad and hooded, Brentford rejoined him. The landscape struck them with its sublime, astringent savagery, barely softened by a dreamy snowfall. So this was home, really? They had died to come back here? They looked at each other and shrugged their shoulders in disbelief. But over there, in the distance, a hazy halo gleamed upon the horizon, and they both knew what it meant: the Fire Maidens of the Air Architecture, the Thirty Sisters of Dawn, were waiting for them, and it warmed their hearts.

"Here," Sson said, pointing at a yellowish shape in the starlit shadow of the Psychomotive. "When I moved the Psychomotive back in time, this is what I found at the exact spot where you forked out."

Brentford drew closer. "Is it . . . de Lanternois?"

"You tell me, Mr. Orsini."

Sson kneeled down and turned the corpse's face towards Brentford. The magnetic crown appeared below the rim of his hood. And it was still there, in his dead eyes: the ecstasy and the fear.

"It's him," Brentford declared, "shortly before I suppose some patrol found him and took him . . ."

"Not to you, but to Peterswarden, curiously . . . as you were still Regent then," Gabriel completed the thought, while hugging and patting himself.

"They may have thought it was some anthropological finding, which would have made it more appropriate for Peterswarden and his committee," Brentford mused, not really convinced by his own argument. He had to admit he had been thoroughly betrayed. But something else was troubling him.

"Did de Lanternois' being here have anything to do with the Psychomotive forking out in time?" he finally formulated.

"Of course," Sson said. "De Lanternois may well have been dead, but the crown wasn't: it still held what was left of his mind. The snow and ice around the body were charged with Odic effluvia from contact with the crown, especially as the effluvia are at their peak at the moment of death, as you yourself have experienced. One full week after the body was taken from here, the place still emitted a strong Odic field."

"And of course, the crown found on the corpse was still functioning. Indeed, Peterswarden may have tried it out on someone—I've recently learned that, the day before the ceremony, a dream interpreter from the Dunne Institute was found roving in the wilderness muttering, 'To the North, to the North.' Presumably, this unfortunate person had time to communicate the latent content of the crown to Peterswarden—not only the magnetic spell but also the memories that had seeped in during the turmoil of death."

"So," Gabriel concluded, "Peterswarden knew that we would either go to Paris . . . or to our deaths at the Pole?"

"I'll let you draw your own conclusions," Sson said. "But this still-active crown was put in the Psychomotive, and being still full of Od, it was attracted to the place of death as it came near to it, as if picking up a signal from its own time frame. It steered you there imperceptibly, and resonated with its own memory, so to speak. It created a chronomagnetic whirl that was strong enough to generate a Black Aurora and send you straight back to where the crown came from."

"You mean it was the remains of a dead man's mind that took us to Paris?" Gabriel wondered aloud. And then he wondered why he wondered. This was precisely what books did, after all.

"The mind creates its own universe," Sson said, somewhat impatiently. "That's a rather standard philosophical tenet, after all, and it's a rather standard magical tenet that it sometimes happens literally."

"It's the way it works that I'm not sure I understand," Brentford went on, shouting to be heard in the suddenly rising wind.

Sson sighed. "Nobody really understands," he began, with visible effort. "But it has to do with the fact that Black Auroras are not exactly void. They're filled with indeterminate particles of invisible dark matter that can turn into solid matter when informed by desire and imagination. We call this the *Materia Prima*, though, as a rule, it's something that we don't like to talk about. This is how the Psychomotive and your bodies were duplicated when you passed through the Black Aurora. And this is how de Lanternois' memories came to life, bringing you, along with the crown, to Paris in 1895."

Gabriel tried to frown in spite of the frost growing on his brow. "You know, I was struck by the fact that Jean-Klein—who should have been much older here if he was a young intern in 1895—did not recognize the Paris of his youth when we got there," he recalled. "He didn't remembered the snow, for example. Could it be that the snow came from *here*, then? That it seeped in, as you said, from de Lanternois' last sensations, and got mixed up with his memories of Paris? So that the Paris we found ourselves in never actually existed, other than in de Lanternois' mind—which was dreaming of Paris . . . while he died in the snow?"

"The Paris we found ourselves in was a Paris where he was dead, remember?" Brentford cut in. "And we saw many things that he could not have known."

"That the mind expresses the whole universe, past, present, or future, is another fundamental philosophical tenet," Sson observed wearily. "Now, if you please, there's something to consider that's a bit trickier. Please look more closely at this corpse, and see if you see something slightly wrong."

Brentford felt he'd seen enough dead bodies these past few days, but he did his best to oblige the wizard. But all he could see was how ugly death was.

"What should I see?" he finally asked.

"It's clear this corpse is not decades old," Ssson said simply. "A few days at the most."

Brentford straightened up in surprise. "Of course! If he left Paris in 1895 . . ." he began.

". . . how is it he died here in 1907 A.B.?" Ssson concluded.

"I don't see how that could be possible," said the drowning scientist in Brentford.

"Although you were, I have heard, close to the source," Sson declared. "It's your friend Helen's stopping of time, for a period that by nature remained indefinite, which has definitively put New Venice off the map, chronologically, and perhaps even *retroactively*, if you can imagine that. Technically, it lies now in the middle of a perpetual vortex of chronomagnetic forces. This means that we can have visitors from any time . . . depending, that is, on their desire to see us."

"Ah!" said Gabriel. "That may explain why Jean-Klein did not look his real age when he was here. He'd been rejuvenated by coming here."

"This fresh air is doing you good, Gabriel," Brentford nodded. "But we didn't only travel through time . . ." he went on, puzzled again. "You said yourself that we were sent to where de Lanternois' mind sent us."

"That seems logical," Sson said. "Time is for bodies; it doesn't make sense outside of them. But the mind knows nothing of such constraints. The dying, delirious de Lanternois created in his mind a variant of the world that, out of time, was as real as the actual Paris, and at the moment of his death, he *desired* it so strongly that when the crown opened a chronomagnetic field within the Black Aurora, it was so charged with this desire that it eventually forked out and became incarnated in another dimension through the Materia Prima— blending memories, fantasies, and whoever happened to be there."

He looked at the perplexed faces that gaped back at him.

"Well, that's my tuppence worth, at least . . . And that's the trouble with magic," the wizard conceded somewhat bitterly. "It always sounds like hogwash when you try to explain it. Now, gentlemen, it's not that I'm bored by this conversation, but we're not exactly sitting by the fireside, and you'll have to tell me—well, what to do with this corpse."

Brentford immediately saw the implication: if they got rid of the body such that the snow patrol never found it, there would be no Parisian embassy, no fork in time, no deaths, no lost Lilian. He had no choice, and there was no time to lose. "We'll pay our last homage here," he said.

"There's a crevasse a few yards from here," Sson indicated. "That's where I dumped—er, where I paid homage to your friends."

Brentford nodded and, aided by a disgusted Gabriel, he lifted de Lanternois' fragile body, so thin from hunger and so stiff from the cold that it felt like a plywood cutout. It took several excruciating minutes in the glare of the Psychomotive lights to bring it to the edge of the crevasse.

"Let's swing him over," Brentford suggested, breathless.

"Nice eulogy," Gabriel smirked. "Are you sure you don't want to destroy his goddamned crown?"

"*Oops*. You're right."

Brentford put de Lanternois down and, with great effort and not a little nausea, removed the crown, feeling as if he were scalping the man, as torn strips of frozen pinkish skin clung to the metal. Brentford felt a deep pity for the French explorer: it must have been maddeningly painful to wear the crown to the point of having it freeze onto his skin.

While Brentford crouched there mulling over the crown, Gabriel pushed the body over the edge of the crevasse with his foot, feeling queasy himself as the body plummeted, with a series of thuds that quickly grew fainter and fainter . . .

Until there was a moment of silence, at which point Brentford busied himself with trying to burn the crown. But its sodden leather straps would not catch fire, and Sson fetched a can of oil and some kindling, and the three of them gave a deep sigh of relief as the kindling caught, and then the leather finally flared, twisting and melting the rest of the crown. And as they watched the blazing metal writhe in the middle of the Arctic night, they could almost see faint pictures of the Paris it contained crackle, shrivel up, and burn out in the flames. Now that snowy Paris will disappear forever, Brentford mused, wondering if all his memories of it would be erased, too.

Either way, he regretted nothing. He had done his duty, and twice over at that: he had saved Paris from the snow that never was and saved New Venice from never being built. With a sigh of weary relief, he ticked them off his list of Twelve Labours. *Go get Orsini*, anyone?

❆

Surrounded by its half-blue, half-red aura, the Psychomotive glided back towards the distant flames that circled New Venice. From a hillock, a furry white shape, firmly planted on its powerful hind legs, watched it disappear. When all trace of the Psychomotive had passed below the horizon, the creature gave a short howl and flapped its huge white wings for the sheer pleasure of feeling them on its back.

II

The Second Death of Colonel Branwell

"I don't want to do it," the Colonel declared, once the Psychomotive had silently glided into its berth at Sson's Uraniborg Castle and the other passengers had gone off with solemn goodbyes to fulfill their own looping destinies.

"And why is that, Benedict?" Sson answered, barely listening as he scanned the approach from the cockpit. He had cut all the alarms from a distance, so as not to warn his snoring, younger self of their arrival from some fourth dimension, and apparently everything was calm. In any case, if there had been an incident a week previously, he would have remembered it.

"Because I lost my son."

The wizard was paying attention now.

"What are you telling me, Benedict?"

"Tuluk was my son. From that Inuk girl I told you about. He died in Paris, in the catacombs, fighting with honour, and I was there. He was killed and they buried him where he died, among the bones and skulls. I don't want to remember this, Woland. Ever. I think I have endured more than my share of atrocities, but if a head is all I can be, at least I want to be able to put in it only whatever pleases me."

"But your son is still is alive somewhere in this city. You understood that part, didn't you? You will see him again."

The Colonel bit his moustache, as he did when he was planning a difficult move in chess.

"Not with these images of him dead in my head. Not after what we've been through. I want to start again with the boy. You know, on a clean slate."

"So it's you that has to go, have I got that right?"

"Aye, aye."

Sson nodded and sighed, wondering when this bizarre night would end.

❋

Through secret corridors, being cautious to avoid running into himself, Woland Brokker Sson took the Colonel back to his cabinet.

"Now," he whispered, taking him out of his bag. "It's very simple. It's the first one who sees the other who dies on the spot. So—if this is truly what you want—all you have to do is keep those black eyes of yours open."

"Ready," the Colonel said curtly.

Sson took this in silently.

"Goodbye, Benedict," he finally said.

"G'bye, Woland," the Colonel mumbled.

Sson took a deep breath and knocked on the door.

"Yes?" a creaking voice boomed from the other side. "What the dickens?!"

Sson did his best to appear innocent. "Benedict? I have a surprise for you. Keep your eyes closed."

"You wake me up to ask me to keep my eyes closed! Have you drunk too much mead, or what? Do you know what time it is, you crazy Norse witch-doctor?"

"You won't be disappointed!" replied Sson. "It comes from Paris."

"Paris? Hmph . . . All right, then, come in. But what the—" The Colonel had opened his eyes. "Is this what you promised me? This awful wax figure of myself?"

Sson thought quickly. "It comes from the Grévin Museum," he said, relieved by the misunderstanding that would save him endless explanations. Still, he felt queasy holding not a wax head but the head of his dead friend, even if the head of his dead friend was, otherwise, very much alive.

"What sort of idiotic present is this, Woland? Do you think I want to spend my half-life watching myself?"

"You're right, you're right, Benedict. It was a stupid impulse. At least, it shows that I think of you."

"I think of you quite often, too," the Colonel grumbled with a reproachful look.

"Well, in any case, I apologize. And I wish you a very good night, Benedict. Goodbye," Sson said, retreating hurriedly. "I'll bring you another surprise tomorrow."

"Oh, and Woland!" the Colonel shouted as the wizard was about to close the door.

"Yes, Benedict."

"Err . . . thank you. For . . . you know . . . what you're doing for me."

"It's my pleasure, Benedict," Sson said, shutting the door, lost in thought.

He hastened, soft-limbed and wheezing, towards his laboratory, taking every precaution not to wake up his sleeping double. He entered cautiously and silently, and found it deserted, but with the fire still roaring in the chimney. He went to one of the ovens that he used for alchemical experiments, and as he opened it, the flames leapt out at him as if happy to see their master again.

With a prayer under his breath that figured in no prayer book, he carefully put the dead Colonel into the flames and turned away as the stench of burnt flesh and hair, and the reek of oil and grease, blended in the smoky air. He closed the oven and wondered what he would find in it one week from now.

But he knew he would never find out. Because he wouldn't be he.

✳

Another round of secret passages took him to another door, which he opened without knocking. He turned a lamp on low and came closer to the white canopied bed that occupied the middle of a room painted black, and lavishly decorated with furniture embroidered in gold knotwork.

"Hervör, my little swan," he said, passing his hands over her face as if to magnetize her. Her eyes lit up, and from the pillow emerged a shining creature of white silver and pale gold, like a statue in armour. Long coils of hair like bronze cables were braided round her head, leaving uncovered the two shell-shaped phonograph horns that were her ears, and her angular cheekbones glistened in the fuzzy lamplight.

"Hervör," he said, as she listened carefully. "I have two things to ask of you. The first is, please could you come at dawn to the north astrological platform, with a broom?"

The creature inclined her head with a gentle squeak of her slender asbestos neck. On her square breastplate, runes flashed in different-coloured gems, asking a question.

"To help me clean the traces of a little experiment. Every remainder of it must disappear. Every one. Yes? And after it is finished, you must not speak to me about it, ever."

The creature flashed its agreement.

"The second is this: I would like someone to take care of the Colonel. I thought of a very able young Inuk called Tuluk, who, I think, works in the Technical Team of the Arctic Administration."

He took a pen and a piece of paper and wrote a few words down.

"I am writing this down, because tomorrow morning I may not remember I gave such an order. You know that my memory is not what it used to be . . . Just show this to me when you meet me tomorrow. Is that all right?"

A flurry of lights answered him.

Sson smiled and passed his hand over Hervör's face again.

"You feel a bit feverish, my little swan. You must have read for too long under your sheets . . ."

The North platform was being lashed by a terrible wind when Sson stepped out onto it, but he briefly stood and welcomed the blast with open arms. Then he flung himself back into the cast-iron armchair that faced the polar sea, and decided that it was time to die. What he had achieved tonight—bringing souls back from a half-imaginary city, taking them one week back in time—had never been done by any wizard before, and would never be bettered. But it had drained him of all his strength, and now he was little better than an empty husk. The other Sson—younger, if only by a week—would have no occasion to perform such a feat, but neither would he have had to cast his best friend into fire.

And with that, Woland Brokker Sson leaned back in his chair, closed his eyes, and put his hand on his heart. He remained there for a while, perfectly motionless. The wind that came from the north ruffled his long white hair, but not only that. By and by, it seemed to ruffle bits of his face and body as well, and then little pieces of the wizard started to flutter and whirl around, blown away as if he were but a heap of paper ashes—the old, torn scraps of a burning *grimoire*. His head, then his shoulders, began to disappear slowly, scattered in a black swarm of confetti and motes of dust, until just half of his face still leaned on the armchair . . . and then there was no face at all, his body thinning out until nothing remained of him but the empty arm-chair facing the frozen sea.

III

The Second Death of Gabriel d'Allier

It was very simple, Sson had explained in the Psychomotive: "Just see him before he sees you."

❄

Once the Psychomotive had been discreetly parked in its berth in Sson's Castle, and its passengers released to live their second lives, Gabriel found himself alone on Beltane Bridge, entirely oblivious of his double. It was as if his chest had opened like a curtain to let the whole of New Venice shine in. His eyes greedily took in the vistas, the endless perspectives, the vertiginous heights, cramming them into his cranium until he felt dizzy. He wanted to take it all in: how the clusters of lamps softly reflected off canals of cracked china; how stalactites of ice hung from lampposts like inverted golden flames; how the snow cracked, as he walked, with the sound of torn gift wrap. Every filigreed shadow, pale on the bluish snow, every carved animal or godly figure on the walls, every warm, muted light behind ruby curtains—it all spoke to him like tarot cards, opening his senses to a code that only his body could crack. He yielded to the city, drifting through the streets, over bridges that looked serene as half-closed eyelids, beneath the ever-changing winks of the moon through shadowy archways, feeling all the while as if the city were following his steps, playing the sly fox with him every time he turned to catch a dome or a tower . . .

But he did, eventually, remember his grim task, and he couldn't avoid arriving at the Blazing Building, where he was supposed to go, even though he wasn't sure he wanted to. But there was no way around it: this story had to end, and life had to return to what passed for normal in New Venice. Spurring himself on like a tired old horse, he headed towards the golden dome, which seemed about to topple over on him, complaining to himself all the way that killing yourself twice in the same night was too much for one man.

❄

It was his luck that as a menial to the Twins (as he liked to call himself) he knew every back door to the Blazing Building. Getting to their apartment was child's play, but then Lemminkainen was always there, guarding it—a task that he was apparently unable to trust to another Varangian guard. Gabriel had speculated in the past that perhaps Lemminkainen, too, was in love with the Twins. Had he said "*too*"? No sane person could actually fall in love with the little buggers.

The lieutenant was slumped on his chair, apparently dozing, with a half-emptied bottle of akvavit on the desk in front of him. Gabriel knew him well enough to know that this was a minor dosage for him and that he would be awake and ready at the merest squeak of a floorboard.

Gabriel took a deep breath and entered the anteroom as casually as a man entering his own home.

Lemminkainen straightened up like a jack-in-the-box and saluted, his cap slightly askew.

"Huh? Mr. d'Allier?" the officer looked puzzled and embarrassed, "I thought you were already in there."

"Almost, Lieutenant. Give me two seconds."

Lemminkainen moved shyly to block the way, blushing like a brick house on fire.

"I must have been mistaken, then. But, if it's not to you there . . . there is someone with them already."

Gabriel could make out a slight note of disapproval—jealousy, as he'd suspected—as he stepped past the lieutenant and reached for the doorknob.

"The more the merrier, Lieutenant," he said softly as he entered, so as not to alert the Twins, "the more the merrier."

✳

The Twins were busy indeed, as Gabriel noticed once he'd stepped quietly through the foyer into their bedroom and slipped behind the purple, peacock-eyed curtains. Now that his memories had come back, he remembered the scene perfectly, but seeing it from a new angle—seeing himself with them—didn't repulse him as he'd first thought it would.

Of course, Gabriel could understand what certain despondent spirits found slightly unsavoury in his relationship with the Siamese twins. He had had his own qualms about it, although they were mostly about his ability to physically satisfy them both. His fears had proved groundless, however, for Reginald and Geraldine could very well take care of each other in his less inspired moments.

In fact, as twins, they were twice the fun; as androgynes, they took that to exponential extremes. Granted, there was something inherently interesting and funny about sexual difference. But compared to hermaphroditism, it had come to seem illogical to him, as well as an awkward waste of potentialities, and more and more often it made him feel that he was only half human. Fortunately, the Twins never mocked his disability except with the utmost gentleness. In the end, Gabriel's only periods of doubt were during their cross-dressing moments, when he quickly got lost in the Who's Who. He guessed he could live with that.

Even now, seen from behind the curtain, the scene didn't seem that strange, really. In fact it had a sort of childish, happy-go-lucky spontaneity to it that was rather refreshing. As for watching himself, he was surprised by his pedantic tenderness and the care he took when inflicting it, which made him a far cry from the rake that others perceived him as being—and that he had vainly tried to become. And the Twins, well, weren't they sweet little wonders, elfin and playful, folding and unfolding themselves like the wings of a white silk butterfly. *Liberty, equality, fraternity*—the motto was wasted on the French, Gabriel thought, being about as credible as calling New Venice "The City of the Sun" . . . but it was tailor-made for Reginald and Geraldine.

It seemed cruel to interrupt this trio, and so Gabriel waited, through the *lento con amore*, the *staccato* and the *allegro*, growing less and less patient as the whole performance gaily gamboled towards the final flourish.

At last his double, declining an encore, put on a fur coat and canvas tennis shoes and left the bed for the bathroom, and Gabriel, a mere wave behind the curtains, followed him there, managing to remain invisible to the Twins. It was eerie to relive the scene from two separate points of view that were each his own. Later, he would remember both points of view precisely: how he had been leaning over the washbasin in front of the mirror, immensely enjoying the fresh water on his face, while simultaneously wondering *Can I do this through a mirror?*

He stopped at the door, panicking.

"Close your eyes," he told himself. "It's not that difficult. It's the way you've lived your whole life."

He braced himself, looked to see where he needed to be, then shut his eyes tightly and stepped laterally so that he would be directly behind himself.

At the sound behind him, Gabriel I lifted his eyes from the white china washbasin and saw himself, eyes squeezed tightly closed, in the mirror like a bizarre double image. A quake of terror passed through him and switched off his heart. He collapsed on the checkered tiles, banging his chin against the washbasin, so that a small gash opened, trickling blood onto the marble chessboard.

"What have I done?" said Gabriel II, the Usurper, opening his eyes and kneeling down above himself.

"What have you done?" said two little voices behind him.

❄

Huddled against each other on their bed, their sheets wrapped tight around them, the Twins stared at him wide-eyed in fear and disbelief.

"What can I do to prove it's me?" Gabriel asked them in a voice that, he had to admit, would have made even a toddler suspicious. Suddenly, an idea came to him. Cautiously, slowly, he leaned towards them and whispered in their recoiling ears a secret that only he and they could know.

Geraldine blushed and pouted. "All right, let's say it's you. Who is *he*, then?"

"A younger me," Gabriel scrambled to explain. "But not anymore—I'm him now, you see . . . ?" He hoped that, given their own background, being born of a dead mother and all, the Twins would be partial to any explanation—so long as it was marvelous.

"Too bad," Geraldine said dreamily. "We could have had fun all together."

"But why did you have to kill him?" Reginald wanted to know. "Wasn't he like a twin to you?"

"Because it's him or me, understand?" Gabriel pleaded. "If he had seen me first, I would be dead. And all my memories of Paris would have been erased. Think of the bedtime stories you would have missed with that loser."

The Twins sighed in unison.

"All right, then. But you could have—"

"I'm, sorry. Can we just say I've had a hard night? Now will your small Highnesses give me a hand in getting rid of that impostor?"

The Twins nodded, still sulking a little.

"Geraldine, will you please get me a curtain cord—a long one, with a tassle? And you, Reginald—unscrew this terrestrial globe." He indicated a splendid Mercator globe at the other end of the room that showed the lodestone and the four rivers of the Pole.

They did not move but looked at him with what he deciphered as pity.

"Okay, one thing after the other, then," he said, a bit embarrassed. "I'm going to fetch him," and headed back to the bathroom.

At first, he thought to hoist his body over his shoulder, but then decided he couldn't bear the thought of that. Instead, he grasped the collar of the fur coat and dragged himself to the bedroom, trying not to look at himself.

He was relieved to find that the Twins had assembled all he needed for the funeral and stood waiting in their dressing gowns, although still slightly wary. He felt sorry to have troubled them.

"All right," he said as kindly as he could, "Would you help me bring all this to the embankment?"

The Twins clasped their arms around the heavy globe, while Gabriel took hold of a bronze candlestick to light their way, his other hand reluctantly dragging his dead self. They opened a door hidden behind the tapestry that uncovered a secret passage. It gently sloped down in a spiral to the platform at the back of the building.

❄

Once on the embankment, the candlestick at his side, his hands shaking from the shock more than the cold, Gabriel took the cord, fastened it around his double's ankle, and made another tight knot to the arc of the globe, while the Twins watched him silently. He tested the strength and tension of the cord and found it satisfying.

He raised the body and sighed. He thought he ought to close the eyes but shivered in disgust at the idea of doing it.

"It's time to throw him overboard," he said, and he grasped the collar again to pull the corpse towards the edge of the canal. But glancing at his dead face, he changed his mind with a nervous realization.

"Wait a minute," he said, something sinking in his stomach. "He's too easy to identify." He turned towards the Twins and said, "All right, your Highnesses. You can go back to bed now. I'll come soon and tuck you in."

Reginald and Geraldine hesitated, looked at each other, and eventually nodded before retreating into the passage.

Gabriel waited for them to disappear. Then, sitting astride his double's chest, he wielded the candlestick in his trembling hand and, finally going berserk, set about bashing the corpse's face to a pulp, his arm swinging faster and faster. It was not as easy as one may have thought: the flesh at first seemed to resist and the bones to rebound. But by and by, after much heaving and grunting from Gabriel, the forehead caved in with a squishy crack, the cheekbones splintered, the teeth burst and the chin twisted and split apart. When his own face was but a mass of bone shards and tartar steak, Gabriel got up on shaking legs. "*Pheww . . .*" he said in a quavering voice, his arms painful with exhaustion. "I've always wanted to do that," he whispered to himself.

Carefully averting his eyes, he grasped the corpse and hoisted it over the edge of the canal. Luckily, the thin layer of spring ice that gleamed on the surface of the water shattered as the body fell in. Dragged by its bronze ballast, it slowly sank to the bottom. The bloodstained, battered candlestick plunged in a second later.

Gabriel blinked and wondered where he was. A faint realization of what he had just done slowly crept into his mind, and a near-retch coated his mouth with bile.

Thoughtful and nauseated, he walked back to the bedroom through the dark passageway, finding his way as usual by trawling his hand to read the bas-reliefs. The Twins were already in their bed, and, he could tell, pretending to sleep. He sat down beside them gently, neatly tucked them in and whispered, "I missed you so much." They did not answer, and so he merely leaned down to put a kiss on each of their foreheads.

Afterwards, feeling very lonely, he walked back to the door, where he noticed a faint glow from the umbrella stand. It was the Kiggertarpoq cane. How could he have forgotten? He took it with a wink to the Polar Kangaroo and walked out of the room.

Lemminkainen saw the blood on his coat immediately. "Don't worry," Gabriel told him reassuringly. "It's mine. We were just playing around."

At the bottom of the canal, his body bobbed gently like seaweed, shreds of torn skin and thin filaments of blood streaming from his broken face, his ankle anchored to the silt by the terrestrial globe.

IV

The Second Death of Brentford Orsini

Brentford couldn't believe that he was back in New Venice. After leaving Gabriel, he'd hung around for a while in the deserted late-night streets, occasionally bending down and touching the cobblestones to convince himself that they were real. Their materiality left him elated. Even the filth and grime and litter of the streets filled him with a sort of well-being, as tokens of the history New Venice didn't want but still had. It all made the city older, and dirtier, but also more human. He understood what Savnock had been trying to get across—that the city was not a negation of nature but the crystal prism through which its rays burned more gloriously.

Around him, New Venice throbbed and hummed in its muted nighttime fashion, vibrating with a nervous energy as if to hide the fact that it was so close to the bone of the world. Somewhere under the hum, Brentford could almost feel the work of the dreamers as they patched the rents of the day and wove the city anew, for it was true that *Sleepers, Too, Are the Craftsmen of the World*, as the motto carved onto the Seven Sleepers' cenotaph observed. And with the satisfaction that everything here seemed to be in order, even if that order was little more than a frail truce with the primeval gods of Chaos, came the realization that for a few days he was still Regent-Doge.

That he also was to be the murderer of a Regent-Doge, however, brought him up short. *Do All, Be All*, indeed. But as Gabriel had said, it all stayed in the family. Speaking of which, he put a note he had written earlier into a nearby dustbin, where he knew the Scavengers would get it quickly. They really were family.

❄

Incognito under his muffler, Brentford continued on, taking a late gondola to the Orsini House, a small-scale but credible three-story replica of a Venetian palazzo hidden behind a nondescript façade. Slipping through the rear entrance just off the canal, he stepped softly, careful not to wake up old Roggero, even if normally the only thing to fear from his faithful servant was that his snoring might collapse the building and crush them all.

Upstairs in his office, however, he knew that the master did not sleep. Brentford remembered how, on this very night, he had stayed up late, working on files and notes and decrees and legislation, as he always did, even though he knew that with only seven days remaining in office these efforts would be wasted, as most of his efforts had been. Brave Brentford, he thought, for whom power just meant more horsepower for more hard work.

Step after step he climbed the stairs to the office, vaguely entertaining the notion that he didn't have to do this. What would happen if he didn't kill the Regent-Doge—who after all had done nothing to deserve death? What would happen if he walked in with his own eyes open? *Innocence* would happen, he knew—deaths and wrongs would be forgotten. But so would his meetings with the Sleepers and the time he had spent with friends. Even if Lavis, Blankbate, Tuluk, or Thomas had not truly died, they had died a human death, and they should be remembered for the sacrifice that they had accepted. And, for himself, he could not, would not, give up the least part of what had been his life, or renounce even a single memory. And so he was to become a murderer.

He found himself on the landing, his hand trembling on the doorknob.

"Now," he told himself, "close your eyes."

He pushed the door open quickly and heard a rustle of paper. It took him a few moments to find the nerve to open his eyes, and when he did so, he found himself facing himself. Death had been quick and merciful. The late Regent-Doge sat seemingly comfortably in his chair, amazement frozen on his face forever. He still had his pen in his hand, as if about to sign his name, and looked more like a wax figure than a corpse. It was not a pretty sight, but Brentford found it curiously attractive.

He carefully closed the door behind him, and as he passed a model of the city on a nearby table, he thought, "What did I tell you? All right . . . it was more than one minute—or maybe not."

He sat in front of his dead self and simply stared at himself, stuck signing papers for eternity. He imagined his mind and that of his doppelganger's to be about equally blank just then. Finally, when the clock struck two, he stood up and pulled together the papers that he had been working on one week ago. There was still time before the Scavengers arrived.

An idea dawned on him. Of course the elections were lost, and de Lanternois out of the way, but there might be something he could devise to make Peterswarden pay for his conspiracy. Though he had himself destroyed all the proofs of a scheme that had not yet happened, he wondered if he might find something useful in the ledgers of the Academy of Arctic Anthropology, as he had a hunch that this budget had been used to bribe some electors. As he was making a note to his staff about it, he noticed the shadows in the opposite corner of the room forming a shape that reminded him of Helen's profile. He sighed and put down his pen.

"All right," he said softly to himself. "I won't become like him . . ."

Instead of charging Peterswarden, he wrote two notes: One asking the Bureau of Buildings to check in their archives for any blueprints regarding a building known as "The Tower of the Sun." The second note was to Lilian, asking her to dinner. He sent them off on his *pneu* machine, and then, as the clock struck three, prepared himself to meet the Scavengers.

✳

He quickly realized that you can't really prepare yourself for carrying your own corpse around on your back, especially down dark stairs and along windswept canals, but that it helps if you can turn it into some sort of allegory. But breathless and trembling from the wind swooshing along the canal, with his own dead body slumped next to him like a drunken tramp, he was still wondering what the hell it all meant when he saw the barge finally gliding towards him.

As the Scavengers moored in front of the palazzo, Brentford recognized Blankbate's bulk. He immediately jumped onto the barge and hugged the Scavenger, until they both found themselves embarrassed.

"I'm glad to see you," Brentford explained.

"I saw you last just two days ago," Blankbate replied, puzzled.

"They have been two . . . long days," Brentford stammered.

"Your note said you have a Monster?" Blankbate asked mercifully.

It was the code name among Scavengers for all sorts of especially cumbersome rubbish, including human bodies. The story went that it came from the fact that the first Scavengers of New Venice had found a century-old corpse made of stitched and patched human remains not very far from the city.

"A sort of Monster, yes," Brentford said, indicating the shape leaning against the wall.

They climbed up the embankment and Blankbate took a closer look. He turned towards Brentford, the bird mask hiding any expression of surprise or disgust.

"You're too hard on yourself."

With a nod, he invited the others to join them, and taking up the corpse with probably more precautions than they would have used if Brentford had not been watching, two of the Scavengers carried it back to the barge. A third had already opened the trash compactor in the middle of the deck. It gaped open, dark and humid, emitting a heady whiff of greenhouse compost and half-rotten food. Brentford remembered his days as a novice, when the Scavengers had initiated him in the mysteries of filth—by smothering him under a heap of it. It was one way of getting acquainted with the city in a most intimate sense. He also recalled the night when he had seen his archenemy, Delwit Faber, paddling in this filthy muck and pleading for his life before being mercilessly crushed by Blankbate. It all seemed such a long time ago, but he could still appreciate the poetic justice.

"You don't have to look," Blankbate said.

Brentford nodded but found he could not turn his head away.

His body was thrown into the compactor, like a dead dog, and it bobbed on the rubbish as the hydraulic walls of the compactor slowly closed, engulfing it with a nauseating squash. Now, his corpse would be turned to plant food for the greenhouses he had once run. He heard the bones crack, like eggs hatching.

The allegory had finally come to him.

V

The Thirteenth Returns

On that sunny St. Mark's day in 1907 A.B.—After Backwards—the white Buildings of New Venice bristled with flags and were heavy with banners, while all along the thronged embankments a cheering crowd waved through a colourful whirlwind of streamers and confetti. As far as the eye could see, a canalcade of ribboned gondolas paraded under draped bridges, crushing brittle pancakes of ice with their gleaming gilded prows.

It was a great day for New Venice, and even Brentford Orsini, the fallen Regent-Doge, seemed to enjoy the occasion.

He sat under a canopy in the leading gondola, observing with a half-smile the crowd above him, perhaps looking for some friends of his in the noisy colourful blur. Sometimes he glanced at Peterswarden, who, totally unaware that his plot had ever existed, now offered him, instead of real threats, a Machiavellian pantomime of cunning smiles and sly looks that Brentford found amusingly grotesque.

It had been strangely soothing to relive these last three days, knowing all the time that the outcome would be a happy ending; deeply soothing to see again people he had seen die or had himself sent to their death, like meeting your loved ones in some crystal corner of the New Jerusalem. They had given the word *holidays* its true meaning, these missing pages from the Penny Dreadful of Time.

The gondola glided away from the shadows and Brentford closed his eyes to the sudden rush of daylight: it was only the pale, feeble Arctic sun, but trapped under his eyelids, it roared with a golden glow. The city persisted for a while, a purple vision that he tried to hold back from the devouring light, but it faded out in the flames, atom after atom, and finally dissolved.

As such, it would be, in any case, a large tax upon the gullibility of readers outside the back streets of Paris.

A. E. Waite, *Devil Worship in France*, 1896

JEAN-CHRISTOPHE VALTAT is the author of *Aurorarama*, the first book in the Mysteries of New Venice series. Born in 1968 and educated at the École Normale Supérieure and the Sorbonne, he lives in Montpelier, where he teaches comparative literature. He has also written a book of short stories, *Album*, and two other novels, *Exes* and *03* (published in English), as well as award-winning radio plays and the screenplay for *Augustine* (2003), which he also codirected.

READ BOOK ONE IN THE STEAMPUNK TRILOGY
THE MYSTERIES OF NEW VENICE

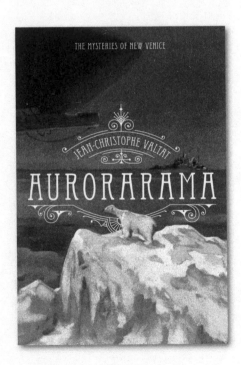

"A magnificent achievement."
—*THE GUARDIAN*

"Combining Arctic adventure with Victorian fantasy, this page-turner is as sparkling and colorful as the northern lights."
—*SAN FRANCISCO CHRONICLE*

$16.95 U.S./CAN.
978-1-61219-131-7
ebook: 978-1-935554-88-2